CASTALIA HOUSE

NON-FICTION

A History of Strategy: From Sun Tzu to William S. Lind by Martin van Creveld
Equality: The Impossible Quest by Martin van Creveld
On War: The Collected Columns of William S. Lind 2003-2009 by William S. Lind
Four Generations of Modern War by William S. Lind
Transhuman and Subhuman: Essays on Science Fiction and Awful Truth by John C. Wright

MILITARY SCIENCE FICTION

Riding the Red Horse Vol. 1 ed. Tom Kratman and Vox Day
There Will Be War Vol. I ed. Jerry Pournelle
There Will Be War Vol. II ed. Jerry Pournelle

SCIENCE FICTION

Awake in the Night Land by John C. Wright
City Beyond Time: Tales of the Fall of Metachronopolis by John C. Wright
Somewhither by John C. Wright
Big Boys Don't Cry by Tom Kratman
The Stars Came Back by Rolf Nelson
Hyperspace Demons by Jonathan Moeller
On a Starry Night by Tedd Roberts
Do Buddhas Dream of Enlightened Sheep by Josh M. Young
QUANTUM MORTIS A Man Disrupted by Steve Rzasa and Vox Day
QUANTUM MORTIS Gravity Kills by Steve Rzasa and Vox Day
QUANTUM MORTIS A Mind Programmed by Jeff Sutton, Jean Sutton, and Vox Day
Victoria: A Novel of Fourth Generation War by Thomas Hobbes

FANTASY

One Bright Star to Guide Them by John C. Wright
The Book of Feasts & Seasons by John C. Wright
A Magic Broken by Vox Day
A Throne of Bones by Vox Day
The Gladiator's Song by Vox Day
The Wardog's Coin by Vox Day
The Last Witchking by Vox Day
Summa Elvetica: A Casuistry of the Elvish Controversy by Vox Day
The Altar of Hate by Vox Day
The War in Heaven by Theodore Beale
The World in Shadow by Theodore Beale
The Wrath of Angels by Theodore Beale

A NOVEL OF 4TH GENERATION WAR

THOMAS HOBBES

Victoria: A Novel of 4th Generation War

by Thomas Hobbes

Published by Castalia House
Kouvola, Finland
www.castaliahouse.com

Title Design: JartStar
Cover Image: Ørjan Svendsen

Dedication

This book is dedicated to Russell Kirk and the Sword of Imagination

PREFACE

THE triumph of the Recovery was marked most clearly by the burning of the Episcopal bishop of Maine.

She was not a particularly bad bishop. She was in fact typical of Episcopal bishops of the first quarter of the 21st century: agnostic, compulsively political and radical, and given, to placing a small idol of Isis on the altar when she said the Communion service. By 2055, when she was tried for heresy, convicted, and burned, she had outlived her era. By that time only a handful of Episcopalians still recognized female clergy, and it would have been easy enough to let the old fool rant out her final years in obscurity.

The fact that the easy road was not taken, that Episcopalians turned to their difficult duty of trying and convicting, and the state upheld its unpleasant responsibility of setting torch to faggots, was what marked this as an act of Recovery. I well remember the crowd that gathered for the execution, solemn but not sad, relieved rather that at last, after so many years of humiliation, of having to swallow every absurdity and pretend we liked it, the majority had taken back the culture. No more apologies for the truth. No more "Yes, buts" on upholding standards. Civilization had recovered its nerve. The flames that soared above the lawn before the Maine State House were, as the bishopess herself might have said, liberating.

She could have saved herself, of course, right up until the torch was applied. All she had to do was announce she wasn't a bishop, or a priest, since Christian tradition forbids a woman to be either. Or she could have confessed she wasn't a Christian, in which case she could be bishopess, priestess, popess, whatever, in the service of her chosen demons. That would have just gotten her tossed over the border.

But the Prince of This World whom she served gives his devotees neither an easy nor a dignified exit. She bawled, she babbled, she shrieked in Hellish tongues, she lost control of her bladder, and she soiled herself. The pyre was lit at 12:01 PM on a cool, cloudless August 18th, St. Helen's day. The flames climbed fast; after all, they'd been waiting for her for a long time.

When it was over, none of us felt good about it. But we'd long since learned feelings were a poor guide. We'd done the right thing.

*

Was the dissolution of the United States inevitable?

Probably, once all the diversity and multiculturalism crap got started. Right up to the end the coins carried the motto, *E Pluribus Unum*, just as the last dreadnought of the Imperial and Royal Austro-Hungarian Navy was the *Viribus Unitis*. But the reality for both was *Ex Uno, Plura*.

It's odd how clearly the American century is marked: 1865 to 1965. As the 20th century historian Shelby Foote noted, the first Civil War made us one nation. In 1860, we wrote, "the United States are." By the end of the war, the verb was singular: "the United States is." After 1965 and another war we disunited—deconstructed—with equal speed into blacks, whites, Hispanics, womyn, gays, victims, oppressors, left-handed albinos with congenital halitosis, you name it. The homosexuals said Silence = Death. Nature replied Diversity = War.

In four decades we covered the distance that had taken Rome three centuries. As late as the mid-1960s—God, it's hard to believe—America was still the greatest nation on earth, the most productive, the freest, the top superpower, a place of safe homes, dutiful children in good schools, strong families and a hot lunch for orphans. By the 1990s the place had the stench of a Third World country. The cities were ravaged by punks, beggars and bums; as in third century Rome, law applied only to the law-abiding. Schools had become daytime holding pens for illiterate young savages. First, television, then the Internet brought the decadence of Weimar Berlin into every home.

*

In this Year of Our Lord 2068—and my 80th year on this planet—we citizens of Victoria have the blessed good fortune to live once again in an age of accomplishment and decency. With the exception of New Spain, most of the nations that cover the territory of the former United States are starting to get things working again. The revival of traditional, Western, Christian culture we began is spreading outward from our rocky New England soil, displacing savagery with civilization a second time.

I am writing this down so you never forget, not you, nor your children nor their children. You did not go through the wars, though you have lived with their consequences. Your children will have grown up in a well-ordered, prosperous country, and that can be dangerously comforting. Here, they will read what happens when a people forget who they are.

This is my story, the story of the life of one man, John Ira Rumford of Hartland, Maine, soldier and farmer. I came into this world near enough the beginning of the end for the old U.S. of A., on June 28, 1988. I expect to leave it shortly, without regrets.

It's also the story of the end of a once-great nation, by someone who saw most of what happened, and why.

Read it and weep.

CHAPTER ONE

My war started May 7, 2016, at the mess night put on by my class at the Marine Corps' Amphibious Warfare School in Quantico, Virginia.

I got killed.

A mess night, when it's done right, is a black tie brawl. It's a Brit thing, very formal-like and proper when it starts, with a table full of wine glasses and funny forks and Mr. Vice proposing toasts and rules like you've got stand up and ask permission to urinate. After enough toasts things loosen up a bit, with the aviators doing "carrier landings" by belly flopping on the tables and sliding through the crystal and the infantry getting into fights. At least, that's how the good ones go.

One of the Corp's better traditions was that we remembered our dead. The mess set a table apart, with the glasses and silver inverted, for those who had gone before us and never came back. And before the fun began we remembered the battles where they had fought and fallen, Tripoli to Chapultepec to Helmand. A bell rang for each, a Marine officer stood up and called that battle's name, and we became pretty thoughtful. Another Marine Corps tradition, not one of its better ones in terms of what happens in battles, was to try to pre-plan and rehearse and control everything so there couldn't be any surprises or mistakes. "Control Freaks R Us" sometimes seemed to be the motto of the officer corps, at least above the company grades. So a couple days before the mess night, the battles to be remembered were each assigned to a captain.

Iwo Jima went to a woman.

We were really steamed. We lost a lot of guys on Iwo, and they were men, not women. Of course, these were the years of political correctness. Our colonel was running for general, and he figured he could kiss ass by being "sensitive to issues of race, gender, and class."

It's hard to remember that we even had women in a military, it seems so strange now. How could we have been so contemptuous of human experience? Did we think it merely a coincidence that all armies, everywhere, that had actually fought anyone had been made up solely of men? But these were the last days of the U.S.A., and the absurd, the silly, the impossible were in charge and normal people were expected to keep their mouths shut. It was a time, as Roger Kimball said, of "experiments against reality."

Like a lot of young Marine officers at Quantico, I was a reader, especially of what the Germans had written about war. They were the masters, for a century and a half, and we were their willing pupils. I remembered, then and always, an essay written by a German general, Hans von Seekt, the man who rebuilt the German Army after World War I. The title, and the message, was *The Essential Thing is the Deed*. Not the idea, not the desire, not the intention—the deed.

So I did it. The moment came on May 7, during the mess night. The bell tolled our battles: Belleau Wood, Nicaragua, Guadalcanal, Tarawa. Iwo was next. The bell. I was on my feet before she started to move. "Iwo

Jima," I cried in my best parade-ground voice.

Our honor was safe that night.

The next morning, I was toast. The colonel's clerk was waiting for me when I walked into the building. "The CO wants to see you at once," he said. I wasn't surprised. I knew what was coming and I was willing to take it.

The colonel generally specialized in being nice. But I'd endangered his sacred quest for a promotion, and in the old American military that was the greatest sin a subordinate could commit.

"You have a choice," he said as I stood at attention in front of his desk. "You can get up in front of the class and apologize to me, to the female captain you insulted last night, to all the women in the corps and to the class, or you can have your written resignation from the Marine Corps on my desk before the morning is over."

"No, sir," I replied.

"What do you mean, 'No, sir?' I gave you a choice. Which one will it be?"

"Neither one, sir."

An early lesson I'd learned about war was that if the enemy gave you two options, refuse them both and do something else.

"I have nothing to apologize for," I continued. "No woman has the right to represent any of the Corps' battles, because those battles were fought and won by men. And people resign when they've done something wrong. I haven't."

"I've already spoken to the Commanding General," the colonel replied. "He understands, and you'd better understand, what happens if word of what you did gets to Congresswoman Sally Bluhose, Chairperson of the House Armed Services Committee. I've been informed several of the female officers here are planning a joint letter to her. If you don't help us head this off, she'll have the Commandant up before the whole committee on this with the television cameras rolling."

"Sir," I said, "I thought when people became colonels and generals and Commandants, that meant they took on the burden of moral responsibility that comes with the privileges of rank and position. That's what I've always told my sergeants and lieutenants, and when they did what they thought was right I backed them up, even when it caused me some problems with my chain of command. Is what I've been telling them true or not?"

"This has nothing to do with truth," yelled Col. Ryan, who was starting to lose it. "What the hell is truth, anyway? This is about politics and our image and our budget. Congresswoman Bluhose is a leading advocate for women's rights. She'll be enraged, and I'll take it in the shorts from Headquarters, Marine Corps. Don't you get it?"

"Yes, sir, I think I do get it," I said. "You, and I guess the CG here at Quantico and the Commandant, want to surrender to Congresswoman Bluhose and what she represents, a Corps and a country that have been emasculated. But the way I see it, and maybe this is Maine talking, if we're supposed to fight, that means we have to fight for something. What's the point in fighting for a country like that? Whatever defeats and replaces it could only be an improvement."

"I don't give a damn how you see it, Captain," said the colonel, now icy calm again. "You are going to see it the way I see it. Do I get the apology or the resignation?"

"Neither one, sir," I said again.

"OK, then this is how it will be," Colonel Ryan declared. "You are no longer a student at this school. As of this minute. Clear out your locker and get out, now. That's a direct order, and I've already cleared it all the way up the chain. You're going to get a fitness report so bad Christ himself would puke on you if he read it. You're finished. You won't come up for major, and you'll clean heads for the rest of your sorry days in this Corps. Dismissed."

As if the colonel would have farted without clearing it first. So that was that. The word spread fast around the school, as it always did. That was a good gut-check for the rest of the class. Most flunked. They parted for me like the sea did for Moses as I wandered around collecting my books and few other belongings. The handful with moral courage shook my hand and wished me well.

One, my friend Jim Sampsonoff, an aviator, said something important. "You're a casualty in the culture war," were his words.

"The what?"

"The culture war," he said again. "The next real war is going to be here, on our own soil. It's already begun, though not the shooting part, yet. It's a war between those of us who still believe in our old Western culture, the culture that grew up over the last 3,000 or so years from Jerusalem and Athens, Rome and Constantinople, and the people who are trying to destroy it. It's the most important war we'll ever fight, because if we lose our culture, we'll lose everything else, too."

"You mean there's more to it than whether we're going to have women in the infantry and gays in the barracks?" I asked.

"You bet," he said. "Look, you'll be heading back up to Maine sooner or later. Take a detour through Hanover, New Hampshire. That's where Dartmouth, my alma mater, is. Go see my old German professor, Gottfried Sanft. He's retired now, but he's the greatest of rarities on an Ivy League campus, an educated man. You need to read some books. He'll tell you which ones to read."

I knew my Marine Corps career was over, but I hung on at Quantico until my EWS class graduated, to make my point about not resigning to apologize for my action. They assigned me to supervise cutting brush around the base, a point the brass carefully made to the mighty "Ms." Bluhose as they ate toads for her. Come summer, I sent in my letter and headed back to Maine.

Was it worth it? Yes. I made early the choice everyone had to make sooner or later, whether to fight for our culture or turn from it and die. As is so often the case in life, what seemed like an ending was really a beginning.

On the way home, I took Jim Sampsonoff's advice and paid a visit to Professor Sanft.

CHAPTER TWO

WHEN President Eisenhower of the old U.S.A. visited Dartmouth in the 1950s, he said it looked exactly the way a college ought to. By the late '90s it still did, despite the fact that they'd built an ultra-modern student center on the traditional green -part of the "foul your own nest" maxim that ruled most campuses from the 1960s on. Those were the days when art was defined as whatever was ugly or shocking or out of place, rather than what was beautiful.

Professor Sanft had retired from the German department in 2012. He was driven out by the weirdos who then populated college faculties—the feminists, freaks, and phonies who had replaced learning with politics. I found him at a house in Hanover, which turned out to be not his residence but the college-in-hiding, otherwise known as the Martin Institute. It seemed some conservative alumni, recognizing that the barbarians were within the gates of their alma mater, had bought a house in town, brought in Professor Sanft and a few other genuine scholars, and were offering Dartmouth students the courses the college would no longer teach, like the great books of Western civilization.

I knew the prof and I would get along when I saw the zeppelin poster on his office door and smelled the pipe smoke curling out the same. The office was a vast clutter of books and papers, pipes and walking sticks, straw hats and the occasional bottle of something refreshing; no old Sandinista posters on the walls here. Professor Sanft, dressed in a white linen suit for summer and the Raj, with a pink shirt and polka-dot bow-tie, bid me welcome. Jim Sampsonoff had written, saying I'd be by. I wasn't quite sure why I was there, but the professor seemed to know.

"Jim says you're interested in getting an education," he opened the conversation.

"Well, I thought I already had one," I replied. "I graduated from Bowdoin with a pre-med major, before I decided I'd rather make holes in people with a bullet than a scalpel. It's quicker and more fun, though the pay is less."

"What do you think an education is?" he continued.

"Going to college, taking some courses and getting a degree, I guess," I responded, suspecting this was not the right answer.

"No, that's just credentialing. It may help you get a job, but it won't help you, yourself, much beyond that. Do you know what the word 'education' means?"

I allowed as I hadn't thought about that much.

"It's from the Latin *ex*, for 'out' or 'beyond,' plus *ducare*, to lead. An education leads you out beyond where you were, in terms of your understanding of life, the universe, and everything. Did Bowdoin do that for you?"

Well, not really, I guessed. But I wasn't sure this was leading me where I wanted to go, either. "Jim said I should see you because you would help me understand why I got fired for doing what I thought was right. Would a real education help me understand that?," I asked.

"Yes, and perhaps a few more things besides," answered Professor Sanft. "There was a fellow named Socrates, some years back, who had a similar experience. Ever hear of him?"

I had, and I remembered something about drinking some bad hemlock wine or some such, but beyond that it was hazy.

"You're in the same situation as most of the students who come to me here," he said. "You know where you are in space but not in time. You don't know where you came from. You live in Western civilization, but you don't know what it is. You don't know that this civilization had a beginning and went through some rather remarkable times before getting to where we are today."

"Without the songs and stories of the West, *our* West, we are impoverished," he continued. "Weightless and drifting, we do not know where we are in history. We are what the Germans call mere *Luftmenschen*—in a free translation, airheads."

The mention of history perked me up. Ever since I was about eight years old, I'd read a lot of military history. I learned to read not so much in school as by falling in love with C.S. Forester's Horatio Hornblower novels, which followed a British naval officer in his career from midshipman through admiral, in the wars of the French Revolution and Napoleon. They were fiction, but rooted in fact. I didn't realize it until much later, but they were also a great introduction to military decision-making.

"In the Marine Corps," I said, "I saw that people who hadn't read much military history could only follow processes, which they learned by rote. They could not understand the situation they were in. They had no context."

"That's an insight most Dartmouth students don't have," said the professor. "And it is what I'm talking about, on a larger scale. Just as your fellow Marines could not understand a military situation, so you can't understand your situation in the war for our culture. Literally, you can't see your place—*situ*—in it."

"Jim said I was a casualty in the culture war. I always thought wars were fought by guys with uniforms and guns. I'm not quite sure what this 'culture war' is all about," I said.

"Sadly, this great culture of ours, Western culture, is under attack," the professor replied. "The universities today are active and conscious agents in its destruction. Indeed, they have generated theories as to why Western culture should be destroyed. Of course, they aren't alone. The most powerful single force in America now is the entertainment industry, and it is also an agent of cultural destruction. Many of the politicians play the game too. The usual code-words are racism, sexism, and homophobia. When you hear them, you're hearing the worms gnawing at the foundation."

I'd been told my high crime was "sexism,"so that clicked, and Col. Ryan was certainly a politician. It sounded as if there were a new battlefield I needed to understand. "So where do I start?," I asked.

"By studying our culture—what it is, where it came from, what its great ideas and values are and why we hold them to be great," Professor Sanft answered. "In other words, with an education." He'd brought me back to where we'd started, though now I grasped what he meant.

"That doesn't mean going back to college," he continued. "You can do it on your own. In fact, to a large degree, you have to do it on your own now, even if you are a college student. That's why we have this institute, and why I'm here. And I can give you a small present that will get you started." He handed me a copy of a book: *Smiling Through the Cultural Catastrophe*. "Another Darmouth professor, Jeffery Hart, wrote this a few years ago. Think of it as a road map, though I've heard it's dangerous to give those to infantry officers," Professor Sanft said.

"Thanks, I think," I replied. Actually, we grunts did get lost a lot, we just tried to keep it a trade secret.

"It tells you what to read, what commentaries are best, and offers a few comments of its own," Professor Sanft said. "The books don't cost much, a tiny fraction of a year's tuition at Dartmouth, but they'll do for you what Dartmouth no longer does. They will make you an educated man of the West."

"Will this give me the gouge on why I'm now a civilian?" I asked.

"Yes," answered Professor Sanft. "But something a bit more specific might also be helpful. Go to TraditionalRight.com. You'll find a video documentary history there about the Frankfurt School."

"Is that McDonald's Hamburger University?" I asked.

"Not exactly," the professor replied. "The Frankfurt School's products are ever harder to digest. It created the cultural Marxism you know as Political Correctness. Cultural Marxism is what killed you, and the video is a good introduction to it. It will help you know your enemy."

I thanked Professor Sanft that day, though not nearly as much as I've thanked him since. I went to the Dartmouth Bookstore and stocked up. Maine would give me time for reading.

When we look back on our lives, incidents that seemed small at the time may take on great importance. That half-hour with Professor Gottfried Sanft changed my life. Most of my years since that day in Hanover have been spent fighting for Western culture, then rebuilding it, piece by piece, once the fighting part was done.

Thanks to Professor Sanft, this was one infantryman who wasn't lost.

CHAPTER THREE

ONE nice thing about Maine is that you can go home again. We Rumfords had been doing it for a couple hundred years. The men of our family, and sometimes the women too, would head out on their great adventure—crewing on a clipper bound for China, settling Oregon, converting the heathen (Uncle Bert got eaten in the Congo), going to war—but those as survived usually came back home again, to Hartland and its surrounding farms.

Whether they returned as successes or failures made little difference. As I'd heard a chaplain say, in his day Jesus Christ was accounted a spectacular failure, so failure wasn't something for Christians to worry much about. We had enough in our family to show we didn't. I was just the most recent.

I wanted time alone to read, think and simply live. I moved into what we called "the old place," a shingle Cape Cod up on one of Maine's few hills. The view down over the fields and ponds somehow helped the thinking part, especially in the evening as the water reflected the Western sky, orange and crimson, fading to black.

No one had lived in the old place since my grandparents died, but we kept it because it had always been ours. It had no electricity, and the well worked with a bucket on a windlass; by modern standards I guess it wasn't a fit habitation. That suited me fine. I was tired of everything modern. I wanted a world with, as Tolkien put it, less noise and more green.

I'd put some money by during my time in the Corps, enough to cover me for some months anyway; the garden and deer in season (or, if need be, out of season) would keep me from starving. The whole country was overrun with deer, more than when white men first came to North America, because there were so many restrictions on guns and hunting. In some places they had become pests; we literally could not defend ourselves from our own food.

Once I got settled, I found the video history of political correctness on TraditionalRight.com. That was a real eye-opener! "Cultural Marxism" wasn't just a name for this stuff. That is what it actually was, Marxism translated from economic into cultural terms, in an effort that started not in the 1960s, but just after World War I. We had been guarding the front door against the Marxists of the old Soviet Union, while the cultural Marxists had snuck in the back. Their goals from the beginning were destruction of Western culture and the Christian religion, and they had made plenty of progress toward both, ruining our country in the process. If every American watched this video, I thought, Political Correctness would be in real trouble.

Next, I took up Professor Sanft's books, "that golden chain of masterpieces which link together in single tradition the more permanent experiences of the race," as one philosopher put it. Homer and Plato, Aristotle and Aristophanes, Virgil and Dante, and Shakespeare and the greatest literary work of all time, the Bible, which was once banned from American schools, which shows as well as anything what America had become.

I had some trouble getting going—Plato isn't light reading—but I found my way in through my life-long study, war, beginning with the *Anabasis* of Xenophon. What a story! Ten thousand Greeks, cut off and surrounded in the middle of their ancient enemy, the Persian Empire, have to hack and march their way back out again—and they made it home. It was as exciting as anything Rommel or "Panzer" Meyer or any other modern commander wrote.

From Xenophon, and Herodotus and Thucydides and Caesar and Tacitus and all the rest, military and not (I did finally make it through Plato, too), I learned three things. Maybe they were basic, even simple. I'm not a great philosopher. But they were important enough to shape the rest of my life.

The first was that these ancient Greeks and Romans and Hebrews and more modern Florentines and Frenchmen and Englishmen both were us and made us. They had the same thoughts you and I have, more or less, *but they had them for the first time*, at least the first time in recorded history. Do you want a thoroughly modern send-up of Feminism in all its silliness? Then read Aristophanes's *Lysistrata*—it's only 2,500 years old. For a chaser, recall the line of 17th century English poet and priest John Donne: "Hope not for mind in woman; at their best, they are but mummy possessed." Pick any subject you want, except science, and these folks were there before us, thousands of years before us in some cases, with the same observations, thoughts and comments we offer today. We are their children.

That led to my second lesson: nothing is new. The only person since the 18th century to have a new idea was Nietzsche, and he was mad. Even science was well along the road we still follow by the time Napoleon was trying to conquer Europe.

Back in the old U.S.A., newness—novelty—was what everyone wanted. Ironically, that too was old, but early 21st century Americans were so cut off from their past they didn't know it, or much else, beyond how to operate the TV remote and their cell phone.

You see, sometime around the middle of the 18th century, we men of the West struck Faust's bargain with the Devil. We could do anything, have anything, say anything, with one exception. We could not tarry, we could not rest, we could not get it right and then keep it that way. Always we must have something new: that was the bargain, and ultimately the reason we pulled our house down around us.

Satan, like God, has a sense of humor. His joke on us was that most of the stuff we thought was new, wasn't. Especially the errors, blunders, and heresies; they had all been tried, and failed, and understood as mistakes long, long before. But we had lost our past, so we didn't know. We were too busy passing around information with our computers to study any history. So it was all new to us, and we had to make the same mistakes over again. The price was high.

The third lesson, and the one that shaped the rest of my life, was that these thoughts and lessons and concepts and morals that make up our Western culture—for that is what these books contain—were worth fighting for. As Pat Buchanan said, they were true, they were ours, and they were good. They had given us, when we still paid attention to them, the freest and most prosperous societies man has ever known.

They were all bought at a price. Christ died on a cross. The Spartans still lie at Thermopylae. Socrates served Athens as a soldier before he drank its hemlock, also obedient to its laws. Cicero spoke on duty and died at the hands of the Roman government. Saints' *dies natales*, their birthdays, were the days they died to this world. Every truth we hold and are held by is written in blood, and sweat and tears and cold hours scribbling in lonely garrets with not enough to eat. None of it came cheap—none of it.

We Victorians, those of my generation anyway, know that fighting for the truth is not a metaphor. We killed for it and we died for it. By the 21st century, that was the only way to save it, weapon in hand. That, too, is nothing new, just another lesson we had forgotten and had to learn all over again.

CHAPTER FOUR

M Y next battle started around the dinner table on Christmas Day, 2016, and I'm not talking about the fight for the last piece of Aunt Sabra's blueberry pie.

It began when cousin John asked me what I thought I was going to do in the way of earning a living. Hartland wasn't exactly a boom town, and hadn't been for a good hundred years. I said I was thinking of farming. That, along with sailing or soldiering, was what we Rumfords usually ended up doing, and like most Marines I'd seen enough of boats to last me a while.

"What you gonna faam?" John asked, the flat, nasal "a" instead of "r" suggesting he hadn't been outside Maine much.

"Waal," I said, talking Down East myself, "I thought I might try soybeans."

"Don't see them much up heah."

"Didn't see wine up heah either 'til Wyly put in his vineyard. I gather his wine is selling pretty well now," I said.

"I'll tell you why you don't see soybeans up here or on many other family farms," said Uncle Fred. "It's oil from soybeans that makes money, and the Federal government makes it just about impossible to transport soybean oil or any other vegetable oil unless you're a big corporation. Under Federal regulations, vegetable oil is treated the same as oil from petroleum when it comes to shipment. You've got to get a hugely expensive Certificate of Financial Responsibility to cover any possible oil spill. You'll never get the capital to get started."

"But vegetable oil and petroleum are completely different. That doesn't make any sense," I replied.

"I didn't say it made sense, I just said that's what Washington demands. It makes no sense at all. Spilled vegetable oil is no big problem. It's biodegradable. But the Federal government mandates a spill be cleaned up the same way for both, even though that's unnecessary. You need to scoop up any petroleum product if it spills, especially into water. But if you just let vegetable oil disperse, bacteria will eat it up. Anyway, the government doesn't care that we lose hundreds of millions of dollars each year in vegetable oil that isn't produced or exported. The bottom line is, as a small farmer, you can't do it."

Great, I thought. First politics gets me thrown out of the Marine Corps, now it's trying to keep me from farming. "Okay, I'll grow potatoes. We certainly grow enough of those here in Maine," I said.

"Only land up at the Old Place that'll grow potatoes is the bottom land. Government won't let you do that neither," said cousin John.

This was starting to get old. "What do you mean the government won't let me grow down there? That's the best land on the place. The rest is just rock," I replied.

"It's the EPA, the so-called Environmental Protection Agency," answered Uncle Fred. "They declared all that ground a protected wetland a couple years ago. It's yours, or ours, but it might as well be on the moon for all the good it does us. We can't touch it."

Protected wetland? Hell, I didn't plan to grow potatoes in the ponds. "That's our property. We've owned it since Andrew Jackson was President. And most of it's dry. How can they tell us we can't farm it?" I asked, betraying how much those of us in the military got out of touch at times.

That got the whole table smiling the thin smile that passes for a good laugh among New Englanders. "Property rights don't mean squat any more," said Uncle Earl, who was the town lawyer. "The government just tells you what to do or what not to do and dares you to fight them. They have thousands of lawyers, all paid by your tax money, and they can tie you up in court for years. You got a few hundred thousand extra dollars you'd like to spend on legal fees?"

I didn't, nor did anyone else, I gathered. "So we're helpless, is what you're saying?" I asked.

"Pretty much, unless you've got a lot of money for lawyers or to buy some politicians and get them in on your side," said Earl. "It doesn't even matter if the law is with you, because you can't afford the fight and they can. If they lose, it means nothing to them; they still get their paychecks from the government. If you lose, you're finished, and even if you win, you're usually finished because the legal fight has left you bankrupt. What it comes down to is that we're not a free country any more."

"What King George III was doing to us in 1776 wasn't a hill of beans compared to this," I said. "We didn't take it then. Why are we taking it now?"

At that point, the women turned the conversation to how Ma's stuffing was the best they'd ever had. It always was.

*

Early next year, that year being 2017, I stopped in at Hartland's one industry, the tannery. My old high school buddy Jim Ebbitt was the personnel department there, and this matter of earning an income was beginning to press a bit on my mind. But I knew the tannery always had some kind of opening, and after my years in the infantry I didn't mind getting my hands dirty. They didn't call us "earth pigs" for nothing.

Jim was glad to see me, but he couldn't give me any good news. "Sorry," he said, "but like every American company, we're having to cut jobs, not add 'em. The problem is this free trade business. What it means is that American workers are up against those in places like Mexico, Haiti, and now all of central and south America, since they expanded NAFTA into AFTA and took in the whole hemisphere. Labor costs now get averaged across national boundaries; it pulls their wages up and pushes wages here down. Of course, we don't actually cut wages, but with inflation rising, we don't need to. We just keep wages steady and cut the number of jobs. Maybe that will keep this plant in business. Then again, maybe it won't. In any event, it means if I had a job to offer you, and I don't, you'd quickly find yourself getting poorer, not richer, if you took it."

"But you just put a lot of money into this plant," I replied. "Hell, it used to stink up the whole town. Now you can't smell it. Maybe that EPA does some good after all."

"You think so?" asked Jim. "You're right that we had to clean up our processes here, and we did put some money into the place. But the main thing we did was move most of the work on the fresh hides to Mexico. That cut 23 jobs here, jobs now held by Mexicans. I guess you can't make Mexico stink any worse than it already does."

"And the EPA still isn't done with us," he added. "They've got another investigation going now, which will cost us tens of thousands in legal fees even if that's all it does. Seems they think we're still doing something to the river."

"River looks clean to me," I replied.

"It is clean. It's cleaner than it's ever been, at least since industry, and jobs, first came to this valley. But that doesn't count to bureaucrats in Washington. They've told us we might have to build a full water treatment plant, which would cost us millions. If they rule that way, it'll be the end of the company here. It would take us 50 years to pay off that debt. There's not that much money in leather any more, not up against the foreign competition."

I thanked Jim for his time and drove back to the old place. My mind was no easier. Next day I'd pull my last ace out of my sleeve and go see my cousin, who had a car restoration place down near Pittsfield. I knew he was doing well, restoring old cars and selling them to the Summer People.

"Sure," Ed said, when I stopped in on him, "business is good and I need a couple folk. I know you'd do good work. But I can't offer you or anyone else around here a job. EEOC won't let me."

"EEOC?" I'd heard the initials, but didn't know much more about it.

"The Equal Employment Opportunity Commission. They come around and tell you how many blacks, Hispanics, women, whatever you have to hire. Of course, all my employees are white, because everybody up here is white. I guess Maine winters are kinda hard on black folk and those from south of the border. Anyway, that doesn't count with them. They've issued an order that the next six people I hire must be blacks. The effect, of course, is that I can't hire anyone, not even you."

This was the nuttiest thing I'd heard yet. "You must be kidding," I replied. "How can they make you hire blacks where there aren't any?"

"I don't know," Ed said. "But I can't fight the EEOC in court. I'm a small business and can't afford it. I just can't expand, is what it comes down to. And you know how badly we need jobs up here."

I did, from growing personal experience. "But someone must care that this is completely absurd," I said. "There has got to be a limit somewhere to what Washington can do to us."

"If there is, I don't know where," Ed replied, obviously a beaten man. "You and I, and most folk up here, are members of the middle class. That means the government doesn't do anything for us, it only does things to us. If you know a way to change that, I'd like to hear it. But these days, unless you're some kind of 'minority,' you don't have any rights. Frankly, it's just not our country any more."

That summed it up pretty well. Somewhere along the line, in the last 30 years or so, somebody had taken our country away from us.

We remembered what our country was like. It was a safe, decent, prosperous place where normal, middle class people could live good lives.

And it was gone.

I was beginning to think that what I wanted to do was help take our country back. How I could do that, and how I could earn a living, were both puzzles. But where there's a will, God often opens a way.

CHAPTER FIVE

A BOUT a week later I got a letter. It was from my old company Gunnery Sergeant, a black fellow and a good Marine. He was also a husband and father—rare among black men by the 21st century—and a Christian. He wrote to ask for my help.

Gunny Matthews had gotten out about a year before I did. He had done his twenty years and had a pension, and felt it was time to move on. He knew that the catastrophe that had overwhelmed many urban black communities in America by the 1970s—crime, drugs, noise, and dirt—was not due to white racism. It was due to bad behavior by blacks, toward other blacks as well as toward everyone else. He wanted to try to do something about it.

It was a measure of America's decay that one of the most important issues facing the country—race—simply couldn't be talked about. Not honestly, anyway. Oh, there was lots of talk about "racism" and how evil it was and how whites were to blame for everybody else's problems. But we all knew it was bull.

The fact was that America's blacks had crapped in their own mess kit.

They had been given their "civil rights," and had promptly shown they could not, or would not, bear the responsibilities that went with them.

Freedom is not doing whatever you want. Freedom is substituting self discipline for discipline imposed by somebody else. But nobody told America's blacks that, so they just went out and did whatever felt good at the moment. The result was a black rate of violent crime twelve times the white rate. Most of the victims of black crime were also black.

Of course, not all blacks were into instant gratification and the drug-using, drug-dealing, mugging, car-jacking, fornicating, and whoring that it brought. But tribal loyalty was strong enough that most of those who lived decent lives wouldn't condemn those who didn't. The rest of America saw that in every city with a black government, which promptly descended into utter disorder and corruption. Detroit turned into 6th century Rome.

As early as the 1970s, the average white American spelled black c-r-i-m-e. That wasn't prejudice, it was statistics. Anywhere near a city, if you were the victim of a random crime, the criminal was almost certain to be black. The only exception was if you were in a Hispanic neighborhood; the Hispanics were rapidly going the same instant gratification route the blacks had taken, with similar results.

Obviously, what was needed was a major crackdown. If a people cannot govern itself, then it must be governed by others. But the white Establishment hewed to the line that said blacks were victims, so their crimes could not be held against them. It was pure Orwellian Newspeak: Criminals became victims, and the victims (at least the white victims) were the criminals because they were "racists." So nothing was done, and blacks were emboldened to believe they could get away with anything.

The result, in time, was a full scale race war, which was in turn part of America's second civil war. The blacks' so-called "leaders," most of whom derived fat incomes from their impoverished supporters, never seemed to care that when one tenth of the population goads the other nine-tenths into a war, it loses.

So Gunny Matthews had taken on quite a job. His letter told me how he'd tried to go about it.

The Gunny had grown up in Roxbury, near Boston, so that's where he retired, "to help the people he knew best," as he put it. There's always advantage in fighting where you know the ground. A number of his friends and relatives lived in public housing, so he picked that as his *Schwerpunkt*, his focus of efforts. In most black communities, that was the worst place you could be. Drug dealers, drug users, prostitutes, the whole ugly smear ran the place, with normal people living in terror.

I'd seen in my job hunt the way government stuck its nose in where it wasn't wanted, messing up people's lives in the process. Gunny Matthews saw the other side of the coin, how government failed to do the things it was supposed to do. If there was one duty any government had, it was to protect the lives and property of ordinary, law-abiding people, regardless of their color. In the United States in the 21st century, it no longer did that.

The Gunny saw the problem in terms of counter-guerilla warfare. The scum were the guerrillas, and the key to defeating them was organizing the locals so they could stand up to the scum. He saw an opening, a "soft spot" as we called it in military tactics, in the fact that one public housing development had been given over to the tenants to manage. They formed a tenants association, and the Gunny helped them draw up rules for tenant behavior, a patrol system that tracked and reported violators, and liaison with the police. As soon as they identified a drug dealer or other scumbag, they got witnesses, brought the cops in and threw the trash out, permanently. Very quickly the place turned around. For the first time in years, the nights were not punctured with gun shots, there were no hypodermic needles in the halls and kids could play safely outside.

Then the feds came in, in the form of the Legal Services Corporation. Legal Services used tax money to pay lawyers to defend "the poor" in court. Only they had no interest in the honest poor. They were always on the side of the scum. They quickly went to court and stopped the evictions, on the grounds that the rights of the drug dealers and their molls were being violated. Just as quickly, the drug dealing, mugging and shooting started up again, and Gunny Matthews and his tenants association were back where they started.

He asked me to come down and give them some help. I knew how to fight enemy infantrymen, not lawyers and judges. But I also knew I couldn't ignore the Gunny's plea. If I was going to do something to take our country back, this was a place to start. So one snowy February day I loaded up the truck and headed to Boston. On the way, I did some thinking.

This wasn't law, I realized, this was war. The Legal Services lawyers, the liberal judges who gave them the rulings they wanted, their buddies in the ACLU, they were just enemy units of different types. More, they were the enemy's "critical vulnerability." The scum depended on them; no lawyers, no scum (a point we have enshrined in Victorian law, where you must represent yourself in court). The tenants had already shown they could kick out the trash, if we could get the lawyers off their backs. So that had to be our objective.

The Gunny had set up a meeting with the tenants association for the night I arrived. They were a pretty down lot when it started. One mother of three kids, the association's leader, tried not to cry when she explained how they thought they'd made a new start, then had it all taken away from them, thanks to Legal Services. They didn't know what they could do, now. If I could help, they'd be grateful. But it's clear they weren't expecting much from a white boy from Maine.

"Okay," I said, "here's where we start. You're in a war. You know that. You've got the bullet holes in your walls and doors to prove it. What we have to do is take the war to the enemy."

"Amen, brother," was the answer. "Are we gonna start shootin' those lawyers?" one voice asked.

"That's tempting," I replied. "But you know that while they won't put the drug dealers in jail, the law will come after honest citizens in a heartbeat. We've got to fight, but we've got to fight smart."

I laid out a plan. The starting point was one of Colonel John Boyd's maxims. Boyd was the greatest American military theorist of the 20th century. He said war is fought at three levels: moral, mental, and physical. The moral level is the most powerful, the physical the least (The old American military, in its love for hi-tech, could never understand that, which is why it kept getting beaten by ragheads all around the world). We would focus our war at the moral level, and use the physical only as it had moral impact.

We'd start with the churches. Most of the black folk who were on the receiving end of black crime were Christians. We'd mobilize the Church Ladies—a Panzer division in this kind of fighting. We'd get them and the black ministers to go to white churches all over Boston and invite their congregations to visit the housing project. We'd let them see what those Legal Services lawyers and their friends among the judges and politicians were protecting. We'd take them through the drug markets, past the prostitutes, over the dazed, crazed addicts lying in the hallways. Then we'd ask them one question: Would they tolerate these people living in their neighborhoods? On the way out, we'd hand them a list of the names of their elected representatives with phone numbers.

The key judge, the one who always ruled in favor of the scumbags, was a federal magistrate, Judge Holland P. Frylass. We couldn't touch him through the ballot box. But I thought there was another way. He was keen on making the folks in the projects live among the drug dealers and muggers and carjackers, but I suspected he would prefer not to do so himself. So we'd hold a raffle. We'd get black kids selling raffle tickets all over Boston. The proceeds would go to purchase the house next door to Judge Frylass's home in that nice section of Cambridge. We'd move in some drug dealers, whores, and gang members and see how he liked a taste of his own medicine.

Then a young mother, carrying one baby with two more grabbing at her coattails, spoke up. "That's all fine, I guess," she said. "But I got a drug dealer workin' right outside my door. Somebody come after him, those bullets will shoot right through my walls and my babies and me. What you gonna do about him?"

"Swarm him," I answered. The physical level of war also had its role to play.

"What you mean, swarm him?" she asked.

"Wherever he goes, or stops, we surround him. Twenty, thirty, fifty of us. We don't touch him. We're just there. We're always there. We're on every side of him. How much business do you think he's going to do?"

"And just what do we do when he starts hittin' out?" asked another woman in the crowd.

"Someone will always have a cell phone. He makes a move, we get it on camera. Then the cops can come in," I replied.

But they knew the ground better than I did. "Hon', we appreciate you comin' all the way down here," began one matron. "I think you've got some ideas we maybe can use. But this sure ain't no boxin' match. When these boys hit out, it's with guns. Some of us gonna be dead if we try swarmin' him like you want."

Now, I knew how to use a weapon, and I guessed I could shoot better than the average drug dealer. But I also knew I'd be the one in jail, not the drug dealer, if I got in a fire fight. And for a young, white, middle class male, jail in the 21st century meant homosexual gang rape. It was funny that the same bleeding-heart lefties who opposed the death penalty never made a peep about a punishment that would have appalled Vlad the Impaler. But I wasn't anxious to have the joke be on me.

Gunny Matthews came to my rescue. "You folks know I've got a good relationship with the cops. You let me work on that one. I'll get us some protection, protection that can shoot back. My question to you folks is, are you willing to do what the man says? We can talk here all night. But we've got to act, not just keep talking. Or give up."

As a German general, Hans von Seeckt used to say, *das Wesentliche ist die Tat*. Always, in war, that's what it comes down to. The important thing is the deed.

The Panzers were ready for battle. One of the Church Ladies got up. She was dressed perfectly for a shopping trip to Filene's in 1955: floral print dress, pillbox hat, white gloves. "I can speak for my church," said Mrs. Cook. "They sent me here as our representative. I don't know whether it will work or not. But the Lord blesses those who try. He may bless us with success, and he will still bless us if we fail. I say we do it." She turned to the young mother with the drug dealer camped outside her door. "Honey, I'm an old lady. If that bad man outside your apartment shoots me, I'm ready to go to Heaven. I'll swarm him, as the man here says, even if I have to do it all by myself."

"You don't have to, Melba." Her neighbor in the project was on her feet, in similar uniform, which events came to show was Urban Combat cammies. "I'll be there too. I've got a heavy purse and a strong umbrella, and I know how to use both of them. We'll swarm this no-account piece of nigger trash all the way back to Alabama."

With that the congregation were on their feet, Amening and Halleluiaing. I could understand now why, back in the 1950s, so many Americans were enraged by the South's segregation laws. It was the Mrs. Cooks they'd made sit in the back of the bus. If young blacks had tried to be like Mrs. Cook, integration might have worked.

What a pity so many chose Malcolm X and Snoop Dogg as their heroes instead.

CHAPTER SIX

I gave the Gunny a lift home after the revival meeting. I was interested in how he thought we could get the police to help. I guessed the cops themselves would want to, but they worked for the politicians, who would probably want them to protect the scum from the Church ladies.

His answer proved to be important beyond our fight to save one housing project. "A number of cops around here are former Marines. We've got a network set up among us," he explained to me. "We're getting together tomorrow night. Can you come?"

"Of course I'll come. You think I'm some staff puke who comes up with a plan, then sends someone else off to execute it? I've done some thinking up in Maine. The real war is the war for our culture. This is a battle in that war. I'm in," I replied. "Do you know a cheap place I can put up for the duration?"

"Sure, stay with us. My wife and I would be honored to have my old CO as a guest," he said.

I was happy to accept.

*

The meeting with the cops was at the Tune Tavern, in Boston's South End, the Irish ghetto. Nobody in Southie was likely to remember anything he overheard in a discussion among cops.

About twenty guys showed up, mostly city cops, with a few state troopers and even one transit cop thrown in. All were former Marines. I hadn't known any of them in the Corps, but they knew who I was and why I was there and they had no problem with that.

Gunny Matthews was too smart to throw the problem on the table and hope somebody had a solution. The old Russian technique, "Let's negotiate from my draft," was more likely to result in action. So after outlining the overall scheme, the Gunny made a simple request: would at least one off-duty cop accompany each swarm that went after a scumbag? Off-duty cops were expected, by regulation, to be armed and to intervene when citizens were in danger, so no politician could go after them for that. But at the same time, no political sleaze-bag could order them not to be there, since they'd be on their own time. Lots of businesses hired off-duty cops as security guards; the only difference here is that we had no money to pay them.

"That's not a problem," said officer Kevin McBreen. "What you're offering us is a chance to do the job we signed up to do, but usually can't because city hall and the effing lawyers and judges won't let us. We're all willing to put some time into this."

"Will it work?" I asked the question, even though the basic plan had come out of my brain housing group. These guys knew the local situation better than I did, and if the plan didn't fit the situation, it was better to scrap it now than to see it fail later.

The cops were quiet. One state trooper finally spoke up, a former commo staff sergeant named Kelly (sometimes I thought half the Marine Corps was named Kelly). I found out later he'd been into Tactical Decision Games big-time, so he knew how to think situations through.

"As far as it goes, I think it has a reasonable chance," he said. "In war, that is all any plan can promise. We're looking for a breakthrough here, in that we're trying to defeat not only the scum but their friends and protectors, the lawyers, judges and pols. The rule in war is, small risk, small gain; big gain, big risk. The potential gain here is worth the risk."

"My problem with the whole proposal is that it doesn't go far enough," he continued. "Down at 2nd Marine Division I sat in on a briefing Colonel Boyd gave. He said strategy is the art of connecting yourself to as many other power centers as possible, while separating your enemy from as many power centers as possible. It was the only definition of strategy I ever heard that meant anything."

"We need some more friendly connections here. We need connections with the press. How this gets covered in the *Globe* and on TV affects the outcome. We shouldn't leave that to chance. The same goes with the legislature. We should have friends there all set to go so the debate tilts our way. In other words, we need some strategy, not just good tactics."

Trooper Kelly was on to something. When I was stationed at Quantico, I'd gotten to know a staffer on Capitol Hill. He explained to me that when the senator he worked for wanted to make a major move, he had a meeting that included other senators' staffers, newspaper columnists, representatives from outside special interest groups, anyone who was in a position to affect the issue. Before the public saw anything, each of these insiders had his assignment: write a column, give a speech, organize a letter-writing campaign, whatever. Then, when the senator acted, all these other things happened as if they were spontaneous. But they weren't. They were all arranged—"greased" was the term my friend used—beforehand.

"Great idea," said one city cop. "But we're just street cops. I don't know how we make this happen. I can't get through to a newspaper editor or a politician. Can you?"

"I can, and so can you," Kelly replied. "We can do it the same way we've come together here: through the Marine connection. A bunch of members of the legislature are former Marines. So's an editor at the *Globe*. I know him, and I know one former Marine in the State House. He can put us on to others. There's even a regular breakfast where former Marines now in politics get together. Most of these guys think like we do. They'll help."

At this point I got one of those brain farts where a whole lot of pieces from a bunch of different puzzles come together to make something new. Boyd called it synthesis.

"Maybe what we need is a new Marine Corps," I said.

"What do you mean?," Matthews said.

"I'm not sure. Let me think out loud here. The Marine Corps we all served in is supposed to fight our country's battles. Yet all the Corps is doing now is fighting ragheads. Those aren't our country's battles. They are just games the politicians and State Department types in Washington like to play to feel important and justify their salaries."

"This battle, for this lousy housing project, is a battle for our country. It's a battle in the real war, the one being fought on our own soil between the people who live according to the old rules and the people who want to break all the rules, and usually do. We need a Marine Corps for the real war."

"I think we're seeing that new Marine Corps in action right here," I continued. "The battle we're planning is just one of what will be many battles, many campaigns, in the war to save our culture. We need a force that doesn't dissolve when this battle is over, that sees the war right through to the end."

The cops were quiet. So was I. I knew what I'd just proposed was scary. I hadn't thought it through; it just came to me. I didn't know where it might lead.

The transit cop spoke first. "Would this be like one of these militias we hear about?"

"No," I replied. "We've all run around in the boonies in cammies enough for that to be old. And we don't want violence. Violence will almost always work against us at the moral level of war. Think of it instead as a general staff for whoever wants to take our country back, wherever we could make a difference. Like we're doing here."

Again, there was silence, a long silence this time. Trooper Kelly spoke again. "I think you've hit on the answer to what's been bothering a lot of us for a long time. We work for a government that doesn't work. No matter how many arrests we make, it doesn't make any difference."

"The whole system is rotten," Kelly continued. "The big boys, the politicians, the lawyers, the judges, the media types, they all live well off the decay. They are scavengers, parasites. But for real people, it just keeps getting worse and worse—crime, lousy schools, rising prices that make our pay and pensions worthless, it's all part of the same picture."

"I hate to say so, but I think this country is finished. It's beyond fixing. We need something new. What you are proposing, skipper, is a start," he concluded.

"In 1775, the United States Marine Corps was founded in another tavern, in Philadelphia," I said. "I think it's time to do it again, here in Tune Tavern. Who knows, maybe we're making history once more."

The transit cop spoke up again. "A new Marine Corps I can see.

Nobody's fighting the battles that need to be fought. But what Marine Corps? Nobody has written a new Declaration of Independence that I've heard of. What kind of Marines are we?"

"Christian Marines." The voice was Gunny Matthews's. "That's what we are, most of us. That doesn't mean we're fighting to spread a religion. But our faith is where our first loyalty must be, because it is the thing we believe in most deeply."

"In 1775, a man could be both a Christian and a United States Marine. Now we have to choose. The reason the government we have doesn't work is that it has thrown our whole Christian culture overboard. I don't care whether someone goes to church or not. But unless people follow the rules laid down in the Ten Commandments, everything falls apart. It seems to me what we're fighting for here, in this housing project, is to make the Ten Commandments the rules again. And that is what this new Marine Corps should fight for, wherever it fights."

"Sign me up," said the transit cop, Meyer. "By the way, I'm Jewish. You may remember we had the Ten Commandments before you did. But we're all in this together. It's the whole culture we have to fight for, our Western, Judeo-Christian culture. I'll still go to synagogue, but I'm happy to be a Christian Marine. After all, Christ was a Jew, and so were his disciples."

And so it began, the Christian Marine Corps, the general staff for our side in the second civil war. I still have the piece of paper that went around the barroom table that day. It has twenty-two names on it. Seventeen of those men gave their lives in the war that was to come. I'm the only one left, now.

But those who died did so knowing they'd made a difference.

CHAPTER SEVEN

THE Battle of the Housing Project began on the last Friday in February, 2017. It proved to be Blitzkrieg, but into Russia.

Friday night usually meant big business for the hookers, pimps, drug dealers, and the rest of the informal economy that dominated the inner cities back then. Boston was enjoying a break in the winter weather, which should have drawn a big crowd out. It did, but not the kind they were expecting. The Panzers were in laager by 3 PM, 243 strong: the Church Ladies. Project residents were the infantry; they would make sure the tanks reached their objectives. The artillery was the press. The Marine connection worked, and we had reporters from the *Boston Globe* plus camera crews from several local TV stations. We also had twenty-five off-duty cops—in uniform and armed—and a couple video cams of our own; I wanted to have our own video tape, edited and ready to hand out ASAP.

Darkness comes early in Boston in February, and as it fell the bipedal roaches started crawling out of their cracks to sell their crack and whatever else. They didn't need any of their own stuff for excitement that night. We had twenty-five swarms just looking for targets, and as soon as one of the scum made an appearance anywhere near the project, he was surrounded. Singing "Onward Christian Soldiers," the Church Ladies and their allies made sure no business was done. One dealer was dumb enough to reach for his piece; before one of our cops could react, a swift umbrella brought him low.

But we faced no stupid enemy. The trash knew how the game usually went. Their friends in high places had already won the first round for them. So they retreated. They backed off, moved on, or went to ground and waited. Monday would see Judge Frylass in his chambers and the Legal Services lawyers before his bench, demanding and undoubtedly getting an injunction.

This time, we were ready for that. We picked a Friday to launch our attack because people would be home over the weekend to read the papers and turn on the TV. The next day, we dominated the news.

To keep the initiative, Saturday morning the leaders from the project and the ministers from the local churches held a news conference. They announced part two of the plan, an appeal to the white churches. Those congregations were prepared when our black Church Ladies arrived on Sunday and invited them to visit the project and see for themselves why we were fighting. We had the logistics carefully planned, with buses lined up, guarded parking lots available near the project and lists where we asked people to commit themselves to come for a tour on a certain date. Anticipating Judge Frylass's action, we had the tours of the project begin on Monday evening.

Frylass did not disappoint us (in war, a predictable opponent is a great asset). With a ringing denunciation of "mob rule," on Monday morning he issued an injunction against any "tactics of intimidation" directed against "the victims of racism and an oppressive economic structure," i.e., the scum.

Monday evening, the scum were back. So were we, again with the black Church Ladies in the lead, but now with white Christians, including some priests and ministers, alongside. At Frylass's order, state cops were present to enforce his injunction. That was just what we wanted. Tuesday's news was filled with photos of Church Ladies and their allies, black and white, being handcuffed and hauled off in paddy wagons while the drug dealers grinned.

The public was enraged, and the politicians started to get scared. In the state legislature, former Marines got the state cops pulled off the case.

Tuesday afternoon, our ministers and Church Ladies, now joined by the Cardinal of Boston, the Mayor, and the Speaker of the Massachusetts House, held another news conference. They announced part three: the raffle to buy the house next to Frylass's and give him a dose of his own medicine.

The public went wild. It was a chance to give one of these Lord High Panjandrums a kick in the butt. The demand for lottery tickets was so great they were bid for on the street at ten times their price.

At this point, our battle went national. Every network ran it as their lead story on the Wednesday evening news, using the video we had prepared. A Senate Resolution condemning Frylass went through by voice vote. Colleagues on the Federal bench began talking publicly about impeachment.

But as is often the case in war, an unpredicted event was decisive. Tuesday and Wednesday evenings had seen repeats of Monday, only bigger. We swarmed the scum, wherever we could find them. Federal Marshals, brought in by Frylass, made their arrests. Now, the televisions were full of businessmen in three-piece suits, white housewives, people from every class and race being hauled off. Wednesday the Cardinal himself was arrested, arm in arm with two Baptist Church Ladies, all singing "We Shall Overcome."

Thursday the crowd started gathering early, around 2 PM. It was huge, it was angry, and it was largely middle-class. Somewhere, somehow, the cry was started, "Let's go see the judge." Everyone took it up. The mob started to move toward the Federal Courthouse. It was a couple miles, and as the march continued the crowd grew. Along the way they found a road crew working and took their tar truck. The crowd took up the chant, "Pillows! Pillows!", and from every window along the route pillows came flying down. Enough had feathers in them to do the job.

They found Judge Frylass in his chambers, having tea. He made a fine sight, tarred and feathered, riding on a streetcar rail for a short journey down to Boston harbor, where he went for a swim. The harbor police fished him out, somewhat the worse for wear.

Friday, it was clear it was over. Every news broadcast and newspaper in the country called it "The Second Boston Tea Party." The President, a man who knew the secret of political leadership was to find a crowd and follow it, announced the Attorney General was personally going to the Supreme Court to ask them to overturn Judge Frylass's injunction. The Court, which had been more a political than a judicial body since Earl Warren, duly complied.

That was the triumph of our Blitzkrieg. It took less than a week.

We then learned why Blitzkrieg didn't work in Russia. The enemy's position had too much depth.

The key to our victory was our starting point, the takeover of the housing project by its tenants. That happened as part of an experimental program sponsored by the Federal Department of Housing and Urban Development, or HUD. Of course, like the rest of the Federal government, HUD was solidly enemy territory. The bureaucrats were leftists to a man (or, back then, woman), and what had happened in Boston horrified them. How dare ordinary people stand up to the government—and win!

So, once the furor had died down and the attention of the press had wandered on to newer things, they quietly changed the rules. There would be no more housing projects with tenant management. Federal bureaucrats would stay in charge, they would not evict the scum, so the scum would rule. And they did.

The lesson for our side was that we could win battles, but not the war. The war had to be fought on the enemy's ground, the vast, incomprehensible network of government rules, regulations, and bureaucracies. That was our Russia, and it was just too big to conquer.

We had to let it fall of its own weight.

CHAPTER EIGHT

A FTER the battle, I figured I'd done what I could in Boston and got ready to head back to Maine. I still faced this problem of finding work. But before I left, Gunny Matthews wanted to get the Christian Marines together again for a "hot wash" critique and to figure where we went from here.

We gathered once more at Tune Tavern. Trooper Kelly led off the critique. "The reason we won here is simple," he said. "We prepared carefully, but did not try to exercise too much control once things began to move. The decisive action, the march on Judge Frylass, was something we did not foresee. But we were smart enough to let it happen anyway. By the middle of the week, everyone knew what we were trying to achieve—cutting the scum off from their supporters in the Establishment. So people could take the initiative, yet all their actions worked in harmony."

"This is what the Germans called mission type orders," I added. "In the German army, an order didn't tell you what to do, it told you what result was needed. You were free to do whatever you thought necessary to get that result. That's why the Germans were able to win so many battles, usually against superior numbers. Mission orders turn everyone's initiative and imagination loose, which is very powerful—far more powerful than an army of automatons with everyone doing only what they are told."

"I was an MP in the Corps," a Boston city cop said. "For most of my time, we were told exactly what to do and how to do it. Then, just before I retired, we got a new CO who understood this stuff, what the Corps called maneuver warfare. He told us, 'I want you to cut speeding on base by at least fifty percent. How you do it is up to you.' And we were much more effective, because each of us did it differently."

Gunny Matthews jumped in at this point. "There are a lot of folks all over the country who want to fight for what is right," he said. "The last time we met here, we did more than plan one battle. We decided to make a difference in the outcome of the whole war. The understanding of war that we share—mission orders, Third Generation war, maneuver warfare, call it what you will—is what the folks out there who believe as we do need in order to win. The question is, how are we going to provide it to them?"

Kelly had an answer. "Captain Rumford had it right when he said we Christian Marines should be the general staff. Remember, German general staff officers weren't commanders, they were advisors. We can't and shouldn't try to muscle in on what other people are already doing to take back control of their own communities. They would resent that, and rightly so. But many of them would be glad to get advice from people who understood war. Because this is war, let's not kid ourselves. And people out there are beginning to realize that."

A cop I hadn't heard from before, Lasky, raised what proved to be the key question. "I agree, but who is going to do the work? I'll put some time in, but I have a regular job that doesn't leave me a lot of time. If the Christian Marine Corps is to be a real organization, we need at least one person to work this full time."

"Don't complain," I replied. "At least you have a job. I'm finding it mighty tough to get one."

"Maybe there's our answer," Kelly said. "Skipper, you've got the time, you know how to think militarily, you're willing to make decisions and act. You ought to do it. You should be the first Commandant of the Christian Marines."

Great, I thought. A job with lots of responsibility, facing well-nigh impossible odds, risking arrest for sedition, all for no paycheck. But I also realized this was the critical decision point if I wanted to help take our country back. "Once to every man and nation comes the moment to decide," the old Anglican hymn says. For me, this was it.

"Well, I do have the time," I replied. "And I was the one who proposed this new Marine Corps, so I also have the responsibility to do what I can to make it real. But I have to tell you, my family fortune ran out around 1870. Does anyone have any ideas as to how I can take this task on and still make enough money to live?"

Kelly did have an idea. "There are now twenty-one Christian Marines, besides yourself. If we each put in $50 per month, that's $1,050 per month for you. Can you live in Maine for that?"

"I reckon I could," I said.

"Can the rest of us pony up that much?," Kelly asked.

"Let's face it, we each spend that every month on donuts," Meyer answered. "I'm good for it."

So were the others, though McBreen looked a little pale when he thought of doing without donuts.

"So that's settled," said Trooper Kelly. "Skipper, now it's up to you.

You can call on each of us for help, and we have a responsibility to look for situations where we can make a difference, not just wait for direction from you."

"But if the Christian Marine Corps is to mean anything beyond this one battle in Boston," Kelly continued, "from here on out, it's sweat, toil and tears, and probably blood too in the end. This is the point where most movements die. The exciting part is over, we all face the press of everyday concerns, and building an organization is slow, dull, frustrating work. It's also the work that makes the difference between talking around the bar and changing history."

"Well and truly spoken, Trooper Kelly," I replied. "In the old American militia tradition, I move we elect our officers, and I hereby nominate you to be the CO, Massachusetts Christian Marines."

The vote was unanimous, and Kelly accepted the post at which he later fell.

"And in the Marine tradition, I propose a toast, gentlemen," I concluded. "To the Christian Marine Corps, and confusion to our enemies." Appropriately, it was drunk in Sam Adams beer.

CHAPTER NINE

To understand what followed, you have to picture what the United States was like in the early 21st century. That's hard to do, because life in the old U.S. of A. had departed so far from everything normal, everything natural to mankind, that any analogy, any description sounds hyperbolic. But it isn't.

Real life, as countless generations had lived it, had virtually vanished into a "virtual reality" devoid of all virtue.

Husband and wife and children, home and household and community, field and farm and village, the age-old lines and limits of our lives, had been shattered into a thousand fragments. Reality was what came through an electronic box, not what you saw out your own front door. Not that you looked out your front door, for fear of what might be looking in, carrying a gun. It might be a stranger, or your own kid, or both.

Everything was political. You chose your words politically, your clothes politically, your entertainment politically. If all three were clean and dull, you were on the right. If they were dirty and suggestive, you were on the left. You had to be one or the other, because everything was.

You lived a lie, one or another, because everything was political and politics was all lies. We were told we were free. It was a lie, because the tentacles of government had a sucker on every sucker. We had elections, and they were lies because all the candidates were from the same party, the New Class.

America's New Class was the French aristocracy of 1789, without the grace. Like that aristocracy, it performed no function beyond living well. Instead of "Let them eat cake," it said "Let them eat free trade." Instead of Marie Antoinette, who had charm and innocence, it gave us Hillary Clinton, who had neither. The French aristocracy held balls, ours held elections. Neither changed anything, but the French gave us good music.

The national sport was voyeurism, done electronically. Day and night, the television, Satan's regurgitation into our souls, paraded the sad lives of other people for our entertainment. No need to peep in the neighbor's windows—just turn on the box. Lucky the citizen who got to do the parading, as he or she thus became real.

Despite our fears, 1984 never came. We got a Brave New World instead.

We stopped making things, and kept getting poorer, but no one put the two together as cause and effect. The GNP continued to rise, because the government kept the statistics.

The solution, we were told, was more technology. We knew less and less, but computers would transmit our ignorance faster. Schools taught our children how to peck at the blue dot on the machine to get a piece of corn.

Or, the solution was big business. The New Class on Wall Street would drive down in their Mercedes to save us from the New Class in Washington. People would find dignity and security by being reduced to commodities. It was more efficient than slavery. You couldn't sell an elderly slave, but you could fire one.

The New Class—cultural Marxists all—told us there weren't any rules, then they set rules. They reached down into society's gutter, plopped whatever they found there on the civic altar and demanded we bow down and worship it. So long as it was sewage—moral, cultural, behavioral—it was fine and good and worthy of adoration. Those who would not bow were ruled out.

We were, of course, collectively mad. There's nothing new about that. From Athens under Cleon through the Tulip Bubble to Party Day at Nuremburg, collective madness has been part of the human tale.

The way to such madness is always the same. Create a false reality, through fine speeches, dreams of wealth beyond avarice, ideologies of revenge and redemption, video screens, whatever.

Stoke the fire hot enough that no one can look away from it. Drive the dance faster and faster, so it entrances, mesmerizes, draws all into it. Think and you'll miss a step and fall. Fall and you'll get trampled. Beat the tom-toms quicker and louder. Dance the Ghost Dance long enough, hard enough, and the bullets will pass through you without touching you.

Thud.

Reality always wins. The farther a people has danced away from it, the more they've done the *danse macabre*.

Americans had done quite a dance by the time we found ourselves in the 21st century. The gap between our virtual reality of techno-driven life-as-entertainment cultural freak show and reality itself was the size of the Mariana Trench. When America's virtual reality collapsed, as it would, the implosion would be stupendous, as it was.

My task, as I settled back into the remains of a Maine winter in 2017 as Commandant of the Christian Marine Corps, was not to bring about the collapse. The nature of man would provide that, all by itself.

Rather, I had to think through what to do when it came. What did we want to rescue out of it? Could we rescue anything? How could a general staff of civilized men who understood war—really understood it, from history, not just by virtue of having had rank in some military bureaucracy—make a difference?

One thing I understood from the outset, again thanks to having some acquaintance with history. The answer did not lie in ideology, right or left, old or new. All ideologies failed and always would fail, because by their nature they demand and create a virtual reality. They all require that some aspect of reality, economic or racial or sexual or whatever, be ignored—more than ignored, deliberately *not seen*. That was a fatal error, always, because whatever part of reality you don't see is the part that kills you.

A meeting in Waterville showed me the way around that problem, and also what we could fight for—not just against.

CHAPTER TEN

I F the Christian Marines were to be the general staff for our side in what was coming, I needed to figure out just what and who our side was. I wanted to get to know them, and, more importantly, let them get to know me. That was the first step in establishing trust.

So one April evening in the year 2017 I drove down to Waterville. When I got there, I could tell Spring was coming to Maine. I could smell all the winter's dog poop melting on the green.

The local chapter of the Tea Party was gathering that night, to hear one of their top leaders up from Washington. I knew enough about the Tea Party to realize it was on our side. Many of the folks in it later became brothers in arms and leaders in the Recovery. But like all such groups in the last days of the American republic, it had a fatal flaw, the nature of which I was to learn that evening.

The fellow from Washington, whose name I long ago forgot, gave the usual pitch the "Inside-the-Beltway" types fed to the local yokels. The gist of it was that the future of the country depended on them (in fact, by that point, it had already been determined); they should respond to what their leaders asked them to do (when it should have been the other way around); and, most important, send money.

After he'd made his pitch, there were a few questions, a bit of discussion of this and that. Then a tall fellow in back stood up. He was dressed in a style from about the year 1945 in a well-cut brown double-breasted suit, wide tie, holding a brown fedora. By Maine standards, he had a good bit to say, and he said it well.

"I appreciate you taking the time to journey all the way up here," began Mr. William Hocking Kraft. "But frankly, you represent the problem, not the solution."

"The problem, put simply, is this. Our leaders always sell us out. Maybe they start out thinking like we do, I don't know. But once they get to Washington, and see how nice life can be once you're a member of the club, the Establishment, their goal becomes joining that club. But our goal is to close it down."

"They—you—always end up getting sucked in to the Republican Party," Mr. Kraft continued. "It holds the keys to the club. And it sold us out long ago. Sure, it tells us what we want to hear, but it snickers and winks the whole time it's talking. The only people it delivers for are those on Wall Street and in the country clubs."

"The fact of the matter is that you can't create what we believe in, a country that follows the Ten Commandments, from Washington. The people in Washington follow only one commandment: Promote Yourself. You have to create it here, not by what you say, but by how you live."

Kraft's words brought to mind something my friend who worked for a Senator had said to me. He said the difference between the Democratic Party and the Republican Party was the difference between Madonna and Donald Trump.

The fellow from Washington slid and slithered as best he could, but it was clear Kraft had said what others were thinking. And he was right. No matter what the group was, it ended up with leaders who wanted to join the club. Those leaders sold their own folks out, because that was the condition of club membership.

I was struck by Kraft's definition of what we wanted: a country that followed the Ten Commandments. That was what the Christian Marines wanted, too. And we needed action, not just words. So when the meeting broke up, I introduced myself.

His reply to my introduction was a surprise. "I already know you, or at least know about you," he said. "I have some friends in the Corps—I'm something of an amateur military historian—and I heard about your raid on the feminists at Expeditionary Warfare School. You showed the rarest of qualities in the American officer corps: moral courage. I would be honored if you would join me for dinner at my home, if you're free."

I was, and Kraft was clearly someone I wanted to know better. We walked out together to his car, an immaculate 1948 Buick Roadmaster. "I'll wait for you here," he said. "Just follow me."

His house was a typical 1920s bungalow, nothing special from the outside, but when I walked through the front door I got a shock. It was like going through a time lock.

Everything was as it might have been seventy years ago. Everything—the big floor model radio (no television), the Brussels carpets on hardwood floors, the appliances, the 1948 calendar on the kitchen wall (as always in Maine, we came in the back door, through the mud room), even the way his wife and children were dressed. It had been a long time since I had dropped in on someone and found his wife in a nice dress waiting to serve dinner.

He introduced his wife as Mrs. Kraft, his young son as Master Billy and his daughters as the Misses Evelyn and Lula Bell.

I expressed my hope that my unexpected arrival for dinner was not a problem.

"Not at all," replied Mrs. Kraft. "I always prepare enough so that if Mr. Kraft brings someone, we have plenty. That is, after all, one of the duties of my sphere."

The feeling of having gone through a time warp was growing stronger.

We sat down in the dining room, with its 1930s floral wallpaper and oak wainscoting, polished mahogany table and built-in breakfront, and Mr. Kraft said grace—in Latin. Mrs. Kraft, and only Mrs. Kraft, served, from the kitchen. Somehow, it all felt right, even though my generation had been taught it was wrong.

"This is sure a change from most places I visit," I ventured, being somewhat unsure how much notice I should give to what then counted as eccentricity, at the least.

"Thank you," said Mr. Kraft. "It has taken some effort on our part, but we have created a home where you can leave the 21st century at the door. Here, at least, things are as they were, and should be."

"We're Retroculture people," added Mrs. Kraft.

"I don't know how much you've heard about the Retroculture movement," Mr. Kraft said.

"I'm afraid we lead a rather sheltered life in the military," I replied. "The only culture we get is the kind that grows on old bread."

"You may remember what I said earlier this evening, at the meeting," he continued. "You cannot create, or, more precisely, re-create, the world we want simply through words, least of all through the words of politicians. You have to do it by how you live. The Retroculture movement is people—individuals, families, sometimes whole neighborhoods—striving to live again in the old ways, following the old rules."

"I'm sure you've been told, 'You can't go back,'" Mr. Kraft went on.

"Like most of what you are told these days, it's a lie. The one thing we know we can do is what we've already done. We can live in the good, wholesome, upright ways our forefathers followed."

"So there is more to this than furniture, clothes and manners?" I asked. The manners were obvious: we were holding an adult conversation at a table that included three children.

"Of course," Mr. Kraft replied. "Things are important tools; our furniture, our clothes, my Buick, all help separate us from the modern world, which is what we want to do. We're like the Amish in that respect. But also like the Amish, the essence of Retroculture is our beliefs, morals and values. We believe what Americans used to believe. We hold the same values, follow the same moral rules our ancestors followed."

"What era do Retroculture people want to live in?" I inquired.

"Any time before 1965," Mr. Kraft responded. "That year marks the beginning of the cultural revolution that destroyed America. Our period is the 1940s, though many of the things you see here are older than that; back then, people didn't throw out their furniture every ten years."

"Many Retroculture people have chosen the Victorian era as the time they want to live in, and for good reasons. The Victorians were astoundingly productive people, building, inventing, creating, conquering, all the things we need to do if we are ever to amount to anything again, other than a Third World country. The basis of their success, of course, was their strong, Christian morals."

"But other Retroculture folks have chosen the 1950s as their era, or 1910, or even the colonial period," Mr. Kraft continued. "The specific time period does not matter, so long as it is a time when traditional American culture was strong."

"Each person, each family decides for itself just how Retro it wants to go. There's no set of rules, except that it must be before 1965 and must include the values if it is to count as Retroculture. Most people follow the simple rule of common sense."

"The colonial period would interest me," I said, "though as a Marine, I was told that bleeding was bad for the other guy, not good for me. I'm not sure I'd like depending on 18th century medicine."

"Don't worry, you wouldn't have to," Mr. Kraft replied. "We had our children vaccinated against polio, I assure you. We have no desire to bring back the tiny braces and little iron lungs. On the other hand, we don't want modern medical technology to keep us alive when our natural life span is over, so we can waste away in some nursing home. When my time comes, I want the doctor to come to the house with his little black bag and give me some morphine to ease the passing, just as he would have done in the 1940s."

"Good luck finding a doctor to make a house call these days," I replied, wondering just how practical Retroculture was.

"We have such a doctor," Mrs. Kraft said. "He's in the Retroculture movement too. When one of us is sick, he comes to the house in his black Detroit Electric automobile from the 1920s."

"You're lucky to have a wife who goes along with all this," I said to Mr. Kraft, thinking how most of my friends' wives would have reacted to the idea of going back to the past.

"The good luck is mine more than his," Mrs. Kraft replied. "These days, women are told they were oppressed and mistreated in the past, and that they will be happier if they can live in the business world, the world of men. That is another modern lie."

"As a wife of the 1940s, I have my own sphere where I am in charge: this home, my family, and my community, where I do a great deal of volunteer work, as women did in the past. It is a more important sphere than the business world where Mr. Kraft works, because it is the sphere where babies grow into children and then into men and women. I, as the woman of the house, hold the future in my hands."

"I agree with that," Mr. Kraft said. "Unless women create good homes and raise the children right, those things go undone. They are not natural to men. We see all around us what kind of children come from homes where the wife is not a mother and homemaker. As Arnold Toynbee warned, our barbarians have come from within."

"As far as all the nonsense about women being oppressed by being given charge of the home," Mrs. Kraft added, "I find quite the opposite is true. Creating a good home is a greater challenge than most matters in the business world, and it allows more room for creativity. The home you are enjoying now is my achievement. How many women in business achieve so much? Or are so loved and honored for their achievement as I am by Mr. Kraft and our children?"

"That you are indeed, Mrs. Kraft," Mr. Kraft replied.

They had a remarkable home life, as I could plainly see. It was the sort of home most people of my generation knew about only from books or plays or family memories. But it was exactly the kind of home we all wished we could live in—not just for the beautiful things, but for the warmth and contentment and absolute solidness I could feel radiating from every corner.

After an ample and excellent meal, Mr. Kraft and I adjourned to his den while Mrs. Kraft did the dishes. As he busied himself filling and lighting his pipe, I started to think. Maybe this was the answer to the puzzle I was facing of how the Christian Marines could explain what we were fighting for. In a broad sense, we knew the answer: a nation where the Ten Commandments ruled. But I knew our program, our goal, had to be developed beyond that to be understood by other people.

The danger facing us was falling into an ideology. Retroculture avoided that danger, because unlike an ideology it was not based on some abstract scheme of ideas. It was simply recovering what we used to have and used to be, which was the ultimate in concreteness. And we could know it would work, because we knew America had worked in the past. Logically, what worked once should work again.

"Just how many of you Retroculture people are there?" I asked Mr. Kraft.

"Tens of thousands," he replied, "and growing fast. You don't hear about us much in the general media, because we represent a rejection of everything it stands for. But we have our own magazines, books, clubs, and societies. We come in all varieties—there is even a group of non-Amish who live like the Amish, what they call, 'plain.' There is growing talk of founding new towns where everyone would live in a certain time period and there would be nothing out of place for that time."

"It kind of makes you wonder what a whole Retroculture country might be like," I mused.

"It would be splendid, as America itself once was splendid, before the squalid sixties," Kraft replied. "Remember, we had a country that worked."

"That is hard to remember now," I responded.

"But people do remember," Kraft said. "Take a look at this—and it is from more than twenty years ago."

He handed me a copy of a poll taken in 1992 by Lawrence Research for something called the Free Congress Foundation. It was a survey of people's attitudes toward the past, and the findings were remarkable. 49 percent said life in the past was better than it is today; only 17 percent said it was worse. 59 percent said the nation's leaders should be trying to take the country back toward the way it used to be. 61 percent thought life in the 1950s was better than in the 1990s. 47 percent said their grandparents' lives were happier than their own—and the margin was 15 percent higher among blacks, whose grandparents had lived under segregation.

When given a menu of times and places in which they could choose to live, a typical suburb in 1950 came in first with 58 percent; in last place was Los Angeles in 1991. When asked for a second choice, the winner, with 32 percent, was a small town in 1900; modern LA again came in last.

56 percent of those polled had a favorable impression of the Victorian period. 45 percent said they saw signs of people and things turning back toward the past—and that it was a good thing.

"For America, that poll represents nothing less than a cultural revolution," Mr. Kraft said. "From the days of the Massachusetts Bay Colony onward, Americans have been future focused. We have always believed that the future would be better than the present, and that the present was better than the past. We don't believe that any more. We believe—in fact, we know, because unlike the future, the past is knowable—what we once had was better than what we have now. Caught as America is in an endless downward spiral of decline, decay, and degradation, we have no reason to hope for our future—unless that future can be a recovery of our past."

"Thanks to a certain professor from Dartmouth College, I've read a bit about our past," I said. "Not just America's past, but the history of our Western culture. My impression is that through most of history, we were past-focused. We saw the past as a model we should try to recapture and emulate. Is what we're seeing here a return to normality?"

"Yes," Mr. Kraft responded. "Most of our culture's great leaps forward have come from attempts to return to the past. The Renaissance is a good example. The Renaissance was an attempt to recover the classical world of ancient Greece and Rome. Of course, such efforts don't exactly recreate the past; 15th century Florence was not the Roman Republic. But the attempt to recapture the classical past created a new synthesis that was brilliant—and that could never have been created by looking only to the future, which is, after all, a void."

"Do you think an attempt to recapture our own past—Retroculture— could give us a renaissance?", I asked.

"Again, the answer is yes," Kraft replied. "Retroculture is something solid, something real people can put their hands on and understand. Most people know how their grandparents or great grandparents lived. They know they were good people who lived decent, satisfying lives. They can grasp the fact that we can live that way again. Once they realize it is possible, once they realize that the saying, 'You can't go back,' is a lie, it is something they want to do. And if they do it, as we have done it in this home, in our lives, they find it works."

"One final question, if I may," I said. "If some people were willing to fight for a country where Retroculture could flourish—not one where it was enforced by law, but where people could live Retro if they wanted to, without any hindrances from the government—would you be willing to help?"

"Of course," Mr. Kraft replied. "At present, Retroculture can't go much beyond home life, because all kinds of government regulations and regulators and lawyers come down on you if you try. As I said, some of us would like to create whole new towns and communities where everyone would live in a certain time. But we know the government would prevent that, because one or another of these victims groups would protest."

"Retroculture isn't political," he continued. "Retroculture is about escaping politics and government and all that nonsense. It's about simply living a normal life, the kind of life Americans used to live. It seems to me that if we're going to talk about a new country, that's the kind of country we should want."

I thought that summed it up pretty well. After drinking a glass of good Port and smoking a cigar to accompany Mr. Kraft's pipe, I bid him good night and headed home through the April slush. Another piece of the puzzle had fallen into place.

CHAPTER ELEVEN

THE summer of 2017 marked the beginning of work. As Trooper Kelly had warned, building an organization proved to be anything but exciting. It was slow, it was dull, it was frustrating. I often felt like I was trying to drive a thousand blind geese through one tiny wicket. But slowly, the Christian Marine Corps grew.

The first thing I did was identify a small group of people I could turn to for advice. I knew better than to think I had all the answers, or all the questions, either. The questions were more important, at least at the start. As Sir Francis Bacon said some centuries back, if you start out with questions, you may end up with answers. But if you start out with answers, you will end up with questions.

The first and most important question was, what did we want to do? We knew the answer to that one: we wanted to take our country back. We wanted to take it back for our traditional, Western, Judeo-Christian culture—in short; for the Ten Commandments.

We realized this was a tall order. We were living in a country where a teacher who posted the Ten Commandments on the wall of his classroom would be fired. (By 2016, in Massachusetts, he would also be fired if he did not put up a state-supplied poster titled "The Ten Commandments of Safe Sex.")

But we also knew the cultural Marxists, seemingly so powerful, had reached what in war is called the culminating point. They were running out of gas. As they stuck their big noses into the business of more and more average people, they were building up a tremendous backlash. Our goal was to shape, strengthen, and guide that backlash.

That was itself a challenge, but one we thought we could manage, God willing. To further limit the task, we decided we would focus on New England.

The second question we faced was, how do we do it? Here too, we had an answer: by offering the other good people who had the same goal our expertise in war. We sought only to be advisors, never controllers—a true general staff.

The secret of success in the culture war would be "leaderless resistance," where people worked independently but with efforts harmonized by shared objectives. The worst thing we could do was create some kind of formal, hierarchical organization. That would be easy for the other side to attack, it would demoralize our own troops by reducing them to pawns on someone else's chessboard, and it would leave us dependent on one or a handful of brains when we could have many brains thinking and acting for us. Also, it would generate office politics as people within the organization struggled for power. I'd seen enough office politics in the Corps to last me the rest of my days.

Ultimately, the Christian Marines did not want to be about power. This, we recognized, was our biggest difference from all the other factions. We did not want power. We did not want a new country built around power, or struggles for power.

Power was itself an evil, maybe the greatest evil. Tolkien was right; the Ring of Power, which is power itself, cannot be used for good. That was another lesson we learned the hard way in the U.S.A. At one time, America had shunned power, refused power, at home and abroad. Those had been our happy days. Then the "Progressives" came along, who thought the power of government could be used for good. Eventually, they decided the power of government *was* good, in itself—because they controlled it.

That's how it always works: power looks good to whoever has it. But it isn't. Our war was in a way the strangest war of all, a war to bury power, not to seize it.

Advisors we would be. In the heat of battle, when someone had to decide and act, fast, we would do that. And our advice itself would be action, because it would counsel action. But in the end, our goal was to return to our plows, Cincinnati, not Caesars.

Only with these questions answered did we turn to the third (too many people started with this one): what kind of organization would we be?

First, we would start small. The old German motto was correct: "Better no officer than a bad officer."

That meant we could not simply recruit former Marines. There were people from other services, and people who had never been in the military at all, whom we would want. And, truth be told, the number of Marines who really understood war was small. The Corps had put strong emphasis on studying war, beginning in the 1980s, but most Marine officers blew it off. Their focus was looking good in the uniform and maxing the Physical Fitness Test, they read nothing beyond the sports page and their only talk was about trout fishing and getting promoted. To us, or to anyone, they were useless.

One of our great fears was that if actual fighting started, civilians who shared our values would turn to retired senior officers for leaders. Most of these guys, the colonels and generals, had never been soldiers. They were milicrats—military bureaucrats. In the old American military, once you made major, further promotion was based on how well you used your knee pads and lip balm, not military ability. If our side ended up led by milicrats, we would be defeated before the battles even began. We would be like the Whites in the Russian Civil War, who got all the old Tsarist generals as their leaders. The Reds got guys like Trotsky, who were serious students of war. We all knew who had won that one.

Because we would stay small, a few hundred men at most, we could avoid formal processes for recruiting. In fact, we avoided formal processes for everything, because the focus of any process becomes the process, not the product. We would accept new Christian Marines only by consensus, and we would consider candidates only on the basis of what they had done, not what they told us. We wanted to see actions, not words: articles or books published, speeches given in places where they counted, people mobilized, victories in free play military maneuvers, and later, as it turned out, in real combat, victories over the New Class—results.

And results, as the old German used to say, was what mattered.

A final rule we adopted was one I insisted on, as only someone who has just learned something important himself can insist. Any Christian Marine had to know the canon of our culture. He had to undergo my baptism by immersion in the great books and ideas of Western civilization. We couldn't hope to fight for that culture, and fight well for it, unless we knew what it was. A few of our recruits came to us with that knowledge—more accurately, that understanding. The rest had to start where I had started. That was true regardless of how well they understood war. An officer should never be a mere technician.

For the next couple years, as we slowly grew in numbers, we kept a low profile. We weren't exactly a secret organization, but we didn't put out any press releases, either. If we succeeded, people would know us by our works, which were all that counted. If we failed, better our failures remained obscure. In any case, general staff officers have no names.

Carefully, we built our cadre. New Christian Marines were recruited, and accepted, one by one. I spent a lot of time doing detective work. When our side won a battle in the culture war, like keeping pro-homosexual propaganda out of the schools, who had provided the leadership? That might be someone we wanted. A Marine from New England was potentially one of us. Where did he stand on the cultural issues? Were there other men who believed as we did in key positions in the state legislature, or the National Guard, or the state police? If so, they could be important to us.

Did we infiltrate the power structure in the New England state governments? Of course, wherever we could. In Massachusetts and lower New England, we didn't get very far; the cultural Marxists were fully in charge there. But we gradually made some key friends in Maine, New Hampshire, and Vermont. Some of those friends became Christian Marines. Others just knew who we were and what we had to offer.

We also infiltrated the active-duty forces. Our goal was not to overthrow the United States government. We were never enemies of the old U.S. Constitution. But we knew that government and its New Class were going to fall, of their own weight, corruption, ineptness, and disinterest in actually governing. We were looking, always, to the time after it fell. We wanted as many active duty Marines—and soldiers, sailors, and airmen—as we could get who would come to New England when it happened, and help us save something worthwhile from the wreckage.

By the first decade of the 21st century, the message that the U.S.A.

was finished, that it was only a question of when it came apart, not whether, found many a receptive ear. Books like Martin van Creveld's *The Transformation of War* had opened quite a few minds. Only the people in the capital, in Washington, could not see it coming. They were like the citizens of Johnstown, Pennsylvania, watching the rain come down in buckets but not thinking about the dam.

For us, in Maine, the dam started to crumble in the Fall of 2020.

CHAPTER TWELVE

Anyone who wondered where we Mainiacs were coming from could find out by sitting down to a typical Maine dinner. Everything was boiled, and if the cook was feeling exuberant that night, it might be seasoned with salt and pepper. Then again, it might not.

Any people with food that bad had to be conservative. And we were, in the old sense of the word: we lived pretty much as Americans had lived all along, and we liked it that way.

The funny thing was, Maine kept electing liberals. The liberals' crazy ideas didn't seem to matter in Maine. They could talk on, as they were wont to do, about this or that group of "victims," and Mainers could nod, because there weren't any of those people Down East. They weren't about to move in next door.

Then, in the Fall of 2020, they did.

The "they," in this case, were the gays. They were our one home-grown minority.

As our culture began to fall apart, in the 1960s, the gays started "coming out." This broke the old rule of "Don't frighten the horses," which had allowed mutual toleration. The rule meant that they were not open about their orientation, and we pretended not to notice it.

By the 2000s, they had become one of the cultural Marxists' sacred victims groups, which meant they were encouraged to flaunt their vice and we were supposed to approve of it. This was justified in the name of "toleration," but toleration and approval are different. You may tolerate things you don't approve. I was willing to tolerate gays, but I would sooner have given my approval to an act involving three high yellow whores, a wading pool full of green Jello, and Flipper.

As usual, Maine had elected a liberal Governor, a former Senator named Snidely Hokem. He'd gotten tired of the Caligula's court that was Washington, where he'd competed hard for the role of Incitatus's hindquarters. But he still liked having his own backside kissed, so he figured being Governor might be about right for him.

To keep up his liberal standing, he had to find one of the victims groups and abase himself and the State of Maine before it. That was a challenge, since our winters kept out most minorities and our women had too much real work to do to be feminists.

The gays provided the perfect answer. So on September 23, 2020, the Honorable Snidely Hokem issued an executive order that each public school in Maine, including every elementary school, had to hire at least one homosexual guidance counselor. The order explained that this was necessary so "students with different sexual preferences would not feel excluded." In order to determine who had what sexual preference, the gay counselors had to be given "unrestricted public and private access" to all the kids.

Suddenly, Mainers found their luxury liberalism had turned on them and bitten them, hard.

It takes a good bit to stir Yankees, but this did. The outrage was widespread. All over the state, parents came to PTA meetings and raised hell.

I expected Hokem to back down in the face of the voters' wrath. After all, he was a politician. But he didn't. Instead, he got on the television and gave a real stem-winder about how "we were all guilty of oppressing people who were really no different from ourselves." Far from condemning them, "we should confront our own homophobia, which is a greater sin than any they might commit, not that what they do is sinful. Let us ask ourselves," he concluded, "whether our children are not safer with these counselors than with the average Roman Catholic priest. After all, the sexually victimized have never led an Inquisition."

I realized it was time for the Christian Marines to go into action. I read in the Bangor paper where the leaders of a number of grass-roots groups were meeting in Augusta, and I decided to join them. Mr. Kraft had the connections to get me in, which he was happy to do. As a student of war, he understood that most crises were also opportunities.

The meeting went as such meetings tend to go. It was full of good people who didn't know what to do because they didn't know how to operate outside the system.

Someone proposed a petition drive. Someone else raised the question, a petition to do what? And who would do it? There wasn't much point in petitioning the state's liberal establishment, which was no different from that in Washington, only smaller.

Others wanted to elect more conservatives to local school boards. But the boards, which knew where the public was coming from and had to run for re-election eventually, were already on our side, most of them. However, they had no authority to countermand a state directive.

Someone suggested, rightly, that we turn Hokem out at the next election. But that would be too late. The gays would be in the schools by then, and they'd go straight to court if a new governor moved to fire them.

I waited 'til everyone had their say, then I got mine. "If we're serious, there is a way to stop this, I think," I said. "The schools need two things to operate: money and students. We can cut them off from both." In war, a frequent route to victory is through the enemy's logistics lines.

"How?" was the simultaneous question from a dozen different voices.

"By going on strike. Until the Governor's order is rescinded, we will neither send our kids to public schools nor pay our property taxes," I replied. The schools got most of their money from the local property tax, and tax bills were due soon. They'd be out of money in six weeks if a strike were widespread. That meant no pay for the teachers. We'd see whose side they were on once they had to choose between their ideology and their wallets.

People took a while to digest this. A voice finally said, "We'd be breaking the law."

"That's right," I said. "It's called civil disobedience. If you remember back to the civil rights movement, civil disobedience is something the liberals did a lot of."

At the moral level of war, it often disarms your enemy when you use his own tactics against him.

The chairman of the meeting, a local woman from a group called Fight for the Family, asked, "What do we do when they come to arrest us—and take our homes away for non-payment of taxes?"

"First, there's strength in numbers," I replied. "I think lots of State o' Mainers are mad enough to join a strike. They can only arrest so many. They can't go after half the population; they don't have enough police, prosecutors or jail space, not to mention that they'd look like idiots."

"Also, it takes time to seize someone's house for not paying taxes,"

I continued. "They have to give warnings, go through all kinds of legal procedures. We'd tie them up in their own knots, for once. And the schools would have dried up and blown away for lack of money by the time they got through all that."

War is a competition in time. If the enemy can't react fast enough, his reaction does him no good.

I could tell the rest of the folks at the meeting liked the idea, the more they thought about it. So I sweetened the pill. "They may try to arrest a few people, to make examples of them and scare the rest," I said. "So what we need are pledges to a strike fund. We'll only ask for the money as we need it. We can build up pledges of a few million dollars, I'll wager; plenty of people are mad enough to pledge. If they come after someone, the strike fund will give his family an income while he's under arrest. It will also pay for his lawyer. If Hokem and his lackies see we've got millions of bucks to fight them with, they'll be less eager to make any arrests."

"If they do arrest us, we can turn that around on them." I recognized the voice, though I couldn't see the face from where I was in back. It was John Fitzgerald, a former Marine major who'd retired around Portland. "Everyone who is arrested, for truancy or non-payment of taxes, should demand political prisoner status. If the state won't grant it, then go on a hunger strike. If the person arrested can't stand such a strike, one of us does it as a stand-in for them. At least half the Catholic priests in the state will volunteer for that duty, I can promise you."

That was the kind of thinking I liked. I'd talk to John afterwards about the Christian Marines.

There was a good bit more discussion, but the momentum was our way. Finally Madam Chairman spoke. "It's time for a vote. We can't make a final decision here; we all need to go back to our people and get their reaction. But we need to decide if we're in favor of it, ourselves. All in favor say aye." The ayes were resounding.

"We meet again in one week. See if your folks are willing to go along. And we need them to sound out their neighbors. This will only work if we have numbers. This meeting is adjourned."

The Christian Marines had done what we existed to do. We'd provided good advice. Now, we had to wait and see what would happen.

As always, the news of what the supposedly closed meeting had done leaked out. Because the media thought they had a scoop, they made the strike proposal their top story on every news program in the state.

The next day, school attendance was down 30 percent. That made the news too, which amplified the effect; the day after it was down 65 percent, then 85 percent. By the end of the week, the schools were pretty much empty.

A few towns had already sent out their property tax bills. Skowhegan was one. After a rally in front of the school, the folks there made a bonfire and burned the tax bills. That made good footage, which put it on the evening TV news all over the country.

In the small town of Waite, they didn't. They didn't have their tax bills yet, so they burned down the town hall instead.

At this point, it was clear the troops were out in front of their leaders. I realized that was a good thing. As long as everyone knows the objective, a unit on the attack does well if everyone advances as best he can. We didn't want to rein our troops in; on the contrary, the challenge for the leaders was using the momentum to drive on even faster. So I called Mr. Kraft.

"How well do you know the lady who chaired the last meeting?" I asked.

"We have worked together before," Kraft answered. "What would you like me to do?"

"Suggest she call a news conference tomorrow morning. At the news conference, she should announce a torchlight parade of all opponents to the governor's plan in Augusta next Saturday night."

"Why a torchlight parade?", Mr. Kraft asked.

"Because I don't think the Governor will feel real comfortable about thousands of torches in the hands of our people in the state capital. Not after Waite. Most of those state office buildings are pretty flammable. Just to make sure Hokem gets the point, she should announce that the people of Waite have been invited to lead the parade."

"Consider it done," Mr. Kraft said. "I know the Fight for the Family people will love it."

They did, and the news conference was big news the next day. By the end of that day, buses were being chartered and convoys organized all over the state.

One rule in war is to game the situation from the enemy's standpoint. If I were Governor Hokem, what would I do? One thing, clearly, would be to mobilize the state police and the National Guard. That meant if Hokem tried to do so, and couldn't, his situation would worsen. We'd be inside his cycle, as Colonel Boyd liked to say. And he'd start to come unglued.

I called Sam Briganti, who was a Christian Marine—a former intel Staff NCO—and a Maine State trooper. "Sam," I said, "I've got a mission for you. We need to box Hokem in, isolate him. I'm sure he's going to turn to the State Police to protect his town from our march. I need you to prevent the cops from responding."

"You're right about the first part," Sam replied. "All leaves have been cancelled and we're waiting for orders. It would really kick his ass if we didn't turn up. I'll have to think about how to do that—and not get caught."

"Let me know if you can't do it, or if you need help from any of the rest of us," I replied. "Otherwise, I'll trust you to make it happen." Sam had a first-rate mind plus determination; I knew that was all the order he needed.

He didn't fail us. The way he went about it showed a good understanding of war. Often, all it takes is some carefully injected ambiguity to force the enemy to abandon his plan. Sam put an anonymous message on the State Police electronic bulletin board: "Blue flu Saturday." He made sure a copy of it went to the Governor's personal email.

Hokem knew what it meant. He emailed the head of the State Police. "Will your guys show Saturday or not?" he asked.

"You can always count on us, sir," was the reply.

"How many of your men and women saw the 'blue flu' message?"

"Virtually all of them, sir. Every trooper has his own computer."

"How many of them will go along with it?"

"We have no way of knowing, sir."

"Then how can you say your cops will be there for me?"

"Because you can always count on us, sir."

Hokem recognized an ass trying to cover itself. After all, he'd appointed the guy. A former Air Force general, no less.

And we knew Hokem's problem was growing, because we were also reading his email.

His back-up was the National Guard. But we had friends there too. The head of the unit in Bangor was one, so I went to see him and told him what we needed to do.

It seemed he'd already been giving thought to the problem. For some years, the Maine Guard had been trying to get the money for new trucks. They'd told the Governor the old ones just weren't reliable any more. So who could he point the finger at if, at some critical moment, they just broke down?

His email went to every Guard unit in the state. "All, repeat all, trucks in 721st Engineers C-4. Impossible to meet any mobilization requirement. Please report status of your trucks."

Mainers aren't dummies, and I doubt there was a Guardsman in the state who wanted gays counseling his kids in elementary school. Suddenly, every National Guard truck in Maine just wouldn't start. We made sure the Augusta newspaper heard of this interesting fact. The Governor read the paper.

At this point, the march was just three days away. Luckily for us, Hokem loved anything high-tech. His smartphone, which conveniently combined audio and video calling with all the privacy of a screen door, never left his sight. One of our guys was a former wirehead Master Sergeant who'd worked for the National Security Agency. It didn't take him long before we were recording Hokem's conversations and filming his meetings.

At precisely 2 PM, on October 3rd, 2020, Hokem convened his last staff meeting. He'd invited only his most trusted advisers, the people who had created him.

"OK, guys, I've got just one question: how can you get me out of this one?" Hokem opened.

"At this point, frankly, I don't know," said his chief fundraiser. "Why in hell did you give that god-damned speech? It sounded like the most radical gay activist in the state wrote it for you."

"That's because the most radical gay activist in the state did write it for me. It came straight from Don Rexrod's office."

"Shit, he's head of the North American Man-Boy Love Association. Even most of the other gays don't like those perverts," said Hokem's chief of staff, Ms. Virginia Teitelbaum. "Boss, if you're dancing to his tune, you've got to tell us why."

"Because Don and the rest of the gays have me by the balls, that's why," Hokem said. "Well, not that way, but you know what I mean."

"No, we don't know what you mean," said Teitelbaum. "We can't help you unless you tell us what the real problem is. You know what you're doing is political suicide. Exactly why have you gotten so far in bed with these people?"

"Now cut it out," Hokem yelled. "I'm not in bed with any gays. I'm perfectly normal. I've got a family, after all. Hell, if I weren't normal I probably wouldn't be in this mess."

"Come on, Snidely. We need to hear the whole story. Now." The voice was that of Fred Farnsworth, the political boss who had found little Snidely Hokem years ago, working at his father's town newspaper.

"OK, here it is," Hokem said. "Years ago, back in the early 1990s when I was on the Senate Armed Services Committee, a bunch of us took a junket out to the Army's training center at Ft. Irwin in the California desert. We figured that wouldn't look like a junket to the folks back home, but the place was close to Vegas. We flew back each night to Caesar's Palace, where we had the usual free suites. Anyway, a bunch of us got plastered at the bar and we spotted some really nice tail. I mean, they were gorgeous."

"We figured, what the hell, we're Senators, right? Who's gonna make trouble for us? So we took them upstairs and started having some fun. Strangely, it was right where they held that Tailhook party."

"I swear, none of us even suspected they were drag queens. By the time I figured out something was where it shouldn't be, we were all in pretty deep. And the bitch, or whatever she, or he, was, was wired for sound. They had the whole goddamn thing on tape! The drag queens gave the tape to a bunch of gay political activists. So when our gay friends call, I listen," Hokem concluded.

Now we had a tape of our own. By the next morning, it was up on the internet.

With the governor's office vacant and the ruling about the gay school counselors rescinded by a very nervous lieutenant governor, the torchlight parade was a festive occasion. During the parade, I spotted Mr. Kraft on a hotel balcony, wearing a smoking jacket and a fez, puffing on his pipe and quietly enjoying the spectacle. I looked him up shortly after the rally ended.

"Not a bad week's work, if I do say so myself," I said.

"It's a start," he replied. By Maine standards, that was a high compliment.

"What do you think should be next on our agenda?" I asked.

"Understanding why we won."

"Why did we win?" I inquired.

"Because we kept the fight within Maine. You call it 'localizing the battlefield,' I believe," he said.

He was right on that. If the Feds had been involved, we would have been overpowered. They would have occupied Augusta with the 82nd Airborne. We wouldn't have been able to get in the town.

"What can we do with that lesson?" I asked, continuing my game of 20 questions. It was a useful game if you were playing with someone who could think.

"The same group that started all this is meeting here this evening. They're the folks you met with, when you came up with the battle plan that worked. Meet us here in my suite at ten o'clock and you'll find out."

I was there, and was somewhat surprised to find Mr. Kraft now chairing the meeting. It seems the rest of the folks had asked him to. They already knew what I was learning: in his Retroculture way, he was a first-rate strategist.

"Meeting is spelled 'waste of time,' in most cases," he began. "So we'll keep this one short. We won this past week because the issue was decided by the people of Maine. If we can decide matters without Washington sticking its snout in, we'll usually win."

"There's an idea I'd like to ask you to take back to your people, the folks in the groups you represent in this coalition. I call it the 'Maine Idea.' And it's what I've just said. We want to decide matters for ourselves. We want to separate ourselves in every way we can from Washington and from the rest of the country. If they want to mess their lives up with all these modern notions, that's up to them. But we want no part of it. We know the old ways were better, and we want to stick to them."

"Our own government up here is rotten," Mr. Kraft continued. "But we can do something about that. This business of putting gays in our elementary schools has awakened the people of this state. We can't fix Washington. So the hell with Washington. The 'Maine Idea' is to shut Washington out."

"How do we do that?" I asked. I liked the theory, but wondered how the mice could keep out an elephant.

"By being Moltkes, not Schlieffens," he replied. "You understand what that means. Moltke did not try to foresee every event in a campaign and plan too much beforehand. He campaigned opportunistically. So must we."

"The first step is to get the idea accepted. Ideas have consequences. When a majority of Mainers share the Maine Idea, opportunities will arise, as one did here in these past few weeks. I'm sure we will have some good Marine advice as to how to use those opportunities," Mr. Kraft concluded.

When Kraft talked, other people listened. They would take the Maine Idea back to their members. And gradually, it would spread along our rocky shore and through our stone-fenced fields.

I waited until the others had filed out; I wanted to extend a private invitation to Mr. Kraft. "You know about our Christian Marine Corps," I said. "You don't have to be a former Marine to join. We'd like to have you. You're general staff material if anyone up here is."

"Thank you," he replied. "You're not the first person to think so. I am honored by the invitation. I have always thought well of Marines. I will be happy to work with the Christian Marines and assist you in any way I can. But I am not at liberty to join you. I wear a different uniform."

I was intrigued by this answer, but Mr. Kraft's tone did not suggest the subject was open for further discussion. So I thanked him for his offer of support, said we would be back to him for assistance, and bid him a good evening.

Which it certainly had been.

CHAPTER THIRTEEN

THE fate of Governor Hokem made it clear that, once Mainers thought about it, they were on the right side in the culture war. While the establishment in Maine remained liberal, it got pretty quiet about it. It was not looking forward to another test of strength with those of us who followed the old ways.

But we knew the feds would come in eventually. They always did. Our victory in Maine had not gone unnoticed in Washington. The forces of cultural Marxism were still dominant there, and they were looking for an opportunity to take us down.

Through the winter of 2020–2021 and into the spring, I worked to build the Christian Marines, and the Christian Marines worked to spread the Maine Idea. Most of the grass-roots groups had gone for the concept, and they were hitting the hustings to spread it around. It wasn't really that hard; most folks already understood that all Washington did was take their money and spit in their face.

I knew the Maine Idea would not become real, however, until Maine had to fight for it. Even if we fought and lost, it would help. The fact that we dared fight the federal government would strengthen people's desire for independence, as the Battle of Bunker Hill did in the first revolution. If we could fight and win—that would give the people of Maine hope that our dream of being free again might become real.

The challenge, and our opportunity, came in the early summer of 2021. The Democrats were back in power in Washington, and their slogan was "A Rainbow Over America." For Maine, that translated into an announcement on June 22 by Ms. Lateesha Umbonga LaDrek, the Secretary of HUD, that her department had purchased two large apartment clusters in Bangor. The current rent-paying residents would be moved out, and 350 black federal prison parolees from out of state would be moved in. LaDrek said the purpose of this action was "to offer oppressed people of color a second chance by letting them serve as ambassadors of diversity to the people of Bangor, who were imprisoned in an all-white ghetto."

Maine seethed. But after years of being told that they were evil racists, people felt morally unable to defend themselves. They dared not speak openly against the trashing of their community.

I knew we had to turn that around. The first step was for us Christian Marines to put our heads together. When we met at the Old Place on June 25th, I put the problem squarely. "I think Maine can stop this, if it will fight. But it has to know it's in the right before it will fight," I said. "You all know the problem. Any resistance to black scum, even by decent blacks, brings screams of moral outrage from the cultural Marxists. Most folks have been so conditioned by this crap they can't stand up to it. They think they're Hitler if they dare defend their—our—community. So we have to win the moral fight first. How can we do that?"

"First, let the feds win a partial victory," said Major Fitzgerald from Portland. "Let them throw the current residents of those apartments out.

They've given them only 30 days to vacate, and the TV news is playing that up. The feds look heartless, as they are when its a matter of white folks. Seeing all those people's lives suddenly disrupted tells Mainers there's something wrong here."

"OK, that makes sense," I replied. "Let the enemy overextend himself. But how do we keep them from moving the black scum in?"

"By moving someone else in first." The speaker was one of our more unusual recruits, Father Dimitri, an Orthodox missionary from Russia. Russia was again a Christian nation, under a new Tsar, and she saw her mission as carrying the Word to the repaganized West. Father Dimitri was one of many Orthodox missionaries working in the States, and he was also a Russian Naval Infantry chaplain. Some of our former "spooks" had brought him in to the Christian Marines; they knew him, and I trusted them.

"What do you mean?" I asked.

"The enemy is presenting these black criminals as the poor, so good people feel it's wrong to oppose them," said the priest. "Of course, with your liberal churches, no clergy tell them that Christianity historically has distinguished between the deserving poor, who are poor through no fault of their own, and the undeserving poor, whose poverty is caused by their own sins. Before the undeserving poor qualify for our charity, they must repent—they must change their ways. Otherwise, we are just helping them along the road to Hell."

"As it happens, I know of some deserving poor who very much need this housing," Father Dimitri continued. "Three weeks ago, a ship brought almost 400 Egyptian Christian refugees into Montreal. Throughout the Muslim world, Christians are being driven out or killed. These are good people who escaped only with their lives. They are survivors of one of the oldest Christian communities, dating to the earliest days to the Church. Why don't we move them into these apartments before Washington can move in the orcs, then dare Washington to throw them out?"

"What are orcs?", Sergeant Danielov asked.

"The word is from Tolkien," Father Dimitri replied. "He was one of the great Christian writers of the 20th century. In his *Lord of the Rings*, which is Christian analogy, orcs are soldiers of the Evil One. Those creatures your government wants to move in to Bangor are orcs, believe me."

"How would we get your Egyptian Christians here?" I asked. "The Border Patrol would never let them in."

"Don't worry, we Russians are very good at smuggling things through northern forests," said the priest, laughing.

"Illegal immigrants are among the liberals' sacred victim groups," said Fitzgerald. "Usually that means trash from south of the border, but we can turn it around on them by bringing in good folks the same way. They'll have to face their own arguments, used against them. That's disarming."

The more I heard, the better I liked Father Dimitri's idea. In fighting merely to keep the orcs out—I'd read Tolkien, too—we were trying to beat something with nothing. That never works. His way, we would launch a pre-emptive strike, occupy the position, and make the feds try to re-take it.

I also knew that by giving refuge to these Egyptian Christians, Maine would be striking at least a small blow in the Third World War. That war had been under way since at least the 1980s. It was a war of militant, expansionist Islam against everybody else. The Islamics had been pushing out in every direction—north into Russia and Balkans and also into Western Europe (immigration can be a form of invasion); south down both African coasts, where the ancient Christian land of Ethiopia was besieged on every side; east into the Philippines (a Muslim Indonesian dagger was pointing at Australia as well); and also West. Since the 1990s, Islam had become the fastest-growing religion in North America.

I knew we would have to fight the Islamics eventually, as we did. Of course, the North American Muslims were all for toleration, as the Koran commands when they are weak. Once they are strong enough, the message changes. The Koran puts it in a way that is hard to misunderstand: "Kill those who join other gods with God (i.e., believers in the Holy Trinity) wherever you shall find them, and seize them and slay them, and lay in wait for them with every kind of ambush."

By accepting some Christian refugees from Islamic terror, we would put Maine on record as to which side we were on in this world war. And it would be hard to find people more civilized than Egyptians; they'd been at it for a good 5,000 years. The Egyptian church even spoke Egyptian, the language of the pharaohs, not Arabic.

"Anyone have a better idea? If not, I say we go with it," I concluded. No one did. "OK, that's settled. Anyone who can help Father Dimitri smuggle the Egyptians in, see him after the meeting. The next question is, how will the feds counter, and what do we do about it?"

"We know how they will counter," said Trooper Kelly, who'd come up from Massachusetts. "We know from Waco and Ruby Ridge and many other places that never made the papers. The federal government has militarized law enforcement. They'll send in INS, federal marshals, probably FBI too, all in combat fatigues, with heavy firepower and armored vehicles. They'll deport the Egyptians back to Egypt, where they'll probably be killed as they come off the aircraft. They'll move the orcs in, and arrest anyone who tries to stop them. And they'll stay to make sure that if anyone objects to the black crime they'll bring, they are arrested for violating their so-called civil rights. Bangor will find itself under foreign military occupation."

"I agree," I said. "That is what they'll do. The question is, do we let them win that way, and count it a moral victory for our side, or do we try to stop 'em?"

We had to think about that one for a while. If we tried to stop them, it meant war at the physical level as well as the moral.

After some talk, our Bangor CO, former Army captain Don Van-derburg, brought us to a decision. "We have two questions to answer: should we stop them if we can, and can we do it? As to the first, it's clear to me," Don said. "Of course. It's my town, my home. And if the feds can rape Bangor this way, the Maine Idea will look hopeless. Most people will give it up. So I think we have to try to stop them."

"I also think we can do it," he continued. "They look like soldiers, but they're not. They're just civil servants in tree suits. Most of them have never studied war. They don't know the terrain, while we do. Plus, we'll have the support of the people, and they'll be invaders. That support translates into all kinds of help, especially information."

"We may be able to do this in a way where no blood is shed. Remember, these guys aren't up for a fight. Most of them just want to make twenty and get out. They aren't our enemies. Most of them share our values and will be privately hoping we win. It's the people they work for who are our enemies. If we can avoid fighting them, they will try not to fight us."

So we decided to resist.

The first part of the operation went according to plan. With some help from folks who knew the back roads, Father Dimitri got his Egyptians in. We hid them in local churches, then on July 23, one day after the apartment buildings were cleaned out, we moved them in.

By now, we had our prep down pat. We had friends in the media, including national media, forewarned and on the scene. We had a dozen clergy, led by the local Monsignor, out front of the buildings to explain what we were doing. The mayor and police chief of Bangor were on hand too, to explain that their city welcomed good people who were in need; it just didn't want violent criminals. We made the evening TV news all across the country, and on the whole the coverage was favorable. We'd taken the moral high ground.

In Washington, an enraged President Cisneros held a news conference the next morning. After denouncing this "racist, insensitive, hurtful, and illegal action by people who want to hold back the future," he announced that a convoy of federal law enforcement agents were on their way to Bangor "to uphold the lawful actions of this government and ensure that justice is done on behalf of Americans of color." Forgetting that his lapel mic was still on, after he had gone backstage, he put it more directly: "I'll show these white crackers who's running this place now."

Like everywhere in the old U.S.A., militias had been sprouting in Maine, although most called themselves a neighborhood watch. Some were nutcases, most were not. Most were made up of decent people who realized their country was falling apart, and when it fell completely the only security would be local security. They were preparing to provide that. The Christian Marines had ties with some of the more serious groups in Maine, and they were willing to work with us to fight the federal invasion.

Equally important, we had a great intel system: the cops. Most of the state police in Massachusetts and Maine and many local police were with us by this time; they realized our values were also their values. The feds needed the help of the cops, didn't realize they'd been penetrated, and provided them the route the convoy would take. The Washington boys were so confident they did the obvious, coming right up I-95.

Our ambush site was near Newport, Maine, where I-95 crosses the marshes at the southern end of Lake Sebasticook on a long, low bridge. The State Cops told us the convoy would leave Boston about 5 AM on June 27, which would put it into Newport around 10 AM the same day. Forewarned, we'd moved our folks into position the night of the 26th.

We were prepared for a real fight, but it was not what we wanted. Dead feds would quickly be turned into martyrs by the media, and most of those guys were privately on our side. The challenge to the Christian Marines was to try to handle this so we won, but with nobody wounded or dead. As always, the physical level of war had to serve the moral level or it would work against us.

I was with an OP we had established just south and east of the bridge. Of course, we'd gone over the plan time and again. More important, everyone understood our objective: defeat them, but don't hurt or kill them. The militias we worked with had the self-discipline to make sure their actions served that intent, even when events outran the plan as they always did and the men had to improvise.

We had a radio in the OP tuned to the state police frequency, and the trooper out front of the convoy broadcast its position every five minutes. Officially, this was so the local cops could clear out the civilian traffic; the feds never thought to ask who else might be listening. Right on schedule, the convoy—a HUMMWV in the lead, then two Bradley Fighting Vehicles, two more HUMMWVs, seven five-ton trucks, and a final HUMMWV as tail-end Charlie—hit the south end of the bridge at 10:13 AM.

We had wired the end panels of the northbound bridge with explosives set for command detonation. From the OP, I could see the whole span, and once all the convoy was on it I hit the detonator. Both panels blew with a roar every fed could hear, even with the vehicles buttoned up.

Immediately, before the agents could figure out what was happening, I broke into their net. "This is the Maine militia," I said in my best command voice. "We have cut the road before and behind you. You cannot move forward or back. We have every vehicle targeted with crew-served weapons, including .50 cals and 90 mm recoilless. If you open fire, you're dead. Lay down your weapons and come out of the vehicles, slowly, one at a time."

At the same instant, a company's worth of infantry, militia and Christian Marines (general staff types also get to mix it up on occasion), were in their faces. We'd positioned them not at the ends of the bridge but under it, along its length (a modern light infantry defense works parallel to an enemy mech column, not across its head). They were equipped with grappling hooks and climbing ropes. As soon as they heard the end panels blow, they swung their grapples for the hand rails and rappelled up. They had weapons leveled at the drivers before the vehicles came to a stop.

This was the critical moment. We weren't bluffing; we did have heavy weapons and we would take the vehicles out if we had to. No one moved, or spoke. The whole thing took less than a minute, but time slowed down so it seemed like hours. Then, slowly, one of the Bradleys started training its turret to the right, as if to look for a target. "Shit," I thought, "the dumb bastard is going to open up."

A sixteen-year old kid from Rockland saved the day for us. He was on the Bradley's left side. He saw the vehicle commander had popped his hatch to come up for a better look. With the agility you lose by the time you're twenty, he was on the vehicle, and the commander got a face full of rifle butt before his head was all the way out. The kid, La Riviere, dropped two smoke and one CS grenades down the hatch, slammed it shut and sat on it, with his AK trained on the infantry hatches.

Two federal marshals came out of those hatches, saw the AK in their faces and gave up. The rest of the crew, choking and puking, came out the rear hatch with their hands in the air—the Italian salute, we used to call it. I was on my feet now, where our guys could see me, gesturing madly and screaming, "Get away from the vehicle!" As soon as our troops and the prisoners were behind the next vehicles in line, I slapped the 90 gunner in our OP on the shoulder and said, "Take that Bradley out."

Like the Russian BMP, the Bradley was an explosion waiting to happen, a tin-clad rolling armor dump that any anti-tank weapon instantly turned into a Viking funeral for its crew. The 90 mm recoilless rifle round hit the ammo and it blew, the turret turning pinwheels in the sky until it plunged sizzling into the lake. The chassis was quickly reduced to a molten mass of metal and treads.

The Feds had seen enough at that point. As Trooper Kelly said, they weren't soldiers. Like anyone in law enforcement, they knew they might get shot at, but a full-scale battle was a different matter. Plus, it had all happened so fast. Engulfed in the smell of real fear, fresh excrement, they crawled out of their vehicles and surrendered.

We brought our POWs, 83 federal marshals and INS agents (no FBI this time), and our own guys down from the bridge on ladders. We had three Bangor city school buses waiting on the parallel secondary road, and bundled everyone on board. The buses were as close as the feds would get to Bangor.

Before we pulled out, we took the opportunity to play some mind-games with the real enemy down in Washington. With a video cam rolling, we turned the .50 cals and 90 mms on the remaining, empty vehicles. The tape of exploding, burning military trucks, HUMMWVs and remaining Bradley, coupled with footage of the line of federal prisoners marching off with their hands behind their heads, went to all the networks. In 24 hours, the whole nation knew Maine had fought the federal government, and won.

Our challenge was to turn a tactical victory into a strategic one. Maine was with us; the Battle of Lake Sebasticook, as it was quickly known, made the Maine Idea real. The slogan appeared overnight on hand-lettered signs in yards, on bumper stickers, on banners hung from highway bridges. But we were nowhere near ready to defeat a full-scale federal invasion, and we knew one was coming.

Washington was still full of fight. President Cisneros, trying to position himself as a second Lincoln, vowed the Union would be preserved, at any cost. Never was the old rule of "first as tragedy, then as farce," so applicable. He announced the 82nd Airborne was on its way to Bangor.

But we had an ancient and effective weapon with which to defend ourselves: hostages. As our militiamen returned to their homes all over Maine, many carried an unusual cargo in the trunk of their car: a trussed-up federal agent. Of course, the feds had specialized hostage-rescue units. But they didn't have enough of them to hit sites all over Maine simultaneously, even if they could find where the agents were hidden.

On the 30th of June, we made the feds an offer, through an open letter to Cisneros printed in the Bangor paper. The key part read:

> We have no desire or intention to harm anyone. We could easily have killed many, perhaps all, of the federal agents who invaded our state. We killed no one, and all the captured agents are now safe. We look forward to returning them to their homes and families as soon as possible. We do not regard them as our enemies. However, our first responsibility is to our own homes and families, which you now threaten. Therefore, we regret we have to say that we cannot guarantee the safety of the federal agents now in our

custody if additional federal forces enter Maine.

To underscore the point, we arranged for CNN to interview several militia units that were holding some of the prisoners. They allowed that if those paratroopers landed in Bangor, or the feds tried any rescue ops, the lot of their policeman would not be a happy one. One unit already had a noose hanging from a large oak tree. It was a bluff, but Washington couldn't know that.

We had a few agents at Ft. Bragg, so we knew within hours that the airlift had been put on hold. Cisneros was waffling.

Meanwhile, the 250 black parolees who were to move into Bangor had been stuck in a couple of motels near Worcester, Massachusetts, waiting for the federal troops to clear their way in. The Justice Department's lawyers had determined that, since they had been paroled, they could not be kept under guard. It seems a few of them got tired of waiting and decided to go have some fun. The date was July 4, 2021.

A summer day in New England is a true joy. That Fourth of July was especially nice. The temperature got up to 77 degrees, with low humidity, a gentle breeze out of the northwest and a few white, puffy, cotton-ball clouds, the kind that children like to see animal shapes in. Sister Mary Frances of the Church of the Blessed Sacrament had brought her Bible school pupils, grades two through five, to a small park on the bank of the West River. They had sandwiches and cookies, toys, a big American flag and sparklers to celebrate the day. Sister Mary Frances had planned to read them the story of the Ride of Paul Revere.

Thirteen of the parolees discovered them there just after lunch. By the time the police found them later in the day, the Sister and most of the children were lying where they had knelt to say the Rosary, praying for the protection that did not come in this life. Sister Mary Frances had been raped repeatedly before being strangled with the chain on her Crucifix.

Perhaps she had bought the three surviving children the time they needed to crawl off into the woods and hide. A posse of state troopers and frantic parents found them there just after dusk.

The media might well have passed over the event in silence, at least outside Worcester; it didn't fit their agenda. But Ms. LaDrek of HUD happened to be in Worcester that very weekend. She had come to open a new high-rise public housing development, modeled on St. Louis famed Pruett-Igoe. At her news conference, she said that the slaughter of Sister Mary Frances and her young charges "was nothing compared to what people of color had suffered in America since the white invaders first arrived. Maybe it would help the white people of Massachusetts have a better understanding of Black Rage. If so, it might be a positive experience for Worcester."

The news conference had been carried live on most of the Worcester TV and radio stations. It concluded with Ms. LaDrek leading the new residents of the housing project into the commons room for a nice lunch. By 12:30, the courtyard in front of the project was filling with Worcester's citizenry, and they weren't in a celebratory mood. They were construction workers, housewives, good Catholics most of them, some coming straight from the noon mass at Blessed Sacrament. Their kids could have been the ones raped and butchered. In a few cases, they were.

The priest from Blessed Sacrament himself, with some of the nuns, led the uninvited guests into the luncheon, chanting the *Dies Irae*. The distinguished Secretary of HUD tried to bolt out the back door, but one of the nuns, a sturdy Irish girl, tackled her. The swift, new elevator whisked LaDrek and a party of escorts to the top floor, where a window was knocked out. The Honorable Secretary of HUD followed the shards of glass down, to a hard and fatal landing in the front parking lot.

It's almost uncanny; our Thirty Years War also started with a defenestration. This time, no angels (or manure piles, if you're a Protestant) broke the fall.

A story like this couldn't be hushed up. The nation was appalled, less by the assassination than what had preceded it.

In Maine, we moved swiftly to take advantage of the public's mood. The militias set up recruiting stations in every shopping center and on each town common. The slogan on a banner over each station read, "The Maine Idea—Defend Our Families." Any male with a weapon could join. The lines ran a block or more long. Within 48 hours we had more than 100,000 men pledged to fight for our state.

In Washington, Cisneros knew he was beaten. The order went to the 82nd Airborne to stand down. Resorting to one of the city's oldest tricks, Cisneros asked Congress to establish a Blue Ribbon Panel to investigate the whole affair. Announcing that "until the panel is appointed and has conducted its investigation, it would be inappropriate for me to comment further," he crawled into the deepest hole he could find. The panel, everyone knew, would take years to complete its work, then issue a report that said nothing. That's what "Blue Ribbon Panels" existed to do.

So we'd won. Some might say it wasn't a good, clean victory on the field of battle. It wasn't, but that isn't how war works. War is politics, propaganda, fighting, maneuvering, luck, all boiled up in one big cauldron. This time, our side had bubbled up to the top.

At least we showed that victory doesn't always belong to the bigger battalions.

Chapter Fourteen

W HEN people read Sun Tzu's saying, "He who knows himself and knows his enemy will win 100 battles," they figure the hard part is knowing the enemy. They're wrong. The hard part is knowing yourself.

After we had rubbed Cisneros's nose in it, some of our guys were feeling pretty cocky. It seemed to them that Maine could go its own way then and there.

I saw it differently. The victory at Lake Sebasticook was genuinely ours. We won it by combining the unexpected, speed, and initiative at the most junior level, which is to say by fighting smart.

But the rest of it was a pure gift from God. As King Philip of Spain of Armada fame found out, God doesn't like it when you presume He's on your side. The next time, the other guy might get the breaks. When the other guy was the whole federal juggernaut, we'd get flattened.

It all came back to something I'd said to my fellow Christian Marines many times: we had to wait for Washington to fall of its own weight. We could drop an occasional banana peel in its path, by setting up a situation where it was likely to embarrass itself. But it was far too strong for us to take on, head on.

Vermont gave us a lesson that way. Our success in Maine had emboldened friends and fellow "racists, sexists, and homophobes" elsewhere in the country. But it had also enraged the enemies of Western culture, the cultural Marxists, who were looking for opportunities to counterattack.

In Vermont—another state with conservative people but a liberal government (God, we were stupid back then)—the governor went on the offensive. He got a law through the legislature that required every Vermont jury to "look like America," which meant it had to be half women, 10 percent black, 15 percent Hispanic, 10 percent gay (the real number would have been maybe 1 percent at most, but these were political numbers), and so on.

Some old-fashioned Vermonters saw an opportunity. Calling themselves the Green Mountain Boys, they declared a "White Strike." No white male would agree to serve on a jury, which would mean the jury could not look like America. Under the new law, that would appear to mean no jury.

The whole thing was a flop. A good number of white males joined up, but a good number wasn't enough. The Green Mountain Boys hadn't thought the situation through. To succeed, they needed near 100 percent support from white men, which they were never going to get. There were still some white male lefties, and beyond them lots more white males who didn't want to listen to the third act of Medea every night over the dinner table from their feminist wives. The courts had to go through more white men than they otherwise would to make up a jury, but eventually they always found enough.

Our cultural enemies won a victory. Their triumph in Vermont allowed them to say their defeat in Maine was just a strange accident; the country was really still on their side.

One Friday evening in late November, 2021, the phone rang. I always hated the damn thing; Ambrose Bierce was right when he defined it, in his *Devil's Dictionary*, as "an instrument almost as useless as the telescope, but unfortunately equipped with an annoying bell." I had to set down my cigar and my book, dump the cat off my lap and walk into the cold back hall to answer it.

Finding one of the leaders of the Green Mountain Boys on the line didn't improve my mood. "We've got a problem," he began.

"You sure do," I said. "You screwed the pooch. Didn't help us any in the process."

"Ayuh. Sorry about that," he replied. "Look, we heah you folks have some sort'a organization that helps think these things through. Bunch of fo'mah Marines, so we'ah told. Any chance we could get theah help?"

"Waal, I don't rightly know," I said, talking Emmett myself. "Sounds to me like you want us to pull you'ah chestnuts out'a the fiah."

"Ayuh, I guess that's what we want, all right," he replied.

I had to think about it a bit. I was tempted to let them sleep in the bed they'd made. On the other hand, the Christian Marines did intend to reach out to the rest of New England, eventually. This was an opportunity to start. We needed to reverse the defeat in Vermont.

"Waal, I guess we can talk about it, anyway," I finally said. "Get your folks togeth'ah at the Norrich Inn Friday night. I'll be the'ah."

By the time we met, I'd done a bit of legal work, with the help of Uncle Earl. It seems Vermont wasn't exactly living up to its own law on this jury business. It couldn't. The problem wasn't the White Strike. Vermont simply didn't have enough blacks and Hispanics to make up the required percentages on the juries. So they were just saying they tried and letting it go at that.

The Green Mountain Boys had about a dozen men at the Norwich Inn that Friday evening, the last Friday in November. After we got to know each other a bit over some supper and cider, I laid out a plan. "Any of you know a lawyer who thinks like we do but doesn't let on?" I asked.

"Sounds like you're talking about my neighbor," one of the Boys replied. "Over pie and coffee in the kitchen, he's as pissed off as the rest of us. He talks funny, of course, since he's a lawyer. 'I have no desire to live in an America that has been Hispanized, feminized, and sodomized,' is the way he puts it. But he always looks over both shoulders to see who's listening before he says it, because he figures he'd lose half his business if his clients knew where he stood."

"It sounds as if he's the right man for a pseudo-op."

"What's that?" another of the Boys asked.

"It's where you dress your troops up in the enemy's uniforms and have them do something embarrassing to the enemy," I answered.

"What we need from your lawyer friend is this," I continued. "Representing the oppressed peoples of the world, he files a suit demanding that the State of Vermont stick to its own law. Trying to get the right percentages of gays, blacks, whatever on a jury doesn't cut it. Each and every Vermont jury must have all the numbers right, or it can't be empaneled. He should file the suit in such a way that it goes straight to the Vermont Supreme Court."

"How the hell does that help us?" asked the first fellow.

"According to my Uncle Earl, who knows his judges hereabouts, the Vermont Supreme Court is as politically correct as they come. He's willing to bet real nutmegs to wooden ones that the court will rule in favor of such a suit. If it does, the Governor either has to repeal his law or go without any juries. In practical terms, that means repeal, which also means we win."

Well, they bought it, and the lawyer filed suit. The Vermont Supreme Court made Uncle Earl look good. It said the law is as the law reads, and the juries have to get all the right numbers of blacks and Hispanics and gays, or they aren't lawful.

But what happened next came as a surprise.

*

The governor, a fellow named Fullarbottom, felt the hollow eyes of all those oppressed minorities fixed upon him. He had been their great hope, a sensitive, caring, feeling white male. Now he had to dump them, and they'd howl like a sackful of cats.

So he went to the legislature with an ingenious proposal. Instead of repealing the requirement that Vermont juries "look like America," Vermont would turn to the rest of America to achieve the balance it sought. Any American citizen could sit on a Vermont jury if his or her presence were required to make a quota. Fullarbottom concluded his message to the legislature with the words, "We are proud to welcome our oppressed black, Hispanic, and gay sisters and brothers as 'Vermonters for a day' to aid us in our battle to reverse two hundred years of white male oppression."

It is in the nature of war that the enemy sometimes makes a good move. This was one. Unfortunately for Fullarbottom, like most good moves, this one had to work fast to work at all. And it couldn't. The Vermont state constitution required that a juror be a legal resident of the state. That meant the governor needed a state constitutional amendment, which in turn required a two-thirds vote in the legislature. And he didn't have the votes, not right off, anyway.

With the rest of the Establishment cheering him on, Fullarbottom launched a campaign to get the votes he needed. The papers, most of them, backed him with editorials; various black, Hispanic, and gay entertainers, sports figures, and other celebrities came to Vermont to support him; President Cisneros himself even paid a visit. In the past, this sort of thing had worked.

But it took time, and that gave our side a chance to counterattack. By 2021, Vermonters who believed in traditional American values had a good grass-roots network. They quickly organized their own campaign, one aimed both at state legislators and at the average Vermonter. They struck some deep chords, especially when they blanketed the state with posters and bumper stickers asking, "Where Will It Stop?" If out-of-staters could serve on Vermont juries, what else would they be allowed to do? Vote in town meetings? Help themselves to the Vermont treasury? Sent their kids to Vermont schools, at Vermont taxpayers' expense?

By January, 2022, it was clear Vermonters were becoming uneasy with Fullarbottom's proposal. The legislature would meet in March. Its members were feeling the public pulse, and getting nervous.

But something was still needed to push them our way, once and for all. We needed an action average Vermonters could do that would scare politicians. The thing that scared politicians most was the danger of becoming un-politicians, of losing their office. The problem was, how could we make them feel that fear when an election wouldn't come until the fall?

Late in January I got an idea, so I drove over to Montpelier to see the head of the grassroots network in Vermont, Sam Shephard. On anything important, I always tried to meet people face-to-face; no fax or phone call or email was as effective in getting things done.

In typical North Country style, we met in his kitchen. "It seems to me," I said, "that we need to appeal to your politicians' patriotism." That was my usual expression for grabbing somebody by the balls. "We need to let them see what happens to whoever opposes us, and we need to make Fullarbottom himself the example."

"Good idea," Sam replied. "How do we do it?"

"I've done a bit of research about your state. You don't have a recall provision in your law, but over the years, a good many folks have said you ought to. My proposal is this: launch a petition drive to recall Fullarbottom. Explain that if you get a majority, not only will it tell the governor to back off his plan to import out-of-state ringers and put them on your juries, it will also tell the members of the legislature you want a recall law. And it will tell the members of the legislature that their own necks are in danger if they vote the wrong way on the jury issue."

"Hmm, that's not bad," Sam replied. "Let me run it by my people. Still, it would have a lot more punch if we could actually toss Fullarbottom out."

"Well, maybe we can," I said.

"How?" Sam asked.

"Leave that to the Christian Marines," I answered.

Sam was good to his word, and his folks bought the idea. Early in February, they announced the recall campaign, and their people got out with the petitions and started knocking on doors. The public's mood had been swinging steadily our way, and the petition drive took off. On the 7th of March, exactly a fortnight before the legislature was due to convene, the "Campaign to Kick Fullarbottom's Bottom" announced that more Vermont voters had said they wanted the Governor out than had voted to put him in.

At this point, Fullarbottom's earlier sense of tactics deserted him. His emotions took over his judgment. On the battlefield, that leads bad officers to order on-line frontal assaults. In this case, it led Governor Fullar-bottom to call a snap news conference.

"I was elected Governor of this state and I will stay Governor of this state as long as I want the damn job," Fullarbottom roared. "I don't care what these people want or what anyone wants. I spent my life working my way to this position. For thirty years, I did all the crappy jobs the Democratic Party asked me to do, squeezing money out of every store owner in Burlington, kissing the backsides of all the party bigwigs, marching in the damn Jefferson-Jackson Day parade with a blintz in one hand and a kielbasa in the other. If the people who elected me wish they hadn't, tough. The office is mine, and I aim to keep it until I don't enjoy it any more."

It seemed Vermont's politically correct governor was, in the end, merely political, and of the Fafnir school of politics—the dragon in *Das Rheingold*. He sought only to lie in possession.

We had the moral high ground. Now we could move to the physical level of war.

*

As soon as Vermont had come up on our radar screen, the Christian Marines had started recruiting. As usual, we had found allies among the cops, including the state cops. One of our state cops arranged to be the Governor's driver.

On Thursday, March 10, 2022, Governor Frank Fullarbottom was on his way home to work on his speech to the legislature. He knew it had to be a good speech, if he were to have any chance of getting his blacks, Hispanics, and gays from out of state on Vermont juries. A very good speech. He was so absorbed in thinking about it that he did not notice when his driver took a wrong turn, down a lonely country lane. Around a bend, where the view was concealed by a clump of pine trees, the Christian Marines were waiting with a pickup truck blocking the road.

There was no violence; that would have worked against us. We had a shotgun pointed at the cop's head, so it was obvious there was nothing he could do. We handled him just rough enough to maintain his cover. As for the governor, he was quickly wrapped up mummy-style in duct tape and tossed in the trunk of a waiting sedan.

The next morning, the Montpelier paper found a message on its email from the Green Mountain Boys. We let them take the credit. It read:

> *Last night Vermont again became a democracy. The will of the people, as expressed by the majority of voters in their petition to recall Governor Fullarbottom, was carried out. Mr. Fullarbottom is safe, well cared for and comfortable. He will be returned to his home the day after his term of office expires. In the meantime, he regrets to announce that he will be unable to carry out the duties of his office.*

Of course, there was an enormous hue and cry from the Establishment, both local and federal. President Cisneros denounced "right-wing fanatics who dare take the law into their own hands." We always thought the power of the law properly belonged in the people's hands, but of course politicians don't see it that way. The FBI was called in, along with ATF, federal marshals, the whole works. We expected that. We also expected no one would look for the Governor of Vermont on a Portuguese fishing boat off the Grand Banks, and no one did.

The good people of Vermont do have a sense of humor. Outsiders have trouble seeing it sometimes, but it's there. They know a typical Emmett joke when they see one. As I drove through the state on my way back to Maine the day after Fullarbottom went on his cruise, I saw a good number of thin smiles.

Vermont juries remained the province of Vermonters. Vermont also got a law permitting recall. Politicians can be fast learners when their careers are at stake.

CHAPTER FIFTEEN

W AR is the extension of politics, and politics may also be an extension of war.

By 2022, the first shots of America's Second Civil War were audible. This time, instead of a few cannon firing at Fort Sumter, its heralds were the popping of thousands of caps. Blacks shot whites because they were white, and Hispanics shot blacks because they were black. Whites usually still called the police to do their shooting for them, though the results seldom justified the cost of the phone call. Koreans and Jews got shot by everybody.

Right-to-lifers shot abortion doctors, who in turn relied on their needles and forceps to terminate potential future right-to-lifers. Farmers shot EPA agents, and the feds threw farmers into jails where they were homosexually raped. Once a week, somewhere in the country, the gays firebombed a church. Somewhere else, once a week, a bomb in a car or a briefcase took out a government office. Insurance companies would no longer sell life insurance to IRS employees.

Like real war in every place and every time, it wasn't pretty. I hated it.

In Maine, our hope was to keep our distance, and increase it wherever we could. That was the Maine Idea, and after we had beaten the feds both on our home soil and in Vermont, most folks were enthusiastic about it.

I was pretty sure the whole political system would go down the drain sooner or later, and probably sooner. But in the mean time, we had to use it intelligently for whatever it could do for us.

The Maine Idea had attracted some folks who understood politics better than I did, and I was happy to let them take the lead. They weren't politicians, just normal people who had done the grass-roots organizing that gave the Maine Idea its clout. An idea, even the best idea, seldom goes very far on its own. A good idea plus lots of people who will work for it leads to a different future.

I was happy to play a fly on the wall in the meetings where Bill Kraft and other grass-roots leaders put together the Maine First Party. They figured that if a political party based on the Maine Idea controlled the state legislature and the governor's office, Maine would improve its chances of saving itself from the coming catastrophe.

They found ordinary people, good people, to run for office. They got candidates on the ballot for every office in the state. They made clear exactly what they were for: a Maine that stood as far apart from the rest of the country as it could get.

They also wanted a place where we could live the way State o' Mainers had lived in times past. When some greasy reporter up from New York asked Bill Kraft what that meant, he replied with the words of the old Book of Common Prayer: we wanted to live a Godly, righteous, and sober life. To most people in Maine, that summed it up nicely.

The Maine First Party faced the Establishment, local and national, with its greatest nightmare: an anti-Establishment alternative the average person could vote for. And vote for it they did. In November of 2022, when all the votes were counted, the Maine First Party held every statewide office and had majorities of better than 80 percent in both houses of the legislature. The Republicans and the Democrats had been wiped off the state political map.

This victory at the ballot box was as important as any victory we ever won on the battlefield. It quickly led to Vermont First and New Hampshire First Parties in those states; as in Maine, they swept into power on a tidal wave of public support. The victories of the home state parties gave upper New England the chance for recovering our freedom when the time came, and laid the basis for the Northern Confederation.

In Massachusetts, the same effort failed. Too many citizens of that Commonwealth found their wealth in the common trough that was government, and they were afraid of loosing their regular ration of swill. They paid for it, later.

I made certain every Christian Marine understood the relationship between war and politics, and politics and war. The actions we had fought, especially the Battle of Lake Sebasticook, made the Maine First victory possible. The victory of the Maine First Party in turn made it possible for us to fight for Maine's freedom, and win. Each victory fed on the other. Neither was possible without the other. Neither had any meaning without the other.

Throughout history, some soldiers have argued that politics should stop when the shooting starts. What fools.

CHAPTER SIXTEEN

B Y the third decade of the 21st century, the dissolution of the United States had reached the point where each year brought a new crisis. The crisis of 2023 began with the Persell Amendment to the Clean Air Act, a measure intended to prevent the smoking of tobacco.

I am not making this up. I know it sounds like satire, but it happened.

In the 1990s and 2000s, as the greatest country in the world turned itself into a cultural toxic waste dump, one of the great issues that absorbed the federal government's attention was—tobacco smoke.

The government and the health industry that lived off the government whooped it up that tobacco smoke was second only to Zyklon-B as the worst thing you could inhale. At first, they just tried to get smokers to quit. But like all bandwagons of the absurd, once their campaign got rolling it rolled over everybody. Soon, they were shrieking that just smelling the smoke from someone else's pipe, cigar, or cigarette was enough to put you in the grave tomorrow, or by next week at the latest. They called it "second-hand smoke."

Of course, you got far more crap in your lungs just walking past a bus, but that didn't matter. Smoking was outlawed far and wide where anyone might smell the smoke. Smokers were literally driven out, into back alleys and onto loading docks for a furtive puff.

A reasonable man, or even woman, might have considered that people had been smoking for some centuries, yet by a miracle the human race had survived. Smokers and non-smokers had even managed to get along, quite nicely in most cases. The secret was etiquette. Good manners dictated that some places were for smoking and some were not, and that where the lines were uncertain, smokers asked the assembled company for permission before they indulged. Previous to the hysteria, permission was usually graciously given, and no one seemed the worse for it.

But by the early 2000s, anti-smoking militancy was the cause of the day. Avoiding tobacco smoke had become the equivalent of Fletcherizing—the 19th century movement that promised sparkling health and a Methuselah lifespan to anyone who chewed each bite of food one hundred times. Americans always were suckers for health crazes.

And politicians were always on the lookout for suckers. So when the Clean Air Act came up for renewal in 2023, Senator Whitman Persell ("Wimpy" to his friends), Democrat of California, saw a chance to score some points with the anti-tobacco harpies. He proposed an amendment whereby anyone who smelled tobacco smoke anywhere might sue any nearby smoker. The plaintiff did not have to prove that the smoker was smoking at the time; the fact that he or she was an admitted smoker was considered proof enough. The amendment encouraged triple damages for "pain and suffering." With the enthusiastic backing of the Cisneros administration and the usual craven collapse by Congressional Republicans, the amendment was signed into law. The Health Nazis triumphantly proclaimed "the end of tobacco smoking in America."

As the law intended, smokers found themselves hunted like rats. A smoker, placed under oath on the witness stand, had to admit smoking or be guilty of perjury. But if they admitted they smoked, they lost the suit, along with their life savings and most else they owned. Repairmen, neighbors, even family members would come into a smoker's home and promptly file a lawsuit, which they won. If someone smelled smoke in someone else's clothes, they sued and won. The Surgeon General even issued a pamphlet suggesting ways smokers could be trapped into revealing their filthy habit, and then sued. It was a virtual reign of terror, enforced by impoverishment.

But the result was not the end of tobacco smoking in America. The result was war. Smokers fought back.

It started about six months after the Persell Amendment took effect. In Pasadena, a little old lady had been sued by a Meals on Wheels delivery-woman who had spotted a telltale cigarette butt in her kitchen garbage. As usual, the smoker lost, and the court ordered her home seized and sold to pay the deliverywoman her winnings. In the final court session on the case, the little old lady pulled a Saturday Night Special out of her handbag and blew away the judge and the plaintiff.

She was shot down herself by an armed guard within seconds, but on her way to court she had sent a letter to the L.A. Times explaining her action.

> *I had nothing more to lose, I would rather die quickly than be left on the street, penniless. And I won't stop smoking. I was born and grew up in England, and I remember how, in 1940, when a Nazi invasion seemed certain, Churchill had posters printed up saying, 'You Can Always Take One With You.' So that is what I will try to do.*

Her story was picked up by the rest of the media, not in sympathy but to demonstrate how all smokers were dangerous extremists. However, smokers got a different message. "You Can Always Take One With You" posters appeared on walls and street signs. Other smokers who had lost everything, or feared they soon would, began shooting. They shot judges and lawyers. They shot the people who had sued them, or other members of the plaintiffs families. They shot government health personnel. One of them shot Senator Persell; regrettably, he survived. They all left the same message: "I had nothing more to lose."

Up in Maine, our Maine First state government saw an opportunity. The Governor proposed, and the legislature adopted, a "Resolution of Nullification" that stated that hereafter, the Persell Amendment would not apply in Maine. Maine folks still had good manners, and we would handle tobacco smoke the old way, as a matter of etiquette.

The feds understood quite well what nullification meant for them; that battle had gone the other way in the 1830s, and the long-ago victory was still an important part of their power. They went to the Supreme Court and Maine was overruled.

But our Governor, John C. Adams, stuck to his guns—or rather, our guns. He wrote to the President and told him the Nullification Ordinance still stood, and that whatever a federal court might rule, no monies based on a Persell Amendment judgment would be paid in Maine. If Washington didn't like it, they could try to send in federal agents again. We Christian Marines made it clear we were not averse to another meeting like the one at Lake Sebasticook, and the state militia raised on the occasion was still available.

Under normal circumstances, Cisneros probably would have sent in federal agents, or troops. But the federal government was by this time caught up in a real crisis, and it didn't have much attention to spare to the tobacco question. Once it was clear we had successfully nullified

Persell, Vermont and New Hampshire did the same, as did the states of the deep South. Elsewhere, smokers kept shooting.

The smokers' defiance had showed the power of leaderless resistance. In former wars and revolutions, effective, sustained resistance required leadership and organization. Without a Continental Congress or a Jacobin Directorate or a Bolshevik Party to guide and direct and order, action could not be sustained. Now, in the 21st century, the internet supplied virtual organization by allowing the actions of one to inspire others, and the actions of those others to instruct and animate more. From the standpoint of the government, it was a nightmare; the rebellions—there were soon many—had no head that could be cut off, no junta or central committee or official spokesmen who could be arrested or assassinated. The ubiquity of the internet meant it could not be silenced, and it could not discipline itself to pass over stories that people wanted to see. For good and for ill, the internet was the sorcerer's apprentice.

Now pardon me, if you'll be so gracious, while I light a fresh cigar.

CHAPTER SEVENTEEN

THE crisis that occupied the feds' attention while Maine reestablished the doctrine of Nullification was one that usually comes in the last days of *ancien regimes*. The currency was collapsing.

In October of 2018, a Big Mac cost $5.99. By October of 2023, it cost $99.99. For $149.99, you also got a small order of fries and a Coke.

The warning signs had been flashing for many years, but everyone in Washington ignored them. As late as the year 2000, the federal government had showed it could balance the budget. But for politicians, doing so had no payoff. The Republicans wanted tax cuts and the Democrats wanted more spending. So they cut a deal where each party would get what it wanted, and we would just borrow the money to pay for it all.

Through the 2000s and 2010s, the deficits soared, as did the national debt and the international trade deficit. Washington ignored all three. Then, in response to the financial panic of 2008, the Federal Reserve bank began printing money. Actually, it no longer had to print it. It could just enter a few keystrokes on a computer and presto, trillions of dollars came into being. No one considered that something created so easily couldn't be worth much.

Wall Street got even richer from all the phoney money, but the real economy, where real people had to try to get jobs, remained in the tank. That kept down inflation, for a while.

The first people to realize that dollars had become green confetti were foreigners. Starting in the mid-teens, the dollar began to lose its position as the world's reserve currency. Gold came back into its own as the only real money, at least internationally. The dollar's role as reserve currency had given the American economy a huge subsidy. When it lost that subsidy, it tanked.

The Federal Reserve responded by creating dollars even faster, by the tens of trillions. All they knew how to do, when a bubble burst, was generate more liquidity to create yet another bubble.

But this time, the bubble was the dollar itself. When that bubble burst, beginning here at home in 2019, creating more dollars made the problem worse. But since that is all the Fed knew how to do, that is what it did.

By 2023, the Fed was creating dollars by the quadrillion. By March of 2024, that Big Mac cost $500,000. By July, it cost $50 million. Financial Weimar had followed cultural Weimar. The middle class was wiped out.

*

In Washington, Republicans and Democrats pointed fingers at each other, each hoping to ride the wave of middle class fury into long-term power. The public remembered that both parties had voted for the policies that brought the dollar down to where it took ten million to buy a single Mexican peso. That meant the political system offered no hope of a solution.

Revolutions and civil wars are the suicide of states. Men and women commit suicide when they are convinced their problems are overwhelming and there is no other way out. Nations rise in revolution or divide in civil war in response to the same conviction: continuation of the status quo is intolerable, and nothing but the death of the state offers any hope of escape from it.

The Federal government's destruction of the dollar, and with it every American's way of life, solidified the public against it. Not only solidified—radicalized. Afterwards, most Americans felt continued rule by such a government was unbearable. They did not yet know how to escape from under it. But they were ready to embrace any possibility. Including suicide.

*

The government's response to the economic catastrophe it had created only deepened the public's alienation. First, Congress indexed its own salaries and those of government employees. That meant their salaries went up week-by-week to keep up with the inflation. The rest of us were left to live as best we could on incomes that fell steadily, in terms of what they would buy.

We weren't the first country to experience hyperinflation, and while everybody's savings were gone for good, it was possible to stabilize the currency by the usual tough measures: stop printing more money, drastically cut government spending, run a budget surplus, and so on. The Feds refused to do any of it. It would have meant cutting off the parasites, the welfare queens, Wall Street bankers, government contractors, and all the rest. Those folks were the politicians' base. The Fed kept on inventing money.

People tried to cope in the usual ways, by buying gold, hoarding foreign currencies, bartering, etc.

The government's next response was to make ownership of gold illegal. If you already owned some, you had to sell it to the government at a fixed price—for paper dollars that in one day were worth half as much as when you got them, a day later a fourth as much, and so on. By this time, people were using $100 bills for toilet paper. It was cheaper than buying the real thing. Maybe that's what economists mean by a "soft currency."

Then, the Feds ordered everyone to turn in all their foreign money as well. Banks were commanded to convert all foreign currency into dollars and send the renminbi and yen and pesos to Washington. By a secret government order, on December 7, 2024, the banks opened all safety deposit boxes and confiscated any precious metals and foreign money found in them. The rightful owners were not compensated, but fined.

Finally, Washington tried to outlaw barter as well. That was hopeless, but they tried. President Cisneros proposed and Congress (with a Republican majority, but in times of crisis the Establishment knows how to stick together) passed a law requiring all citizens to show receipts for any new goods in their possession. Failure to do so resulted in immediate confiscation, plus fines. Enforcement was given over to the IRS, on the reasonable grounds that it had always presumed guilt unless innocence could be proven by documentation. Armed teams of IRS agents would burst into a home, demanding receipts for anything they thought looked new. They still went through the motions of getting a warrant, but "probable cause" included the fact that the family was not starving. If they had food, they were presumed to have bought it. If they had no receipts for it, the food was confiscated too. And they were fined for having it.

Down east, we suffered along with the rest as our money turned into litter. But the Christian Marines' notion that most crises were also opportunities had caught on. Just before Christmas, 2024, I got a letter from Bill Kraft asking if I would join him and a few others in a meeting with Governor Adams on December 27.

I went, though going wasn't easy. Like most people in Maine, I had food and wood for heat, but gasoline was $1.5 billion a gallon by December, so my truck was up on blocks in the barn. I hiked down to Pittsfield, where I got a train for Augusta. We'd gotten passenger trains running again and, like most retro things, found we liked them. The one I rode was pulled by a steam engine converted to burn wood, of which we had plenty, so the fares were affordable.

There were about twenty people at the meeting, most of whom I more or less knew. They were the folks, up from the grass roots, who had put the Maine First Party together. I wasn't sure what I would have to add to a political gathering, but I knew I'd learn a few things.

The governor began by saying something a lot of Mainiacs had been thinking. "Gentlemen, we've let this whole thing go too far already. Maine has shown it can act independently of Washington. The inflation problem has stymied us, because the currency is controlled from Washington. But we have to be able to think our way around that—and then do something. We cannot get peoples' savings back, but there must be a way we can give them a currency that doesn't lose value faster than it can be printed. I called you here to get your ideas on how we might do that."

"Why don't we just print our own money?" asked a fellow from Skowhegan.

"We've thought of that," the governor replied. "We're willing to do it; I don't care whether Washington likes it or not. The problem is, what do we back it with? The full faith and credit of a government, even our government, doesn't mean anything any more. Our economists tell me any paper currency we issue will quickly lose value, the same as the dollar has."

Bill Kraft spoke up. "As usual, history shows us the way to handle this. In the 1980s and 1990s, a number of other countries, faced the same problem. They solved it, and we can solve it by doing what they did."

"What did they do?" Governor Adams asked.

"They established a new currency," Kraft replied. "But to maintain its value, they only issued as much of it as they could back with foreign currency or gold. To guarantee that, they gave all authority to issue the new money to an independent Currency Board. The government could not give an order to run the presses. Once people understood that, they came to trust the new money. And it held its value."

"Where do we get the gold or foreign currency to back our new money?" the Governor responded.

"We seize and sell or lease abroad all the federal assets in Maine that might be worth something," said a fellow I didn't know. He turned out to be Steve Ducen, an economist who had worked in Washington as long as he could take it, then fled up here. He had a prosperous apple farm near Lewiston, now. "Start with the national parks; Japanese hotels will lease them in a heartbeat and put in golf courses. They'll bring in Japanese tourists by the planeload, and we'll feed 'em all the raw lobster they can eat."

"Asia is booming, and we can cash in on that," he continued. "American antiques are all the rage among wealthy Chinese. Maine has plenty, and we can make more. I'm already selling more than half my apples in Japan, Korea and Singapore. With some clever marketing, we could sell potatoes, maple syrup, you name it. People who eat dogs and sea cucumbers will eat anything."

"We don't need to look just to Maine folks for foreign currency," added John Rushton, President of the First Bank of Portland. "We can allow any American citizen to set up a gold or foreign currency account in a Maine bank. They bring their dollars up here, sell them for whatever they'll bring in foreign currency, and set up an account. And, if they export, instead of having the Feds turn the payments they get from abroad into worthless dollars, they can have them paid right into one of our banks. They can withdraw either the foreign money, or ours, as they choose."

This sounded good to me, but I saw one question no one had addressed. So I asked it. "How do you keep the feds from getting into these accounts electronically and sucking the foreign money out?"

Bill Kraft had the answer—a perfect Retroculture answer. "There won't be any electronic records," he said. "Remember, we had banks long before we had computers. We just go back to doing it manually, with passbooks and account ledgers and the like. We run these accounts just the way they would have been handled in 1950—or 1850, for that matter. In effect, we just pull the plug."

I had to admit that was the ultimate electronic security system.

*

We did it. Maine began issuing Pine Tree Dollars in March, 2025. We soon got the kind of prices people remembered from before the U.S. dollar began its long slide. A loaf of bread again cost 15 cents. A pound of hamburger cost 20 cents. Gas stayed expensive at over $50.00 per gallon; we had no Maine oil. But horse feed was cheap because we grew our own.

Within six months, Pine Tree Dollars were in demand throughout the United States. Foreign currency flooded into Maine from the rest of the country, most of which was exchanged for Pine Tree Dollars. Within Maine, prices were stable, for the first time anyone could remember.

Washington was unhappy, of course, but it was now too weakened morally to dare any serious countermoves. Beyond denouncing us all once again as "racists, sexists and classists," the only action the Feds took was to order the U.S. Customs Service on Maine's borders with Quebec and New Brunswick, both of which were now independent, to seize all Pine Tree Dollars as well as gold and foreign currency held by people trying to cross.

Bill Kraft asked me if the Christian Marines could help out on this one. I said I thought we could. I had preached all along that we had to wait for the Federal Government to fall of its own weight. Now, it was down for the count. It would thrash around on the mat for a while, but I knew it would never get on its feet again. So we could be bolder.

On July 2, 2025, a mixed force of Maine Guard and Christian Marines arrived at the border crossings and rounded up the Customs officers. We gave them a choice. They could join the new Maine Customs Service and follow Maine laws, or stay with the feds and get shipped south. Most of them lived in Maine and were happy to join us. They despised Washington as much as we did.

Just thirteen Customs agents said they wanted to remain with the Feds. We took them down to Augusta, where on July 4, in festive fashion, they were paraded in their U.S. Customs Service Uniforms. We then bent them over, cut the seat out of their trousers, painted their backsides red and bundled them all into a boxcar with waybills for Washington, D.C. As their train pulled out of the station, the Governor led the crowd in a rousing toast to Maine, a sound dollar, and liberty.

CHAPTER EIGHTEEN

I N September of 2025, little Suzy La Montaigne, age seven, came home from her elementary school in New Orleans, Louisiana, with a headache and sniffles. Three days later she was dead. Ten days later, so were all but three of her classmates and her teacher. A week after that, only a handful of the students in her school were still alive, and people of all ages were dropping dead on the streets of the community her school served.

When scientists first began fooling around with genetic engineering in their labs, real conservatives warned there would be consequences. When man plays God, bad things happen. But companies perceived that money could be made, so genetic engineering took off. It quickly permeated the food supply. As the technology continued to be developed, word of how to do it spread. Unlike nuclear weapons, genetically engineered diseases did not require much in the way of facilities to develop. Kids could do it in the basement—and soon some of them were.

No one ever figured out whether N'Oleans flu, as it came to be known, happened as an accident of genetic engineering or was deliberately created as a weapon of war. If it were the latter, we never determined who used it on the American South, or why.

People did figure out, fast, that N'Orleans flu spread easily, like other flu, but it had a mortality rate of about 80%.

The Plague was back. Contrary to what Americans had been taught, the Middle Ages were a highly successful society. What brought them down was disease. Ring around the rosy, pocket full of posies, ashes, ashes, we all fall down. Dead. It's an old rhyme about the Plague. You still hear children sing it, not knowing what it means. When N'Orleans flu hit, they found out. In response, people did the only thing they could. They panicked.

*

To understand the Great Panic of 2025, you have to realize that by that time, no one trusted any American institution. The hyper-inflation had destroyed what little remained of the federal government's legitimacy. The media was equally mistrusted. People had figured out what was called news had been reduced to another form of entertainment. The culturally Marxist academics and mainstream clergy were taken seriously only by each other.

The average American's life was dominated by one emotion: fear. He feared crime, he feared for his job, he feared the government, he feared for his children, and, most of all, he feared the future. His fears were realistic. They reflected the reality that pressed in on him from every side.

So when this new fear arose, the fear of plague, of a new Black Death lurking in every bus and elevator, shopping mall and office building, he panicked. The Establishment tried to reassure him, to deny the evidence, to damn those who had warned about genetic engineering as technology-hating Luddites. But it was all lies and he knew it. He knew the Establishment lied about everything.

People simply fled. They gathered up their children and ran for the country. It was the only reasonable response, the only possible response. It didn't work, because the country soon filled up with people, which is what other people were trying to avoid. So they fled further. Woods and fields became gypsy camps. Like the gypsies, when they needed food or clothing or weapons, they stole them. Their money wasn't worth anything anyway.

The woods were pretty in autumn that year; the East had one of its most spectacular seasons for color, the maples decked in brilliant oranges and scarlets. Soon, there were less attractive sights under the trees.

At first, the country people welcomed and helped the refugees. Rural areas were still largely Christian. People there helped each other, and felt it their duty to do the same for the newcomers. But too often, the city people brought their ways with them—crime, drugs, noise, and dirt—as well as N'Orleans flu. The rural folk caught the scent of fear, and feared themselves. Soon, militias were being organized in church basements, and bends in country roads became the settings for ambushes. The red and yellow leaves, dying, offered themselves as cheerful shrouds for human dead; no one would bury the bodies for fear of contamination. The carrion-eaters had a feast that winter.

The panic was finally suppressed in 2026 by two old Russian generals, General January and General February. The winter was a harsh one almost everywhere. Just another sign of climate change, the experts said. As the snow fell and the mercury plunged, people started walking home. The risk of a rapid death by disease seemed preferable to a slow and agonizing death by starving and freezing, or murder. By Spring, the country people had their woods and fields to themselves again. However, they did not disband their militias.

Citizens demanded that the government do something, now that they couldn't run away. And government did. It got a ruling from the Supreme Court that said people with disease were "disabled," so that any preventive measures like a quarantine would be illegal discrimination. No one was surprised. And they all knew there was nothing they could do about it.

*

In Maine, of course, things were different. The government in Washington was merely a polite fiction for us, and we paid as little attention to its Supreme Court as to a headline in a supermarket tabloid. We moved promptly to protect public health.

Anyone who showed early symptoms of N'Orleans flu was quarantined, along with all other members of their household. We had very few cases because we also put controls on entry into Maine. The lack of motor traffic due to the price of gas meant most people coming came by train, and there weren't many of them; the American tourist was an extinct animal. All trains had to stop while passengers got a quick blood test; those who didn't pass were put on the next train back. The airports and the Interstates had a similar rule; the rest of the roads we closed. Washington squawked, of course, but we didn't bother to reply. Vermont and New Hampshire soon joined us, which reopened the border roads. The deep South states also adopted a policy of quarantine; they too were starting to act in concert.

The fact that we learned early how to control our borders and who and what crossed them was central to our survival. As the 21st century moved on and the world was engulfed by wars, every surviving state had to shut their borders down tight. Anyone who had the slightest laxness in border controls was quickly hit by a genetically engineered disease. Those growing parts of the world where the state had disintegrated were depopulated.

It's funny how all the experts in the early 21st century were predicting a future of globalism and the international economy, where people and goods moved freely throughout the world. The reality is, it now takes two years to get a European visa, and when you get there, you face two weeks of medical tests at your own expense followed by six weeks of quarantine even if you pass. And that's if you're coming from another state. If you're from someplace where the state has disappeared, you can't go there. Illegal immigrants are shot on sight.

CHAPTER NINETEEN

T HE next two years, 2026 to 2027, were the last of the American
Republic. In Maine, we were effectively running our own show.
We still sent tax money to Washington, but those taxes were
paid in U.S. dollars, not Pine Tree Dollars, so they didn't mean much to
us. In effect, we just shipped some green paper south for recycling.

In Augusta, Governor Adams and the Maine First Party put through a
change to our state constitution. It required that every major issue be put
to the people of Maine in a referendum, and it also allowed Maine citizens
to put on the ballot any issue for which they could get 5,000 signatures.
That gave the government back to the people, where it had originally
come from. It also meant that whenever government did something, it
had a majority of Maine folk with it.

The Maine First Party in addition set a rule that it would only consider an issue in the legislature if a majority of Maine towns said they
couldn't deal with it in town meeting. That moved most decisions back
to the local level, where they belonged.

We were all poor, but thanks to the Pine Tree Dollar, we weren't getting poorer. We ate a lot of cabbage and potatoes—the Eastern European diet—and we huddled around the woodstove in winter, but we didn't starve or freeze. As we had hoped, Asian firms lined up to bid for leases on what had been the national parks in Maine, and the foreign tourists came—and spent. Our economy began to revive.

We knew we had one serious, long-term problem: energy. The only oil in Maine is that left over from frying fish, and our gas was a product of Boston baked beans. Bio-diesel or ethanol wasn't a solution, given our poor soil, which we needed for potatoes anyway. But electricity was.

In a referendum on March 11, 2026, 83 percent of the people of Maine voted to open negotiations with the independent Crown provinces of New Brunswick and Nova Scotia on damming the Bay of Fundy. With the strongest tides in the world, the Bay of Fundy offered a vast reservoir of power which could turn electric turbines. Both of the former Canadian provinces were agreeable; they were also desperately short of energy, along with almost everything else, now that the rest of Canada was no longer there to subsidize them.

Of course, none of us could afford to build such a vast engineering work. But private industry could. We offered the concession on a build-and-operate basis, with a 99 year monopoly on selling the power. On February 28, 2027, the State of Maine, with New Brunswick and Nova Scotia, signed an agreement with the Great Wall Construction and Power Company, a Chinese consortium. Work began that Spring, on a project that would take thirteen years before the first electricity flowed. In the meantime, we would continue to burn wood in our stoves and locomotives (we started building steam locomotives again, at the old Boston & Maine Railroad shops in Waterville) and see our way around the barn with a tin lantern, as our ancestors had.

We even told a good New England joke on ourselves. What did

Yankees use for light before they had candles? Electricity.

Thanks in part to our poverty, we began to rediscover real life. Family took on renewed importance. If people were to survive, they had to look after each other, and the family is where that starts. Family members still on the farm sent food to those in town. The kids working in the Asian-owned resorts sent money back to the old folks on the farm. Families set up new businesses to make the basic tools we needed again; plows and buggies proved more useful than computers.

Real life has always meant working, not waiting to be entertained, and there wasn't much time for entertainment when fields were waiting to be cleared, plowed, sown, and reaped. That was healthy and good. So was the kind of work we did as we returned to the soil and the sea. Dirt is what used to flow from the video screen, not what you run through your fingers as you decide when to plant or water. Maine's cold sea was cleansing to her sons who turned to it again, in wooden boats propelled by sails or oars, seeking the cod that were once again essential to our survival.

With automobiles stopped for lack of gas, the people who lived nearby took on new importance. What had been mere places again became communities. Families helped other families, trading skills; one could farm, another could teach, a third could saw and hammer. As in the Great Depression of the 1930s, the local doctor took his fee in vegetables and eggs.

Life had gotten harder, but somehow also cleaner. We didn't know it then, but this was the beginning of the Recovery.

Up in Hartland, still at the Old Place, I worked the farm. Now, there was no EPA to tell me I couldn't plant, and the town needed whatever I could grow. A neighbor was breeding work horses, solid, gentle Belgians, and I got a team from him. I built a wagon, and, with the help of our local blacksmith, a plow, and went to work clearing stones and planting. It was nothing fancy, just corn, potatoes, and cabbage, but it fed the folks working in the tannery, who in turn made leather we could sell overseas.

*

To my regret, it proved too soon for me to play Cincinnatus. In October, 2026, after the harvesting was done, Governor Adams called. Would I venture the trip to Augusta again? He and a few other folks needed some help thinking about Maine's future, and felt the Christian Marines had a role to play in that. Of course, I said I'd come. At least this time I could drive a wagon to the train in Pittsfield instead of walking.

We met on October 28, in the governor's living room. He understood that informal meetings usually get more done than formal ones. Besides the governor and myself, the gathering included General Sam Corcoran, who was the Adjutant General of the Maine Guard, a few of his unit commanders, and some leaders from the various militias around the state.

Governor Adams made sure we each had a bottle of hard cider lying easy to hand, to lubricate the flow of ideas. Then, his back to the fire and his meerschaum pipe in his hand, he explained why he had called us together.

"Gentlemen," he said, "I do not know what the future has in hold for the United States of America, but I cannot believe it is happy. We have already seen things that, merely twenty years ago, would have been unimaginable to most citizens. Through our own efforts, we in Maine have escaped the worst of it, so far."

"But we have already had to defend ourselves with force," he continued. "We must presume we shall have to do so again. As I see it, that means Maine needs an army. I have asked you here today to begin the process of creating one."

"Of course, I realize we have some military units," the Governor went on. "We have the Guard and Reserve units of the U.S. armed forces. We have our militias. And, not least, we have the Christian Marine Corps. But I wonder if these separate units constitute a real military—the kind Maine will need if she has to fight a war?"

General Corcoran replied first. "Governor, as you know, the Guard's first loyalty is to Maine, now. We swore an oath to defend the U.S. Constitution, but Washington abandoned that Constitution long ago. It abandoned it when the Supreme Court began finding things in it that just aren't there, like a 'right' to an abortion. It abandoned it when Congressmen became professional politicians instead of the citizen legislators the Founders envisioned. It abandoned it when the Executive branch bent the powers of government to force political correctness down everyone's throat."

"Above all, the government in Washington abandoned the Constitution when it deliberately misread it to rule God out of public life. The Founding Fathers committed the nation's future, to God. I have no doubt that if those men could come back now and see what the federal government has become, they would say it is the very opposite of everything they intended."

"I think there is an easy solution to your problem," he continued. "Just turn the Maine Guard into our army. Let us take over these militias and other groups here. We'll teach them how to be real soldiers—to salute, march and drill, to wear the uniform right. I'll give you a better-looking army than anybody else has got, I promise you that."

At this point I realized we were on the verge of making a big mistake. It was time to speak up. "General," I said, "I appreciate your loyalty to Maine and to what we all believe in. But quite frankly, Maine needs a fighting army for what is coming, not a parade-ground army. Remember the Sukhomlinov Effect: the army with the best looking uniforms always loses."

"What would you recommend?" Governor Adams asked.

"I agree we should bring all our units together—militias, Guard, Christian Marines, whoever is willing to fight for Maine," I replied. "But forget about uniforms and drill. The first thing we need is training. Real training is free-play training, where you go against someone who can do whatever he wants to defeat you. That's the only way to train for real war. Do it with paint guns, BB guns, and eventually live fire."

"Live fire force-on-force training? You're nuts," the AG replied.

"Other countries have done it, and do it today," I shot back. "Go train with the Chileans some time. They do it. They learned it from the Germans. The rule is, 'Offset your aim.' It works, if you trust your troops. And if we want an army for modern war, the first rule has to be, trust your troops."

"That's only the beginning," I continued. "We need all promotions to flow from exercise results: winners get promoted, losers don't. Otherwise we'll end up with leaders whose best ability is kissing ass. I saw enough of that in the Corps to last me a lifetime.

"We need to reward initiative, not obedience: everyone, at every rank, must be expected to take initiative to get the result the situation demands. Discipline is key, but the modern battlefield requires self discipline, not imposed discipline. Armies of automatons lose.

"We need soldiers who love their weapons, not soldiers who are afraid of their weapons, like those in most U.S. units. We need leaders who love making decisions and taking responsibility. We need to reward people who take initiative, even when it doesn't work, instead of those who do nothing in order to avoid mistakes. We need units that can move, shoot and fight fast—faster than any enemy, because in war, speed and time are everything."

"Pardon me, but just where did you learn all this stuff?" the AG asked. "I know you were a Marine captain, but I can tell you Army captains don't think this way. Frankly, it's new to me too."

"There were a bunch of us pushing this way of thinking and fighting in the Marine Corps," I replied. "We called it maneuver warfare or Third Generation war. Historically, it is the German way of war—or the Israeli way, if you prefer. The Israelis got it from the Germans, though they don't like to talk about that."

"What you and your men learned in the U.S. Army, general, is the French way of war, Second Generation: focused inward on process instead of outward on results, prizing obedience over initiative, centralizing decision-making, and seeking strength through brute force instead of through speed and tempo. When the French and German styles of war clashed in 1940, the French army went down to defeat in just 43 days. It had more tanks than the Germans, so the cause wasn't equipment. The reason was doctrine: the way each side thought about war."

"It seems to me you have a point," Governor Adams said. "What you are describing as the German army is also the way the most successful corporations have learned to do business: lots of initiative at every level, always trying something new, moving fast and focusing on the customer. Are you saying that Maine's army needs to be like Silicon Valley instead of General Motors?"

"That's right," I responded. "The American armed services follow the old industrial model: Henry Ford's production line. Instead, we need to be military entrepreneurs. The tie-in with military doctrine is direct. Around 1990, the Marine Corps put out a field manual on maneuver warfare called FMFM-1, Warfighting. Somebody else slapped a new cover on it and put it out as a guide for businessmen—without changing a word in the text."

"Well, before I became Governor of this state, I was in the business of making paper," Adams said. "We learned to run the paper mill just the way you describe running a military, and we beat the pants off our competition. I think if a small state like Maine is to have an army that can win, it needs to go at it the same way."

"As I said, it's all new to me," the AG allowed. "But I do know that Maine cannot afford the equipment or the logistics I was taught to depend on. So I guess we have to do something different. Captain, can you show us how?"

"Sir, it isn't just me," I replied. "All Christian Marines understand maneuver warfare. Plus, the Jaeger or 'Hunter' tactics infantrymen use in maneuver warfare will be natural to most of your Guardsmen. After all, most of them are hunters. I'm sure some of your officers and NCOs have studied the Germans on their own. I can't do it for you, but together, I know we can make this work with Maine soldiers."

"Captain, it seems to me the man who understands this new way of war best ought to lead us into it," Governor Adams said. "I am prepared to offer you the command of Maine's forces if you will accept it."

"Thank you, Governor, I am honored," I replied. "But I think General Corcoran should be the commander. I would suggest that I serve instead as Chief of the Maine General Staff. In that role, I would advise General Corcoran, as other members of the General Staff would advise commanders of other Maine units. We would also establish a central office of the General Staff here in Augusta to do contingency planning. But we would not replace the commanders the units now have—that goes for leaders of our Maine militia units as well."

"Is that agreeable to everyone?" the Governor asked.

It was. I knew the militia leaders would appreciate not being bumped downward in units they had created. And the AG's dignity was intact. The meeting had shown he was open to new ideas, though he wasn't likely to come up with them himself. That's OK, I thought: I can play Max Hoffman to his Hindenburg.

"That settles it, then," Governor Adams said. "That's the kind of meeting I like, short and decisive. I trust you'll also be available to advise me, Captain Rumford—or should we make you a general now?"

"Captain is enough for me, Governor," I replied. "In the German Army, authority went with position, not with rank. I think that's a good way to do it. It keeps people from thinking too much about getting promoted."

"Fine. General Corcoran, I trust you will be accepting of the captain's advice?"

"Yes, sir. It's clear he knows a lot of stuff I don't. I just want to serve Maine as best I can," the AG replied.

He seemed to mean it too. It reminded me of what the Kaiser said in August of 1914 when he introduced the Crown Prince to his General Staff officer. "What he advises, you must do."

The next day, I traded my hotel room for a boarding house in Augusta It was clear I'd be spending the winter there, working with the Guard to integrate the militia units into our new armed forces and getting the training program going. Of course, we already had our Maine General Staff: the Christian Marines.

We didn't announce any of this, not yet. No reason to give Washington something else to howl about. By the time they found out, we'd be more than ready for them—or anything else that might come our way as the old U.S.A. dissolved.

For the melting pot had become the refinery. The United States boiled and bubbled and flared with fear and loathing: black against Hispanic against white, woman against man, gay against straight, neo-pagan against Christian, enviro-freak against corporation, worker against boss, west against east. It cracked and separated along every line imaginable, and some not.

Ex uno, Plura. Thank you, "multiculturalism." See you in Hell.

CHAPTER TWENTY

O N July 27, 2027, the blacks of Newark, New Jersey rose against their oppressors and took over the city.

The rising itself was hardly unusual. For years now, urban blacks had regularly celebrated the coming of summer by rioting. It followed a standard pattern. After about a week of hot weather, the Boyz of the F Street Crew would drop in on their G Street opposite numbers and toss a Molotov cocktail into an abandoned building. Since most buildings in most American cities had been abandoned, this was no big deal. To keep face, the G Street Roaches would return the favor. Then, honor assuaged, the two Crews would band together and visit another neighborhood, where a few more buildings would be set ablaze. By this time, others were getting the message, and the gangs began to move out beyond their usual turf. A general *Pax Diaboli* prevailed when it was time to riot, and the borders were relaxed so everyone could join in.

The real sport was not the rioting and burning, but the looting. In effect, the whole city had a blue light special going. The merchants were cleaned out, but unless they were Koreans or Jews they usually weren't burnt out; the gangs wanted them around next year so the street fair could continue. The merchants still made money, thanks to the hundreds of percent markups on the stuff they sold the rest of the year.

Where were the police and the government? The police, like most else, had long since divided along white/black lines, and white cops no longer went into black sections of town, for the good reason that they might be shot if they did. Many black cops and local black politicians were in bed with the gangs, who really ran the place because they controlled the streets. All the politicos wanted was a portion of the take, which they got. In return, they did the Oppressed Victims' Boogie anytime higher authority threatened to mess with the gangs. One hand washed the other.

The real losers in all this were the honest, working blacks, still a majority, who lived in a state of perpetual terror. They hid during the riots, swept up afterwards and otherwise kept their mouths shut. Until that July 27th.

The rioting started in the usual way. It had been blazing hot in Newark for more than a week, with nighttime temperatures staying in the 90s. On the 25th, a few fires were set. The tomtoms beat through the night, and on the 26th the looting began. But that evening, outside the Mt. Zion A.M.E. church, the script changed.

The congregation had gathered about 5 PM, more for safety than worship; black rioters usually didn't fire-bomb black churches. The preacher, one Rev. Ebenezer Smith, delivered an unusual sermon:

> For more than a century and a half, blacks in this country have been battling their oppressors. But we have forgotten something important. We have been so busy fighting oppression that we have forgotten to ask just who our oppressors are.
>
> Maybe at one time our oppressors were white men. White peo-

ple. But that is not true any more. I have never seen a slave owner, or a slave dealer, or a slave. They were all dead long before I was born, before my father and his father were born.

I have never met a member of the Ku Klux Klan. There may still be a few of those somewhere, but I doubt if there are any within a hundred miles of Newark. If I did meet a Klansman in his white sheet, I would laugh.

I have never been oppressed by a white man. But I have been oppressed by other black men almost every day of my life. So has everyone in this church.

We are oppressed when we fear to walk home from the bus stop, because another black man may rob us. We are oppressed when our schools are wrecked by black hoodlums. We are oppressed when our children are shot by another black child for their jacket and their shoes. We are oppressed when our sons are turned into crack addicts or crack dealers by other blacks, or our daughters are raped by other blacks, or taken into prostitution by other blacks.

We Christian blacks are more oppressed today than we have ever been in our history. Our lives are worse than they were in the deep South under segregation. They are probably worse than they were when we were slaves, because then we were at least a valuable piece of property. The black toughs with guns who terrorize this city and every black city in this country do not value us at all. They shoot us down for any reason, or for no reason at all!

It is time for us to fight our real oppressors, the drug dealers, the whore-mongers, the gang members. The fact that they are black

*makes no difference. They are our black oppressors. They are
not our brothers. They are worse enemies than the white man
ever was. It is time for us to fight them, and to take our city
back from them.*

He then equipped his congregation with baseball bats and led them out
into the street.

Singing "Onward Christian Soldiers," they proceeded to beat the crap
out of any gang member they caught. Other honest blacks, seeing what
was happening, came out and joined in. Some had guns, others had
ropes, kitchen knives or tires and gasoline cans.

When they turned the corner onto Newark's main street, a bunch
of gang members opened fire on them. A few fell, but the rest came on.
They mobbed the gang members, hanged a few from the nearest lamppost
and necklaced the rest, stuffing a gasoline soaked tire around their necks
and setting it on fire.

The internet was the command and control system. Video of burning
Boyz soon filled the cell phone screens, and more decent blacks poured
into the streets. By midnight, it was full-scale war, blacks against orcs.
It turned out there were still a lot more blacks than there were orcs. The
gangsters, pimps, whores, drug-dealers and drug-users ended up *lume-
naria*, in such numbers that the street lights went out, their sensors telling
them that it was dawn. It was.

The next day, for the first time in decades, Newark knew peace. The
citizens had taken back their city. The corrupt mayor and his cronies fled,
and the Rev. Ebenezer Smith was acclaimed as the city's new Protector.
He appointed a Council of Elders to help him run the place, and ordered
armed church ushers and vestrymen to patrol the streets.

Across America, men and women of every race cheered Newark's Protector. When the good Reverend Smith appealed for help restoring his

city, it came. Every part of the country sent shovels, bricks, mortar and money. Construction workers, white and black, came with bulldozers, trucks, and cranes. The NRA offered a thousand pistols to help arm the new City Watch, and the Carpenters' Union built gratis a handsome gallows on the town square, complete with three traps, no waiting. The Council of Elders voted to make car theft, drug and handgun possession, and prostitution hanging offenses.

*

It took a while for the politically correct establishment to react. But they did, because they had no choice. One of their most useful lies was that they represented the oppressed. Now, their own slaves had rebelled and taken over the plantation.

On August 3, 2027, as Newark was beginning to pick itself up off its knees, the Establishment tried to kick it in the head. The governor of New Jersey, a Republican woman, with the former mayor of Newark standing beside her, announced that "the rule of law and due legal process must be restored in Newark" (a place where for decades all the law and due process had protected was crime and criminals). To that end, she was ordering the New Jersey National Guard to occupy the city, restore the mayor to office and arrest Rev. Smith, his Council of Elders and his City Watch. She announced they would be charged with murder, conspiracy, and "hate crimes."

The next day, the lead elements of the New Jersey Guard, with the mayor hunkered down in a Bradley Fighting Vehicle, entered the city. They were met by a vast crowd of Newark's citizens, carrying Bibles and hymnals, led by their clergymen. They laid down in the street before and behind the convoy to block it, then approached the Guardsmen, not to threaten them but to plead for their help.

The moral level of war triumphed. Faced not with rioters but with crying women and children quoting Scripture to them, the Guard fell apart. The Guardsmen were ordinary citizens themselves, and like most normal people, they thought what had happened in Newark was great. The black Guardsmen took their weapons and went over to their own people, and the whites and Hispanics went home with the sincere thanks of Newark's citizens. The mayor was dragged out of his Bradley, marched by Newark's new soldiers to the town gallows, and hanged.

In Washington, the Establishment sensed that if they lost this one, it was over (they were right about that). So on August 5, President Sam Warner, a "moderate" Republican who had won with 19 percent of the vote in a 13-way race, announced he was sending the 82nd Airborne to take Newark back for the government. In a move so politically stupid only a Republican could have made it, he waved around a Bible and said, "The United States Government will not allow this book to become the law of the land."

That was the final straw. All across the country, Christians held rallies for Newark. Busloads of militiamen, mostly white, headed for New Jersey to help the city defend itself. Military garrisons mutinied, with the 2nd Marine Division at Camp Lejeune moving on Ft. Bragg, the base of the 82nd Airborne. That didn't come to a fight, because the Christians in the 82nd took over the post and announced they would not obey orders. In New York State, the Air National Guard painted Pine Tree insignia on their aircraft and said they would bomb any federal troops approaching Newark.

*

Here in New England, our friends in Vermont beat us to the punch. On August 8, Governor Ephraim Logan of the Vermont First Party addressed an emergency session of the State Legislature. In Vermont fashion, his words were few but to the point:

> Vermont was once an independent republic. We joined the new United States because they represented what most Vermonters believed in: limited government, serving the people, guided by virtue.
>
> The government now in Washington represents none of these things. It seeks to run and regulate every aspect of every person's life. It lords over the people, far worse than King George ever did, and it regards citizens as nothing but cows to be milked for money. It lives and breathes vice of very kind, and holds virtue in contempt.
>
> The federal government no longer represents the of people of Vermont or the United States. I do not know what other Americans will do, but I know what Vermont should do. It is time for us to resume the independence we won, and voluntarily surrendered. I ask you for a vote of secession from the United States and the restoration of the sovereign Republic of Vermont.

The Vermont First Party held a large majority of the seats in the legislature, so the outcome was foreordained. It was the moment they had long been waiting for. Most of the legislators from other parties joined in too. On August 9, 2027, Vermont became a republic again.

In Maine, we moved swiftly to follow Vermont. Our Resolution of Secession was passed on August 22, by a referendum, with 87 percent of the voters saying "Yes." New Hampshire's legislature had already voted secession on August 14.

We knew we were all in this together, so when the governors of the three states met in Portsmouth, New Hampshire on October 12, Columbus Day, and recommended we join together as the Northern Confederation, it was accepted by our people. Our flag was the old Pine Tree flag of America's first revolutionaries, with its motto, "An Appeal to Heaven."

The Confederation would be a loose one, like the original American Confederation; we had all had enough of strong central governments. We would have a common defense, foreign policy and currency, and no internal tariffs, but otherwise each state would continue to handle its own affairs. The three governors would make up a Council of State to handle common problems; that would be the only federal government, and the capital would rotate every six months among the states so no federal bureaucracy could grow.

Elsewhere in the old united States, South Carolina seceded on August 24, followed quickly by North Carolina, Georgia, Alabama, Mississippi, Louisiana, Tennessee, Arkansas, and Kentucky. Their representatives met in Montgomery, Alabama in early September and formed a new Confederate States of America. Virginia, dominated politically by the non-Southerners in northern Virginia, held back this time, as did Florida and Texas; the latter two feared the reaction of their large Hispanic populations if they left the Union, and for good reason. As it turned out, the Union wasn't much help.

The Rocky Mountain states pulled out too, and established a new nation named Libertas. Oregon, Washington and British Columbia had long been calling themselves Cascadia; they had had their own flag since the 1990s. They quickly made it official. A few more states set up independent republics, while the rest waited to see what would happen.

At General Staff Headquarters in Augusta—now the General Staff of the Northern Confederation—we knew what was going to happen—war.

We also knew it wasn't going to be a War Between the States, not this time. That would be part of it, but probably just the beginning. The deep divisions that ran through America's "multicultural" society in the early 21st century did not follow state boundaries. Yet those divisions would be the most important ones in the war that was to come.

As Chief of the General Staff, I faced two main responsibilities: getting the Northern Confederation's forces ready for war, and developing contingency plans. To that end, I called a conference of our principal officers, including the Guard leaders from Vermont and New Hampshire, in Augusta on October 30, 2027.

CHAPTER TWENTY-ONE

W HEN met over breakfast at Mel's Diner, a few blocks south
of the State House. That was where our General Staff did
most of its important business. The office was useful for doing calculations and research, nothing more. The old American military
had loved offices and Power Point briefings because they helped avoid
decisions. Our objective was precisely the opposite.

We had just eleven people at our breakfast: no horseholders or flower-
strewers allowed. They were militia leaders and Guard commanders, plus
the commander of 2nd Battalion, 8th Marines, Lt. Col. John Ross. He'd
brought his whole battalion, with their families, north from Camp Lejeune to join us, on an LPH he stole from the Navy by boarding it at night
and giving the squids a choice between sailing for Portland or walking
the plank. The ship and the battalion together gave us an amphibious
capability that would later prove useful. Father Dimitri, now our liaison
with the Russians, was also there. The Tsar was friendly and willing to
offer discreet help.

Over hot cider—coffee was an import we couldn't afford—I started the session with a question. I knew most folks were thinking about what we did not have and could not do, and I wanted them to look at the situation creatively, not despairingly. So I asked, "What are our main strengths (pun intended)?"

Three militia leaders answered at once, "Our infantry."

"That's a good answer," I replied. "Your militiamen are not only fine infantry, they are light infantry, which is an important distinction. They are hunters, which is what light infantrymen must be. They understand ambushes, stalking the enemy, staying invisible, because that is what you must do to hunt any game, including human. What about our Guard infantry?"

"Frankly, it's not as good," said Lt. Col. Seth Browning, who led one of the New Hampshire units. "We got too much training in the American Army, which never understood light infantry tactics. They think you defend by drawing a line in the dirt and keeping the enemy from crossing it, and attack by pushing the line forward. Their tactics are a hundred years out of date, or more, if you've ever looked at the tactics of 18th century light infantry. Roger's Rangers could have cleaned the clock of any infantry unit in the modern American Army."

"How do we fix that?" I asked.

"Can we get some General Staff officers as instructors?" another Guard commander asked.

"Sure, if you need 'em," I replied. "Do you?"

For a bit, the only sound was chewing. Then Sam Shephard, head of the Green Mountain boys, who'd learned a few things along the way, said, "If we know the right tactics, why can't we teach them to the Guardsmen?"

At this, the National Guard commanders looked uncomfortable. They saw themselves as the real soldiers, because they had uniforms and ranks and knew how to salute. I needed to break this mind-set down, be-cause what makes real soldiers is an ability to win in combat, not clothes or ceremonies. But I also wanted to go easy on their egos. So I asked, "Are any of the militiamen also Guardsmen?"

The militia leaders chuckled at this. "Lot's of 'em," Shephard replied. "I guess we don't need to keep that secret any longer. We infiltrated the Guard years ago."

"Why not have them lead the training in the new tactics?" I asked. "That way the Guard would train itself."

I saw the Guard leaders relax at this point. Nodding heads indicated agreement. "OK, we'll let you make that happen," I said. I'd just given them a mission-type order: they knew the result we needed, and that it was their responsibility to get it. I wanted to get them used to that.

"John, what about your Marines?" I asked Lt. Col. Ross. "How modern are their tactics?"

"Well, as you know, the Marine Corps never made the transition to Jaeger tactics," he replied, using the German word for true light infantry, which translates as "hunter." "But I've worked on my unit a good bit. What would help us most is some free-play exercises against militia units, using paint-ball and BB guns. Is anybody willing to play?"

"Sure," Sam Shephard replied. "we'd love to kick your butts."

"You may, at first," Ross responded. "At Lejeune, when Marines played paint ball against the local kids, they almost always lost. But you'll find we learn fast. And I suspect we can teach you a few things about techniques. The American military was pretty good at those."

"What else are we good at?" I asked. "Is our infantry our only strength?" Silence told me folks were thinking too small. They knew we didn't have the gear American militaries were used to, so we seemed weak. "What are we fighting for?" I added.

"Everything," answered the New Hampshire AG, General George LeMieux. "Our lives, our families, our homes, our culture, and our God. If we lose, we lose all of them. The cultural Marxists will throw us in gang-run prisons, take everything we own away from our families, probably take our kids away and turn them over to homosexuals to rear. We'll all be 're-educated,' like the South Vietnamese soldiers were after their defeat, and forced to worship the unholy trinity of 'racism, sexism, and homophobia.' Our only other choice will be to grab our families and what we can carry and run for New Brunswick, and hope we can find some country in the world that will take us as refugees."

"What are the federals fighting for?" was my next question.

"For pay, maybe. For a government most of them hate, unless they are blacks or Hispanics or gays, and sometimes even then," was John Ross's answer.

"Does that make a difference?" was my final question. The faces all said Bingo at once.

"It makes all the difference," Ross answered. "That's why the Vietnamese and the Lebanese and the Habir Gedir clan in Somalia and the Pashtun in Afghanistan were able to beat us. We had vastly superior equipment. But they had everything at stake in those conflicts and we had very little. Now, we have everything at stake, and if federal forces attack us, they will have little. That doesn't guarantee we will win, but it means we can win, because we will have the will to fight and they won't."

At this point Browning broke in. "John, I agree we have better infantry, and we have the will to fight. But what about all the things we don't have? What about tanks, artillery, antitank weapons, an air force, and a navy? How do we fight without them?"

"We've been working on all those, Seth," I replied. "Maine already has a Light Armored Regiment, based on technicals— four-wheel drive trucks carrying .50 cal machine guns or 90mm recoilless rifles—and other 4Xs as infantry carriers. Ross's outfit brought a few Marine Corps LAVs, which give us a powerful core unit. We'd like to raise another Light Armored Regiment in Vermont and New Hampshire, also equipped with technicals. We've got the weapons, and any good body shop can make the conversion."

"One ship has already arrived from Russia, and more are coming," said Father Dimitri. "We are sending you machine guns, mortars, which will be more useful than artillery in your terrain, anti-tank mines, thousands of RPGs, shoulder-launched anti-aircraft missiles, and anti-aircraft guns. And a special present from the Tsar himself for Captain Rumford: 100 T-34 tanks, which should be here next week."

"Shit, T-34s?" said General LeMieux. "I guess beggars can't be choosers, but those date to World War II. They can't possibly fight American M-1s. Couldn't you spare us something a little more modern, like T-72s?"

"T-34s are exactly the right tanks for us," I replied. "They are crude, simple, and reliable. They always start and they always run. If they do break, any machine shop can fix 'em. We don't want tanks to fight other tanks. That's what anti-tank weapons are for. The best way to stop an M-1 is with a mine that blows a tread off. We want tanks for real armored warfare, which means to get deep in the enemy's rear and overrun his soft stuff, his artillery and logistics trains and headquarters, so his whole force panics and comes apart."

"The Tsar guessed the Chief of your General Staff would understand tanks and what they are really for," said Father Dimitri.

"As usual, older and simpler is better," I added. "Retroculture also has its place on the battlefield."

"What about an air force?" Browning asked. "We'll get killed from the air."

"No air force has yet won a war," I replied. "Air power is pretty much useless against light infantry in our kind of terrain, because it can't see them. Night and bad weather still protect vehicles effectively, unless they can find columns on the roads. Our shoulder-fired SAMS and Triple-A will make them fly high, and from 20,000 feet they can't see or do much. Plus, we have some ideas for fighting their air force in ways they won't expect."

"And we will have an air force of our own," I continued. "We have mobilized ultra-light aircraft and their owners, which we'll use to help our infantry see over the next hill. We'll have other light planes for deeper reconnaissance and also to serve as fighters to shoot down drones. As has been the case since World War I, the most useful function of aircraft is reconnaissance. Bombing serves mostly to piss the enemy off and make him fight harder, especially when it hits his civilians, which it usually does. Remember, there is no such thing as a precision weapon in real war."

"And we've got some guys working on a navy, too," I added. "It won't have ships like the U.S. Navy, but it will have a sting to it."

"Don't get me wrong," I concluded. "The feds will have a lot more gear than we will. But there are tactical counters to most of it. The more automated a weapon or a system is, the less it can deal with situations not envisioned by its designers. And the feds are deeply into automation and systems. Any system is fragile, because they all have lots of pieces, and if you counter any piece the whole thing falls apart. We'll just have to be imaginative and creative and out-think their systems. Other people have done that, like in Afghanistan. So can we."

"It's clear the General Staff has been doing some good work," said Fred Gunst, who led a battalion of militia in southern New Hampshire.

"But general staffs are supposed to be about planning. I'd like to know what kind of campaign plans our General Staff is developing."

"You're right, and we haven't been idle there either," I replied. "The most important planning is for mobilization and deployment. We've got some stuff in draft for you to take back and talk to your people about. We need their feedback to know if where we're going is practical.

"But the gist of it is simple, as plans in war must be," I continued. "We will have three types of forces. The first will be active-duty, mobile forces. We want to have the two regiments of light armor, plus one heavy armor regiment with the T-34s. With those will be three regiments of motorized infantry, in trucks, of three thousand men each. Each regiment will have some heavy mortars for artillery, but we want to keep the focus on infantry. We want lots of trigger-pullers, not mechanics and communicators and other support personnel.

"They will be the first line of defense. Behind them will stand ten more regiments of light infantry, made up of first-line reservists. They will be subject to call-up in 24 hours. They will be usable anywhere, but long-distance transport will have to be provided with civilian vehicles. Tactically, they'll move on their feet.

"Finally, behind them will stand a universal militia, which will include every male citizen of the Northern Confederation between the ages of 17 and 55. We've got enough AKs and RPGs coming from Russia to give one of each to every militiaman, plus a machine gun and a light mortar to every squad of twelve, which will be divided into three fire teams. They will operate only in their local area, because we can't transport or feed all those folks. But they will form a web of resistance to any attacker which will set him up for a counter-attack by our mobile forces and mobilized light infantry.

"We've already done some gaming, both of deployment plans and possible enemy options. We're looking to do more, so identify your best war-gamers and we'll tell them what we need worked on. More minds beget more options."

"Great," said Gunst, "but you haven't answered my question. What about campaign plans. We need something like the Schlieffen Plan. Aren't you working on that?"

"No, and we won't," bellowed a deep voice behind me. Startled, I turned around to find Bill Kraft. Big men can move remarkably quietly. "We want to be Moltkes, not Schlieffens," he continued. "War cannot be run by time-table, like a railroad. Like Moltke, we know what we want to do. If the federals attack, we want to draw them in, encircle them, and wipe them out. But exactly where and how we will do that depends on what the enemy does, which can never be foreseen with certainty. We are gaming some possibilities, as we should. But we must be prepared to act creatively and above all quickly when the federals move, according to the situation they create and the opportunities it gives us. The key to good planning is to understand what can be planned and what cannot."

"I agree with that," said General LeMieux. "It always drove me nuts in the U.S. Army the way they would develop some elaborate operations plan, and then become prisoners of the plan because it took so much time and effort to create. When the enemy did something unexpected, we would still follow the plan as if nothing had happened. Of course, that was in an exercise, so nobody paid a price. But God help them if they do the same thing against us."

"I suspect they will, and I also suspect He won't," I replied.

CHAPTER TWENTY-TWO

THE federal government in Washington believed in only one thing, but it believed in that strongly. It believed it wanted to remain a government. All the privileges of the Establishment depended on that, and the people who ran Washington couldn't imagine living without those privileges. So they were prepared to fight for them—at least so long as they could hire someone to do the actual fighting for them.

They quickly found an important ally in the United Nations. The Washington Establishment was just one part of the Globalist Establishment, and they all stuck together. They shared a common belief in three things: A New World Order that would replace the state with an international super-state, in effect a world-wide European Union; cultural Marxism; and that everything, everywhere, should be decided by people like them. Globalism still faced a serious opponent, Russia, and Russia blocked any armed action to support Washington by using her veto in the Security Council.

But by working through the General Assembly, the U.N. came

through in September with what Washington needed most: money, real money, not worthless greenbacks. It provided Washington a ten trillion yen loan, with more to follow.

The Feds used the money wisely. They started paying what was left of the old U.S. armed forces in yen. Virtually all the Christian soldiers, sailors, Marines and airmen had resigned, and what was left were willing to fight for Washington, as long as they got paid.

The flow of yen also brought the federal army new recruits, mostly black gang members from the inner city, immigrants straight off the banana boat, and women. The gangs demanded they be accepted whole and designated as military units, with names like the Bad Boyz Battalion and the West Philly Skullsuckers, on the grounds that "forcing them into a white male structure would deny their unique cultural richness." The result was units that spread drugs and mayhem throughout the federal army but ran as soon as someone shot at them. The immigrant outfits had Spanish as the language of command, and their officers would do anything for a bribe and nothing without one. The all-female infantry battalions were issued cardboard penises so they could take a leak in the field without wetting their drawers.

With a motley collection of remnants of regular units, some urban National Guard outfits happy to get paid in yen and assorted other rabble, the federals made their first moves. In October, they invaded Indiana, which had declared itself a republic. The Indiana government had forbidden any defensive measures as provocations, with their Republican governor promising that "my good friends in Washington are wholly opposed to violence in any form." He was first on the list of sniper targets when the two remaining battalions of the 82nd Airborne dropped on Indianapolis; they got him as he ran for his limousine. A brigade of black gangs from Baltimore and Philadelphia took Fort Wayne and spent three days looting and burning the place, with the enthusiastic help of some local Boyz. The videos of panic-stricken whites fleeing their burning suburbs and the blackened corpses of necklaced Koreans outside their looted stores told the rest of us what to expect.

Other states that had seceded but failed to organize a strong defense got the same treatment: Iowa in December, Nebraska and the Dakotas in January and February, Kansas in March. Taking these rural states proved easy; all that was required was a coup de main in the capital with some airborne forces, followed by show trials of secessionist leaders and their public executions. The favored method was the use of all-female firing squads.

But news soon began filtering out that the capitals and a few other cities were all that the feds controlled. Local militias sprang up in the countryside, and any federal troops who ventured far from town were found swinging from trees or impaled on pitchforks. Soon, the cities and towns emptied, as people went to live with relatives or friends or fellow church members who had farms. Federal garrisons and their Quisling politicos had to be moved and supplied by air, and the planes and helicopters accumulated lots of holes from hunting rifles. But the U.N. kept real money flowing in, and Washington grew more confident.

*

On March 25, 2028 President Warner announced a major coup. He had negotiated a treaty with Mexico recognizing Mexican co-sovereignty over Texas, New Mexico, and Arizona. In his speech to Congress, Warner said, "We are recognizing and healing an old wrong, that hateful war in which white *Norteamericanos* tore these states from the bosom of Mexico. Mexican-born citizens now make up more than 50 percent of their populations, and it is only just that they should feel part of their homeland. To insist otherwise would be to deprive them of their human rights. We have no doubt that Mexican co-governance will benefit all the citizens of Texas, New Mexico, and Arizona, as they may now fully share the vibrant culture of our southern neighbor."

As the treaty allowed, on March 27, the Mexican Army moved north across the Rio Grande. In Brownsville, Laredo, Las Cruses, and Nogales, they were met not by smiling senoritas and Mexican hat dances but with bullets and Molotov cocktails. It wasn't just the Anglos who fought them, so did many of the Hispanics. These people had emigrated to get away from the brutal Mexican Army and the corrupt and incompetent Mexican government. Unlike liberals in Washington, they had no illusions about what Mexican co-rule meant. It meant rule by torture, ballot-box stuffing and *la mordida*—the bribe.

The state governments reacted fast and well. They mobilized their National Guards and the remains of the two U.S. Armored Divisions at Ft. Hood joined them. Then they called for volunteers and seceded from the Union. In Houston, Governor John Dalton spoke of "a treasonous and tyrannical regime in Washington that has plunged Santa Ana's knife into the back of Texas." Washington responded with a drone strike that destroyed the Alamo.

From Mexico City, U.S. Ambassador Irving P. Zimmerman emailed Washington that "the regular Mexican Army, which has benefited greatly in recent years from American aid and training, will quickly suppress such disorders as nativist-extremist elements may generate." The reality was that the Mexican Army was the same inept outfit it always had been, useful only for massacring unarmed peasants. Texans weren't peasants, and they most certainly weren't unarmed.

The Mexican troops never made it beyond the border towns.

Hemmed in by roadblocks made of trucks and buses, their vehicles set on fire by gasoline bombs and their troops shot at from rooftops and from behind every door and window, they melted into a panicked mob. A few managed to surrender, and a few more made it back across the Rio Grande. The rest littered the streets like dead mayflies.

But the war didn't stop at the border. Texas swiftly organized its forces and counterattacked into Mexico, with Arizona and New Mexico providing diversionary attacks. The government of the Republic of Texas had the good strategic sense to announce that its only enemy was the despised government in Mexico City, not the people of Mexico. It invited Mexicans to join its march, and thousands did. A mixed force of Texans and Mexican rebels took Monterrey on April 24, and by May 11 they were in San Luis Potosi. What was left of the Mexican Army concentrated at Queretaro for a battle to defend the capital.

But that battle was never fought. The Texan invasion gave the Indian population in southern Mexico the opportunity for which it had long waited. On April 25, with the fall of Monterrey, Indian rebels in the Yucatan proclaimed the rebirth of the Mayan Empire at Chichen-Itza. Nahuatl-speaking Indians, the last remnants of the once-fearsome Aztecs, announced the rebirth of their kingdom in Tenochtitlan three days later. Indian columns, some led by feather-clad priests and Jaguar warriors and others reciting the *Popul Vuh*, marched on Mexico City. The Texans pinned down the Mexican Army, so there was nothing to stop them. Mexico City fell on May 21. On the 23rd, an Aztec high priest cut the beating heart from Mr. Ambassador Zimmerman and offered it to the Hummingbird Wizard atop the Pyramid of the Sun at Teotihuacan.

*

Reeling from the fiasco in the Southwest, Washington cast about for something it could do that might work. The U.N. was not about to cut the money off, but the federals wanted more than money. They were working hard to persuade the U.N. to send troops.

The Security Council was still a non-starter. Russia did not want to appear to side too openly with the rebels in an American civil war, but it had used its veto once and could do so again—which is why the U.S. Navy made no attempt to block the arms that were arriving in Portland on Russian ships. In Washington, the feeling was that if Federal forces could win a major victory, Russia might have to go along with sending a U.N. peacekeeping force that would define "peace" as putting the federal government back in control.

The Joint Chiefs of Staff met with President Warner on June 15, 2028, to give him their considered advice. The seceded Rocky Mountain states, they opined, were effectively protected by the guerrilla war in the Midwest. To support a major offensive in the Rockies, federal forces would require secure supply lines, highways and railroads, in the conquered states west of the Mississippi. But their supply lines were not secure.

The Confederacy was too strong to take on until Washington had the rest of the U.S. back under its control as well as major U.N. help. Talks were under way in Beijing about securing large-scale Chinese assistance; an expeditionary force of as many as 20 Chinese divisions was being openly discussed. Mao's successors had little liking for regional rebellions elsewhere, given their own vulnerability to the same. But they would only act as part of a U.N. mandate, which brought the problem full circle.

That left us.

The Joint Chiefs recommended initiating a full naval blockade of all

Northern Confederation ports, coupled with round-the-clock air, drone, and cruise missile attacks. After about 30 days, the ground war would begin. The main attack would be up I-95, roughly along the New England coast; once Maine was beaten, New Hampshire and Vermont would be cut off from the sea and surrounded on three sides. Their situation would be hopeless.

The best of the federal regular forces, the remains of the old U.S. Army and Marine Corps, would carry out the main attack. A supporting attack would be launched from New York state into Vermont by the 42nd National Guard division, an outfit recruited almost entirely from Harlem.

President Warner noted that the naval blockade would be difficult politically, because of probable Russian reaction. Otherwise, he seemed ready to approve the plan.

But his Secretary of Defense wanted to say something. She had represented Harlem in Congress, and after her defeat by a Black Muslim candidate the administration had given her the defense job to maintain her visibility; she was one of its biggest supporters in the black community. The 42nd Division was her baby—in fact, she had carried several of its babies, until the abortionist had restored her shapely figure—and she wanted it to have its chance to shine.

"Mr. President," said the Honorable Kateesha Mowukuu, "I am the only black woman at this table. We have heard what these white men have to say. I would remind you that in this war, white men are our enemy. Now you will hear what a black woman has to say, and I expect all of you to listen with respect."

"Blacks have been the only true warriors in history. White men can't fight. It's because their noses are too small. Courage comes from the nose, not the heart, as the African spiritual healers you call witch doctors have long understood. That's why black warriors eat their snot! What do you white folk do with your snot? You wrap it up in a little white surrender flag and put it in your pocket. So you don't have no courage.

"All the great warriors in history have been black. Caesar was a black man, and so was his enemy, Hannibal. The Spartans were black. They just dyed their hair blond, to fool their enemies into thinking they were weak white people. Charlemagne was a black man. In French, *charlemagne* means 'kinky hair.' The Vikings came from Africa, which is where they got those helmets with horns on them. Gunpowder was invented by ancient Zimbabwean scientists, who made it from elephant shit. You ever hear an elephant fart? Black scientists knew there had to be some juju behind that.

"All of America's military heroes were black people. Washington was a black man. We know that because he came from Washington, D.C., which is a black city. General U.S. Grant had a black grandmother, and so did Robert E. Lee. In fact, it was the same black woman, which is why they looked so much alike. Eisenhower is really a black name, and General George Patton got his pearl-handled revolvers from his black grand-daddy, who took them off Simon Legree.

"This racist white-boy society of yours has dissed the black man big-time. You've throw'd 'em in jails and cut off their tails. You've put AIDS in their veins and cocaine in their brains. You've made black mean slack and crack, Jack, and we ain't gonna take it no more!

"And now the black warriors of our black 42nd Division, which I will rename the 1st Division, will teach these racist, sexist, Yankee crack-ers what happens when they mess with the black man," Ms. Mowukuu concluded. "And they don't need no help from nobody!"

President Warner was torn. His mind told him the Joint Chiefs' plan made considerably more sense, militarily and otherwise, than that of his

Secretary of Defense, but he had long ago conditioned himself to turn off his mind whenever the magic word—racism—was mentioned.

"Thank you for that helpful contribution," he replied. "I am sure all of us respect what a black woman has to say." The Joint Chiefs' heads nodded in unison. "Would the Chiefs care to comment on the Secretary's proposal?"

"Mr. President, may I make a suggestion?" said the Army Chief of Staff, General Wesley. "We all deeply appreciate the Secretary's brilliant remarks. But the Army already has a 1st Division, with a long and distinguished history. May I recommend that the 42nd Division be renamed the Numero Uno Division instead? That would avoid any conflict and also honor its members from Spanish Harlem."

"Ms. Mowukuu, is that agreeable to you?" asked President Warner.

"I believe deeply in multiculturalism, Mr. President, as you know," replied the Secretary of Defense with a gracious nod. "I am prepared to accept that modification."

"Are there any other comments?" asked the President. There were none.

"The Secretary's proposal is therefore unanimously approved," he said. "I think we have seen here how we can all learn if we open ourselves to what our sisters and brothers from diverse backgrounds can offer us. Ms. Secretary, you have the deep respect and gratitude of your country."

The gratitude of what remained of America was small compared to that offered by the General Staff of the Northern Confederation, once Ms. Mowukuu's plan became known to us.

That took all of about 24 hours. One of the Massachusetts State Police who was a Christian Marine had a brother on the White House Secret Service detail. He was in charge of the electronic security of the Oval Office.

CHAPTER TWENTY-THREE

As usual, we gathered around the coffee-stained, ring-marked back table at Mel's. The General Staff had grown somewhat with the addition of men from Vermont and New Hampshire, but the Operations Section was just twelve officers, which was the most who could fit at the table. I made sure Mel didn't get a bigger table.

We had Washington's invasion plan. The question was, how could we take advantage of it? Once everybody had downed their buckwheat cakes and venison sausage, I asked for ideas.

"I know the 42nd Division," said one of the new guys from Vermont, Fred Farmsworth. "Our Marine Reserve unit played against them in an exercise a few years ago. It was a joke. When we attacked, they broke and ran—and everybody knew we were just shooting blanks. I could keep the 42nd Division out of Vermont with a couple of Boy Scout troops armed with slingshots."

"Do we want to keep them out?" I asked.

The old hands smiled; they knew we had an opportunity to use the "let 'em walk right in" defense, and on the operational level too. Seth

Browning, who had traded his Army National Guard rank of Lieutenant Colonel for a captaincy in the General Staff and a pay cut, laid out the obvious. "The 42nd Division can only come on two routes," he said. "They can come up I-91, or they come up via Whitehall and the east shore of Lake Champlain. I'd bet on the Champlain approach, because I-91 is hemmed in by mountains and they'll be scared of our infantry in the mountains. They're flatlanders, and the land east of Champlain is fairly flat. Plus, they can get into Vermont directly from New York state, and they'll be more comfortable with that. If we guess wrong and they do come up I-91, our militia can keep 'em on the road and our mobile forces can shift quickly and cut them up with *motti* tactics."

"A good analysis," I replied. "What should our intent be if you're right and they attack via Whitehall?"

"That's easy," said John Ross, who I had dual-hatted as commander of our motorized forces and member of the General Staff. "We let them come well in, then pocket them with their backs to Lake Champlain. Being Army, they'll see water as an impassable obstacle rather than a highway. Once we have them trapped with their backs to the lake, they'll cave."

"What about the folks in Vermont between West Haven and Burlington?" said Sam Shephard. "They'll take this kind of hard."

"Sadly, that is war," said Father Dimitri, now the informal Imperial Russian advisor to the Northern Confederation General Staff. "We Russians know well the cost of letting an invader come. But we also know it can bring decisive victory to the defender. Their sacrifices will be well-rewarded. The Tsar has authorized me to tell you that he will follow your first major victory with diplomatic recognition of your country. I think the destruction of the 42nd division will count as such a victory."

"OK, then, we know our intent: pocket the whole 42nd Division against Lake Champlain and wipe it out. The Plans section can lay out our deployment accordingly. What else do we need to decide here?" I added.

"What if they try a naval blockade? Our report from the White House meeting leaves that unclear," asked Don Vanderburg, also a recruit to the General Staff; he'd shown earlier that he could make decisions. "And what if they go through with the JCS proposal for an air campaign?"

"Our satellites indicate they may attempt to intercept the next Russian ship bringing arms into Portland," answered Father Dimitri. "They have stationed two American destroyers and an Aegis cruiser off the Maine coast. If they try to stop our ship, the Imperial Russian Navy will uphold the principle of freedom of the seas. You do not have to worry about that."

"An air campaign does face us with some problems," I added. "They can unquestionably do serious damage to civilian targets. History tells us that will just make our folks fight harder, but of course we want to prevent it if we can. Militarily, an air threat is only significant if we have to move operational reserves fast, by road or rail. I don't anticipate that here. Plus, our anti-aircraft guns and shoulder-fired SAMS will make most of their pilots fly too high to see or hit much."

"I think we may have some operational, not just tactical answers to their air," said Captain Ron Danielov, a former Marine Corps Scout/Sniper sergeant who was in charge of special operations. "As you know, a special operation is an action by a small number of men that directly affects the operational or strategic level. I think we may be able to do one targeting their air power. I'm playing around with some ideas, talking with Ross's guys and a couple of the trash haulers from the Air Guard."

"Fine," I replied, "but we need to move fast. How soon will you be ready to pull something off, or tell me that you can't?"

"One week," Ron answered.

"In war, one week is a long time," I said. I allowed my subordinates to come up with their own solutions to problems, but I insisted they be quick about it.

"Sorry, but that's what it takes," Ron responded. "We're not just doodling and day-dreaming, we're rehearsing some stuff to see if it works. You can't make a special operation up as you go along; it's too fragile for that. You've read McRaven's book too. You know that."

I had and I did. His reference was to a book by a U.S. Navy SEAL officer, Bill McRaven, *The Theory of Special Operations*, published way back in 1993 by the old Naval Postgraduate School. That and the U.S. Special Operations Command's Pub 1, *Special Operations in Peace and War*, were good guides to a kind of war where smarts could make up for numbers and equipment. I knew Ron was right.

"OK, you've got your week," I replied. "If they start bombing before then, we'll just suck it up and take it."

The first bombs fell three days later, on June 19, 2028. Cruise missiles came in just before dawn, targeting the State Houses in Maine, New Hampshire, and Vermont, National Guard Armories, and power plants. The damage was extensive but largely symbolic. The State Houses and armories were empty, and the power plants were down for lack of fuel. Three waves of bombers hit us after the cruise missiles, going for bridges, rail lines and railway shops, fuel depots (also empty), and the Portland docks. In Washington, President Warner announced "the beginning of precise, surgical air action to compel the northern rebels to surrender to lawful authority."

In Augusta, a precise, surgical cluster munition dropped by a U.S.

Navy F-35 hit the schoolyard of St. Francis Elementary during noon recess. Thirty-three children died, along with seven teachers and the parish priest.

We had expected the hits we got, other than the schoolyard. Railroads are easy to blow up but also easy to repair, and we had the trains moving again by midnight. Engineer bridges were ready to go in strategic places, and those were up quickly too. Railroad rolling stock was hard to replace, but we had scattered it around the country and didn't lose much.

Video of the St. Francis schoolyard was on the internet within forty-five minutes of the attack, and the images broadcast around the world brought further air attacks to a screeching halt. Japan said in no uncertain terms that if there were further civilian casualties, there would be no more yen.

We also had an amazing stroke of luck—or perhaps something more than luck, since St. Francis was involved. The F-35 that dropped the cluster bomb was shot down. Our few anti-aircraft weapons were deployed to protect our mobile ground forces, not our cities. But a Russian instructor happened to be showing some of our troops how to use the SA-18 shoulder-fired anti-aircraft missile at a small base just south of town. They heard the bombs hit Augusta, and when one of the American jets screamed overhead on its way home, the instructor took a shot and got it. The pilot came down alive.

I immediately sent one of our few helicopters to pick up the U.S. Navy pilot and bring him to St. Francis. Pilots seldom see their handiwork up close. They pickle their bombs, run for home, and its Miller Time at the club. It's all a video game for them. Unlike infantrymen, they're not prepared to see the other guy's eyes bug out when you twist a bayonet into his guts.

I called the school and stopped the removal of the bodies. Then I went over there myself and met the helo as it came in. The helo crew had told the pilot what he'd hit, and he was already shaking when I met him at the bird. With a video camera stuck in his face, I forced him to walk through the blood, guts, and tiny severed limbs, lifting each sheet and staring at his handiwork. He managed to maintain his composure until the third kid, a little blond girl whose torso was ripped half away. He had a little blond daughter about the same age, and he came unglued. The camera caught his face in an unforgettable image of horror and agony, just before he puked himself dry. By the tenth kid, he was begging me to shoot him rather than look at any more. I made him keep looking. When he'd stared into the eyes of every tiny corpse, I ordered him locked up in the town jail under close watch, not so he couldn't escape but so he couldn't kill himself.

I got back to headquarters to find a message from Governor Adams, asking me to meet him down at Mel's as soon as possible. When I got there, I found the mayor, a couple of the Governor's advisors, and Bill Kraft already with him. The subject of discussion was what to do with the Navy pilot. The two most popular alternatives were putting him on trial as a war criminal or hanging him that afternoon in the St. Francis schoolyard.

"Well, what does the General Staff advise in this case?" the Governor asked me.

"Waal, I don't know," I said in my best Maine accent. "Since we seem to be deciding to hang him now or hang him later, I guess I'd as soon hang him now. It'd make the people of Augusta feel a little better, anyway."

"It sure would," the mayor added.

Bill Kraft had been sitting to the side, smoking his pipe, looking into a book and making it clear that he didn't much care for meetings like this. I expected he'd also favor a prompt hanging. Instead, he gave me a look of icy contempt and said, "I would have expected at least an attempt at military reasoning from someone in the uniform of a General Staff officer."

After that face shot, I knew I was going to get a lesson in military reasoning. Bill's lessons were usually good ones, even if they sometimes felt like a cut glass suppository wrapped in sandpaper.

"Here as elsewhere, the correct question is, how do we use this situation to strike most powerfully at our enemy?" he went on. "Merely doing what makes us feel better betrays a lack of self-discipline. Our object is not to feel good, but to win."

"I thought we'd already done that by putting this guy on YouTube as he cracked up," I replied.

"That was an excellent start," Kraft said. "But why not carry it further?"

"How?" asked Governor Adams.

"Send him home," Kraft replied.

"You mean just let him go after he killed our kids?" the Mayor asked.

"Exactly," Kraft answered.

"How does that help us?" the governor inquired, knowing Kraft well enough to realize he was probably on to something.

"The Chief of our General Staff should be able to answer that question," said Kraft. "Regrettably, in his hurry to get here he seems to have left his brain in his wall locker, so I will explain." There was the suppository.

"If we send the pilot home, we toss a hot potato into the lap of the federal government. They have three choices, all bad. They can let him out in public, in which case he will tell a story of horror that will undermine public support for the war. They can arrest him for war crimes, which will let all their military personnel know that if they make a mistake, their own government will sacrifice them. Or they can send him back to his unit, where he will undermine the will of his fellow pilots to drop bombs anywhere but in the ocean or open fields. Whatever they do helps us, while the pilot is no further help to us if we keep him here. So we should send him home."

As usual, Bill was right. We all saw that, and we all knew he was right about self-discipline as well. As the weaker party, we had to do what would hurt the enemy, not what would make us feel good.

So that's what we did. We announced that as a humanitarian gesture to the pilot's family, we were releasing him, and we invited the federals to send a plane under a white flag to pick him up. That made us look like the good guys to the world, and the video of a U.S. Air Force transport coming into the Augusta airport with its insignia covered by white patches didn't hurt either.

The pilot gave a weepy interview to the press on his departure on June 20, saying that the war was a terrible thing and he hoped nobody would drop any more bombs.

He said the same thing to a bigger clutch of newsmen when the plane landed at Andrews.

Then, to our delight, facing three unpalatable choices, the federal government did the worst possible thing. It chose all three.

First, it let the pilot appear on all the TV talk shows to cry about what he had done. Then, it arrested him. When the military screamed, it dropped the charges, so it looked like it was condoning war crimes. Finally, it sent him back to his unit, where he spread his horror story to everyone he could talk to, so those pilots dropped their bombs in the ocean from then on.

*

It was not the end of the air campaign. For several days the sky was quiet. Then, on June 23, federal aircraft began buzzing our towns at night with sonic booms, not dropping any ordinance but reminding us they still could. On the 25th they hit two bridges with laser-guided bombs, after warning us well beforehand so all traffic could be stopped. On the 26th, they began hunting our locomotives with anti-tank missiles We didn't have many engines; we needed every one of them and couldn't let this continue. I called in Ron Danielov. He'd had more than his week, and it was time to see if a special operation could help us out.

"Waal, what've you got for us?"

"I've got three operations set up and ready to roll. You can use any of them or all of them," Ron replied.

"What are they?" I asked.

"The first, and most powerful, is aimed at Washington itself. We've got six moving vans sitting in southern Virginia, each with about 10,000 pounds of explosives in it. The drivers are our men. On signal, they will take those trucks on to the six bridges that connect Washington with Virginia, park 'em, set the timers, and dive into the Potomac. They're all good swimmers who can reach the Virginia shore. When the bombs go, they'll take several spans out of each bridge, cutting Washington off from the south."

"What about civilian casualties?" I asked. "We can't ignore that problem without giving the feds license to ignore it too, and it's our best air defense."

"The trucks have powerful loudspeakers that will play a recorded message, 'This is a bomb. Get off the bridge immediately.' That starts as soon as the drivers punch out, and goes for fifteen minutes before they blow. If anyone tries to enter the truck or move it, the bomb goes off automatically, so the delay won't effect the operation."

"How long will the bridges be down?"

"A few days, but that's enough. As soon as the Confederate government knows they're blown, Confederate forces will enter Virginia and the governor will proclaim the state's secession from the Union."

"Holy shit, you set that up?" I replied, astounded.

"Well, I pushed it over the edge, anyway," Ron replied. "Virginia has wanted out, and the Confederates have wanted Virginia in, so the ground was already laid. When I told them we'd cut Washington off from Virginia long enough for them to move, they decided this was the time. Remember, that's what special operations are about: hitting on the strategic level, or at least the operational level. Blowing the bridges would just be tactical, and that's not a special op."

"If Confederate forces are on the Potomac opposite Washington, the feds' capital will be untenable. They'll have to move it which will be an enormous problem for them, given the size of that government. It will effectively incapacitate them for months," I said, thinking aloud.

"Now I hadn't thought of that," Ron admitted.

"If that's your first act, and it's a good one, I'm almost afraid to ask for the second," I said. "But bombing them won't keep them from bombing us. Have you got something that will?"

"The second operation helps with that, and also assists the Confederates' entry into Virginia," Ron answered. "We've done a little recon at the Oceana Naval Air Base and at Langley Air Force Base, near Norfolk. One of our guys got into both, driving a beer delivery truck. You know a beer truck will never be stopped on an air base. Anyway, they've got the planes lined up wing-tip to wing-tip in nice straight rows on both bases, so they look pretty. I've got four teams down there with an 81 mm mortar each, and they can just walk their fire up and down the rows. I figure they can take half, maybe three-quarters of those aircraft out."

"Not bad," I said, "but the feds will still have plenty of aircraft. That will disrupt them for a few days, maybe a week, but no more."

"We know that, which is why we have a third operation planned," Ron replied. "The target is the other base where most of the sorties against us are flown from, Dover, in Delaware. We're gonna hit the single most vulnerable point on any air base: the Officers' Club on Friday night."

"Now that's better," I reflected. "Pilots are a great deal harder to replace than aircraft. How many of the fly-boys do you expect to wipe out, and how are you going to blow the place?"

"Our intel is that there are usually 100 to 150 aircrew, pilots and NFOs, at the Club on the average Friday night. But we're not going to blow it. We're going to take those guys and bring them home."

"Home? What do you mean? I don't get it," I said.

"Here," Ron replied. "We're going to bring them here, to the N.C. When we take the place, we're going to hold the federal aircrew hostage and demand a transport aircraft to bring them here. When they get here, they'll serve as hostages. We'll chain one to every locomotive, every factory, every strategically important target, so if the feds hit those targets, they'll kill their own men. My guess is that the federal government will order them to do that, but their pilots' accuracy will diminish drastically."

"I love it! I love it! That's brilliant! Ron, if you make that one work, you'll get the Blue Max!" I cried. "Skorzeny himself would shake your hand if you can pull it off. Is that the kind of thinking they taught you Scout/Sniper guys?"

"We didn't write it with the runes for nothing," Ron said.

"OK, my answer on all three is GO! And the ideas are good enough I'll back you up even if they don't work," I said.

"Aye aye, sir," Ron replied. "And they will work, subject to the old German artilleryman's caution: all is in vain if an angel pisses in the touchhole."

*

This time, the angels were on the side of the smaller battalions. One of the trucks broke down, and we'd overlooked the railroad bridge which was sloppy map work on our part, but otherwise the attack on the Washington bridges did what it was supposed to. It triggered the move of Confederate forces into Virginia and that state's joining the Confederacy, which made Washington untenable for the federal government.

The feds picked Harrisburg, Pennsylvania as the new federal capital. Not only did the move prove disruptive, they lost their local support base of government employees, most of whom couldn't move because there was no place to put them. Deprived of the federal payroll, much of northern Virginia became a ghost town. The Pentagon was turned into the world's largest nursing home, specializing in patients with Alzheimer's. It wasn't much of a change. In the former District of Columbia, the Capitol and the White House were vandalized, partly burned and finally taken over by bums and crack heads as places to squat. Having ruined the nation, they became ruins themselves.

*

The mortar crews at Langley found the aircraft still parked in tidy rows and walked their fire from one end to the other. They destroyed about fifty airplanes.

At Dover, our team of special operators found almost 300 guys in the club. It seems the base CO had called a meeting of all aircrew for a mandatory lecture on sexual harassment, in response to a complaint by the bar girl that some pilots had been looking at her. It took two C-17s to carry them all to Portland. The feds howled when we staked them out at all the worthwhile air targets, but the tactic worked even better than we expected. When President Warner ordered the air attacks continued, the remaining American pilots simply refused to fly. The air campaign was over.

As Father Dimitri had promised, the Russians took care of the threat of a naval blockade. On July 4, 150 miles outside Portland, the American destroyer USS *Gonzalez* ordered the Russian freighter *Belyy Rossii* to stop. The ship, which was loaded with RPGs, machine guns and ammunition intended for us, refused. The American ship put a five-inch round into the *Belyy Rossii*'s bridge, killing the captain and seven crew members. Ninety seconds later the *Gonzalez* was blown out of the water by three torpedoes from the Russian submarine which had been escorting the *White Russia*.

In Washington, where the federal government was beginning the process of packing to move, the Navy demanded immediate and forceful military action against Russia. President Warner, remembering the Trent Affair in the first American Civil War, demurred. "One war at a time, gentlemen, as President Lincoln said," were his words to the JCS. It was a wise decision, but it effectively took the U.S. Navy out of the war against us.

*

That left us to face the renowned 42nd Division (as it continued to be called by everybody except the American Secretary of Defense). That wasn't a threat, it was an opportunity.

The deployment of our own forces was complete. The militia was mobilized in western and southern Vermont and southern New Hampshire, to provide a web within which the regular forces would maneuver and to guard against an attack up I-91.

We knew the first enemy objective was Burlington, where they intended to turn inland away from Lake Champlain and follow I-89 to the Vermont capital, Montpelier. After a thorough reconnaissance, the General Staff determined that we would attempt to pocket the 42nd Division around Vergennes, trapping them between Otter and Lewis Creeks with their backs to Lake Champlain.

Accordingly, we moved a regiment of light infantry, with our few artillery pieces, into the area along Lewis Creek, stretching east to Monkton Ridge. Their mission was to prevent any advance north. They did not entrench, but set up a mobile defense in depth based on small teams that could ambush enemy infantry and call in fire on enemy vehicles. Another light infantry regiment plus the local militia held the eastern flank from West Rutland, along Lake Bomoseen and Lake Hortonia, through Middlebury to Monkton Ridge. Their mission was to prevent the enemy from going east. Vergennes lay too far west to cover, so we evacuated the population and garrisoned it with light infantry who had been trained in urban combat. They expected to fight cut off from our other forces. Operationally, their mission was to draw as many enemy as possible into the area and hold them while we encircled.

I established the headquarters of the General Staff in Middlebury, about fifteen miles from where Lewis Creek empties into Lake Champlain. Here was stationed our Mobile Force, under John Ross. It consisted of his Marine battalion on dirt bikes, both of our light armor regiments, our heavy armor regiment with its T-34 tanks, and a regiment of motorized infantry. The mission of the Mobile Force was to undertake the actual encirclement of the 42nd Division. That was the *Schwerpunkt* of the whole operation.

The 42nd Division had been mobilized in late June, but had done virtually no training. Its encampment, at and around Camp Smith on the Hudson River, had been a circus of drugs, drinking, and debauchery. After three white officers were murdered, most of the rest went home; blacks were promoted from the ranks to replace them. On July 10, three Death Battalions of gang members were added to the division, which turned mere chaos into complete pandemonium. Finally, on the 21st of July, 2028, the monster started crawling north.

For the New York towns in its path—towns on supposedly friendly soil—the passage of the 42nd Division was an envelopment by hell. Stores were looted. Whites were mugged, raped, or shot. Homes, barns and businesses were burned. The division's march was a traveling riot.

Since the federal government could not control the internet, the images of rape and pillage were broadcast into every American home. Secretary of Defense Mowukuu, when asked to explain the depredations of her division on its own citizenry, replied truthfully that they were no worse than what the people who made up the division had been doing for many years in the areas where they lived. Most Americans failed to find that reassuring.

Vermont actually got off easier than New York. We had evacuated the towns we knew the 42nd would pass through. The remaining homes and businesses were put to the torch, but none of our civilians were hurt and most movable property was saved.

Our militia was sure they could hold a line against an invasion as pathetic as this one, and they were right. But I would not let them, because I didn't want to stop the 42nd Division. I wanted to destroy it. Once they understood that, they went along.

On July 31, the lead element of the enemy force hit the forward edge of our defense in front of Lewis Creek. We let them penetrate as far as the creek itself, then started chewing them up in small ambushes. The main body of the division did exactly as we hoped when it hit resistance in Vergennes. It figured this would be the decisive battle, and halted while its reserves came up. On the morning of August 2, I told John Ross to attack.

John put the T-34s right up front, figuring they would cause "tank terror" among the drunken, untrained, undisciplined horde. They did, and the enemy fled back toward the Lake. By the evening of the 2nd the encirclement was complete.

That same afternoon, I went out to find John. He was down by the southern end of the pocket, figuring that if a breakout was attempted that was where it would come.

When I stuck my head into Ross's CP, which was a single command version of the LAV, I was almost impaled by a German spiked helmet coming out. Below the helmet was a vast, rotund figure that could only be Bill Kraft, clad in the dark blue uniform of a 19th century Prussian officer. Down the trouser legs ran the wine-red stripe of an officer of the Prussian General Staff. I must have done a double-take, because Kraft looked at me and said, "Don't you remember why I turned down your kind offer to join the Christian Marine Corps?"

I had to think back a bit, but I did remember. Bill had said, "I wear a different uniform." Now I knew which one.

"We were wiped off the map in 1947." Bill said, "but Prussia is more than a place. As Hegel understood, it is also an ideal. Prussians still exist, and so does the Prussian Army, a bit of it anyway. Now, it's fighting again, here, for what it always fought for: for our old culture, against barbarism. Someday, we will win."

"Well, this is a good start," I replied, with what I thought was suitable

New England understatement.

"It's only that," Bill said. "What do you intend to do next?"

At that point John Ross stuck his head out of the LAV. "We've just gotten a radio message from someone claiming to be the commander of the 42nd Division. They want to surrender."

"I guess that answers your question, Bill. It's over, and we can go home," I added.

"Wrong answer," Bill shot back. "All that means is you've won a tactical victory. The operational question is, what are you going to do with it?"

I saw immediately that Kraft was right. I'd gotten too wrapped up in the immediate situation and was failing to think big—a serious mistake for a General Staff officer.

"Since you are our Prussian advisor, can I start by asking your advice?" I responded.

"Strategically, just as restoring the union is the federal government's objective, ours is fracturing it further," he replied. "I think this battle, and the conduct of the 42nd Division on its march here, gives us an opportunity to bring New York state into the Northern Confederation."

"Do we want New York in the Confederation?" I asked. "We want people who share our traditional values, and I'm not sure they do."

"Most of the people in upstate New York do," Kraft responded. "We don't want New York City. But most of upstate is conservative, and it is also rich in land and industry. It would be an asset."

"OK, then, how do we go about it?" I inquired.

"You are Chief of the General Staff. You should be able to answer that question. I gave you a hint of where to start," Kraft replied in good Prussian style.

I took some time to ponder the matter, while *Herr Oberst i.G. Kraft* filled a fresh pipe and Ross prepared to move up to meet with the 42nd's commander. I knew what Bill Kraft meant by his hint: the reference to the 42nd's conduct on its march. The people who lived in the area it passed through hated its guts. Now, the 42nd was ours. Bingo!

"I guess the first thing we do is turn what's left of the 42nd over to the people of New York," I said to Bill.

"Right," he replied. "That takes the moral high ground. We become the agents of justice."

"I suspect they'll hang every one of them from the nearest tree," I said.

"Right again, and that will split them from the federal government," Kraft said. "The feds will scream that they're all guilty of murder, which means their own government will be a threat to them. What do we do then?"

"We move in to protect them from their own government."

"I think you've got it," Kraft concluded.

It worked out pretty much the way we had outlined it. It took us a couple days to round up the POWs. Then, with one light armored regiment and two motorized infantry battalions, we escorted them back in to New York. We followed the 42nd's own route of advance in reverse, and along the way we dropped off batches of POWs for the locals to deal with as they saw fit. Mostly, they saw fit to slaughter them on the spot. CNN covered the whole thing, and after what people had seen of the division during its advance, most Americans cheered.

By the 5th of August, we were in Rensselaer, just a few miles up the Hudson from the state capital at Albany. We had about 1,000 POWs left.

That evening, President Adams delivered a televised speech to his nation. After denouncing the vigilante justice taken by the New Yorkers as the usual "hateful racist" stuff, he promised that "this government will not rest until every American citizen who participated in this lynching is brought to justice. I have directed the FBI to move in force into New York state as soon as the military situation permits." So every New Yorker knew that the forces of the Northern Confederation were now their best protection.

Just after midnight, Governor Adams rang me up on the satellite phone. "John, Governor Fratacelli of New York just called. He and his cabinet are prepared to secede from the union if we can protect them. What should I tell him?"

"The federals don't have any significant forces in position to invade New York," I replied. "If they are prepared to mobilize their state to fight, we can protect them in the interim. But what about New York City? We sure don't want that."

"Neither do they," he replied. "I've already discussed that with him. We cannot decide on admitting them into the Confederation. New Hampshire and Vermont would have to vote on that, as would the people of Maine. But New York does want in, and it also knows it can't get in unless it dumps Babylon on the Hudson. They are ready to do that."

"Then tell him I can have a battalion in Albany by daylight."

"Do it," Governor Adams ordered. So we did.

By the time the legislature met to hear the governor at ten in the morning on the 6th of August, our troops were patrolling the city. The legislature, with the images of the 42nd Division's march fresh in its mind, voted overwhelmingly to secede. In an ingenious move, they gave the city of New York to Puerto Rico, on the grounds that it had far more in common with that place than with the rest of the people of the state of New York. Puerto Rico was too smart to take it, but at least New York state was free of it.

I brought up two more motorized infantry battalions to secure the new border, which was set at the George Washington bridge. Following the vote for secession, the governor mobilized the Guard, called upon the local militias to help defend the state and began setting up a state military. Unlike the Northern Confederation, the New York Guard included a potent air force: a whole wing of F-16s, trained in ground support.

In the east, the federals were now reduced to a narrow belt made up of Pennsylvania, Maryland, New Jersey, and Delaware, connected by a thread through New York City with Connecticut and Massachusetts. That connection was lost on July 15, when Connecticut seceded.

On July 18, I received a discreet inquiry from the Confederate military staff in Richmond. Would we be interested in a joint offensive on Harrisburg? Quietly, they had been moving strong mobile forces into the Shenandoah Valley, preparing to roll north.

CHAPTER TWENTY-FOUR

I scheduled a meeting with Governor Adams on the 19th to discuss the Confederates' offer. I saw no reason to refuse it. So far, the war with the federal government had been going just as we planned it, at small cost to ourselves. When that happens, a General Staff officer should become wary. War never works that way for very long.

My phone rang at 7:19 on the morning of the 19th. The officer in charge of the governor's security detail was on the other end. "John, I've got bad news," he said, breathing heavily and obviously shaken up. "Governor Adams is dead. He was shot just six steps outside the Governor's mansion, as he left to meet you down at Mel's. It was obviously a professional job. He took one round in the head from a .50 caliber sniper rifle. We didn't hear a report, so the weapon was either silenced or it was a long-range shot or both."

I was stunned; John Adams was a competent leader and also a good friend. But I knew this was war, and stunned or not I had to think. "How do you know it was a .50?" I asked.

"Because there's nothing left of his head," the security officer, Lieutenant Bob Barker, replied.

Good reasoning, Sherlock, I thought. U.S. Army special operators used a silenced .50 cal sniper rifle. The silencing wasn't very effective, so the shot had to have been taken at long range. Good shooting at long range also suggested federal spec ops boys.

"OK, Bob, secure the site and get the governor's remains in for a fast autopsy. We need to confirm that it was a .50 caliber round from a standard U.S. Army sniper rifle. I'll take it from there."

My job was to get the sniper team before it could leave town. I immediately sent out three messages. The first was to all local regular forces, ordering them to sweep the area, starting with long-range vantage points that overlooked the shooting site. The second was to mobilize the militia and get them searching. The third was to the Augusta radio stations—with electric power down because of the fuel situation, everybody carried a battery-powered transistor radio—announcing the governor's assassination and requesting all citizens to search for and apprehend any suspicious parties.

As I expected, the old "hue and cry" brought the best results. When Mrs. Seamus McGillicuty heard her dogs making a racket out by the chicken coop, she got suspicious and called the militiaman three doors down. He phoned in a report, took his shotgun and covered the coop. We had troops on the scene in fifteen minutes, and they soon had in custody three very fit men in black jumpsuits with trademark Delta Force mustaches.

I ordered the prisoners taken to the town jail, then went over to meet them myself. I was 90 percent certain who they were, but I needed to be absolutely sure before accusing the federal government of war by assassination. The first rule of good propaganda is to make sure the facts are accurate.

A crowd surrounded the building—word always spreads fast in situations like this—and our men had difficulty getting the suspects into the jail in one piece. Governor Adams had been more than popular. He had been honored by a people grateful for a public official who had put his country ahead of himself. Under the old American republic, that type had almost disappeared.

I had the prisoners marched into the interrogation room. "Gentlemen," I began, "I regret to say you have been caught out of uniform. Black jump suits may be your unofficial uniform, but I am afraid unofficial doesn't count. Under the laws of war, I can have you taken out and shot right now. However, I am prepared to be lenient. If you will give me your names, ranks, and serial numbers, as the laws of war require you to, I will grant you POW status and treatment." Names, ranks, and serial numbers were all I needed to confirm they were from the American military.

I got back nothing but distant, silent stares.

"Very well, we'll do this the hard way," I continued. "Until you are prisoners of war, you have no protections." I pointed to the shortest member of the group. "Rack him." I ordered.

A few months back, a grizzled old Yankee in worn but clean overalls had approached me down at Mel's. He said he was too old to fight, but he wanted to do something for the cause. So he'd turned his skill as a cabinet-maker to creating a device he thought our military intelligence branch might someday find useful, namely, a rack. Would I accept it as his service to the Northern Confederation?

His patriotism touched my heart, and my head remembered a line from one of my favorite songs;, the auto-da-fe song from Leonard Bernstein's *Candide*: "Get a seat in the back near the rack but away from the heat." So I thanked our good cabinetmaker and asked if he could deliver his rack to the old town jail, one of those marvelous 19th century prisons with crenelated battlements and damp stone walls that hint of dungeons and people hanging by their thumbs.

We marched all three probable-Deltas down to the rack room. I'm not sure they believed we really had a rack until they saw it. When they did, they looked rather grim. "Perhaps you've heard of the Retroculture movement?" I inquired gently. "We find it has wide potential application."

Our rack operators were members of the Society for Constructive Anachronism, who had never had anything more lively than department store manikins to experiment on. The prospect of real groans excited them to no end, so they were quick about getting Shorty strapped in. A few preliminary twirls of the capstans took the slack out, and the boys were smiling with satisfaction when we heard the first snap, crackle and pop.

To the disappointment of the torture team, it was over after the first few screams. The assassin on the rack didn't give in. One of his friends did. "His name is Glenn C. Pickens, his rank is First Sergeant in the United States Army, and his serial number is 199-66-6703," called out the youngest-looking soldier, who was turning rather green. This was just what I'd been counting on. It is easier to suffer yourself than to see a friend and comrade suffer.

"Thank you very much," I answered. "Release him," I ordered the racketeers, "Now, do we have to go through this again, or are you two willing to give what the law requires you to?" They were, and did.

By noon, we had the official announcement out: the federals were waging war by assassination and we had the names, ranks and serial numbers of their assassins to prove it. Our people's anger over the assassination was channeled into supporting the war effort even more strongly.

The American people were made more uneasy about their own government. In Tokyo, the Diet dissolved in a riot as the opposition demanded an end to the subsidies. I considered that vital result to be my personal memorial to my friend, John C. Adams.

Our lieutenant governor, Asa Bowen, stepped into the governorship, and the governments of New Hampshire and Vermont agreed that he should continue to be unofficial head of the joint war effort. He did not have John Adams' mind, or his voice, but few did. I just hoped he had the sense to recognize good advice and make reasonable decisions.

As always in war, time was precious and pressing. I met with Governor Bowen the evening of the 19th, amidst preparations for his predecessor's funeral, to discuss the Confederacy's proposal for a joint advance on Harrisburg. I recommended we agree.

I explained to the governor that the federal government was disorganized by its move from Washington, more and more of its forces were being sucked into the guerrilla war in the trans-Mississippi, and the citizens of what remained of the United States were tiring of the war. We could almost certainly achieve an operational victory, cutting the U.S. off completely from the Atlantic seaboard. A strategic victory was possible, because the American government might not survive another major defeat.

Governor Bowen said he agreed, but he could not make a decision without the agreement of New Hampshire and Vermont. I hoped we didn't have a leader who wanted "councils of war," but I made allowance for the fact that he was new and seemed somewhat nervous. Had we made any plans with the Confederacy, he wondered?

We had. The Confederates would advance with one armored and two mechanized divisions up the valley of the Shenandoah, cross the Catoctin mountains, and, following Lee's route through Gettysburg, move on Harrisburg from the south. I thought they would do better to follow I-81, which would allow the Catoctins to protect their flank much of the way, but they wanted to avenge the wrongs of history by having Lee win this time. Making allowances for cultural differences among allies—southern Cavaliers and Yankee Roundheads—I agreed.

In turn, we would play the *chi* force to their *cheng*, using our better operational mobility to strike indirectly. While their mech forces were tracked, most of ours were wheeled. We would concentrate in the westernmost counties of New York, then with all our LAV and motorized infantry units cut into Pennsylvania on I-90. From Erie, we would strike straight south at Pittsburgh via I-79. That would cut the federals' east-west road and rail connections. Once Pittsburgh was liberated—we expected its white ethnic communities would welcome us—we could move east on Harrisburg on the old Pennsylvania Turnpike, go west toward Columbus, Ohio to stir up trouble there or just wait until we saw what the federals were going to do. In any case, we would make sure the feds faced a threat to all of Pennsylvania, not just one city, which would tend to fragment their response.

Governor Bowen nodded, saying only that he wanted to run the plan by a few other people before signing on. Another sign of indecisiveness, I thought; great. He probably meant Bill Kraft, who had been part of the team designing the operation, so that wasn't a problem. The General Staff advisors to the other governors would pull them along. But we would lose time. How many days, I wondered?

By the 23rd, I still didn't have a decision, and I knew Governor Bowen was not the right man to lead a war. That was the day the federal government formally departed Washington for Harrisburg. We wanted to strike while they were in transition to use the chaos of the move to our advantage. Our forces were in place between Buffalo and Chautauqua, and the Confederate Army wanted to roll. All I needed was a green light, but I couldn't even get an appointment with Bowen. His secretary told me privately that he was in a state of nervous collapse and wouldn't see anyone.

At 3 PM on the afternoon of the 23rd, Warner, the last president of the United States, gave a final speech on the White House lawn. After pledging to "fight the forces of racism and bigotry wherever they may appear," he joined the vice president, senior cabinet members and the majority leaders from the House and Senate on the presidential helicopter for the flight to Harrisburg. The feds had organized a rousing welcome for him there, paying every bum, drunkard and whore for miles around to turn out and cheer.

Just south of the Mason-Dixon Line, a single engine light plane had been cruising in lazy loops over the Monocracy River, which marked the most direct route from Washington to Harrisburg. At 3:27 PM, its pilot spotted the HMX-1 V-22 following the river about 3,000 feet below him, and dove on it. The crash turned both aircraft into a fireball that could be seen as far as Hagerstown.

The kamikaze pilot, Mr. Montgomery Blair of Clinton, Maryland, had sent an email to the *Washington Post*, marked to arrive at 4 PM. In it he wrote, "I have given my life that the Tyrant's heel may finally be lifted from Maryland's shore, and in revenge for the murder of the Northern Confederation's brave leader, Governor John Adams of Maine. Sic Semper Tyrannus." The Leaderless Resistance had struck again.

In Harrisburg, as soon as the news was known, General Wesley, Chairman of the federal Joint Chiefs of Staff, appeared on a balcony above the crowd that had been gathered to welcome President Warner. After announcing the death of the president, the vice president, the speaker of the House, and most of the cabinet, he said, "The line of succession envisioned in the U.S. Constitution had been broken beyond repair," which wasn't completely true since there were still some cabinet members, but that didn't matter. "I'm in charge here," he went on, "and the United States is now under martial law. Civilian government is suspended for the duration of the war for the union. The duty of every citizen is to remain quiet."

Ever since the presidency of Jimmy Carter, way back in the 1970s, the United States had made an international pest of itself by insisting that every other country conform to its notions of democratic government. Now, it was payback time.

In New York, at the U.N., the speakers were lined up at the rostrum to demand that all subsidies to the American government be cut off, since America was no longer a democracy. China led the charge in the Security Council, its ambassador unable to conceal his glee at the chance to hoist the canting Americans on their own petard. Tokyo had its own unpleasant memories of military rule, and made it clear its days as paymaster for Washington were over. The Tsar's representative worked quietly behind the scenes to line up the votes. General Wesley's request to speak to the U.N. was turned down. On the 25th, the Security Council voted to end all grants and aid to the United States, and the General Assembly passed its own resolution of agreement. The chickens had finally come home to roost for the liberals and neocons alike.

And that was the end of the United States of America. Its epitaph was the same as that of all states dependent on mercenary armies: *pas d'argent, pas du Suisse.* That's French for No Silver, No Swiss. The remaining states, defying a martial law that had no soldiers to enforce it, declared their independence. General Wesley's government was quietly interned at the Shady Acres home for the mentally indigent by the government of Pennsylvania.

It was over. We were free.

On the 28th, as I sat in my office enjoying a victory cigar and going over the plans for demobilization, Captain Vandenburg stuck his head in. "The Black Muslims are taking over Boston."

CHAPTER TWENTY-FIVE

Summertime, and the blacks were uneasy. It had been hot in Boston over the last week, and July was the usual month for the usual riots. Now, Massachusetts would have to look to itself to put them down. There was no more 82nd Airborne standing by just in case. But it shouldn't be all that hard. The traditional "whiff of grape" from the Massachusetts State Police usually sent the rats running for their holes, once they'd looted the Koreans and Jews. No reason it should be any different this time.

I clicked on the radio and caught a reporter speaking from the Boston Common. "A green flag is flying from the State House, and fires have broken out throughout Back Bay," he was saying. "Columns of cars and trucks festooned with green streamers, full of armed blacks, have been moving through central Boston, heading across the Charles River into Cambridge and west on the Mass Pike toward Brookline and Suffolk. I see people dressed in white moving onto the Common for what appears to be some sort of rally. We're told to expect an announcement soon from the State House, where General Hadji al-Malik al-Shabazz now has his headquarters."

This didn't sound right at all. What were the blacks doing on Boston Common and in Cambridge? That wasn't their turf. Green flags? Some Muslim general? Did the looters bump into a Shriners' parade and the two get mixed? I needed to get the gouge on this, fast, so I called John Kelly, our Christian Marines' Massachusetts commander and now a colonel in the State Police.

"Colonel Kelly's not in his office at present," said his worried-sounding secretary. "Would you care to leave a message?"

"No, I need to talk to him right now," I replied. "Patch me through to him over your radio net."

"I'm sorry, sir, I can't do that. Our radio net is being jammed," she told me.

Shit, what kind of rioting blacks have an electronic warfare cell? "OK, don't worry about it," I told her. "I'll get a hold of him another way."

We had a Christian Marines' satellite phone network which we didn't use unless we had to. I punched in John's number, and after about 20 rings he picked up. "Ire, thank God," he panted, using an old nickname earned by my sunny disposition. "We've about had it here. At least you can get the word out."

"Word about what?" I replied. "What in hell is going on? Isn't this the usual summer ghetto free-fried-chicken-and-watermelon riot?"

"No way," Kelly replied. "This is a Black Muslim operation to take over all of Boston. It's organized and it's disciplined. They've already moved their command element into the State House. I'm trapped with about 20 other state cops on the top floor of the left wing of the building. John, I'm afraid it's the Little Big Horn for us."

My mind immediately began racing, thinking of what we could do to put together a quick rescue mission. If there was one person I didn't want to lose, it was John Kelly. "Do you have any way out of there?" I asked, which was a dumb question since he'd already said he was trapped.

"Negative," he replied. "They're using gas, and we don't have masks with us. We're trying to throw the gas grenades out the windows as they shoot them in, but they've already gassed us from floor to floor. I've lost a lot of guys, John, and I'm afraid we're all toast unless you can get here in a big hurry. I'm expecting another assault within half an hour, and we've got nowhere left to go."

How fast could we move? We had a few helos down at Portsmouth, New Hampshire. That was about 50 miles from Boston, as the crow flies. We had to get a scratch crew together, and they'd have to plan en route. About all we'd be able to do is hover over Kelly's wing of the State House and lower some lines.

"Can you get to the roof from where you are?" I asked John.

"Negative," he replied. That meant we'd have to try to lower the lines near windows and hope they could grab them, then pull themselves up. It would be a desperate attempt, but it was a desperate situation. Better a wrong action than no action.

"OK, John, hold on as best you can. This time Major Reno is coming through. Let me get things in motion and I'll call you again," I said.

"Thanks, Ire," he replied. "Thanks for everything, not just this. Whatever happens to us, what the Christian Marines have done has made a difference. In the end, that's all that counts. Out here."

I immediately rang up the CO of the helo outfit at Portsmouth and explained the situation to him. He said he'd have a crew in half an hour. It would take another half hour, at the least, to get to Boston. If we made it in time, there was still an excellent chance the helicopter would get shot down as it sat over the State House, a big piñata for everybody to blaze away at. But we had to try.

I also called Governor Bowen to let him know what I was doing. As usual, he wouldn't take my call, which saved me having to get his approval. If he'd disapproved, I would have gone ahead anyway.

I picked up the sat phone and called John Kelly again to let him know the cavalry was coming. It would be close, but we had a chance. Like last time, it rang and rang. Finally, I heard a click. "Who dis?" a voice said in an accent I recognized all too well. Maybe it was one of Kelly's men.

"Put Colonel Kelly on," I ordered.

"Allah is Great! Allah kill all da white devils!", the voice replied. "All da white devils burn in hell! Ha ha ha ha...."

It was over for John. I hoped it had been quick.

*

I canceled the rescue mission, then sat back to think. Should the Northern Confederation get involved in this? Massachusetts was not a member of the Confederation. It had remained loyal to the federal government until there was no federal government. We didn't owe Massachusetts anything. And if Boston burned, maybe that was just desserts for all those decades of Kennedys and Welds and liberal cultural rot. Whenever anybody had tried to defend our old Western culture, they'd screamed "Intolerance!" and shut them down. Now, we could let them see what kind of "tolerance" they would get from the Black Muslims.

On the other hand, Massachusetts still held a lot of good Christians within its borders. John Kelly had been one. I remembered the folks around the table at Tune Tavern, in south Boston, where the Christian Marine Corps was founded. What was happening to them now, and to the rest of the Irish Catholics in that neighborhood? And if the Black Muslims succeeded in Boston, what effect would it have on the blacks in upper New York state's cities, which were part of the Confederation? Islam had spread there as well, as it had among blacks in virtually every city in the old U.S.A.

I recognized it was time for some Prussian advice. Bill Kraft was still in town, waiting for our big victory banquet that was scheduled for August 4, a date he had insisted upon for reasons he wouldn't explain. I found him comfortably ensconced in a Victorian garret at his boarding house, his nose in Sigismund von Schichtling's criticism of von Schlieffen.

"You hear the news from Boston, *Herr Oberst?*" I asked, thinking I could take him by surprise with the latest scoop.

"Indeed," he replied. "It's not surprising. It's the opening of Phase Two."

"Phase Two of what?" I inquired, slightly deflated but curious.

"America's Second Civil War," he answered. "You didn't think it was over, did you?"

"Well, I guess I did," I said. "I hoped so, anyway. You think what's going on up in Boston is of more than local importance, I take it?"

"Very much so, as you will see," he responded. "The war in America has just intersected the Third World War, which has been going on for at least fifty years. You know the war I mean: the war of Islam against everybody else. Have you forgotten how we ended up with Egyptians in Bangor?"

"No, but I didn't connect the two," I said. "Are you suggesting what's going on in Boston has been planned elsewhere?"

"Your naiveté would be charming, were you not Chief of the General Staff," he scolded. "I am expecting a call shortly from Geneva." Following the demise of the United States, the UN had relocated to the old League of Nations building there. "While we wait, you might wish to rummage about the 'Bismarck' shelf among my books. He will be more relevant than von Moltke to what is coming."

"Instead, why don't you put your book down and let me tell you what I'm thinking?" I said.

Kraft obliged graciously, overlooking my shot back at him, and I shared with him the conflict in my own mind about whether we should get involved in Boston. He listened, expressionless, and let me say my piece.

"Seen only within itself, this question is difficult, as you've found it," he replied once I was done. "But it is transparent if we see it in its larger context."

"What we are, John, is the West. We are Christendom, at least its remnants. It was for the West that we left the United States, once that country was taken over by the cultural Marxists, who are enemies of Christendom. The Northern Confederation is a Christian nation, or it is nothing. We've already seen where nothing leads, and I do not think we will make that error again."

"Islam is an enemy of Christendom, and a deadly one. It has been our enemy since its beginning. All of North Africa, the Levant, Turkey, these areas were once Christian. You can ask our Egyptians what happens to Christians in those places now."

"If we are part of Christendom, then we must fight the Islamics, because they will attack us as soon as they think the odds favor them. If they succeed in Boston, they will try the same thing in every one of our cities. Nor should you think the appeal of Islam will be only to blacks. They will shape and tune their message to white audiences as well, and they will penetrate them. They will use any means that work. Saudi Arabia used to pay tens of thousands of dollars to any American citizen who would convert to Islam."

"John, let me put it to you as a question," Bill concluded. "We decided we were on Christendom's side against Islam when we accepted those Egyptian Christian refugees in Bangor. Then, we took on someone else's fight. Do you think we can walk away from the same conflict when it's being fought on our own southern border?"

Again, I realized I'd thought too small. Bill sometimes missed some of the trees, but he always saw the forest. "I guess you're right, because that's the strategic perspective," I said. "But what do we do about Governor Bowen? If he has to make a decision on this grand a scale, he'll break out in assholes and shit himself to death."

"The Bowen problem will soon solve itself," Kraft answered. "He is permanently on the edge of a nervous breakdown, and one day he'll go over it. Meanwhile, the governors of Vermont, New Hampshire, and New York are for intervention. I've already talked to them. So is a majority of Maine's state legislators. They are prepared to call an immediate referendum on the issue if you, as Chief of the General Staff, formally recommend the Northern Confederation intervene. The Egyptians in Bangor will go to every town and farmhouse in the state to explain what Islam is and does. I think it will carry."

"How long will that take?" I asked.

"Two or three weeks, at least," Bill replied.

"What do we do in the meantime?"

"Develop our plans and deploy our forces."

"What happens to Boston before we get there?"

"The Black Muslims take it over. The whites will have to fight their way out. For reasons I don't yet understand, the Islamics are trying to encircle the city and keep the whites in. They may be planning to use them as hostages."

"If they do, will it keep us from moving into the city?"

"We shouldn't move into the city," Bill said. "Casualties would be enormous, and much of Boston would be destroyed. In fighting for our culture, we don't want to destroy its monuments. The way to take a city is by siege. Remember, cities can't feed themselves."

"We'll plan our deployment accordingly," I concluded. "Please convey my thanks for your assistance to the Prussian War Ministry."

Bill grinned. "I will do so with pleasure. I'm sending dispatches to Koenigsberg this afternoon."

"Not Berlin?"

"Sadly, we Prussians remain exiles, even in Germany."

As I was putting my cover on and walking out Bill's door, the telephone rang. He motioned me to wait as he picked it up. "It's Geneva," he said in a stage whisper after the caller had identified himself. Bill said little, other than, "As I expected." After the call was finished, he turned to me. "The U.N. General Assembly has given its approval to sending a Muslim expeditionary force to Boston, under the U.N. flag. Russia will block it in the Security Council, but that won't matter. It's only a fig leaf, anyway. The real actor is the World Islamic Council, made up of every Muslim nation. I'm sure the expeditionary force was on its way before the Black Muslims made their move in Boston."

"So for the first time, a World War will be fought on north American soil," I reflected. "I guess we couldn't luck out forever." I took my leave from Bill and went back to General Staff headquarters to set the new deployment in motion. It looked like there wouldn't be any demobilization in our future for a long, long time.

*

Within twenty-four hours of the U.N. vote, the first transports began landing at Logan airport, carrying a battalion of infantry from Muslim

Bosnia. That was America's reward for helping establish a Muslim state in Europe in the 1990s. Two Egyptian squadrons of U.S.-made F-16s and a Saudi Arabian F-35 squadron flew in to provide air cover; it was clear our New York Guard F-16 drivers would get some air-to-air action in this war. Three days later an Islamic naval task force arrived off Boston, including Iranian, Pakistani, and Indonesian destroyers and frigates, plus transports carrying 20,000 Egyptian and Iraqi combat troops equipped with tanks and artillery. Their equipment was the best oil money could buy. As Bill Kraft had suspected, this whole thing had been coordinated from the outset. Otherwise, it would have taken the Islamics months to respond with forces this large.

On August 15, the people of Maine voted for war. The rest of the states in the Northern Confederation had already done the same, in their state legislatures. A Governor's Council met on the 16th, in Concord, New Hampshire, to make the formal decision. Bowen maintained a zombie-like detachment, saying not a word. His secretary said he was so doped up he could hardly walk. I was past anger, and felt genuinely sorry for him. He had never sought the office he now held, much less expected to be the man responsible for deciding questions like war or peace. Why didn't he resign? No one would have thought worse of him for it. War proves many men inadequate to their tasks. It usually forgives those who get out of the way so others, more able, can do the job they can't.

On August 17, as darkness fell, we began infiltrating Northern Confederation forces into Massachusetts. I expected enemy air attack, so we moved in small groups, on back roads, at night. Speed of advance was not important. The Islamics had established a perimeter roughly along Route 128, and so far showed no signs of moving beyond it. I had begun to suspect that their planning didn't go beyond securing Boston, and they weren't sure what to do next.

With the enemy's far superior fire power, I knew we couldn't stop them with a perimeter defense if they tried to break out. Instead, we put small outposts forward, a couple miles outside of Route 128. Their job was to watch, report, help the refugees who were still slipping out in some number, and block any supplies from going into Boston. Behind them, I set up a network of light infantry ambushes running as far west as Worcester, south to Fall River, and north to Methuen. It was good light infantry country, especially against an enemy who would probably stick to the roads. I kept our LAV and tank forces dispersed in small, concealed laagers north of the border on I-95 and west of Worcester along the Mass Pike. If the Islamics tried a major break-out, there would be plenty of time to concentrate to counter it, if in fact we wanted to concentrate. In the face of their air power, I thought we might try to use our mobile forces in *motti*, the famous Finnish enveloping tactics, just like our light infantry. If the enemy comes at you with a spear, you usually do better breaking the shaft than trying to dull the point.

By the 25th, our forces were in place. The Massachusetts state legislature met in the Worcester train station and formally applied to join the Northern Confederation, putting all state forces under our command at the same time. There was no reaction from the Islamics, beyond some air reconnaissance missions. We doubted those saw very much.

Boston was now besieged by land, but the Islamics had control of the sea, which meant they could stay in Boston as long as they wanted, just as the British did during the American Revolution. I spent my days considering what we could do about that and wondering just what they were up to in Boston.

*

We soon got an answer to my second question, and found out why the initial Black Muslim eruption had tried to trap as many whites as possible. On September 1, 2028, "General" al-Shabazz, who until the uprising had been known as Willy Welly in the upscale Roxbury nightclub and whorehouse where he played the saxophone, called a news conference to announce that "the triumph of the Prophet will begin in Boston, on the Common, on September 3, 2028." All news media, including those from the Northern Confederation, were invited to cover the festivities.

At ten A.M. on September 3, the General Staff gathered around the TV in our temporary headquarters in Worcester to see the show. Al Jazeera gave us a ringside seat. I figured we would get a parade of some sort, sermons from various mullahs, and maybe some indication of what the Islamics would do next. At some point the Sitzkrieg had to end.

The ceremony opened with General al-Shabazz giving a raving, largely incoherent sermon about "the sword of the Prophet" from a platform set up in front of the State House. Behind him were an array of mullahs from various Islamic countries, plus the commanders of the Islamic Expeditionary Force in their blue U.N. berets.

Then, twenty whites, obviously prisoners, were marched out in front of the platform. Several were in the torn and bloody remains of a uniform of a Massachusetts state trooper. I stared intently at the screen. My God, that's John Kelly! I couldn't be sure, because the prisoners' backs were to the camera, but the way the guy carried himself was just like John, both hard and loose, ready for anything. I prayed silently, Lord, let it be John. Let us have him back. Then I stopped short, realizing we didn't know the script for this play. John might be better off dead.

A mullah was introduced as the Ayatollah Ghorbag from Qum, in Iran, and he came down from the platform. Standing in front of the first prisoner, he said, in English, the Islamic formula:

"There is no God but God, and Mohammed is his prophet." The prisoner responded by repeating the same words back to him, making himself a Muslim. The Ayatollah then handed the new convert a crucifix, which he dropped on the ground and stomped.

The shabby little rite went on, working slowly down the line of whites. Then, after seven worms in a row had turned, somebody dropped their lines. The Ayatollah was standing before the man next to the state trooper I thought might be John. The prisoner repeated the magic words: "There is no God but God, and Mohammed is his Prophet." The Ayatollah held out the crucifix. But the trooper drove his shoulder, hard, into the new Moslem's arm, reached out for the crucifix and snatched it from the startled Ayatollah. I could see the side of the trooper's face as he turned—it was John! The Christian Marines' Massachusetts commander held the crucifix up, kissed it, shouted "Vivat Christus Rex" and drove his big, black Mass state trooper boot into the Ayatollah's groin. The mullah bent doubled, and John smashed both his fists and the crucifix down on the back of his neck. Ayatollah Ghorbag went down like a bag of manure.

Around the television, we all yelled "Arugah!"

Black Muslim guards poured out from around the platform and fell on John. I expected them to kill him on the spot, but they just held him down. The unconscious Ayatollah was carried off, another mullah took his place and the ceremony resumed.

But John's courage proved infectious. When the Muslim cleric said the formula to the next man in line, he said nothing back. So it went, until they came to the only woman in line. She was straight-backed, had certainly seen her 65th birthday, and looked every inch a Boston brahman. Before the mullah could say anything, she announced, "I am Mrs. Elliott Cabot Lodge. I was baptized in the Church of the Advent,

I was married in the Church of the Advent and I shall be buried from the Church of the Advent. Nothing you may say to me will make the slightest difference."

If the mullah didn't understand all she said, her expression was unmistakable. It perfectly summed up the words, "High Church Anglican." Wisely, he passed her by. Between her example of Christian courage and John's, only two other prisoners converted to Islam.

General al-Shabazz then took the podium again, to announce that all the "white idolaters" the Black Muslims had captured would be given an opportunity to convert to Islam. "Those who refuse," he shrieked, "will die a dog's death!" Uh-oh, I thought. Here it comes.

The guards grabbed those who had remained true to their Christian faith, shoved them together and marched them across the street onto the Common. There, crosses were waiting. The Islamics made sure the Al Jazeera cameras got a clear view as the prisoners, starting with John, had nails driven through their wrists and their feet into the wood of the cross, which was then erected. John said the Nicene Creed, in Latin, as the hammers pounded. Mrs. Lodge wept, but she didn't scream.

Death by crucifixion is slow, and Al Jazeera didn't stay for the end. An Egyptian soldier we captured later told us John Kelly took two days to die.

The Islamics set up an assembly line process on every side of the Common, where the ceremony went on all day, every day. Most whites had managed to escape the city, but we figured they had captured between fifty and one hundred thousand. Thousands converted. Thousands refused. The Common soon was crowded with crosses, to the point where it looked like a convention of short telephone poles, each holding the broken body of a Christian martyr. They even had special, tiny crosses for the children, who gasped and wheezed out their breath looking over the little lake where the swan boats used to sail.

As can happen in a siege, the advantage of time had turned. The Black Muslims could hold Boston forever, so long as they controlled the sea. But we had to do something. We couldn't just sit there and watch our fellow Christians—and some Jews, Meyer one of them—die horribly.

The people of the Northern Confederation were with us, every man and woman, now. They knew why this had to be our fight, and why we could not let Islam get a foothold on our shore. They would accept the casualties of a direct assault. But the Islamic Expeditionary Force had so many troops in the city that I was sure any direct assault would fail.

Their critical vulnerability was the sea. That's where we had to attack.

CHAPTER TWENTY-SIX

BACK when we were establishing the armed forces of the Northern Confederation—just Maine at the time—I had sent one of our Christian Marines, Captain Rick Hoffman, formerly of the U.S. Navy, down to Portland to see what might be done about creating a fleet. Hoff had his work cut out for him, since our only ship was the LPH John Ross pirated when he came north.

I hadn't paid much attention since to what Hoff was up to, partly because we hadn't needed a navy yet and partly because he had a mission order and could be trusted to carry it out. I figured by now he ought to have done something, so I ordered him to our HQ in Worcester to help plan a naval battle.

"Waal, do we have a navy or don't we?" I asked the good captain when he reported in, "I hope we do, because we sure need one right now."

"We have a navy of sorts," Hoff replied. "It's nothing the old U.S. Navy would have called a navy, but I think it can fight."

"Can it cut the Islamics in Boston off from the sea?"

"I think it can, if we use a combined arms approach," Hoff replied.

"What do you have in mind?" I asked.

"We've developed two types of warships," Hoff explained. "I should call them warboats, because they're pretty small. The first is a gunboat, armed with either a 'Stalin's organ' multiple rocket launcher or a Russian 240 mm mortar. They are converted fishing boats, which means they can carry plenty of ammunition but they're slow. Our second type is torpedo boats, converted from speed boats."

"Did the Russians send us torpedoes?" I asked.

"No. They don't have torpedo boats any more, and the experiments we tried shooting their submarine torpedoes from converted speedboats were not very promising: We're using spar torpedoes."

"Spar torpedoes?" I asked, not sure I'd heard right. "Hell, those disappeared with the Civil War. I'm all for Retroculture, but isn't this taking it a little far? How will our crews survive ramming a torpedo on a stick into a Muslim destroyer?"

"We're a little more modern than that," Dick replied. "We're up to about the 1880s. After the Civil War, in Europe, navies developed spar torpedoes that could be towed behind and off to one side of a torpedo boat. Instead of ramming the target, the torpedo boat could cut ahead or astern of it, and the towed torpedo would still hit the ship's side. That's the kind we've got."

"Still sounds pretty risky to me," I commented.

"War is dangerous," Hoff reminded me.

"Well, you should have the advantage of surprise, anyway," I responded. "The Islamics certainly won't be expecting a type of attack no one has made in more than a century. How do you plan to use your boats to cut Boston off from the sea?"

"There, I need some help," Hoff answered. "We can't do it alone. It has to be a combined arms operation—the old rock-paper-scissors trick.

If we have surprise, and I think we will, I believe we can sink or disable the five warships the Islamics now have off Boston. Once the warships are gone, the transports are dead meat, and we can set up a blockade. What we can't do is deal with the warships they will send to replace those we sink, because by then they'll be on the lookout for our torpedo boats.

"The best answer to those ships are our F-16s. But they can't operate near Boston so long as the Islamics have air cover out of Logan. So our navy needs to take out that air cover to allow our aircraft to keep their ships away."

"Can you do that?" I asked.

"Yes, I think so," Dick said. "I've talked to the boys in Utica, and they'll launch a massive feint toward Boston with every F-16 we've got at the same time we make our torpedo attack on the Islamic warships. That will make the Islamics launch their aircraft in response. Assuming our torpedoes hit, the way will be clear for our gunboats to blow the hell out of Logan airport. When the Muslim F-35s and F-16s get back, the only place they'll have to land is in the ocean. After that, our F-16s will have clear skies to defend the approaches to Boston from any more ships the Muslims may send."

"OK, you've thought this through well," I said. "Combined arms is the answer. As always in war, the outcome is in the hands of Dame Fortune, but you've done everything possible to make her job easy. How soon can you do it?"

"It will take about three days to infiltrate our gunboats and torpedo boats into the Boston area," Hoff answered. "Their weapons systems are concealed, so they look just like other coastal traffic, which the Islamics haven't blocked. We want to attack at first light with the torpedo boats, when their warships will be silhouetted by the dawn and we can come out of the shadows. The gunboats will already be in Boston's outer harbor, posing as the fishing boats they were. Utica is ready now, so let's say we make D-day September 10th, four days from now. We need to move fast, or there won't be any unconverted whites left alive in Boston."

"There may not be any by the 10th," I said, "The one thing Muslims seem to do efficiently is murder. Anyway, I'll need that time to get our ground forces in position to attack. We should move when you do, and we'll need to bring up artillery. A good artillery stonking should rattle them. But I fear we'll still face heavy urban combat, which is the nastiest job on the face of the planet."

"I'll leave that part to you. I'll be busy enough playing 'Canoes vs. Battleships,'" Hoff said. "But I do have a question for you. All the attempts at forced conversion to Islam we've seen in Boston, and all the crucifixions, have been of whites, Hispanics, and Asians. What has happened to Boston's black Christians?"

"Hmm, that is a good question," I answered. "To be honest, I hadn't thought of it. I guess I just assumed they were being left alone because they were black. But we shouldn't assume that. Islamics don't like black Christians any better than white Christians, as they've shown by slaughtering hundreds of thousands of them in Africa. I'll look into it."

*

After Hoff left for Portland to get his Navy moving south, I asked our intel officer, Capt. Walthers, what he knew about the fate of Boston's blacks. He hadn't asked the question either. But he said some blacks had fled through our lines, with the white refugees, and he'd see if he could find out what they knew.

I went back to work, writing the orders to deploy our forces close-in around Route 128 in preparation for the assault. The Islamics still had not attacked us with air, but I didn't want their air recon to pick our movements up and tip them off something was coming. So we still had to move at night, on back roads, in small units. There were plenty of houses and barns to hide in during the daytime.

That evening, just after I'd finished giving the last motorcycle courier movement orders for the artillery, Walthers rang me up.

"Skipper, I've got someone you may want to talk to, a black fellow who got out of Boston just last night. He says he knows you, and he knows what's happening to Boston's blacks. His name is Matthews."

"Shit, Gunny Matthews? Yes, I know him. Send him up to my office."

"Aye aye, sir. He's on his way."

Mathews was the hero of the Christian Marines' first battle, the Battle of the Housing Project. I'd lost touch with him since. Whatever the Islamics were doing to Boston's blacks, it was great to know he was still among the living.

My door was open, as usual, and I soon saw a very downcast Gunny Matthews standing in it. I got up to shake his hand and congratulate him on his escape. He wouldn't take my hand, and he wouldn't look me in the eye. That wasn't the Gunny. "What's wrong?" I asked. "Are you hurt?"

"Terribly hurt, sir," he replied. "But I did it to myself. You don't want to shake my hand, sir, not after what I've done."

"Sit down," I ordered. "Now, what's this crap all about? You're still a Christian Marine, and you're still my friend. What happened to you?"

"No sir, I'm not a Christian Marine any more. I'm not a Christian any more. I have some information I think you should hear, sir, but once I've told you, and told you how I got it, I'll be gone. I'm not fit to be around decent people no more."

"As your commander, I'll be the judge of that," I replied. "Tell me what happened to you, what you did, and most important, what you know about the fate of Boston's black Christians."

"Yes, sir. Well, sir, you know what's been happenin' to the white folks in Boston. Back in our churches, we wondered whether the Black Muslims would do the same to us. A few days after they started crucifying white Christians there on the Common for everyone all over the world to see, they began rounding up black folk, too. We all knew people who disappeared. Some came back as Muslims. They told us they'd seen other blacks refuse to convert, but they didn't know what happened to 'em."

"So, sir, I decided to try and find out. I went straight to the Black Muslim's headquarters in the State House and told 'em I wanted to become a Muslim. I figured if I volunteered, they'd trust me more, and maybe I could find something out."

"So I did it. I said the words, 'There is no God but God, and Mohammed is his Prophet.' I turned my back on Jesus Christ, sir, and I denied him. That's why I said I can't be a Christian Marine any more. Of course I didn't mean it, it was a, what did you used to call it? Something French, oh, yeah, it was a *ruse de guerre*. But still I said it, so I guess I'm no Christian any more."

"But it worked, sir. They'd had a few other people just come in and volunteer, but not many, so I was something special. They gave me the rank of major in their Black Muslim army, and some Arab handed me a whole bunch of his country's money. They put me on the staff that was overseeing the conversion of other black people to Islam. There, I found out what they're doing to black Christians who won't convert."

The Gunny paused, whether for breath or for drama I didn't know. "And what are they doing to them?" I asked, playing my part.

"They're selling them, sir. As slaves, back in the Arab countries.

When a plane or a ship arrives with Muslim troops or equipment, it doesn't go home empty. It goes back filled with black Christians, sir, to be sold as slaves."

"You're sure of this?" I asked, realizing we'd just been handed a potent weapon if it were true.

"Yes, sir. I've got proof. I've got it with me." Gunny Matthews reached into a canvas bag he'd been carrying and hauled out a bundle of hand-written notes.

"The Arabs, once they had the black folk who wouldn't convert rounded up, told 'em what was gonna happen to them. They thought they'd get some more converts to Islam that way. And they did get a few. But most black Christians are strong folk, sir. They're like the church ladies you remember. They wouldn't deny their Jesus, their Lord and Savior."

"After they'd been told they were goin' back into slavery, when I could be alone with them, I told 'em that if they wanted to write their families and tell 'em where they were going, I'd try to get the letters through. These are their letters. I'd still like to get them to their families, like I promised, sir, but I thought you might have some use for them first."

"Gunny, you done good," I said, with a grin on my face. "I think it's safe to say I—we—will make very good use of those letters. Are you ready to go on the air, letters and all?"

"Sir?"

"Gunny, the forces of the Northern Confederation are about to attack, to liberate Boston. You have just given me the keys to the city. If you'll do it, I'll call a news conference where you will tell the whole world's media what you just told me, and you'll show them the letters. I'll time it so it hits Boston right before our assault. I suspect every black in Boston, including the Black Muslims, will go for the throat of the nearest member of the Islamic Expeditionary Force as soon as he hears what his allies have been up to. We'll have those camel-drivers between two fronts and they'll collapse in a heart-beat. You've given me the most powerful psychological weapon since Germany shipped Lenin to St. Petersburg in 1917."

"I'll do whatever you want to help my people, sir. All my people, black and white," the Gunny replied. "I know I'm not a Christian any more, but to me, all Christians are still my people."

"Gunny, listen to me. You're still a Christian, as good a Christian as any and better than most," I said. "Remember a guy named Peter? He denied Christ three times before the cock crowed, and he was the rock on which Christ built his Church. Jesus knew what he did. And Jesus knew what you were doing. I even suspect he put you up to it. Your idea was too good not to come from the Holy Spirit.

"I don't know what the one unforgivable sin is, but it surely isn't using a *ruse de guerre*. Not only are you still a Christian Marine, when you get to Heaven, I suspect they'll have a special big show when they give you your crown, with all those good Church Ladies belting out some Gospel number to shake the rafters. You've done good, real good. And you've helped save the lives of lots of other Christians, including my troops."

I could see relief dawning in the Gunny's face. That was good. Planting a seed of hope in the man was all I could do now, because we had a city to storm.

*

September 7, 8, and 9 were days of gut-wrenching tension. Our troops and warboats were moving into position. Gunny Matthews was briefing key members of the international press on the fate of Boston's blacks, with release embargoed until noon on the 9th. The weather forecast for the 10th was good for our navy; some morning fog then clear, with light winds. Our infantry was deployed to attack, not on major routes, such as I-90 and I-93, but on all the back roads and minor streets. The Islamic Expeditionary Force had focused on defending the major roads, leaving the small stuff to their Black Muslim allies. I was relying on Matthews' message to clear them.

Meanwhile, all I could do was wait and gulp down Maalox. Bill Kraft reminded me of what von Rundstedt did when he got the word that the Allies were landing on the beaches of Normandy. He went out into the garden and trimmed the roses. He had already done all he could, and anything more would just get him into his subordinates' knickers where he shouldn't be. It was a useful lesson, but it didn't untie the knots in my stomach.

The first action opened on schedule at noon on the 9th. At a massive press conference with reporters from all over the world, Gunny Matthews told his story. We beamed it into Boston, live, on radio and television. Then, the Gunny read, over the air, all the letters he had brought out with him. We knew they would authenticate his account in the minds of our Boston listeners, because the names and family events mentioned in them would be recognized. Those who heard the words of their own wife, husband, child, or grandparent would tell others the letters were real.

By the evening of the 9th, Boston was crackling with light weapons fire, and the deeper reports of tank guns and RPGs were starting to be heard. Boston's blacks were turning on their false Islamic friends.

At first light on the 10th, among the fog banks drifting outside Boston's harbor, the lookouts on the five Islamic destroyers and frigates spotted some small boats messing about at low speed. Some were fishing boats, others the kind of speedboats used to run hashish between ship and shore in a trade both sides made money from. Nothing seemed unusual, on a blockade that had never been challenged. The lookouts knew the infidels had no navy, and besides, it was time for morning prayers.

Precisely at prayer time, the speedboats gunned their engines and turned sharply toward the Muslim warships, on courses that would take them across their bow or stern. The spar torpedoes ran about 20 feet outboard of the torpedo boats and 100 feet astern. The morning calm was broken by the deep booming of underwater explosions as 250 pound charges blew truck-sized holes in the Prophet's war galleys.

At the same time, the Islamic air controllers at Logan Airport picked up a mass formation of incoming Northern Confederation F-16s on their radar. Within minutes, Saudi F-35s were scrambling to intercept, followed by everything else that could fly. No one noticed that on the fishing boats near the end of the runways, crewman were taking the canvas covers off tubes planted amidships. The first rounds from our gunboats' mortars and rocket launchers began landing on the runways and support facilities at 06:40. There were no Islamic warships to interfere.

Our zoomies badly wanted to get into furballs with the Islamic fighter aircraft, but I had forbidden it. Our pilots were better, and I was sure we would win, but I was also sure we'd take some losses. Never fight an enemy you can destroy without fighting. True to their orders, our F-16s turned tail and fled west when they picked up the lead Saudi F-35s closing on them. The Islamic aircraft turned back also, jabbering on their radios about how the Christian dogs were hopeless cowards. They got back to Boston to find Logan a burning heap of wreckage. Some tried to land anyway and became one more wreck amid the potholed runways. Others tried putting down on highways; the ones that made it were captured by our advancing infantry. Most ditched in the bay.

With the Muslims' air force wiped out, our F-16s launched a second strike, this time for real. They finished off two Islamic warships that had remained afloat after our torpedo attacks, sank the Islamic transport ships, then strafed and cluster-bombed the Muslim armor and artillery.

Our ground assault had also kicked off at first light. Our infantry walked into a city-sized civil war. Everywhere, blacks were fighting troops from the Islamic Expeditionary Force. Militarily, the result was to open the door to us, since the blacks had gone after the Arabs who were mostly on the main roads. The back streets were clear.

Without any direction from General Staff headquarters, our forces moved to encircle the regular Islamic units. That made me proud, because it showed that the concept of achieving a decision through encirclement had taken hold. The effect in this case was a double encirclement: first a ring of blacks around the foreign forces, then an outer wall of Northern Confederation forces around the blacks.

The question was, how would the blacks react? Would they fight both us and the foreign troops? Or would they welcome us as friends and liberators? Around noon on the 10th, I realized this would be the decisive question. It was not something I could determine sitting in an office in Worcester, no matter how good our communications were. I had to be there to get a feel for it. So I grabbed the chopper we kept ready at the door, and had a motorcycle recon squad meet me at Waltham. I took a soldier's bike and the rest of the squad led me into the city.

A major pocket had been closed just south of Waltham, along I-90, between Newtonville and Route 128. In it was most of the Islamic armor, which had been put there to block an armor thrust by us that never took place. We'd blown bridges on I-90 before and behind the armor, so it couldn't move. On the other hand, we didn't have the heavy weapons to take it out. Tactically, it was a Mexican stand-off, but operationally they were toast because their shipping was gone.

John Ross and his Marines had led the column that created this pocket. I found him on I-90, just west of the blown bridge that cut the road back to Boston. In our army, he wasn't surprised to find the Chief of the General Staff arriving on a dirt bike.

"How's it goin', John?" was my formal greeting.

"It's goin' good, best I can tell," Ross replied. "From what I hear on the net, the rest of the Arabs are either caught in pockets like these guys, or are running for the harbor, where they'll find their ships sunk."

"It's over for the Islamic Expeditionary Force," I said. "All that's left is for us to cut up their U.N. blue berets and use 'em as toilet paper. But it's not them I'm worried about. It's the local blacks. How are they reacting to you?"

"None of them are shooting at us, and I've made sure we don't shoot at them," John answered. "The black civilians have welcomed us and given us some good intel. Of course, most of them are Christian. You see the markings on our vehicles?"

I hadn't. John took me over to the Dodge pickup he was using as a command vehicle. Painted on the side was a white shield with a red Crusader cross. "You'll find this on just about every vehicle in our army. The men came up with it on their own, as we waited in our jump-off points," he said. "The cross tells the locals we are friends."

"But the black troops are Black Muslims," I said.

"I think most of them are galvanized Muslims," John replied. "And they all know what their Muslim brothers have been doing to fellow blacks who wouldn't convert. I think many of them would come over to us, if we could talk to them."

"Why don't we try?" I suggested.

I broke a whip antenna off a vehicle, tied my handkerchief to it and started walking forward. John Ross came with me, as did a Catholic chaplain, Father Murphy.

The Black Muslims had built a small barricade of trucks and overturned cars between themselves and us. Beyond it, further west on the pike, they had a larger barricade built the same way between themselves and the Arabs. Periodically, the Arabs sent a tank shell into it, and the blacks responded with light weapons fire.

As we approached the smaller barricade, we could see weapons pointed at us. "Stop," a voice called out. "What d'ya want?"

"We want to talk with you," I replied. "The white flag means parley, not surrender."

After about a minute of silence, another voice called, "Who do you want to talk with?"

"All of you," I answered.

Again, silence. Then a black man in cammies carrying an AK stood up on the barricade. "OK, come on," he said.

We climbed over the barricade and found a couple hundred Black Muslim militiamen gathered in front of us. Their faces showed uncertainty, not hate. They were caught between one enemy and one might-be enemy, which was not exactly a comfortable position. The man who had told us to come on said, "I'm Captain Malik al-Shawarma. What do you have to say to us?"

"What's your real name?" I asked.

He hesitated a moment, then answered, "John Ross."

Our John Ross grinned, then said, "I'm John Ross too. Glad to meet a cousin I didn't know."

That got a few chuckles, which was a good sign. "Captain Ross, I've got two things to say to you and your men," I said. "First, you've been had. You've been conned, you've been swindled. This Nation of Islam stuff was made up by a guy in Detroit. You're not Muslims and we're not devils. The whole Black Muslim bit itself is just Father Divine and the Reverend Ike and the Kingfish all over again—a few folks who get rich by selling you their shit."

"Most of you, maybe all of you, became Black Muslims not because you believed it as a religion, but as one more way to 'get Whitey.' Well, it's been almost 200 years since Whitey was selling you as slaves, like your new Arab friends are doing with your real friends and family members. In your hearts you know that what your mother or grandmother taught you is true: Jesus Christ is Lord. He's the One sitting up there, the One we'll all meet some day. It's not some damn camel-driver who sits at the right hand of God.

"We all get conned on occasion. I got conned by a car company once. I bought a Saab, which is what you do when you own one. You got conned by Louis Farrakhan and a bunch of rug merchants, and you bought a false religion. Once you realize that and dump this Black Muslim garbage, we have no quarrel with you, nor you with us.

"So second, we don't want to fight you. And I don't think you want to fight us either. If you do, you'll lose. The whole Islamic fleet is now on the bottom of the bay. Our aircraft will sink any new fleet that comes within 250 miles of Boston. You've got no way out—except to join us instead of fighting us."

"What do you mean by 'join you?' " one militiaman asked.

"First, renounce Islam. Then, turn in your weapons and go home," I replied.

"Most of us know we was had by Islam," Captain Ross said. "Anything that makes slaves of black people is our enemy. But we want to kill these Arabs. They sent my own grandmother into slavery. Can we keep our weapons until that's done?"

"No," I replied, "because we don't want to kill the Islamic Expeditionary Force. We want to capture them all, then trade them for the black Christians who chose slavery over renouncing their faith."

"You mean you're gonna get our people back?" Captain Ross asked, his eyes wide with surprise.

"That's exactly what I mean," I answered. "Anyone who is strong enough to accept slavery rather than renounce Christ is someone we want as a citizen, we don't care what color he is. We care about what a man believes and how he behaves. The black Christians of Boston are our people, and we want them back too."

The militiamen looked at each other in astonishment. They'd been told what the white devils wanted was to put every black they could lay hands on in the kind of camp where they only came out through the chimney. And here we were telling them we wanted to bring back the blacks the Arabs had enslaved.

As usual, the moral level of war was the strongest. A voice came from the crowd, "You got a deal." The rest nodded their agreement.

"OK, start stacking your arms over here," I said. "I need volunteers to team with my men and talk to the rest of the Black Muslims in this city. Our deal is open to everyone. Who's willing to help?" More than one hundred hands went up.

After tossing his AK on the pile, one militiaman came up to me. "When we accepted Islam, or thought we did, they had us say, 'The only God is God, and Mohammed is his Prophet.' What can we say now to become Christians again?"

I turned to Father Murphy for an answer. "You've already been baptized, son?" he inquired. The militiaman nodded yes. "Well then, you're still a Christian. Jesus Christ sees your heart. He doesn't need any magic formula to know you are His."

"Isn't there anything we could do to give up Islam?" asked another from what had become a growing group around the priest.

"Well, I suppose there is," Father Murphy replied. "Are you willing to take Communion from a Catholic priest?"

Again, the nods said yes. And with that, Father Murphy took some crackers from an MRE and a half-drunk bottle of Ripple found among the rubble and said Mass. As he intoned the Words of Institution, more and more of the former Black Muslims gathered around him, until he had them all. Both John Rosses and I knelt with them to receive the Body of Christ. I still don't know how the crackers from one MRE provided the Host for all those people, but they did.

*

The battle was over in one day, and thankfully, our casualties were light, as was the additional damage to Boston. By the 11th, the encircled elements of the Islamic Expeditionary Force knew their fleet was destroyed and their exit closed, so they asked for terms of surrender. We assured them they would be treated as POWs and exchanged for Boston's blacks, provided they left their equipment undamaged. They agreed, and we inherited a huge park of the latest tanks, artillery, and air defense weapons. For real war, most of it was inferior to the older, simpler gear we already had, but we still found ways to use it. 70-ton tanks work fine as coast artillery.

With the revelation of the Islamic trade in black slaves, the Black Muslims essentially ceased to exist. The vast majority turned Christian, and were welcomed back by the church ladies as prodigal sons. "General" al-Shabazz became Willy Welly again, and took up his sax in the cause of the WCTU. Some people wanted to hang him, but the consensus in

Boston was that the Martyrs of the Common would rather have a convert than a corpse.

Boston again became the capital of Massachusetts, and Massachusetts, now shorn of its long-standing liberal illusions, was accepted into the Northern Confederation. Connecticut and Rhode Island came in, too, giving us a solid, defensible block of the old northeastern United States. Again, I had hope of demobilization and peace.

But our war wasn't over yet. The next battles would be against poisons within.

CHAPTER TWENTY-SEVEN

O N September 15, just after lunch, I was finishing packing up my to move back to Augusta when Gunny Matthews stuck his head in the door. This time, he was smiling. Not only had he played a central role in liberating Boston and saving his fellow black Christians from slavery, his own pastor had backed me up in telling him he had been faithful through it all.

"Come on in, Gunny," I said. "Pardon the mess, but General Staffs live on paper. Even this short operation has generated plenty for the archives."

"Don't you use computers, sir?" the Gunny asked in wonder.

"Just as paperweights," I replied. "The only electronic security in the age of computers is not having any computers. The only computers in our army are in the Agency, where we have a nest of nerds who hack the other side's computers."

"Retroculture again, sir?" the Gunny asked jokingly.

"Ayuh, that's what it is," I replied. "I never did trust any machine that wasn't run by steam."

"Well, sir, I guess it's Retroculture I came to talk to you about, in a way," the Gunny said. "At least Retroculture may be a solution. I came to talk to you about a problem, maybe a big problem, facing the Confederation."

I could tell Gunny Matthews had a piece to say, so I leaned back in my chair, put my boots up on the desk and reached for a fresh cigar, a good Connecticut Valley maduro. The Gunny knew from old times that meant he had the floor.

"Sir, let me put it to you straight. The biggest problem I see facing the black community is bad blacks."

"Now, you know we have a lot of good black people. You saw that in the Corps, and in the Battle of the Housing Project. Everybody saw it in Newark. The problem is, in most places, it isn't the good black people who run the black community. It's the bad blacks. It's gang leaders and drug dealers and drug users. It's muggers and car-jackers and burglars. It's pimps and prostitutes, beggars and plain-ol' bums. It's people who just won't work for an honest living."

"Sir, you know and I know the Northern Confederation isn't gonna live with this. It's not the old United States. The Northern Confederation is for people who want to live right, by the old rules. They won't tolerate having little pieces of Africa all over the place. And they shouldn't. Africa's a mess. I'm thankful for that slave ship that brought my ancestors over here, cause otherwise I'd be livin' in Africa, and I don't think there's a worse place on earth.

"Sir, I'm not talkin' to you just on my own account. I've been speakin' with a lot of folks, back in Boston, in the churches. We don't want to go on livin' like we have been, surrounded by crime, drugs, noise, and dirt. We know that if we don't clean up our own act, the white folk in the Confederation are gonna clean it up for us. We want to do it ourselves, to show folks what good black people can do.

"What I'm here for, is to ask if you can help us find a way to do that," the Gunny concluded.

"Hmm," I said, "Do you have any ideas about solutions?"

"Yes, sir," Gunny Matthews answered. "We've had a group working on some ideas. But we don't know what to do with them."

"OK, let me see what I can do," I said. "Give me a few days, then call me."

The Gunny took his leave, and I followed him down the stairs to pay a call on Herr Oberst Kraft. He'd been expanding his political network into the new states, and he'd know who to talk to.

The smoke from my cigar mingled fragrantly with that from Kraft's pipe, and he offered me a glass of Piesporter Michelsberg Spatese '22 to wash down both. I laid out what Gunny Matthews had said to me, and asked if he could help make the political connections. The Northern Confederation didn't have any real central government and didn't want one, so what we needed to do was present something to the governors of the states.

"Your black friend is perceptive," Kraft said when I concluded. "In fact, at the political level we have already recognized the black problem as the first thing we have to face, now that we have an interval in the war—and no, the war is not over yet. But this can't wait. No one in the Confederation has any intention of tolerating disorder in our black inner cities. It represents everything we revolted against when we left the United States."

"We have some ideas ourselves about how to solve it, and we have no hesitation in taking whatever measures are necessary, however harsh," Kraft continued. "The will is there. I'll tell you, quite frankly, that some well-placed people simply want to expel every black from our territory, and I think a majority of our citizens would agree."

"I could understand that, and I think Gunny Matthews could too, given the black crime rate," I replied. "But I also know there are good black people, good enough that they'll work and even fight for the same values we believe in," I continued. "Don't forget the blacks in Boston who chose slavery over renouncing their Christian faith. I read Gunny Matthews' effort as a message from the same kind of people that they're now willing to do what it takes to get back their own communities. If they can do it, then the blacks could become an asset to the Confederation."

"I don't know," Kraft replied. "Perhaps you are right. The black community was an asset as late as the 1950s. But we cannot allow it to remain what it is now: a burden the rest of us have to carry."

"Are you at least willing to hear what Matthews and his people want to do?"

"Yes, we can listen. But remember, *das Wesentlich ist dem Tat*. We will only be satisfied with actions and with results, not intentions."

"Agreed," I said. "Will you set it up so they can make their pitch to the governors?"

"Yes," Kraft answered. "But not to the governors alone. This matter is too important for that. The meeting will be carried live on radio, so every citizen in the Confederation can participate."

*

On the afternoon of the first Sunday in November, the governors of the states in the Northern Confederation met in Albany, New York, to hear the leaders of the "Council Of Responsible Negroes" present their proposal. Even our Governor Bowen attended, though he looked like death warmed over. The session had been scheduled for a Sunday afternoon so the Confederation's citizens could gather around their radios without missing work or church.

Since the liberation of Boston, what to do with the Confederation's blacks had become the number one topic of public discussion, thanks to my promise to bring Boston's black Christians back out of slavery. The deal was not a popular one. For too long, "black" had meant "criminal" to too many whites. Fortunately the governors realized I had made a military decision, one that had allowed us to re-take Boston with a minimum of fighting. Our troops, who for good reason did not relish combat in cities, understood it too, and they explained it to their families and neighbors. Otherwise, I might well have been in for some tar and feathers myself.

Anyway, it was clear that Gunny Matthews, the director of the Council Of Responsible Negroes, or CORN, had a tough row to hoe. The question was, could he and his people come up with something this late in the game that would change both black behavior and white attitudes?

The meeting was chaired by the governor of New York, since it was meeting in his state. Meetings of the governors had no authority to make decisions for the Confederation; each state had to decide matters for itself. After throwing off the heavy hand of Washington, we had no desire to create much in the way of a new central government. Such sessions were held, infrequently, purely for purposes of gathering information and sharing common concerns.

Facing the row of governors were the four leaders of CORN from the four states that had significant black populations: New York, Connecticut, Rhode Island, and Massachusetts. Gunny Matthews represented both Massachusetts and CORN as a whole; he was the organization's president. In fact, he had put CORN together in the few weeks since Boston was re-taken, building on work a handful of blacks had been doing since the 1980s. These pioneers had realized the black community's problems were mostly of its own making, and while they took a lot of crap from the cultural Marxists, they had persevered and slowly grown. Now, many blacks had turned to them for help and hope.

The governor of New York opened the session with a few remarks that reflected what most people in the Northern Confederation were thinking:

"Your Honor, we are here today to discuss the most urgent matter facing our Confederation, now that the United States no longer exists and our borders are, at least at the moment, quiet. Within those borders we hold people, black people, who are a threat to the rest of us. Blacks threaten to be what they have been for many decades: an economic burden and a source of disorder, crime, violence, and even, as we saw in Boston, war. Unlike the United States, the Northern Confederation will not live with this threat. A state's first responsibility is to maintain order, and we will. However, if blacks themselves can successfully end the threat and permit all citizens of the Confederation to live in harmony, that would be the best possible outcome. We have come together today to hear from you, as representatives of the black community, proposals to that end. You may proceed."

Folks in the N.C. liked their leaders' speeches to be short and to the point. The governors understood that. So did Gunny Matthews.

"Gentlemen, thank you for this opportunity to speak," the Gunny said. "As the leader of the Council Of Responsible Negroes, I do not dispute anything the governor of New York has said, because it is true. As a whole, the black community did become a burden on, and a threat to, the rest of society starting sometime in the 1960s."

"But it was not always that. As late as the 1950s, any of you could have walked safely, alone, through the black neighborhoods in your cities. You would have found intact families, with married fathers and mothers, who supported themselves and contributed by their work to society. You would have seen small but neatly-kept houses fronting clean streets. The people there would have welcomed you. If you were hurt or in need, they would have helped you. Their skins may have been black, but their hearts were as white as yours."

"I say this because it proves that negroes are not inherently disorderly or criminal. It is not in our genes. The catastrophe that overwhelmed the black community over the last sixty years came from following the wrong leaders and the wrong ideas. That has happened to other peoples as well. To white people. It happened in Germany and it happened in Russia. You fought against it here in America. Other peoples have turned from their wicked ways and lived, and we can do the same.

"We know we must take strong measures, painful measures, to rebuild a negro civil society. We are prepared to do that. And we will do it, for ourselves, if you will let us.

"Now here is our proposal: First, we will put an end to black crime. Any negro who commits a crime involving violence or threat of violence, who breaks into a home or business, or steals a car, will hang. Any negro accused of such a crime will be tried within 48 hours, the jurors will be selected from the residents, black or white, of the street where the crime was committed, the trial will be over in 24 hours, and the sentence will be carried out within three days. We'll build gallows in every park. We'll gibbet the hanged corpses on every street corner. And we negroes will do the hanging.

"Not only will we hang every drug dealer, we'll hang every hard drug user. Anyone, black or white, on the street in black neighborhoods will be subject to random drug testing. Anyone who fails the test will be dragged to the nearest gallows and hanged. The drug test itself will count as the trial.

"Second, we will enable all negroes to work, produce, and contribute to society instead of taking from it. For decades, regulations imposed by the U.S. government made it impossible for most blacks, and many whites, to start a small business. Anyone who tried was visited by dozens of inspectors and regulators demanding something or other under penalty of law. Now that government is gone, but the new members of the Confederation, New York, Massachusetts, Connecticut, and Rhode Island, still have many such regulations of their own. They have minimum wage laws that price negro labor out of the market. They have zoning laws that prevent a negro homeowner from running a boarding house. They have laws that allow only union shops to bid on state contracts.

"Before welfare, negro communities had a thriving small scale economy. If you will allow us to get the regulations and regulators off our backs, we will build our own economy again.

"Third, we will make certain no more negro children grow up in cities. Cities have always provided rich soil for vices of every kind. The other reforms we have proposed will help, but the city will never be as healthy, physically or morally, as the countryside. Therefore, any negro family that has or wants children will be resettled on a farm. Our states have vast amounts of land that used to be farmed but now lies fallow. World prices for food are rising. Life on a small farm will not make negroes rich in money, but it will give them richer lives.

"We will buy the farmland we need for rural resettlement. We will pay for it by sharecropping. No one will be forced to sell to us, but many whites own more land than they can farm, and they will profit if they sell. The Amish and the Mennonites have volunteered to teach urban negroes how to farm. We know we can do it, because most of our people used to farm.

"This is our proposal. If you will approve it, we are ready to put it into effect within 90 days. We ask you to give us three years to prove that it works. If it does not work within that time, we will know black people cannot live in this country, and we will leave. I will personally lead our people back to Africa.

"Our question to you is, will you give us a chance to show that our people can live good, productive lives as your friends and neighbors?"

*

The governors' body language told me Gunny Matthews' proposal had hit them hard. It was a serious offer from a serious man. It meant no more shuckin' and jivin'. If it didn't work, the blacks would leave the Northern Confederation. The only real risk to the rest of us was the possibility of three more years of black disorder if it didn't work. I figured we could live with that risk, especially since the potential payoff was a lot more land under the plow in a world increasingly short on food.

The governors asked a few questions, then turned the meeting over to the citizens of the Confederation. Anyone could phone in their question or comment, and the response was broadcast live so everyone could hear it. I was happy to hear that most people seemed to react as I did: they were willing to give the blacks a chance, especially since they promised to leave in peace if they failed.

By about nine that evening, the callers had dwindled, and the governor of New York moved to end the session. He did so with a surprise. "Ladies and gentlemen," he said, "I know we are accustomed to allow every state to make its own decisions. But on this matter, and undoubtedly on others in the future, we need a common policy. I therefore propose we take a lesson from the state that gave birth to our Confederation, the State of Maine. I propose we submit this proposal to the people, in a referendum held throughout the Confederation." Each state had to make its own decision on that proposal, so the meeting adjourned.

I had quietly mobilized the militias around each city that had a substantial black population, in case of trouble. There wasn't any from the blacks, but in Lawrence, Lowell, and Methuen, Massachusetts, the Puerto Ricans rioted.

The Massachusetts militia quickly encircled the affected areas in each city, then blockaded them. They turned off the water and gas, stopped all food deliveries, and waited. It took about 48 hours for the first Puerto Rican refugees, cold, hungry and thirsty, to approach the militia's perimeter. There, by my orders, they were turned back.

Meanwhile, the Massachusetts legislature passed a resolution expelling all Puerto Ricans in the three cities from the Commonwealth. Once that law was in place, the militia announced over the radio that Puerto Ricans would be allowed to leave each city by one exit. The exit was chosen to be convenient to a railroad, and after the PRs had been fed, given water and allowed to warm up, they were packed into boxcars for a short trip to Boston harbor.

There, freighters were waiting, along with John Ross's LPH and his Marines. The PRs were led on board the merchantmen, and on November 17, the convoy set sail on "Operation Isabella." It anchored off the small Puerto Rican port of Aguadilla on Thanksgiving Day. The Marines came ashore in case there was resistance—there wasn't—and the human cargo was landed. Our men were back on board their amphib and sailing for home in time for turkey with all the trimmings, and Massachusetts had a double reason to be thankful. After that, there were no more riots.

By December 15, all the states in the Confederation had accepted the governor of New York's idea for a nationwide referendum on the CORN proposal. It was held on January 3, 2029, and it passed by 58 percent.

Surprisingly, the referendum got strong majorities in virtually every black ward. The lesson we taught the Puerto Ricans probably helped, but the fact was that most blacks were ready for a change. After all, most of the victims of black crime were also black.

Inner-city crime quickly vanished. The shiny new gallows stood mostly unused after the first few weeks. The black militant act everyone had groaned under for decades simply collapsed. As Dr. Johnson said, the prospect of being hanged concentrates the mind wonderfully.

What astonished many of us, including me, was how quickly the out-migration to the countryside began. Even though most urban negroes had been born and reared in the city, they seemed to retain some ancestral memory of a happy country life. We didn't have to force them to head for the farm; they wanted to go. Churches, white and black, worked together to find landowners who would accept negro sharecroppers, sharecroppers who, unlike those in the old South, would eventually own the land they cleared and farmed. The Amish and Mennonites proved to be excellent teachers. Within a year, over a third of the urban black population was relocated on farms. By the end of the three years given by the CORN plan, the only negroes left in the cities were old folks without kids and a few black professionals. Gunny Matthews and the other negroes who had seen through the professional victim hokum had brought their people home.

Today, in the year 2068, our negro farmers are the bedrock of our agriculture. Their products make up more than 30 percent of our exports. Black and white folk still mostly keep to themselves socially, as is only natural, but they work together for the good of our nation. The black visionary whose vision finally came to pass was not Martin Luther King, but Booker T. Washington.

If you visit a one-room negro country school, at recess you may hear the children jumping rope to this cheerful little song:

*

Hang him high

Or hang him low,

To the hangman

He will go.

Hang the fat

And hang the thin,

Bow his head

And stick it in.

Hang the young

And hang the old,

Hang the bully

And the bold.

If he steals,

He must know,

To the hangman

He will go.

*

It's always been true that children learn their lessons best at play.

CHAPTER TWENTY-EIGHT

HOPE, they say, is a fool, and perhaps so was I. But I had hope the new year of 2029 would see normal life begin to return to the Northern Confederation. With the war in remission and the black problem on its way to solution, our main difficulty was that the economy was in the tank. We were caught in a depression worse than that of the 1930s, a lot worse.

As in Russia in the 1990s, the breakup of the country had severed so many trade relationships that industry came to a standstill. There were no raw materials, no spare parts, no markets. The Pine Tree Dollar held its value, because we stuck to the rule of not printing any we couldn't back with gold or foreign exchange. But to get foreign exchange, we needed to export. To export, we needed to make things. And to start making things again, we needed to loosen the money supply, which we couldn't do because we couldn't print more money. Our empty wallets told us why economics is called "the dismal science."

Bill Kraft worried that voters would demand we start issuing money we couldn't back. That didn't happen. Folks weren't about to forget why the old U.S.A. fell apart. There was no nostalgia for decadence. People just took in their belts a notch or two, huddled together in the one room that had heat and looked for opportunities to work.

Slowly, those opportunities came. With the Federal government and its OSHAs and EPAs and EEOCs gone, someone with an idea could just set up shop. In Massachusetts, one of the companies on Route 128 made a breakthrough in battery technology and began manufacturing power-packs for European and Japanese electric cars. In New York, a crazy retired colonel started building small dirigibles using carbon fiber frames, as replacements for helicopters. They cost only one-tenth as much to operate for the same lift, and foreign orders started coming in.

A computer wizard in Providence came up with a terminal that gave the user hard copy as he typed, thus guaranteeing he would never again lose days of work because the system crashed. He called his device a "printwriter," and it sold like, well, typewriters.

I was tempted to go into business myself, making a practical and highly gratifying attachment for the telephone which would, upon de-tecting voicemail on the other end, immediately zap the receiver with a gazillion-volt charge and turn it into a blob of melted celluloid. Regret-tably, my General Staff duties proved too demanding to allow a diversion into business.

Most new businesses weren't fancy or high tech. Rather, they rep-resented a step back into the early years of the Industrial Age. They were small shops, located near rivers and railroads, making things peo-ple needed: plows and hoes, carts and wagons, frying pans and treadle sewing machines and hand operated washers.

It wasn't clear at the time, but these NIPs—New Industrial Pio-neers—marked the real new wave the Tofflers and other fat fools had predicted. Only it was the opposite of everything they had foreseen.

First, it centered on making things. It turned out that passing around information among computers was just a video game for adults. It wasted vast amounts of time, produced nothing, and caused living standards to fall faster than a whore's drawers. By moving back into the Industrial Age, the NIPs began laying a sound base for a stable prosperity.

Second, in the real new wave, enterprises were small. Bigness did not result in efficiency. On the contrary, anything big—government, business, an army, whatever—created a labyrinth in which incompetents could hide, breed, and "make careers." Instead of a "world economy," we found ourselves moving toward many small, local economies where maker, seller, and buyer all knew each other and understood what worked.

Third, the new wave marked the end of rampant consumerism. A dose of reality, in the form of hard times, taught people what was important: a few useful things, made by hand by real craftsmen, built to last for generations. Some people called it the "Shaker Economy," and that wasn't far off the mark.

These were the beginnings of a Retroculture society, though at the time they were actions driven by necessity, and we saw them as nothing more. An invisible hand was at work—not that of Adam Smith's market, but the infinitely more powerful hand of God. For the first time in generations, we were willing to be the sheep of His hand, and let His wonders unfold.

*

But in the year 2029, that all lay in cloud. We were scrambling to make ends meet, all of us. The General Staff had quickly demobilized the army, all but three battalions which were stationed as quick reaction forces, one in Connecticut and two in New York. Local militia were responsible for keeping the borders closed. It was less than a bare-bones arrangement, but the Confederation didn't have the money to do more, and the men were needed at home to hammer and forge, plow and reap.

The first crisis of the year came in April, right on April Fool's day. I scented that something was in the wind, because for the previous three weeks, no one had been able to find Governor Bowen.

This wasn't merely a case of the governor being unavailable; we were accustomed to that. He had vanished! No one had any idea where he had gone, not even the nurses who took care of him or his wife. What made it all the stranger was that, for many months, he had been unable to leave his bed.

Bill Kraft proved unusually unhelpful. He'd gone home to Waterville and he declined to return to Augusta. Nor would he let me come up there to see him. He told me flat out it would be a waste of my time and his. I suspected his was a Taoist withdrawal—inaction as a form of action—but that didn't help clear up the mystery. The legislature was out of session, nobody moved to recall Bowen by referendum, so all I could do was sit like Mr. McCawber and wait for something to turn up.

Around 10:30 in the morning on the first of April, my phone rang. On the other end was Major Jim Jackson, formerly a Marine reservist in Vermont and now the NC General Staff rep in Montpelier. "We got some funny goins' on here," he said, "and I thought you ought to know about 'em. As we speak, I'm lookin' out the window at men and women both, all headed toward the state capitol and all carrying weapons. They don't look like our sort of folks, either. Most of the men have long hair, and the women seem to be the horse-faced sort. If its some kind of April Fool's gag, they're doin' a good job of keepin' a straight face."

"If this call is an April Fool's joke, it'll be on you, because I'll have you clapped in irons 'til May," I replied.

"It isn't," Jim replied. "I'm now seein' a few flags. They appear to be green."

"Shit, more Muslims?" I asked.

"I doubt it, here," Jim answered.

"Who else would have green flags?"

"Deep Greeners," Jim answered. "Vermont's still got a good number of 'em. They've kinda gone to ground since Vermont First took over, but they didn't die off. If I were to bet, I'd bet that's what I'm lookin' at. They're seedy enough. And no one else would give women guns."

Deep Greeners were the Khmer Rouge of environmentalism. They believed nature was a gentle, sweet, loving earth goddess who had been ravished by Man the Despoiler. The earth could again be a Garden of Eden, if only man could be removed. That this would leave no one capable of appreciating the garden did not occur to them. Deep Green was the most radically anti-human ideology humans had yet invented, in that it called for man to eliminate himself. There were, of course, exceptions: Deep Greeners were fit to live. But nobody else was.

"OK, Jim, go check it out, and try to stay out of trouble," I ordered. "Alert the local militia, too. I'll be over as soon as I can get there, with part of the Battle Squadron."

The Battle Squadron was a new unit established after demobilization from two infantry companies. It answered directly to the Chief of the General Staff. Mostly, I used it as a cadre unit to experiment with new tactics, techniques and weapons and to train other units. In battle, they were a force I could use to intervene personally. In this case, they had some interesting gear I wanted to try out, stuff the Marine Corps had developed in the 1990s as part of "non-lethal warfare."

We were ready to move out just before noon when Jim Jackson called again. "I was right, it's Deep Greeners," he said. "They've taken over the capitol building and most of the downtown. Nobody's done any shooting, so far. I've got one of the handbills they're passing round, and it's what you'd expect: demanding an end to all industry, especially the NIPs, condemning logging and farming as 'rape.' They even say we should burn down all our towns and cities and make everyone live like they do, in huts and holes in the hills."

"Who's leading them?" I asked.

"Your governor, Bowen," Jim said.

"What? Bowen's there?"

"Standing tall and strong on the capitol steps, in the midst of a speech that's gone on for two hours already and gives no sign of stoppin'," Jim replied. "When I left, he was sayin' that oxygen is a precious resource, and no one who didn't worship Mother Gaia should be allowed any."

"What action have you taken?" I asked, knowing that as a General Staff officer, Jim would have done more than collect information for someone else to act on.

"The local militia is mobilized, and we're quietly evacuating the citizens from downtown," Jim answered. "We'll put the area around the capitol under siege as soon as that's done. I'd like to avoid any shooting if we can."

"We're thinking the same way," I said. "I'll be there with a company of Battle Squaddies by this evening. Out here."

*

We rolled in around eight that night. The militia had sealed off downtown Montpelier, with the Deep Greeners inside. They weren't allowing any food in, but hadn't turned off the water or gas yet. We weren't quite ready for a confrontation, nor did the Deep Greeners seem to want one. They thought that if they ran up the Deep Green flag, Vermont would rally to them. It didn't.

We could just wait them out. But I saw this as an opportunity to demonstrate the Confederation would not tolerate putsches. Every state, and the Confederation as a whole, now allowed initiatives and referenda. If Deep Greeners wanted to change our course, they could put their ideas on the ballot and let people vote. Unlike the late United States, we had a legitimate government.

Our Battle Squadron company had brought along a gadget I thought might force the issue. It was a sonic weapon, developed by the French decades ago, that caused people to lose control of their muscle functions—including their sphincter. Basically, they flopped around like fish and shat their pants. What could be more appropriate than making Deep Greeners soil themselves? We also grabbed some local fire engine pumpers to use as water cannon; overnight, our troops welded shields on them to protect the operators from rifle fire.

We attacked at first light on April 2nd. The sonic weapon was on a LAV. It led our column right up to the capitol, followed by three fire engines and infantry with gas grenades. The Deep Greeners, with Bowen, now in the pink of health, out in front, met us on the lawn of the capitol building. They were carrying weapons, but they didn't point them. Evidently, they hoped we would massacre them in front of the television news crews, creating martyrs for their cause.

Instead, we turned on the sound weapon. The effect was immediate. The Deep Green crowd hit the deck, involuntarily, as they lost all muscle control. We didn't even need the fire hoses or the gas.

As soon as we turned the sonics off, our infantry moved in and started handcuffing the Deep Green warriors and tossing them in wagons. I directed the media reps to come in close, real close. They quickly got a strong dose of *eau de excrement*. Holding their noses, the TV and radio announcers reported the smell-o-rama, which sent their audiences into howls of laughter. That took care of the PR danger of them being portrayed as martyrs. No one becomes a hero by crapping his drawers.

So ended the Deep Green putsch. By noon on the 2nd, downtown Montpelier was returning to normal, and the governor of Vermont met with the legislature to determine the fate of the putschists. It was quickly decided that since they were unsatisfied with life in Vermont, they ought to go somewhere else.

Cascadia had a strong Deep Green party, and the government there had been following events in Vermont with interest. They volunteered to take the expellees, and on the morning of April third we dumped them on two Air Nippon Airbus 600s and sent them on their way to Seattle. To help Cascadia appreciate what it was getting, we did not give them an opportunity to change their pants.

*

That was not quite the end of the matter. On the evening of the 2nd, I had received a telegram from Bill Kraft, commanding "Return Bowen to Maine immediately." So I tossed our good governor in the back of my LAV, to find in Augusta on the 3rd a welcoming committee of Kraft, the leaders of the legislature, and the town jailer, who was there to escort the Hon. Mr. Bowen to the slammer.

Bill and I adjourned for dinner at Mel's. When we'd ordered our codfish cakes and boiled potatoes, which was all the menu offered in those hard days, I gave the Herr Oberst my best hurt puppy look and said, "Old friend, you set me up, or at least I think you did."

"I did not set you up," Kraft replied, somewhat on the defensive. "If I'd told you what I knew, you would have acted just as you did anyway."

"What did you know?" I inquired.

"I knew Bowen's sickness was an act," he replied. "At first it was real. He was overwhelmed by the responsibility of being a wartime governor. Like most politicians in the old United States, he'd spent a lifetime learning how to avoid decisions. When he had to make some, he came unglued."

"But that passed. By the time of the governors' meeting in New York, he was over it. I was getting reliable reports that when he thought he was alone, he was quite spry. Once I figured out he was acting, the question was why? If he just wanted to be governor of Maine and serve his people, he had no need to pretend he was sick. So who or what was he serving instead?"

"I got a break, thanks to one of the oldest engines of human history, female jealousy. Bowen's wife had noticed that one of his nurses, a certain Miss Levine, spent increasing amounts of time with him. He brightened notably when she entered the room, and was sufficiently indiscreet to ask for her if she wasn't there. At the same time, he grew colder toward everyone else, including his wife."

"Naturally, Mrs. Bowen thought they were having an affair. Afraid of causing a scandal, she approached me quietly for advice. I suspected something more was going on. So I arranged for Miss Levine to get a telegram calling her home to attend a sick momma. Along the way, her journey was unexpectedly interrupted when the train made a water-stop. She was escorted to a waiting automobile, and thence to a small fishing shack on the coast. Interrogation techniques soon proved they have not lost their efficacy."

"It seemed Miss Levine was a devoted Deep Greener. She did appeal to Bowen's amorous propensities, but those just opened the door. Bowen had absorbed a great deal of cultural Marxism under the old regime, and his breakdown came in part because he found himself heading a government that rejected everything it stood for. She worked her feminine wiles to convince him he could become a hero by embracing Deep Green and leading it to power. That restored his health, and also gave him reason to keep his cure secret until he could find a way to act."

"Did you know Bowen was involved with the Deep Greeners in Vermont?" I asked.

"Yes," Kraft replied. "Miss Levine had established that connection for him. Threatened with the gallows, she agreed to become a double agent. She convinced Bowen he had to communicate with the Vermonters in writing. I got copies of all the letters."

"Why didn't you tell me all this?" I asked.

"I was afraid you would counterattack too soon. It's a bad American habit. We needed to let our enemy commit himself irrevocably before we acted."

"And what will happen to Bowen now?"

"He will be tried for treason, convicted, and hanged by the neck until dead," Kraft replied.

*

The wheels of justice ground coarse but swiftly in the Northern Confederation. Bowen went on trial before a jury of his peers on April 7. The weasel first reverted to his helpless invalid act, then suddenly recovered his health to offer a stirring defense of cultural Marxism. The jury literally laughed in his face. The prosecutor gave the court Bowen's treacherous letters to the Vermont Deep Greeners, and on April 10, it took the jurors less than fifteen minutes in deliberation to find him guilty.

Bowen's lawyer—we had not yet recodified the laws and eliminated lawyers—knew his client was as guilty as Judas, and hadn't spent much effort suggesting otherwise. Instead, he focused his efforts on avoiding the death penalty. He presented the court with a stack of glowing character references. The prosecutor pointed out they were all written by former politicians or lobbyists whose palms Bowen had greased under the old American regime.

The defense then called a variety of clergymen—and, foolishly, some women, including one purporting to be the Episcopal "Bishop" of Maine. Bill Kraft, a traditional Anglican despite his Prussian commission, referred to her as "the Vestal". They testified that the death penalty was unchristian. The prosecution responded by offering the local Monsignor as a witness. He methodically catalogued passages from the writings or sermons of each defense witness where they had departed widely from Christian doctrine. With a twinkle in his venerable eye, he then recounted how the church itself, in its salad days, had not hesitated to turn the most hardened of sinners over to the secular arm for the ultimate sanction—while praying, most sincerely, for their souls.

Bowen's attorney's final trick was to call Mrs. Bowen to the stand. Perhaps he thought conjugal bonds would inspire her to plead for mercy, and that a faithful wife's tears would sway the court.

But Mrs. Bowen proved to be made of sterner stuff. Her plea to the court, while not what Bowen's lawyer had hoped, was most eloquent.

"Your honor, men of the jury, perhaps you can imagine how hard it is for me to say what I must. Perhaps you can't. Asa was a good husband, and I think I've been a good wife. I loved him, and I think he loved me. I know I love him still.

"That's what makes it so hard. If I were angry with him, or jealous because of his unfaithfulness, it would be easier. But I'm not. I wish with all my heart that he and I could simply walk out of this building together and go home.

"But I know I must honor a higher love, my love of this state of Maine. And I do love her. I love her rocky spray-swept coasts and quiet forests, her old ways and silent people. And I know Maine's women, no less than her men, must do their duty by her.

"My husband betrayed us. There is no other way to put it. He tried to sell us out to people who would have destroyed us. I know what kind of people they were. Asa used to bring them by the house all the time, back when we were still the United States. They were always going on about this cause or that, somebody who was a victim, somebody else who was an oppressor. I'd invite them out to see our garden, a nice garden. But they couldn't see it, or me, or anything. All their brain was taken up by some ideology, so they couldn't see at all. And what they could not see, they would destroy.

"If my Asa had succeeded with these Deep Greeners, this State of Maine my family has loved for more than 200 years would have vanished. It would not have been the same place. I don't know what it would have become, but it would not have been the same. It would not have been Maine.

"I would like to ask mercy for my husband. But I do not have the right to do that. All those generations who went before us, who carved our state from the wilderness with lives of toil and hardship, who gave all they had to make us what we are, forbid me. What Asa did might have reduced all their labor and pain and sacrifice to nothing. No one has a right to do that.

"My husband is guilty of a terrible crime. I thank God he failed in it. But he did it, and he must pay the price. I will miss him, and mourn him the rest of my life. But I cannot ask you to spare him. Do your duty, as I have done mine."

*

The judge, along with the rest of us in the courtroom, was deeply moved by Mrs. Bowen's speech. His voice rang throughout the chamber as he sentenced the Honorable Asa Bowen, the former governor of the great State of Maine, to hang by the neck until dead on the 15th of April. Those of us who remembered what April 15th had meant in the old U.S.A. found it a most appropriate day for hanging a government official.

The gallows were set up in front of the State House, still a burned-out shell thanks to federal bombing, but a symbol of Maine nonetheless. The whole town turned out for the hanging, and other folks came from all over Maine, despite the difficulties of travel. I was pleased to see that many parents brought their children. They weren't too young to learn that the wages of sin are death, that Maine was recovering its nerve.

Right at noon, just after the factory whistles blew, Bowen stepped out of the horse-drawn paddy wagon, draped in black, that had brought him from the town jail. Before him walked a priest reading Psalms. Bowen kept his dignity, mounted the platform unassisted and stood on the trap. The executioner, in his black mask, hooded Bowen and bound his legs. The noose was slipped over his head and tightened. The priest offered a prayer for Asa's soul; most of us bowed our heads and joined in the Amen. It was the state's duty to execute justice, but God could be merciful. At exactly 12:10, the hangman pulled the lever and Bowen dropped. It was a clean kill.

It was also time for lunch.

CHAPTER TWENTY-NINE

OWN at Mel's, the talk was about our new governor. The problem was, we didn't have one. We'd never had an election to choose a new lieutenant governor after Governor Adams was assassinated and Bowen moved up. While most matters were handled directly by the people, through referenda, if the war heated up again we'd need someone who could make decisions, fast. The Roman republic had elected dictators in times of crisis. We didn't need to go that far, but we did need a governor, and this time it had to be a good one.

Everybody knew who that was: Bill Kraft. He believed what we believed, he could make decisions and he understood war. But Bill was not about to cooperate.

"*Nolo episcopari*," he growled when the speaker of the state legislature asked him if he'd take the job—"I don't want to be a bishop," the ancient answer a priest is expected to give when he is selected for that honor. The difference was that Bill actually meant it.

I added my voice to the many telling him he had no choice, Maine and the Confederation could not do without him, we could not afford another mistake, and so on. He would have none of it. When he got up from his half-eaten meal and marched out of Mel's, I knew he was serious. I'd never seen Bill leave a table while it still had something edible on it.

At the Speaker's request, I joined him and a few other political movers and shakers at his office after lunch. Sam Gibbons, the speaker, was clearly worried. "I think we all expected Bill Kraft to replace Bowen, as soon as we knew what Bowen had been up to. I know the folks back home in my district want him. Bowen's treason upset them in a serious way. They feel Maine could go the way of the old U.S.A. if this sort of thing continues. They know Kraft and what he has done for us, and they trust him. If I have to tell them he won't do it, they'll really start to worry where we're headed. They just won't understand, and frankly, neither do I."

"Have you ever visited Bill Kraft at home?" I asked.

"Nope," Sam answered. "Bill doesn't really like politics, or politicians, even ones who agree with him," Sam explained. "He does like Marines. Have you been there?"

"I have," I answered. "And I think I understand why Bill is afraid of the governorship. He lives a quiet, ordered life, a retro-life if you will. That's his anchor, and it enables him to think creatively and boldly without becoming unstable. My guess is he fears the celebrity life of a political leader would overturn that. He's probably right. 'Innsbruck, ich muss dich lassen' is a sad song."

"I can understand that," Gibbons said. "We all feel it. I'm a lot happier back on my farm than here in Augusta. But in Bill's case we have to get him by it. No one else can make the people of Maine confident in their leaders right now, after Bowen. What if we just put his name on the ballot, hold an election and let him win, which he would?"

"I seem to remember another popular military leader named Sherman who faced the same kind of political draft," I said. "His answer was, 'If nominated I will not run, and if elected I will not serve.' I suspect we'd hear something similar from Bill Kraft."

"Isn't there some way we can order him to do it?" Gibbons asked.

"He only takes orders from the Kaiser," joked one of the other politicos.

Bingo! As the light went on in my brain housing group, I could feel a big grin spreading over my face. Herr Oberst Kraft had played one on me by letting me go after the Deep Greeners without a full sheet of music. Now, it was payback time.

The others saw my idiot grin. "You got an idea?" Gibbons asked.

"I do," I replied. "I think I can arrange for Bill to get an order from the Kaiser, or more precisely from the King of Prussia—they're the same person."

"Who is it?" asked another politico.

"The head of the House of Hohenzollern."

"I didn't think Germany had a Kaiser any more," Sam said.

"Technically, it doesn't," I answered. "But technically, Prussia doesn't exist any more either. I don't doubt Bill's Prussia is real, but its place is in his heart, not on the map. That Prussia has a king, and its king is the head of the House of Hohenzollern. If he orders Bill to accept the governorship of the state of Maine, he'll do it. As a Prussian officer, he'll have to."

"How do we get to this king?" Sam asked.

"Through his dear friend and cousin—that's how the kings of Europe addressed each other, even when sending a declaration of war—the Tsar of Russia," I said.

*

Following our little meeting, I walked a few blocks to the small
wooden house that was the Imperial Russian Embassy and the residence
of the Russian ambassador, Father Dimitri. In the front room that was his
office, the samovar was bubbling beneath the double-headed eagle, and
from the kitchen the ambassador brought out *blini* and a tin of caviar.
"Thanks," I said. "You know all we eat up here any more is fish. You
wouldn't have a nice beefsteak back there, would you?"

"Not on Friday," Father Dimitri answered, laughing. "Besides, fish
is good for you. Caviar especially. Health food. And it goes so well
with vodka," a large bottle of which adorned the silver tray bearing the
imperial coat of arms. I helped myself to a generous glass.

I explained our problem to the good priest, and why we needed assistance from his sovereign. He knew first-hand what Bill Kraft had done
for Maine and the Northern Confederation, and why we needed him to
be governor. He also knew this would be the best joke ever played on the
formidable Herr Oberst, and his eyes danced with laughter.

"I know His Imperial Majesty well enough that I can say he will assist
in this," Father Dimitri concluded. "Give me ten days, then check back
with me to see where things stand. I would guess that Prince Michael, the
rightful King of Prussia and German Kaiser, would be willing to oblige
my Tsar in such a matter, but I cannot be certain."

We left it at that, and I returned to my office and other business,
principally the business of trying to control our borders. As bad off as
we were in the N.C., others had it worse, which meant they wanted to
move in with us. We couldn't allow that. By the early 21st century, it
was evident around the world that any place that got things working was
immediately overwhelmed by a flood of people fleeing places that didn't

work. Unless it could dam the flood, it drowned. It was dragged down to the same level as the places where the refugees were coming from. We didn't intend to let that happen to us.

About mid-afternoon on April 23rd, I was going over reports from New York militiamen of shootings of would-be illegal immigrants when the door of my office was flung open with a crash that nearly tore it from its hinges. Filling the doorway was Herr Oberst Kraft, in full dress Prussian uniform including *Pickelhaube* and flushed, beet-red face. (The old saying in Berlin was that there were two kinds of Prussian officers, the wasp-waisted and the bull-necked; Bill tended toward the latter.) "Do you know the meaning of this?" he bellowed, waving some documents in my face.

I quickly guessed I did, but my gut told me to be careful. It was always hard to tell whether Bill was genuinely angry about something or just keeping up his reputation. If he really was as mad as he looked, I might be in for a hiding. Bill Kraft was no athlete, and big as he was, as a Marine I knew I could take him if it came to that. But I also knew I could never do that to him. I owed him too much. If he really was going to pound me, I'd just have to sit there and get beat up.

"*Moi?*" I replied. "*Mais mon colonel…*"

"Cut the froggy-talk, you little worm," he yelled. "How dare you cook up some forgery in the name of the King of Prussia! You want some *Froschsprache*? That's *lese majesté*, you maggot, and the penalty for it is death! I ought to run you through with my saber just as you sit and let your pathetic soul dribble out all over your damned reports."

"May I see the papers you're holding?" I asked, beginning to understand the cause of his wrath. He thought we were making light of his All-Highest.

"Here," he said, stuffing them into my face. "But you can drop the charade. I'm sure you wrote them. Who did you get to forge His Majesty's signature and mail them from Germany?"

What he handed me was a letter from Prince Michael von Hohenzollern to Herr Oberst Kraft, on royal stationery, ordering him to accept the governorship of Maine if he were elected to it.

"I am certain this letter is genuine," I told Kraft. "Furthermore, I believe I have a witness. Will you accept the word of the Russian ambassador?"

That brought Bill up short. His face began to show a different expression—less anger, and more dawning wonder. "Is it possible His Majesty really has sent me orders?" he asked. "I've served him since I was a boy, but I never thought he knew I existed. How could this be?"

"Will you come with me to Father Dimitri's?" I suggested.

"Yes, I guess," Bill replied, cooling down but still wary. "You know, when I first received the envelope with the Black Eagle of Prussia on it, my heart almost stopped, not from fear but from hope. Then I realized it had to be some trick. If it is..." His face started to redden again.

"It isn't," I said, skirting dangerously close to the edge of the truth. "Let Father Dimitri explain."

It took us about fifteen minutes to walk to the Russian embassy. Bill's face was blank, his mind far away. The private world in which he had always lived was taking on a new reality, and it was both wonderful and terrible to him.

My own thoughts were penitent. In what I had conceived as a good joke, I had trespassed on the core of my friend and mentor's being. It does not do to laugh and make merry before the Ark of the Covenant.

Father Dimitri received us with the inevitably generous Russian hospitality and a good priest's sense that we were on perilous ground. Bill took a glass of tea but didn't even look at the tempting *zakushki* placed before us. He handed the letter from Prince Michael to Father Dimitri. "Captain Rumford tells me you know something about this," he said in a slow, flat voice that told me he was pulling hard on his own reins. "Is it genuine?"

Father Dimitri, who also spoke German, read it carefully. "Yes, it is genuine," he replied. "I can confirm that in writing with St. Petersburg if you want me to, but there is no question about it. These are orders for you from your King."

"How do you know?" Kraft asked the priest. My stomach was wadded up tight as a fist around a grenade with the pin pulled. If Bill took Father Dimitri's answer the wrong way, my relationship with him might be shattered irreparably. If that happened, I knew I'd have no choice but to resign as Chief of the General Staff. I could not function without his guidance and support. I would also have lost a good friend.

"You may recall that on the day Governor Bowen was hanged, you were approached about the governorship, which you declined," said Father Dimitri. "Your refusal concerned many of Maine's leaders deeply. They felt that you alone could restore the people's confidence in their leadership after Governor Bowen's treason."

"Later that day, one of them came to see me and asked my assistance. He did something that you may dislike, but that you must also admit is not improper in emergencies. He asked my help in contacting your superior—your King."

Every language has one phrase that captures the essence of its speakers' culture. For German, it is *"Wer ist ihrer Vorstehener?"*—Who is your superior?

"I communicated the situation here, and your central role in the creation of an independent Maine and the Northern Confederation, to my superior, His Imperial Majesty Tsar Alexander IV," Father Dimitri continued. "He expressly directed me, when he assigned me here as his ambassador, to take such actions as I believed necessary to uphold the independence of the Northern Confederation. In my dispatch, I told him I believed it necessary for you to be Maine's next governor, if the Confederation were to endure."

"You may remember, Herr Oberst, that our Tsar was once a soldier himself, a general in the Russian Army. He understands *Auftragstaktik*, that wonderful Prussian contribution to the art of war. He therefore trusts his subordinates—or replaces them. Trusting me, he laid my case before his fellow sovereign—by rights—the King of Prussia."

"Prince Michael read my description of the situation here in Maine. He is a Christian prince. Desiring to support the effort to rebuild Christian civilization in North America, he sent you his order to accept the governorship if the people offer it to you. It was his decision, no one else's. The order is genuine, it is from him to you—he knows who you are and what you have accomplished—and it expresses his wish."

Bill Kraft sat unmoving, unblinking, almost as if in a trance, his eyes fixed a million miles away, or more than a century back. East Prussia, Allenstein perhaps, a clear day in early fall with a hint of the steppes in the east wind, his regiment drawn up on parade, himself on horseback in front. The Kaiser, Wilhelm II, stops his horse, smiles, commends the appearance of his men. Explains his intent for the coming maneuvers, *gut, alles klar.* Oh, and you'll soon be coming back to Berlin—plans division, West, in the *Grossgeneralstab.*

Slowly, Bill came back to us. "Father Dimitri," he began in a soft, almost inaudible voice, "I thank you for what you have done. It goes without saying that I will accept whatever orders my King gives me. But to me, what has happened here touches on much more than any order. I must know this letter is genuine. Forgive me, but I must ask if you are prepared to swear that what you have told me is true?"

The good priest's Bible lay open on his desk, to the Psalm appointed for the day. Reverently, he took it, kissed it, closed it, and laid his right hand on it. "I swear, before God the Father, God the Son and God the Holy Ghost, before the Blessed Virgin Mary, Blessed Michael and all angels, and Nicholas, Tsar and Martyr, that what I have told you is the truth."

"Thank you," Bill said quietly. Then he turned to me. "May I ask what your role was in this?"

It was time to face the music. "I was the one who asked Father Dimitri for his help in reaching Prince Michael. I'm the one who went over your head."

"Thank you also," he said. My stomach began to relax. I'd made it over the bar.

Bill took a couple deep breaths, as if coming up for air after a long dive into some hidden depth. Gradually, he was reconnecting with the world.

"May I not tempt you with some Sevruga?" asked Father Dimitri. I knew Bill was very fond of caviar, and this was the best.

"I'm sorry, I just can't right now," Bill replied. "I have eaten and drunk too deeply of other things this day. If you will excuse me, I need to be alone for a while."

"Of course, we understand," Father Dimitri replied kindly. "But before you go, I have something else for you."

From his desk drawer he removed a small box, richly worked with gold, looking like a Faberge egg. "This came with today's dispatches. Prince Michael sent it to my Sovereign, with a request that he send it on to you. The box is a small token of esteem from Tsar Alexander."

Slowly, Bill moved to take the box. He stared at it for a long time.

Then, almost reluctantly, he opened it.

Inside was the Pour e Merite—the Blue Max.

*

After Bill had gone and I had recovered with more than a few glasses of vodka, I looked seriously at Father Dimitri and said, "I don't know what you've learned from this day, but I learned that I won't be playing any more jokes on Herr Oberst Kraft."

With a gentle smile, Father Dimitri replied, "You still don't understand the Russian sense of humor."

CHAPTER THIRTY

THE election for governor was held on May 15, and Bill Kraft was elected with 83 percent of the vote. He had opponents. In Maine, the law made it easy for candidates to get on the ballot. We didn't want any rigged two-party system like in the old United States, because the two parties soon became one party with a common interest in keeping everyone else out. But most folks in Maine knew what Kraft had done for us, and they wanted to give him a chance to do more.

Governor Kraft was inaugurated on May 20, and since the other N.C. governors all decided to come, they got together for a meeting. There, they agreed that Kraft would remain the supreme decision-maker in military matters, just as the two previous Maine governors had been. States rights notwithstanding, everyone knew what war required.

I was called before the governors to tell them where the implementation of the peace agreement with the Muslims stood. The World Islamic Council had agreed to return the black Christians kidnapped from Boston and sold into slavery in return for the Islamic POWs we held. But so far, nothing had happened.

I'd been communicating directly with the Egyptian military author-
ities in Cairo, who were in charge of the exchange for the Islamic side.
At first, I'd been troubled by an incessant gurgling sound on the phone;
I figured it was some kind of recording or EW device. Then one of our
intel guys with some experience in the Middle East explained that the
Egyptian general was just smoking hashish in his water pipe as we talked.
After that, I understood why not much was happening.

However, the Egyptians did tell me they had collected some 3,000
of our blacks in camps outside Cairo, ready for exchange. To get things
moving, I proposed we tell them that as of June 1, unless the exchange
was underway, we would forbid all our Islamic prisoners to practice their
religion. No prayers five times a day. No Korans. And we'd send 'em all
to work on pig farms.

Most of the governors liked that idea. But Bill Kraft was uneasy.
"Gentlemen, I have to tell you this whole business troubles me. It's gut
instinct, and I can't put my finger on it. But I feel in my bones that when
we bring these black folks back to Boston, we're bringing in trouble."

"They won't be in Boston very long," New York's governor responded.
"Thanks to CORN, blacks are already moving out of the cities, back to
the land, in substantial numbers. We're not seeing the usual crime or
unrest among those who remain. The good blacks have taken their community back from the scum. It seems to me these blacks coming back
are good Christian folk who'll help that process along."

"What would be the effect if we repudiated our agreement with the
black community to get their people back?" the governor of Rhode Island
asked me.

"Militarily, it wouldn't be a problem," I replied. "The blacks know
we won't tolerate disorder and we have the muscle to put it down."

"But I think CORN has shown us the way to make the Confederation's blacks into contributing members of our society. If we broke faith with them, we would undermine their new direction," I added.

"Of course, as a soldier, my word is my bond. If the Confederation broke the deal I made—a deal that saved Boston from widespread destruction—my honor would be at stake. I would have no choice but to resign immediately."

The governor of Massachusetts broke in. "If I may speak bluntly to Governor Kraft, does he expect us to agree to break our agreement with the blacks just because he has a gut feeling?"

"I cannot expect you to do that, and I don't," Kraft replied. "But as those of you who have been in war or studied war know, sometimes your instincts are your best guide. Are you willing to agree to repatriate the blacks slowly, into a few limited areas, until we see how it goes?"

In the old days, politicians would have rolled anyone, military or civilian, who offered an argument like Kraft's. The game was just to win the immediate squabble so someone could look good by making someone else look bad. But the cold shower of reality we had all taken in the break-up of the U.S.A. had changed things.

"I know Governor Kraft's achievements as a soldier," the governor of New Hampshire said. "If he says his soldier's gut instinct troubles him about this, I'm troubled too. In the world we now live in, it pays to be careful. I don't see any harm in some sort of quarantine of the people we're getting back. Being too soft is what brought our old country down. I'd rather risk being too hard."

The word "quarantine" seemed to do the trick. We didn't know what these people might be bringing back with them. It would have been risky for the Muslims to impregnate our blacks with a genetically engineered disease because of the risk it would spread to their own people, but it wasn't impossible.

The governors recommended that the matter be handled as a national security issue, which put Kraft in charge and left me to work out the details. Before the end of the day, the General Staff had selected a couple areas in Roxbury where returnees would be held for three months, until we could be sure they were not infected. The migration to the countryside had left places enough there for them. The remaining local residents could go or stay, but if they stayed they would be stuck there for the same three months. The governors seemed comfortable with that.

In the absence of any word from Cairo, on June 1 we implemented our threat. We made sure Al Jazeera got pictures of their POWs shoveling pig manure. We also made clear it would continue until the prisoner exchange began. The next day, Cairo called, and on June 7 the first planeload of our blacks landed at Logan. It took off the same day filled with Egyptian POWs returning home.

Boston received her heroes gratefully, but she also accepted the quarantine. The people of Boston had learned some lessons, including patience. They knew that when the Confederation acted, it was for the common good. In the 21st century, it was wise to be prudent.

For about six weeks, everything went smoothly. The number of black returnees grew steadily. Some local folks had deliberately stayed in the areas where they were quarantined, to help them reintegrate. It turned out that in almost every case, the experience of being sold into slavery had strengthened their Christianity, not weakened it. These people would be assets to our society.

Then, on July 23, I got a phone call from the head of the public health office in Boston. "Captain Rumford, I don't like making this call," the fellow said. "I hope what I'm about to tell you is wrong. In the last week, we've had fourteen deaths among the blacks who returned from Islamic countries. They all showed the same symptoms. Now, we've got three local people from the quarantined areas showing those symptoms."

"What are they?" I asked.

"First, inflamed swelling of the lymph glands, usually surrounded by a ring. Then, fever, chills, diarrhea, and internal bleeding leading quickly to death."

History told me immediately what we were facing. Black Death.

"It's the plague, isn't it?" I asked.

"Yes, it's plague. But there's a difference. Normal bubonic plague responds to antibiotics. This one doesn't. The doctors have tried every antibiotic known, with no positive results."

I gave orders to tighten the quarantine by evacuating all areas bordering those where the returnees had settled. No one was to be allowed in or out on pain of death. Snipers in full MOP gear were positioned to enforce that order. The prisoner exchange with the Islamics was also suspended immediately.

We had a network, established in the 1990s by the Marine Corps, that tied us into scientists who were specialists in biological warfare and genetic engineering. I immediately pulled a team together to go to Boston and figure out what we were facing. If it was genetically engineered, we needed to find out how before we could develop a vaccine.

Meanwhile, the black returnees continued to die. We had comm with them, of course, so the picture was clear. Just as in the Middle Ages, the houses filled up with dead, the living too weak to drag out the bodies. Some dropped in the street, where the dogs and rats feasted on them.

We sent every medicine we had, but none made any difference. Some white doctors and nurses went in as volunteers. Since this plague took at least six weeks before symptoms appeared, they could relieve some suffering before they too went down. By then, we hoped to have a cure.

The scientists worked frantically, but without success. The problem was, there were many ways bubonic plague or any other disease could be genetically engineered to get around the usual vaccines and medicines. Finding which genes had been altered and how took time—too much time for those who had been infected. By the end of September, they were all dead, including the local residents who had remained and the volunteers who had gone in to succor them. Roxbury was a cemetery.

Yet even as they died, those black Christians accomplished something. They did not rage or rail or issue demands. They prayed together, and died together, quietly helping bear one another's burdens to the end with a Christian patience that inspired us all. In so doing, they worked powerfully to change many whites' late 20th century image of blacks from whiners who always demanded something for nothing or punks with guns to an older, truer picture: a good, faithful people who suffered without complaint and humbly served both God and their neighbor. In a society that was beginning once again to accept such qualities as virtues, that was no small legacy. It did much to ensure that blacks had a solid future in the Northern Confederation.

*

Nor did their deaths go unavenged. In the Muslim countries where Boston's blacks had been sold as slaves, the buy-back program had slowly gathered them in camps, in preparation for the POW exchange. There, they had been injected with the engineered plague. The Islamics thought this safe enough, since the disease took about six weeks to manifest symptoms and was not contagious until it did. That was plenty of time for them to be shipped off to the infidel.

Only now it wasn't because we had halted the exchange. So the plague broke out in the camps. There, too, the blacks died, but in the process they infected their guards. Arab countries not being noted for their efficiency, their quarantines had holes in them, and the bacteria crawled through. Soon, plague was raging through the slums of Cairo, Istanbul, Tehran, and Islamabad. By the Fall of 2029, thousands were dead or dying and hundreds of thousands were infected.

We still held the Islamic POWs, and I thought turnabout was fair play. I asked our scientists to come up with a different genetically engineered variant of plague, one that would mimic the symptoms of the Islamic variant but not respond to the same vaccines or treatments. Genetic engineering had become all too easy in the 21st century. Some teenagers working in a basement in Stockholm cooked up one bug that gave a week-long case of diarrhea to anyone who ate either rutabaga or herring, thus wiping out Swedish cuisine. We had the right stuff in a couple weeks' time, and as soon as we had inculcated it in the POWs by mixing it with their hummus, we sent them home. Our blacks were dead or dying, so the POWs were no longer of any value to us as commodities.

The Islamics took us for fools, welcomed their heroes with open arms, and ended up with a mix of plagues it took them three years to sort out, at the price of millions of dead. It was a small lesson in not playing games that advanced, disciplined societies could play better.

Governor Kraft's gut instinct had saved us from a similar catastrophe, but it had been a close call. The lesson, once again, was that closed borders were essential to survival. It wasn't just movements of people that had to be controlled. It was easy enough to send a bacillus by shipping container or mixed in a bulk commodity. Foreign trade fell drastically throughout the world as every import had to be quarantined, examined, and tested. Only what was local was safe, and even at home we developed a neighborhood watch to report any suspicious basement laboratories. This didn't require a police state. People were eager volunteers, because they knew the mortal danger genetic engineering posed to everyone.

It was funny, at least for those with a sense of irony, the way Americans in the early 21st century had howled about the stupid mistakes of earlier generations in pursuing "better living through chemistry" and similar scientific great leaps forward. As they scorned their forefathers, they made the same blunder on a vaster scale. Genetic engineering rolled Frankenstein's monster, "The Fly," and the Black Death all into one, yet they hailed it. Computers reduced their operators to mindless androids while hooking them on the drug of virtual reality, yet they were the miracle machine no one could do without.

It wasn't a case of those not knowing the past repeating it. They knew, yet they repeated it anyway. That's what brings civilizations to their end.

We in the Northern Confederation were lucky, once again. We figured out early what everyone who survived earned eventually. Just because a technology exists doesn't mean you have to use it. Those who depart from the ways of their ancestors do so at their peril.

CHAPTER THIRTY-ONE

B Y the 21st century, America had become a country of many universities and little education. Her colleges were mostly diploma mills crossed with asylums for the politically insane: howling Bluestockings, inventors of Afrocentric history, mewling advocates for the blind, the botched, and the bewildered. Frequently, these defectives pooled their neuroses and formed a coalition that took over the campus, turning it into a small, ivy covered North Korea. Any student who dared dispute their ideology of cultural Marxism swiftly felt the hand of revolutionary justice.

Students still arrived, despite appalling tuition bills, because they needed the sheepskin. America had come to value credentials over performance, so anyone without a college degree remained a bottom-feeder for life. Universities were a classic socialist set-up: a monopoly that produced crap at high prices. Many were little more than vending machines; insert your $250,000, pull the lever, and get your diploma.

Inflation proved the ax that finally killed the silly goose. The American republic's final hyperinflation wiped out college endowments, destroyed the middle class that footed the tuition bills, and finally made worthless the massive government grants and subsidies most universities had come to depend on. The professors were still paid, but in money worth so little a month's paycheck couldn't cover lunch. It got so bad some of them had to go out and get jobs.

The break-up of the union and the fall of Washington closed the doors of every college and university. Young people had real work to do, and no state government had spare cash to fund phony education. Frankly, nobody much missed institutions that had long since abandoned their function, which was passing the higher elements of our culture on to the next generation. So it was something of a surprise, in early September, 2029, to see students once again matriculating. The way it happened was even more surprising.

Sometime in March, an organization based in Zurich called the Foundation for Higher Learning had approached the former presidents of Yale, Harvard and Dartmouth and asked whether they could start their schools going again if funding were provided. They said they could, and immediately found themselves with a hundred million Swiss francs each—an enormous sum in our poverty-stricken economy. Lured by huge salaries, their professors re-gathered. Students were offered full scholarships, plus stipends that amounted to enough money to feed a whole family. People without much cash realized their college-age son or daughter could be their main wage-earner, and applications poured in.

At the time, I'd been occupied with both the Boston problem and our succession crisis, and I hadn't paid the whole business much mind. Three hundred million Swiss francs was an economic Godsend, because it enabled us to increase our money supply. It was many times what we were earning in foreign exchange from all our exports put together.

I had gotten a nose full of political correctness at Bowdoin, so I guess

I should have known what to expect. But that seemed ages ago, and I figured reality would impress itself on campuses just as it had on the rest of our society.

I was wrong. Quickly, all the old games started up again. The course catalogues were filled with crap like "Women in Judeo-Christian Societies: Three Thousand Years of Phallic Oppression and the Symbolism of the Bagel," "The African Origins of Chaos Theory" (a course which was quickly denounced as insensitive and withdrawn), and "Salons in the Camp: Lesbian Contributions to Line and Column Tactics in 18th Century European Warfare."

An informal contest developed among the three colleges to see which could be the most PC. The Harvard faculty collectively led a love-in that "introduced students to the richness of man-boy relationships." Yale countered with an "auto-da-fe" in which every heterosexual male student had to choose a sin from a PC list—"sexism," "homophobia," "good table manners," and so forth, and parade around campus wearing a signboard bearing their confession. Dartmouth erected a Temple of Artemis in the center of the green and forced all male students to prostrate themselves before the goddess, on pain of expulsion it they refused.

Seeking to establish itself as the best of the worst, Dartmouth called a faculty workshop for October 12, Columbus Day, "to discover means for reversing Eurocentrism and white male domination over the North American continent." Faculty leaders from Yale and Harvard were invited to attend.

*

On October 2, I received a note from Governor Kraft me to asking meet with him the next day and to bring along Ron Danielov, head of our

Special Operations forces. We gathered in his small office that afternoon.

"Are you both familiar with what is happening in our so-called institutions of higher learning?" Bill opened.

"I guess everybody is," Ron replied. "It's in all the newspapers. I can tell you, people aren't happy about it. We all thought we were through with this kind of crap."

"We soon will be," Kraft replied. "As usual, there is more to it than meets the eye. Do you know where these colleges are getting their funding?"

"From some foundation in Switzerland," I said.

"That's a front," Bill replied. "Some friends in Europe did a little sniffing around for me. The real source of the money is the UN, specifically UNESCO, the UN's cultural branch. It's been a den of vipers for as long as anyone can remember. Now, with UN money, it hopes to poison us the same way it's poisoned so many other places. Only that's not going to happen."

"Where do we come in?" I inquired.

"Conveniently, the worst malefactors are gathering at Dartmouth College on October 12," Bill answered. "They are meeting in Dartmouth Hall, in room 105, which is a small auditorium. I'm going to be there."

"Do they know that?" I asked.

"No, and they won't until I walk in," Bill replied.

"Mightn't that be a bit dangerous?" I cautioned.

"I intend it to be dangerous—for them," Bill answered.

"Here's my plan, and here's where you come in, sergeant. About mid-morning, I will crash their meeting. I'm simply going to barge in, march up to the front and grab the mic. There, I'll explain what political correctness really is and why we will not tolerate it, or its advocates, in the Northern Confederation."

"Sergeant, I need two things from you. First, I need snipers concealed in 105 Dartmouth where they can cover the stage. If any of the freaks, phonies, or faggots try to rush me or shout me down, I want them shot. They are going to hear this speech whether they want to or not."

"No problem," Ron replied. "I hope you don't mind if I'm one of those snipers myself. I'd enjoy taking a few of those bastards out."

"Be my guest," Bill answered. "But you still need to be able to run the second part of the operation. Once I've said my piece and left the stage, I want a massacre. I don't want a single one of those idiot-logues to leave that room alive."

"Press will be there, so you can't just blow the building up," the governor continued. "I want to kill the people who've earned death, but no one else. And I want the media, including television, to record and report the whole thing, in every detail."

I was taken aback by Kraft's sudden bloodlust. In the past, we had generally been careful to minimize casualties, especially among people who were at least nominally our countrymen. Knowing a General Staff officer has no right to keep his opinions to himself, I spoke up.

"Excuse me, but there's something here I don't get," I said. "When the Vermont Deep Greeners led an actual revolt, we made every effort to avoid killing them. Now we've got a bunch of crazy professors just holding a meeting, and we're going to slaughter them like so many pigs. Why?"

"A good question, captain," Governor Kraft replied. "It has two answers."

"First, the Deep Greeners were deluded, but they were not deluders. They had swallowed the poison of ideology, but they did not know it as such. They thought what they were doing was good. And a proper concern for the environment is good. We Christians call it stewardship.

They had simply gone too far, in both their goals and their choice of means.

"Because they erred, they had to pay a price, and they did. The price was banishment. Had we set their lives as the price, we would have gone too far. It is useful to remind ourselves that we are all fools on occasion.

"It is otherwise with the slime now oozing its way toward Dartmouth College," the governor continued. "These people are not the ensnared, but the setters of snares. They are the deluders, the tricksters, the deceivers who serve the One Deceiver.

"They know political correctness is bunk, and deconstruction a mere parlor game with words. Why do you think they devote their efforts so assiduously to youth? Young people have not seen enough of life to tell what is real from what is not. So they drink the poison unaware.

"This mutilation of innocence in the service of death, the death of culture and the death of truth, deserves death. That is what it shall receive. Let it be to each according to his works.

"And that leads into the second answer to your question," Kraft went on. "By giving each what he has earned—which is to say, by acting justly—we make the point that at least in the Northern Confederation, our culture, Western culture, is recovering its will. We are no longer afraid to act on what we know is right. You know Von Seeckt's saying, captain: *Das wesentlilche ist die Tat.*

"Oh, we've known, most of us anyway, that what was preached in our universities was garbage. Most of the students themselves have known it, ever since political correctness reared its ugly backside in our faces in the late 1960s.

"But we were cowed. We were frightened out of acting on what we knew, because we were told it wasn't nice, it wasn't tolerant, it didn't respect the rights of others. Those arguments were themselves provided by the politically correct, to create the opening wedge for an ideology that, once empowered, showed not the slightest shred of tolerance for any dissent, or dissenters.

"But that's all done with. We're becoming men again. Men have the will to act. This act, I promise you, will speak in a voice no one can misunderstand. This trumpet will not sound uncertain."

The governor turned to Danielov. "So then, can you give me my massacre?" he asked.

"Easily," Ron replied. "Our snipers are good enough to take out the right people and not hit the wrong people, even in a melee, which this will become as soon as the first shots are fired.

"But I think there's a better way," he continued. "You want to send a signal that we are recovering our will. Killing our enemies does that, but I think how we kill them can make the signal stronger.

"In killing, the hardest thing to do, the greatest challenge to the will, is to kill up close, with cold steel—to plunge your sword or bayonet or dagger into your enemy's guts and twist. Will you allow us to do it that way here?"

"I like it. Yes!" Governor Kraft replied. "Let the trumpet sound loud and clear."

"What about the women?" I asked.

"These women despise anyone who looks upon them as women," Kraft responded. "They spit on the word lady. If a man opens a door for them, they kick him in the shins. They demand to be treated equally. Let it be unto them according to their wish."

*

Ron knew what was wanted, so I left it to him to make the arrangements. Precisely because I still wasn't comfortable with the idea of a massacre, I felt a need to be in Hanover on October 12th. I needed to show myself that I could do what I was ordered even when I was uncomfortable with it. On the other hand, I didn't want Danielov to think I was looking over his shoulder, and I knew I'd be recognized. The targets might suspect something if they spotted the Chief of the General Staff wandering around town.

In the end, I decided just to go home to Hartland, where I could get a better sense of the public's reaction. I wasn't at all sure our folks were ready for this. Up home, I was still just "that Rumford kid," and people would let me know in a hurry what they were really thinking.

On the morning of the 12th, I hitched up the wagon and headed into town. The general store had a generator, powered by a turbine in the stream that flowed by the tannery, because they still had a good-sized freezer. The ice cream in the freezer plus a television made the store the town social center. There'd be enough of a crowd that I'd get a good sense of public opinion.

The PC congress at Dartmouth was well known to folks, since the papers had been talking about the affair at some length. When I got to the store around 9:30, a good crowd had gathered, and they had hard words for the goings-on. Time had not dimmed their memories of what was worst about the old U.S.A., and this political correctness crap was at the top of the list. More than one neighbor said we ought to take the lot of 'em out and shoot 'em. I took that as a good sign, but still wasn't sure how people would react when we actually did it.

The television was covering the conference, live, and the other side was laying the groundwork for us as well as if we'd written the script. The speakers were a succession of whiney women and faggy men, all bemoaning this or that oppression and blaming the world's ills on white males.

The comments from the Hartland peanut gallery got increasingly nastier; we all felt like we'd gone through a worm-hole into a tour of the Inferno conducted by Catullus. The main sentiment seemed to be, "Why are we still putting up with this stuff?"

By around 10:30, I began to fear the local crowd would go home before the action started. Just at the point when Farmer Corman said, "If I want chicken shit, I got plenty to shovel at home" and headed for the door, the picture changed.

From the back of 105 Dartmouth, the camera showed Governor Kraft marching in the side door, to gasps, then boos, hisses and shouts of anger from the gutter worshipers. Bill's 300-pound bulk tossed those in his path aside like bumboats around a battleship as he climbed toward the stage. Grabbing the mic from some stingy-haired bitch reading a poem about making love with her Labrador, the governor bellowed, "Sit down and shut up!"

They did. *Auctoritas* has that effect, even on the illegitimate.

"Fellow revolutionaries," were Kraft's next words. Recovering quickly from their initial shock, a few of the snakes hissed at him.

"You doubt that I am a revolutionary?" he replied to the hisses. "Oh, how very wrong you are. Very wrong indeed, as you will shortly learn."

"Now 'fellow', I confess, is merely a bit of polite rhetoric. After all, I cannot address you as 'ladies and gentlemen'. You would be offended, about which I care not a fig. But it would be untrue. You are neither ladies nor gentlemen. Considering how long you have coupled with demons, I'm not sure there is any humanity left in you at all."

No one was moving toward the door of the Hartland general store now. It was so quiet you could have heard a mouse fart. Like all effective leaders, Bill wore the masque of command well.

"You see, I am not one of the beguiled," Governor Kraft continued.

"I know whence you come. I have studied your history. You are not descendants of the hippies, despite your bedraggled appearance. You are not the offspring of Quakers and Anabaptists, for when you say 'peace,' you mean 'war.' You did not grow from the Suffragettes, nor the civil rights movement, nor apostles of tolerance such as Roger Williams."

"For your father in Hell, no less yours than Lenin's and Stalin's and Mao's, is none other than Karl Marx himself. Your poison, the poison of political correctness which you have striven these many years to inject into the Western bloodstream, is nothing less than Marxism translated from economic into cultural terms."

At this, one aged crone on the Dartmouth faculty, Professorette Mary Ucistah, realized the danger. The governor was about to unveil PC's ultimate secret: where it came from and what it really was. She jumped to her feet and cried, "Come on, people, let's shout this pig down. You know the chant: Two, Four, Six, Eight, We Know Who the People Hate!"

Their eyes fixed on the professor, few television viewers noticed Bill look up slightly toward the rafters and raise his eyebrows. Ron read the signal correctly. 105 Dartmouth rang with one shot from a sniper rifle, and Ms. Ucistah's brains splattered across the backs of her colleagues. Everyone in the room froze.

"Thank you for the courtesy of your attention," Bill said quietly.

"As I was saying, the sewage which you have poured for decades into the once-sweet grove of academe is Marxism, nothing less. The derivation is obvious. Like classical, economic Marxism, cultural Marxism is a totalitarian ideology. From Marxist philosophy, it derives its vision of a classless society—a society not of equal opportunity, but equal condition. Since that vision contradicts human nature, society will not accord with it, unless forced. So forced it will be. Thank God, you never got control of the power of the state, not in full. But on campuses like this one, where you did gain power, you made your totalitarian nature clear. Cultural Marxism was forced on everyone, and no dissent was allowed. Freedom of speech, of the press, even of thought were all eliminated. Anyone who challenged you, student or faculty or administer, was driven out.

"Like economic Marxism, your cultural Marxism said that all history was determined by a single factor. Classical Marxism argued that factor was ownership of the means of production. You said that it was which groups—defined by sex, race, and sexual normality or abnormality—had power over which other groups.

"Classical Marxism defined the working class as virtuous and the bourgeoisie as evil—without regard to what members of either class did. You defined blacks, Hispanics, feminist women, and homosexuals as good, and white men as evil—all, again, with no attention to anyone's behavior.

"Classical Marxists, where they obtained power, expropriated the bourgeoisie and gave their property to the state, as the representative of the workers and peasants. Where you obtained power, you expropriated the rights of white men and gave special privileges to feminists, blacks, gays, and the like—Marcuse's revolutionary class.

"Classical Marxists justified their actions through a warped economics. You justified your actions through a deliberate warping of the language: deconstruction. Deconstruction claimed to prove that any text, past or present, illustrated white male oppression of everyone else, just as economic Marxist analysis claimed to prove the exploitation of the working class. Deconstruction was in fact just political scrabble. Compared with it, classical Marxist economics was at least intellectually challenging. But then, most of you never had minds.

"But that is not all I know about you," the Governor continued. "I have visited, through history, the fetid holes where your cultural Marxism grew. I have read Gramsci, the Italian Communist who pioneered the translation of Marxism from economics into culture as early as the 1920s. I know Adorno, and his Frankfurt School that in the 1930s crossed Marx with Freud. I have studied Critical Theory, the product of that school that carried the bacillus into American universities. I know the whole, sordid story of your sorry ancestry among the exiled refuse of European Marxism, the story of how failed intellectuals worked for what is now almost a century to stab our culture in the back.

"But as I said at the outset, I too am a revolutionary. My revolution—our revolution, here in the Northern Confederation—is against you. Marxist revolutionaries of every yellow stripe, wherever they obtained power, brought revolutionary justice. Anyone or anything that furthered their revolution was just, anyone or anything that opposed it was unjust. And the unjust were liquidated, by the millions.

"Now, by your own standard, you will be judged. You have opposed our revolution, so you stand condemned.

"You are condemned, let me hasten to add, not by me alone, nor merely by those who live today in our Confederation. Your jury is every man and woman who for three thousand years has labored and fought and died for Western culture, the culture you sought to sacrifice to your own pathetic egos.

"And that jury's sentence is death."

At those words, the doorways to 105 Dartmouth filled with our men. Each wore a white surplice with the red Crusader cross emblazoned on a shield over the heart. Each held a Roman gladius, the short, sharp stabbing sword of the Roman legionary, in his right hand. Through the doorway closest to the stage, a choir of monks filed in. Mounting the stage, they began chanting the *Dies Irae*. At that signal, the soldiers set to their work.

The hall held 162 politically correct luminaries—163 if you count Ms. Ucistah's corpse. The work of slaughter went quickly. In less than five minutes of screams, shrieks and howls, it was all over. The floor ran deep with the bowels of cultural Marxism, and at least in the Northern Confederation, it was dead.

As intended, the television showed the whole thing, the faces frozen first in terror, then in death. It was not a pretty picture, even to those of us who had seen war. As the cries turned to moans, and the moans were replaced with nothing but an occasional twitch of a limb unconnected to any living brain, the *Dies Irae* too softened until the choir was silent.

Then, Governor Kraft, who had stood like some human Matterhorn overlooking the carnage, moving and unmoved, turned and walked slowly, as if in solemn procession, toward the door. As he did so, the choir broke again into song, now in a major key, strong and soaring: the *Non Nobis*. "Not to us, Oh Lord, but to Thee be given the glory."

In the Hartland general store, I had kept one eye on the television and the other on my neighbors. Perhaps my own ambivalence made me overly sensitive, but Kraft's massacre was a high-risk move, and public reaction would determine whether it worked or blew up in his face.

State o' Mainers are born with poker faces and stuck tongues, so at first it was hard to judge. But as the massacre proceeded, I began to notice a few thin smiles, the sign a Yankee likes what he's seeing.

After Kraft left the stage in 105 Dartmouth, Farmer Corman reached up and turned off the set. "Waal," he said, "I don't know about the rest of you, but I thinks that deserves a toast. Here's a jug of my best cider, which I brought in to sell, and I see some glasses theah on the shelf." The glasses and the jug quickly went round.

"Heah's to our Governor, the State of Maine, and our own Johnny Rumford, who've had the courage to do what we should have done a long time ago." As the glasses were raised, a kid in back shouted "Hip, hip, hurray!" Three cheers rang out, and I bowed my thanks for good neighbors and a people who deserved their liberty.

*

Bill Kraft had gambled and won. No one in the Confederation regretted the loss of the treasonous intellectual scum who, perhaps more than anyone else, bore the responsibility for what had happened to the old U.S.A. But I felt there was still some unfinished business, and a few days later, back in Augusta, I asked Bill if he would stop by my boarding house lodgings some evening so we could talk.

He came on a cold November night. Knowing that the route to Bill's heart and brain lay through his stomach, I had stopped by Father Dimitri's to wheedle something special. Not only did the good priest provide the tin of caviar I had hoped for, he threw in a few bottles of vintage Port, Bill's favorite drink. "Just lubricating the wheels of government," he said smiling as I thanked him and his Tsar for their generosity. He knew one good bottle often accomplished more than many memos.

Bill arrived around eight and caught sight of the sideboard as he was shucking off his field-gray greatcoat. "I'm pleased to see the General Staff has been maintaining a productive relationship with the Russians," he said jovially.

"Tanks and caviar are a happy combination," I replied.

"Especially when it's Sevruga," Bill added, quickly pouring himself a glass of Port and diving into the tin.

"I'm glad to see you've gotten your appetite back," I joked.

"Nothing picks up the spirits better than a good massacre," he mumbled through a mouthful of black pearls. "An 'Un-rest Cure,' you know."

"Having a bit of Saki with our caviar?"

"Reginald would approve, I'm sure," he almost purred. Bill's ecstasies, like his rages, were something of an art form.

Seeing an opportunity to turn the conversation the way I wanted it to go, I asked, "I wonder how many of the young men growing up today in the Northern Confederation will ever have a chance to read Saki?"

"Not many, I guess," Bill replied. "That's always a problem with revolutions. You lose a lot of good things too."

"Is it time to start getting some of them back?" I asked.

"What do you have in mind?" he said.

"A real university. You know what that is. It's a place where people study Latin and Greek, read Aristotle and Cicero and Thomas Aquinas, learn Logic and Rhetoric, and come to appreciate the classics of our English language—Jane Austin and Chesterton and Tolkien and, perhaps, even our friend Saki."

"I would like to see that too," Bill said. "But can you read Chesterton on an empty stomach?"

"Who was it that said, 'If I have money, I buy books, and if there is any left over, I buy food and clothes?' "

"Virgil, I think," he answered. "But I'm not sure our fellow citizens are Virgils."

"Why don't we ask them?"

"You mean a referendum?"

"Exactly. Remember the first truth about modern war: you have to trust the troops."

"True enough," the Governor said. "And you have to take risks. The risk here is that if it's voted down, it may be hard later to bring the issue up again."

Bill chewed thoughtfully for a while as he pondered my idea. "OK,

I'll do it," he decided. "I'll make the proposal to the other governors, and I'll campaign for it in public. If we lose, we lose. If we win, we'll be on the road to rebuilding our culture. To me, that's ultimately what it's all about, everything we are doing."

*

The other governors agreed the people should decide, and the vote was held on December 24th, 2029. The citizens of the Northern Confederation decided to give the future a Christmas present. The measure passed with 63 percent of the vote.

There was a general feeling that since Dartmouth College saw the death of the old, ideologized, corrupted education, it should also be the place classical education was reborn. Besides, we wanted a college devoted to teaching undergraduates, not a research university.

From every corner of the Confederation, real scholars emerged from hiding, hiding they'd been driven into by cultural Marxism, and offered to teach, even though the salary was small. Many had no PhD; their work was their credentials. Most proved dedicated and effective teachers.

Autumn, 2030, once again saw students matriculating. The number was small—there were no stipends this time—but they were earnest. They came for knowledge and understanding, not a sheepskin. Small farms and factories cared little about degrees. At least in the N.C., civilization was returning.

CHAPTER THIRTY-TWO

FOLLOWING the Dartmouth massacre, life became pretty quiet in the Northern Confederation. I had given up hoping the war was over. But gradually, as things stayed peaceful, I came to think life had again taken me by surprise. Maybe it was over, at least for us.

It was hard to call it peace. In the 21st century, a nation lived on guard every moment or it didn't live very long. Border control was as necessary as food or water or air. One moment's inattention, one contaminated refugee or shipping container slipping through, could mean death for thousands through a genetic bomb.

We still has some disaffected folks at home, Deep Greeners, cultural Marxists, animal rightsers and the like, but they kept a low profile. We'd made it clear what would happen to them if they didn't. Besides, like everyone else, they were busy trying to eat, stay warm, and maybe make a little money.

Our poverty continued to cleanse us of our sins, as the Dark Ages had cleansed Europe of the sins of the late Roman Empire. Consumerism, materialism, careerism, and the "me first" attitude of early 21st century

America faded before the demands and rewards of real life. People began to see our Shaker economy as something good. Plain living strengthened old virtues and revived honest pleasures, like the smell of a fresh-mowed field of hay and a cow's kiss on a frosty morn.

Summer and winter, one thing grew stronger: Christian faith. We had some Jews, too, of course, and they were welcome. And each place still had its town atheist and village idiot. But our deep roots were Christian, and they were not touched by the frost. On the contrary, with the tares frozen, faith sprouted everywhere. Catholic or Protestant, high church or low, made no difference. We all knew what we shared was more important than what we differed about.

This was real Christianity, too, not social gospel or social club Christianity. It was Christianity that changed the way people thought and lived. No longer was this world the most important. It was the place where people got ready for the world to come, through self-sacrifice, serving others, and obeying God's laws because they loved God. Like our wise medieval ancestors, we were learning to put *beatitudine* before *felicitas*. Being saved was more important than being happy.

It was clear we would never turn back to the vulgar carnival that was late 20th and early 21st century life. But being human, we did hope for a somewhat easier time of it, for hot water and frequent trains and the power to run machines that made things we could sell.

Here, the Christian virtue of patience stood us well. The great project to dam the Bay of Fundy was moving forward. When it was complete, we knew we would have an abundance of white coal: electricity. With plentiful, cheap, clean energy, we could be prosperous despite our lack of most other resources, so long as we worked hard and maintained our morals. Switzerland isn't poor.

When in the Spring of 2031 the former Canadian provinces east of

Quebec asked to join the Northern Confederation, our people voted yes. The Brunswickers, Labradorans, PEIers, and Newfies shared our faith and morals, language and culture, and would be assets despite their current poverty. Our economies would be integrated by the electrical grid anyway, so we felt we might as well make it official.

The reception of the former Canadians on July 4th, 2031 completed the Northern Confederation. We had reached what Mr. MacKinder would have called our natural limits. Unlike in the 19th century, those limits were now marked not by great rivers or towering ranges of mountains or uncrossable deserts, but by chaos.

*

To see how lucky we were in the N.C., all we had to do was peer over our southern border, into what had been Pennsylvania and New Jersey.

Right after the remnant of the Washington government in Harrisburg fell into history's dustbin, Pennsylvania's future had looked bright. The sweep of our OMG through Pittsburg had left the white ethnic communities in control of that city. The state had resources: coal, oil, good farmland. It had a functioning government. It seemed to have fine prospects.

Unfortunately, it also had Philadelphia. Already by the late 20th century, much of Philadelphia resembled some former colonial entrepot on the West African coast. The remnants of civilization, buildings, paved streets, electric wires, even that *summa* of urbanity the streetcar, still filled the view of the passer-by. But of civilized people there was small sign. Instead, mile upon square mile was crammed with jobless, skilless, feckless blacks. Beneath the human decay, every other kind of decay spread.

Up the Delaware, there was more of the same. East of the water gap, and not far east, you were in the urban bush. Camden, Trenton, New Brunswick, Newark ran the line of the new Underground Railroad, moving drugs, guns, whores, and gang members up and down, back and forth in an endless journey to nowhere. Newark's fame as the Aframerican Florence had proven brief. Within a couple years, the corruption and incompetence of black leaders had brought it back to where it started.

Hell was like that. By great effort, you could make a difference, for a little while. But then people got tired, and it all slid back into Hell.

New Jersey never established itself after the union broke up. There was no effective government, and soon no government at all. Gangs, mafias, tribes provided the only order and security, if those terms had any meaning. Within a year of Pennsylvania's independence, Philadelphia had de facto joined the Jersey tribal territories.

Soon, the tribes started raiding. First it was just into the suburbs, for whatever they could steal. Then they started burning whatever they couldn't steal. Kidnapping became the leading sport once the goods were taken or trashed; you could get someone to pay for their kid or their grandma.

Pennsylvania tried to stop it with the Guard, but around Philidelphia the Guard shattered on ethnic lines. Many blacks went over, with their equipment. Whites fled west into the countryside, but the raiding parties followed them. Pennsylvania's rural areas had been depopulating for generations, and the few people remaining were mostly old. They were easy pickings. By 2030, all the territory up to the laurel highlands was Indian country.

At the beginning, Pittsburgh could have helped, but it had never given a shit about Philadelphia and wasn't about to start. Then, the no-longer-working Pittsburgh white working class started coming apart. It had given birth to its own culturally black lower class, "whiggers," its own children. The poisonous culture of drugs, sex, and degraded "entertainment" that overwhelmed the urban blacks proved no respecter of color lines. Soon, whigger gangs were turning Pittsburgh into another Philadelphia, and the country folk west of the Alleghenies were living in fear of white savages with painted faces and Mohawk haircuts. It turned out the dark mills where their grandfathers had labored were less Satanic than crystal meth and punk rock.

On March 14, 2031, the last Pennsylvania governor packed up what was left of the state treasury and fled across the Maryland border into the Confederacy. A raiding party of Camden Orcs burned the state house the next day. Pennsylvania had become a geographic expression.

What happened on our southern border was repeated in most of the other industrial states: Ohio, Illinois, Michigan, even Wisconsin and Indiana, though there the rural areas were strong enough to establish *limes* behind which they lived in comparative safety. They did it partly by fighting and partly by buying the barbarians off with regular shipments of food and house coal.

A few folks in the N.C. argued we should intervene. But when they put the proposition on the ballot, 83 percent of the voters said "No." Our people realized we could not export our success, not that way. We'd get drawn into the briar patch with the tar baby, and in the end would have nothing to show for it but a long butcher's bill. The cultural base had to be strong enough locally to allow our old, Western culture to rebuild itself, and in these states it wasn't. The rural areas had too few people, and in the cities, too many whites had gotten caught up in the cultural disintegration of early 21st century America to the point where they had lost the old ways.

The only answer was depopulation, and that was happening. People died in the fighting, the massacres, the raids, and the sieges. They died of hunger and cold, especially in the cities in midwestern winters. Mostly, they died of diseases, diseases created in labs as weapons of war. Lacking any but the most local political organization or security, they could not protect themselves from the new weapon of mass destruction, the genetically engineered epidemic. By 2038, the population of the industrial Midwest was one-tenth what it had been in 2000. The great cities lay deserted and in ruins. Happy the womb that was barren.

Behind our sealed borders, we survived. As things stood, we could hope for little more. Survival itself was tough enough in the New World Disorder of the 21st, formerly the 14th century. We survived because we still believed in our old culture, and were ready to do whatever it took to keep it alive. In turn, it kept us alive. That was the ancient bargain, the bargain that had governed the West from its beginnings until the apostasy of the Enlightenment.

Because we knew what we owed to our Christian culture, deep in our hearts we wished we could do more for it, more than keep it alive in our northern redoubt. We recognized the limitations on our power, and the primacy of our one absolute interest, staying alive—no Trotskyites, we. Still, as we smoked our pipes in our cold rooms, we dreamed.

*

On a frigid, early December day in 2032, St. Nicholas' Day to be exact, Bill Kraft asked me to stop by his place in the evening. Bill wasn't very social, even with Marines, and an evening invitation meant he had something on his mind. He needed to ruminate, and was inviting me to serve as his cud.

I trudged across the snow, already crisp enough to walk on top of, about eight o'clock. Although Augusta was our capital, already by that hour it was shuttered, with most folks in bed. I saw only two sleighs out on the freshly-rolled streets. The pinholes of my candle lantern sent a wild display shooting along the silent surface of the snow. Shaker pleasures, I thought to myself, smiling. In the truck the white stuff would have just been something to get through.

I found Bill as always, smoking his pipe and reading. He offered me such luxuries as a Maine governor now had at his disposal: a good fire and a bottle of Father Dimitri's vodka well iced on the windowsill. Together they warmed me up.

"Thank you for coming by to see me so late," our Governor said. That touch of Spanish court etiquette was a sign Bill had carefully worked out what he was going to say and would proceed to unroll it like a Torah scroll. My function was to let my ears attend.

"Like many of us, I am distressed by what is happening to those who believe as we do in the wreckage of what was our country," he began. "I would like to do something to help them, and by that I don't mean sending potato peelings and tracts." That last was accompanied by a sharp look. I knew what Bill was thinking: the time-honored Anglican response to the needs of others.

"My model in matters of state is Prince Bismarck," Bill went on. "He knew when to make war, and more unusually, he knew when not to make it. I have no intention of dragging the Confederation into more war for the benefit of peoples elsewhere, even those who believe as we do. It wouldn't benefit them in any case, and I know how our citizens voted when that proposition was made to them. I voted against it myself. Still, I think there may be another way.

"What we did here, in the creation of our island of sanity amidst the chaos, we did with few resources, no fancy weaponry, not even any real soldiers beyond John Ross's Marines. We succeeded because we had some people who understood war. They knew the history and the theory of war. They had educated their minds to think militarily. They understood von Seekt's rule, that in war, only actions count. They could put thought and action together."

"What if, very quietly, we offered that same ability to our friends elsewhere in the old United States?"

"Waal, that's a thought," I replied in non-committal Maine fashion. "When you say, 'very quietly,' do you mean without letting folks up here know we're doing it?"

"No," Bill replied. "We're not about to go back to the Imperial Government games Washington used to play. The people of the N.C. would vote on this proposition as on any other. By quietly, I mean in ways that don't get our armed forces into shooting matches."

"Hmm," I responded. "That might be easier said than done."

"History shows a way, I think," Bill suggested. "Remember Liman von Sanders?"

General Liman von Sanders, I knew, had headed the German military advisory mission in Turkey during World War I. He turned the creaky Ottoman armies into far more effective opponents than the Allies had expected. One whole British army was compelled to surrender to them outside Baghdad, the first time that had happened since Yorktown. And there was Gallipoli.

"A military advisory group, you mean?" I asked in turn.

"Precisely," Bill answered. "It could help our friends at small risk or cost to ourselves, and would keep us accurately informed about the wars now raging on our continent."

The latter point was important. Our own security demanded that we be up to the minute on what was going on elsewhere, because it could quickly arrive on our doorstep. At present, our information was spotty at best, because we didn't have our own people on the scene.

"Well, I think that might have some merit," I said after chewing on the idea and my cigar for a while. "Obviously, the group would be small, and so long as things are quiet I could spare a few general staff officers. It would be a good education for them. Have you given any thought to who ought to head it up?"

"Yourself, of course."

"Me?"

"As you said, it would be a good education."

Ouch. There was the patented Kraft suppository. I shot Bill a resentful glance, but I couldn't fairly reply. Even though I was Chief of the General Staff, he was better educated in the art of war and we both knew it. So I stood up, clicked my heels (as much as they'd click in heavy wool socks, having left my wet boots on the landing), and replied, "*Yessir, Herr Generalfieldmarshal*, sir!" Bill caught the sarcasm.

"Now don't be snotty," he shot back. "If you've done as you should in developing your subordinates, they'll carry on for you quite nicely in peacetime. If something happens here, we should be able to get you back quick enough. Remember, there are wars going on all over the place, some none too distant from our own frontiers. Would the Chief of the General Staff rather spend his time in bed?"

That got my Marine back up. "I'll march to the sound of any guns I hear, humping a full pack, and still get there a damn sight before you do," I replied.

"Good, then it's settled, as far as we can settle it. The rest is up to the people of the Northern Confederation," Bill said. Over and out.

Slowly, I realized I'd been had once more. Oh well, I thought, the places I'd be going were mostly warmer than Maine, and maybe they offered something besides potatoes and codfish to eat. Still, a small voice told me I'd just added one more layer to the legend of the dumb Marine.

The proposition was put to the people on January 15, 2034, in this form: "Shall the Northern Confederation, within the limits of its resources and without engaging its armed forces, offer military advice to those people in the former United States who are fighting for traditional Western, Judeo-Christian civilization?" It passed, though narrowly: it got just 53 percent of the vote. But that was enough to open the door and send me through it.

And the world I was to find beyond was stranger than any beheld by Alice.

CHAPTER THIRTY-THREE

O NE of the rules of America's second Civil War seemed to be that those who started off best, ended up worst. In that respect it was like the first Civil War. The South's star had shone most brilliantly at the beginning, at Bull Run, on the peninsula with Lee and in the Shenandoah Valley with Jackson. After those brief shining moments, the industrial and financial sinews of the North put forth their strength and the South withered. Plus, the Union found two generals who could competently command armies, and the South had only one.

When the union broke up a second time, the Confederacy resurrected itself smoothly, almost as if it had been there all along. The southern Senators and Congressmen again left Washington for Richmond. Old Senator Sam Yancey of Georgia was elected Mr. Davis's successor and installed in the Confederate White House. On Monument Avenue, the trivializing statue of tennis player Arthur Ashe was replaced by a heroic cast of the black Confederate soldier. Southern officers and men of the former U.S. Army turned in their Yankee blue uniforms for Confederate gray.

The Confederate economy took some shocks from the usual loss of markets and suppliers, but the South was big enough and prosperous enough to recover quickly. Beyond the low-level guerilla war between blacks and Hispanics that had been going on in south Florida since the 1980s, there was little internal disorder. All in all, for most Southerners, not much seemed to change.

In fact, it hadn't, and that proved to be the Confederacy's undoing. The southern wing of the old American Establishment held on to power. The politicians were the same people, the university presidents and newspaper editors and television commentators were the same types, and the leading businessmen played up to those in power, interested only in maintaining their status as members of the club.

These people all belonged to the "New South." A product of post-World War II Southern prosperity, the New South abjured the old Southern ways and culture. It embraced the rules of political correctness, found the Stars and Bars offensive, and lived the hedonist modern lifestyle. It favored Bauhaus architecture, not neo-classic columned porticoes. It listened to rock and rap, not Stephen Foster, and read Günter Grass, not Walker Percy, much less Sidney Lanier. It shuddered at the Southern Agrarians and sought its heroes among the carpet-baggers.

The wealthy, ugly, overgrown crossroads of Atlanta, Southern only in its inefficiency and corruption, was the New South's home and shrine. Charleston it regarded not as a wonder and an inspiration but as some sort of antediluvian theme park. The recovery of Southern independence and the restoration of the forms and symbols of the old Confederacy were, to the New South, not the triumph of The Cause but an unavoidable embarrassment, hopefully to be mitigated by time.

Because the New South ruled the new Confederacy, the recovery of Southern independence did not bring with it any recovery of will.

After a brief revival incident on proclamation of the Southern Republic, the old slide continued. Crime resumed its racial cast and upward trend, with the same old judges letting off the same old criminals. The schools—attendance centers, as they were already called in Mississippi by the 2000s—continued to turn out illiterates who had learned only that their own feelings were the most important thing in the universe. Television and other video entertainment (the South had plenty of electricity, thanks to coal and TVA) still sucked out brains like an ape sucking an egg. Ted Turner became Secretary of Education in Mr. Yancey's second cabinet.

But the New South was not the only South. Outside Atlanta and Miami and Charlotte, the Old South still lived. It hung on in the small towns and the hollows, on the farms and the shrimp boats, and in the real Southern cities: Charleston and Savannah, Montgomery and Natchez and Vicksburg. It resided among the country people—black as well as white—and the old folks and the Independent Baptists, and also among a genuine southern intelligentsia who did read Walker Percy and knew the Southern Agrarians and realized the whole civil rights business was just a second Reconstruction.

Unlike the New South, the Old South had will. It didn't have to recover it. It had never lost its will, the will to preserve and restore the old Cavalier Southern culture.

It took about two years for the Old South to figure out that the New South despised it no less than the Yankees did. By 2030, the first rumblings of discontent could be heard. From country pulpits, Richmond was denounced in the same words earlier reserved for Washington. That year in Mississippi, an initiative put a referendum on the ballot to open each school day with a Christian prayer. When it passed by 78%, the Supreme Court in Richmond struck it down. A few months later, the

Commanding General of the Confederate States Army asked the Senate Military Affairs Committee to end the recruitment of women as "incompatible with Southern chivalry." The Committee responded by demanding the general's dismissal. In the truck stops and the Garden Clubs, heads shook and tongues clucked.

In most of the Old South, race relations were not a problem. Contrary to Northern propaganda, they had never been, for the simple reason that local blacks and whites got along. They lived largely separate social lives, but when they came together, they did so courteously, with understanding of the roles and responsibilities proper to each. That's the way people work things out when they live side-by-side for centuries and are left alone by ideologues.

The cities of the New South were a different story. There, a black underclass had formed by the late 20th century. Nurtured on phony resentments and imagined injustices, that underclass generated its own little Africa of crime, drugs, noise, and dirt. The government in Richmond proved as vulnerable to mau-mauing as its Washington progenitor, and with no will to contain it, black terror soon spread its bloody hand into an ever-widening circle of the white community.

In the Old South, eyeholes were cut in sheets. But the courts and police remained mostly in New South hands, so the Klan stayed in the hollows, where it wasn't needed. Alienation between people and government grew like kudzu in a wet July.

By 2032, the guerilla war in south Florida could no longer be mislabeled a crime problem. In Dade county, the body count from battles between blacks and Hispanics was upward of a hundred a week. Gangs and militias ran a network of feudal fiefdoms. If anyone, including grandmas pushing prams, ventured off their turf they were dead meat. Raiding parties of blacks were working steadily north, while Cuba threatened to send troops to protect the Hispanics.

In March, 2032, the Confederate Congress finally ordered the army to take over Florida and restore order. Had the CSA been allowed to do what was necessary, the Confederacy's disintegration might have been checked at that point.

The Confederate Congress, being New South, had no stomach for anything of the sort. Instead, it laid a set of rules of engagement on the forces it sent to Florida that made them first impotent, then laughingstocks, and finally targets. All crew-served weapons were forbidden, and individual weapons could be used only to return fire, not initiate it. Fleeing felons could not be shot. "*De facto* local authorities" were to be respected and negotiated with, not rounded up and hanged—and the Army had to negotiate in Spanish if the locals demanded it. *Habeas corpus* remained in force. Black and Hispanic ombudsmen were to accompany the troops to investigate any charges of racism or insensitivity, with Confederate soldiers subject to courts-martial on either charge.

It was the same old cultural Marxist crap as used to flow out of Washington, for the simple reason that the same people were sitting in Richmond who had sat in Washington. Just as when the Soviet Union fell apart in the 1990s, the *nomenklatura* simply transferred its allegiance to the new system, kept the same jobs and got richer.

By the Fall of 2032, the Confederate forces sent into south Florida had been pushed into enclaves by the effects of their own rules of engagement. As in intervention missions by the old U.S. Army, force protection had become the top-priority mission. A military that is most concerned with protecting itself can't do anything else, so the local tribes and gangs became bolder than ever .

Ominously, blacks and Hispanics began concluding local nonaggression pacts so they could cooperate in raiding into white areas up north.

On October 2, a column of over three hundred vehicles and almost 5,000 gang-bangers hit Tallahassee, sacked the city for three days and made it back to Dade with a train of loot that stretched for seven miles along the highway. The Confederate Army threw up a roadblock, but the raiders, wise to their enemy's weaknesses, literally pushed their way through it without firing a shot. Not having been fired upon, the Southern soldiers couldn't use their weapons.

This pathetic display of impotence on the part of an army with a noble fighting heritage enraged the Old South. Rallies, marches, and torchlight parades were held in protest in all the Southern states, with hundreds of thousands of people turning out. When one came right down Monument Avenue in Richmond, old President Yancey joined it himself, telling the crowd he was "disheartened and dismayed by the disgrace to our ancestors and our flag." In response, the Confederate Congress removed itself to Atlanta, where it passed a joint resolution "reaffirming the South's commitment to a diverse, tolerant, and multi-cultural future."

*

New Orleans had long been a strange Southern amalgam. Physically, it was one of the finest cities of the Old South, not just in its unique French Quarter, but also in the old Anglo section along St. Charles Avenue, the site of America's most beautiful homes and quaintest streetcar line.

Its population was another matter. Run since the 1970s by the usual corrupt and inept black city government, the city had long been a hellhole of violent crime and sexual perversion. The scenes in the French Quarter on a Friday or Saturday night would have given pause to a citizen of Sodom. A walking tour of the Garden District was dangerous even in daylight.

The city depended on tourism, but the breakup of the union put an end to most of that. Under the Confederacy, there were some half-hearted efforts to sweep the French Quarter's dirt under the rug, but the lowest class grew steadily more worthless and more violent. From events in Florida, it drew the lesson that it could get away with anything. On the prematurely stifling evening of May 17, 2033, it erupted.

At first, there was some organization, as much as gangs could manage. Columns headed out into the suburbs and surrounding countryside to loot and kidnap. But Louisiana wasn't Florida, and the local refinery workers, shrimpers and good old boys had long ago put together the Coon-ass Militia, as they called it. The black raiding columns were met not with roadblocks but ambushes. The Coon-asses knew how to hunt, and the raiders who left New Orleans did not return.

The state government in Baton Rouge was corrupt but white, and it swiftly mobilized the official State Militia and marched on New Orleans. Mississippi sent reinforcements, and from Richmond President Yancey ordered CSA units to assist—this time with heavy weapons. Within ten days, New Orleans was sealed and under siege.

The blacks responded by letting loose the red cock. It wasn't merely random mob action, which usually concentrates on liquor stores and leaves civic monuments alone. It was systematic self-destruction. The mayor of New Orleans, Mr. Tsombe "Big Daddy" Toussaint L'Overture Othello Jones, climbed up on a Mardi Gras float, a vast statue of Aunt Jemima pouring syrup into a pool where high yellow beauties wrestled with "White Planters" and harangued the crowd in Jackson Square. "The white folk like things pretty. The white folk love this beautiful city. Well, I'm here to tell tha white folk that this here city ain't gonna be beautiful no more. Blow it up! Tear it down! Burn it to the ground! That's the word we have for tha white folk of Dixie—burn, baby, burn!"

This, their final promise to their glorious city, the blacks accomplished. The cathedral on Jackson square was blown up by the New Orleans's police SWAT team. The little cafe across from it by the river, famous for its beignets and cafe au lait, was bulldozed with city equipment, as were the gardens of the square itself. Bourbon Street was burned, along with Tulane University. Audubon Place, which the 20th century writer George Will said contained "America's noblest collection of stately homes," was first burned by the city fire department, then razed. The stately, ancient Perley Thomas streetcars of the St. Charles Avenue line were stacked in a pile, doused with gasoline and set on fire. A mob then ripped up the tracks, heated the rails over bonfires and twisted them around trees, just as Sherman had done to southern railroads during the first Civil War. By the tenth of June, everything that had made New Orleans what it was lay in smoking ruins. Like Dresden in 1945, the city was no more than a bend in the river, covered in ash.

The Confederate Army, state, and militia forces around the city were strong enough to have intervened, but they did nothing. The orders to move in never came. No one believed the blacks would really destroy one of the South's most historic places until they did it. And when they did, the authorities in Baton Rouge and in Richmond were too stunned to react.

In Atlanta, the New South Congress did react. Blaming the death of New Orleans on "racism and intolerance that tried the patience of loyal African Americans beyond endurance," they called for a series of "reforms to eliminate the symbols and substance of the South's racist heritage." The first reform was to abolish both the Confederate national flag and the battle flag as the nation's emblems. In their place, they raised over the Congress's temporary quarters, the Atlanta Convention Center, a new flag that showed a rainbow on a U.N.-blue background. Beneath the rainbow was a black-and-white dove, behind and beneath which floated a sprinkling of silver stars, one for each Confederate state. The banner was immediately nicknamed "the Pooping Pigeon."

Charlotte, Raleigh-Durham, Alexandria, Baltimore, Birmingham, Little Rock, and other New South cities promptly raised the new flag. The Old South stuck with the old flag. Pointedly, the St. Andrew's Cross still flew over the Confederate White House in Richmond.

*

Often, a people will put up with unimaginable abuses on matters of real importance, but rebel when their sacred symbols are defiled. So it proved in the new Confederacy. The official replacement of the old Confederate flag with the Pooping Pigeon recalled the people of the Old South to their founding tradition: rebellion. On June 23, Coffee County, Alabama, announced its secession from the Confederacy, "in order to uphold and preserve the traditions of our Southern people and culture." Ironically, Coffee County was peopled almost wholly by blacks.

As the news of Coffee County's action spread, it set off a chain re-action. All over the South, towns and counties, cities and some whole states—Mississippi was the first—seceded from the Confederacy. They still recognized Mr. Yancey as President, and called themselves True Confederates, but they would have no more of Atlanta, the Confeder-ate Congress, and the New South.

The New South responded in mirror-image fashion. New South cities withdrew their recognition from the executive branch in Richmond and from most of the state governments as well, pledging their loyalty to the Congress in Atlanta. That Congress elected a new President, a Dr.

Louis Greenberg, formerly head of Duke University. True Confederates replied by electing a new Congress, which once again met in Richmond. This time, there were no holdovers from Washington.

By the winter of 2033, two states existed on one territory. There was no geographic separation, beyond urban and rural. One city owed allegiance to one government, one to another. So far, there was no shooting, but it was obvious the situation was too unstable to endure. In the New South cities, militias were being organized by combining black gangs and weapons were smuggled in. In Richmond, President Yancey was desperate for peace, but the Confederate Army was thinking about the war it knew was coming.

*

On March 4, 2034, Bill Kraft asked me to stop by his office.

"John, I received a letter this morning via our embassy in Richmond from the Commanding General of the Confederate States Army. He is of course aware of the vote up here to provide military advice to people elsewhere in the former United States who share our beliefs. The True Confederates meet that standard, without a doubt. Are you ready to do some traveling?"

"Have they formally asked for our assistance?" I asked.

"They have," Bill replied.

"Well, it should be an interesting war," I said. "When do you want me to leave?"

"Tomorrow."

CHAPTER THIRTY-FOUR

As ordered, on March 5, 2034, I left for Richmond. I thought about who to take with me, and decided in the end I didn't want anyone but our Spec Ops chief, Sergeant Danielov. A sergeant would help get me out of trouble, other officers might get me into it. Besides, if I screwed up, Ron wouldn't tell anyone.

I could have asked the Confederates to send a plane for me—due to the fuel shortage, we didn't fly ours unless we had to—but I didn't want to come hat in hand. So I decided to travel like everyone else did.

From Augusta, I took the steam train to Portland. I had to admit I enjoyed bucketing along through the Maine countryside at a stirring 40 miles per hour, the smells of summer mingling with the wood smoke from the engine, the rail joints and the locomotive exhaust playing their leisurely, syncopated song. Old pleasures rediscovered are better than new, because you can muse on your grandparents and great-grandparents enjoying the same things.

At Portland, we booked passage on a freighter sailing for Norfolk, Virginia. There weren't enough people traveling to support passenger

liners, but most freighters had space for half-a-dozen folks. Ours was a
Maine vessel, sail with auxiliary diesel, the *Silas Lapham* out of Castine
with a cargo of used cars, newsprint, and live lobsters. I noticed .50 cals
mounted on either side of the quarterdeck. Pirates were operating out of
Philadelphia.

We left Portland harbor on the evening tide, picking up a strong
breeze off the port quarter aft, the remains of a Nor'easter, as we headed
south. Dano turned green and spent the night communing with the
leeward rail. I enjoyed the sharp sea air and a cigar, then turned in. We'd
be in Norfolk on the 29th.

Like so many activities from the past, traveling by ship gave me time
to think. The question I needed to think about was, what was I going to
do? Our objective was to help the True Confederates. In our Germanic
way of war, help didn't mean fiddle and diddle at the margins. Help
meant win, win decisively, completely, finally, in such a way that the
victory could never be reversed. Icy cold and lightning fast, as somebody
used to say.

Did that mean keeping the peace or tilting the balance toward war?
And what kind of war could our True Confederate allies wage? I'd known
a few Marine generals from the old Southern aristocracy. They were fine,
upright, honorable men, solid as old Stonewall himself on matters of
morals and character. But they seemed to have the notion that it wasn't
quite gentlemanly to make a decision. And the people they chose for
their staffs… John Randolph of Roanoke's simile came to mind: Like a
rotten mackerel in the moonlight, they shined and they stank.

War, as von Moltke said, is a matter of expedients. You need to know
what result you want. That was clear enough in this case. But as to how I'd
get there, that would have to depend on what I found, and who. In war,
the power of personality is immense. You get a Napoleon, you conquer

Europe. You get a Napoleon III, you end up in a chamber pot at Sedan. Sam Yancey even in his younger days had been a cautious, lawyer-like fellow, and few men get bold as they get old. But it isn't only the people at the top who count. Sometimes it's a guy at the bottom who takes the action that gains the decision.

Such soliloquies, along with the volume of Horatio Hornblower I always took with me when I went to sea, made the few days pass agreeably. The *Silas Lapham* carried enough canvas that we bowled along at eight knots or better.

Once Ron got his sea legs, we liberated some lobsters from the tank in the hold and dined in style each night on the quarterdeck. Good sergeant that he was, Dano had a couple bottles of *Piesporter Spatlese*, the companion God intended for lobster. As we drained the last on the evening of the 12th, I remembered the old Marine rule: don't whistle while packing for deployment. Detached duty had long been good to captains.

We awoke on the 13th to find ourselves back in the 21st century; a pilot boat was leading us through the minefields into Norfolk. The Confederate ambassador in Augusta had cabled our arrival, and a young CSA officer was on the dock to meet us and whisk us around customs and immigration. He introduced himself as Captain Charles Augustus Ravenal of the Palmetto Horse Guards.

Captain Ravenal was splendid in his high-collared gray uniform and mirror-shined cavalry boots with silver spurs. In the simple, forest green hunting jacket that was the uniform of the Northern Confederation, I looked like Grant opposite Lee. Captain Ravenal's darkey driver bowed us into a Mercedes limo with the CSA crest on the doors and Confederate battle flags on the front fenders, and we were soon speeding up the Interstate toward Richmond. Dixie was indeed rich.

Southerners are good at small talk. Mainiacs aren't, but we listen carefully. As the captain went on, I got the sense he was uncomfortable about something. So in Maine fashion, I went right at him. "Something's bothering you, Captain. If it's that we smell like lobsters, well, most folks up north smell like fish, 'cause it's all we've got to eat. If it's something else, why don't you tell us about it?"

"I am truly sorry, sir, if I have in any way offended," Captain Ravenal replied. "We are all deeply grateful for your time and trouble in coming here. But to be entirely honest, sir, there is a small matter that gives us some difficulty in our protocol."

Welcome to the South, I thought. Up our way, protocol meant seeing that the other guy was warm and had something to eat. "I am certain we can resolve the matter easily, Captain, if you'll tell us what it is," I replied.

"Sir, we are all aware that you are Chief of the General Staff of the Northern Confederation," Captain Ravenal answered. "You will be accorded every honor due to your position. Our difficulty, sir, is that formally your rank is that of captain. That required that you be met by someone of similar rank, which is why I am your escort. Again, I assure you no offense was intended."

"None taken, Captain," I replied. "I rather like the rank."

"Thank you, sir. But you will be meeting with our generals and our President, Mr. Yancey. Normally, a captain would not be included in such circles, and there is some concern about seating arrangements, precedence, and the like. We do not wish to offend, as I have said."

"No problem, Captain. Sergeant Danielov and I are happy to stand in the back."

"Er, sergeant, sir? Would you expect the sergeant to accompany you, sir? I assumed he was your servant."

"Sergeant Danielov is head of Special Operations for the Northern

Confederation. In effect, he's a Commander-in-Chief. Besides, he might have something useful to say."

"Yes, sir. I'm afraid we have made arrangements for the sergeant to stay in our NCO quarters."

"Is the NCO mess good?" Dano asked.

"The specialty is Tennessee barbecue," Ravenal answered.

"Then I'm not moving. Captain Rumford can go to the meetings. I'll just potter around on my own."

"I'm certain that will be agreeable with us," Ravenal said, making a mistake of serious proportions.

"Captain Rumford," Ravenal continued, "if I may put forward an entirely unofficial proposal, for which I take full responsibility, would you possibly be willing to take on a higher rank while you are our guest here in the Confederacy? It would make our situation a great deal easier, in term of providing the hospitality which is our duty as officers and gentlemen. Please understand that I intend no disrespect to the rank you hold up North. It's just that, well, things are different down here."

I remembered how my Senate staff friend back in Washington in the old days had always been given three-star rank when he spent time with the American military. He found it funny as hell, but without that, they didn't know how to deal with him.

"If that would make your situation easier, Captain Ravenal, I have no objection," I said. "After all, we are allies, and I hope we will be friends. Anything I can do to assist, I am ready to do. What rank did you have in mind?"

"Whatever you think suitable, sir, so long as it is of a general officer grade."

This was too delicious an opportunity to pass up. I could play a joke on the South and on Bill Kraft at the same time. "How about Field

Marshal?" I suggested.

The captain's eyes popped. But he recovered quickly, and said, "I am certain that would be agreeable with our people, sir. In fact, there has been some discussion about introducing such a rank in our Army, and I know some of our officers would find such a precedent useful. Thank you, sir."

As I settled back into the leather upholstery of the Benz for the remainder of our drive, I suspected this might be a long war.

*

Now that I was formally an Exalted High Wingwang, Richmond was rich with hospitality. I was met by a 500-man honor guard, all in first Civil War uniforms, though much too well fed to be real Confederate soldiers. For quarters I was given my own mansion, right off Monument Avenue. The butler was even white. For a solid week I was toured about in the daytime and feted and admired at balls and cotillions in the evenings. Not a lick of work was done. It was just like Richmond in 1863.

When I gently reminded Captain Ravenal, who I had asked to remain as my escort despite my promotion, that I had come south to do more than drink Bourbon and admire the fine figures of Southern ladies, he seemed surprised. "The town would be deeply disappointed if it did not get to meet such a distinguished visitor," he explained. "President Yancey would be deluged with complaints from the fair sex. The brilliance of your campaigns up north has our newspapers calling you 'the new Moltke,' you know."

"That's butter without much bread," I replied. "I only know how to be silent in two languages. But I also know the South wants its guests to be happy. Would you do me the favor to convey the message that this guest would be happier if he could do some actual work?"

Putting it that way seemed to do the trick. Three days later, on March 23rd, I was invited to a briefing on the situation in the South by the Commanding General of the Confederate States Army, General Loren Laclede. Following the brief and a formal luncheon, I would be received by President Yancey.

The CSA headquarters wasn't a building. It was three whole city blocks in downtown Richmond, mostly highrises, filled to overflowing with staff officers. To take me there, instead of the usual Mercedes, I was met at my door on the 25th by an elegant barouche with a cavalry escort. Another honor guard was waiting on arrival; I found out later there was a brigade's-worth of ceremonial troops in and around Richmond. General Laclede received me in a gorgeous uniform, complete with that nice Latin American touch, a sash, amongst a vast entourage of other generals and colonels. Great material for a couple of mine-clearing battalions, I thought.

After coffee in his mahogany-paneled office, furnished with Second Empire antiques and decorated largely with pictures of himself, General Laclede escorted me to the briefing room. It was nothing less than a thousand-seat auditorium, and every seat was taken. On the stage, three huge screens were set up for the Power Point slides.

Shit, it's the Pentagon all over again, I said to myself. Just as the Confederacy had gotten the old American politicians, it had also built its military on the old American senior officer caste. I knew what was coming: a highly choreographed presentation of absolutely nothing.

I was right. For three hours we sat in wonderfully comfortable chairs as one staff officer after the other delivered a scripted, meaningless patter. The maps did indicate which areas were held by the New South and which by the Old, but the newspapers had published the same maps long ago.

Beyond that, we heard about the weather in each area, the roads, the telecommunications, the general locations of units; endless equipment rosters and readiness reports, most of which I knew were bullshit.

There were other things I can't remember because I accidentally offered the most appropriate comment on the whole affair. I went to sleep.

It was rude, no doubt. But Southern gentlemen dealt with it with Southern manners. They pretended it hadn't happened. When the lights finally came up again, Capt. Ravenal discreetly elbowed me awake. General Laclede then took to the stage himself, summed up by thanking his regiment of briefers for a splendid performance, and asked if I had any questions.

"Just one, General," I replied. "What are you going to do?"

I thought of quoting von Seekt to them, but realized that if any of these buffoons spoke a second language, it would be Spanish, not German.

"A most important question, Field Marshal Rumford," Laclede replied. "It is one which we have under study. Fourteen Colonels in my G-3 section have been working on it for most of the summer. Those are all full colonels, I might add, not lieutenant colonels. We have more than fifty contractors and consultants supporting them. Confidentially—this is the first my own staff has heard of this, and I apologize for surprising them—President Yancey is thinking about appointing a Blue Ribbon Commission of retired senior officers to investigate the matter and give us the benefit of their recommendations. I can assure you, we are considering every possible aspect of the situation in the most thorough manner."

"When do you expect to make a decision?" I asked.

"Well, sir, I am not certain I am prepared to put a time line on it. I would certainly need to consult further with my staff before attempting to do so," Laclede replied. "After all, I'm just the coach," he added, smiling benignly on his vast staff horde. They smiled back, with the grin of the apparatchik who knows that nothing is likely to disturb his comfortable routine anytime soon.

I realized further questions were pointless. It was the worst of the French way of war combined with the worst of the British: endless staff actions and a commander who played umpire. I'd seen it all before, in the Marine Corps and, even more, whenever we did a CPX with the United States Army. Like the French Bourbons, the Confederates had forgotten nothing and they had learned nothing.

We adjourned to a splendid lunch, including a concert by the CSA band and chorus. If these guys ever did win a war, they'd put on one fine victory parade. But in this case, someone else would have to win the war for them. I now understood why New Orleans had gone as it did. Nobody could decide anything.

My session that afternoon with Confederate President Yancey confirmed my depression. He was a splendid old gentleman, earnest, decent, upright. Over and over, he impressed upon me his urgency to do the right thing. Unfortunately, in war the right thing is never clear, so he too would do nothing.

On the way out of the Confederate White House, I told Captain Ravenal to ask Sergeant Danielov to come see me that evening. Dano might have found out something useful. I certainly hadn't.

"You want to see your sergeant, sir?" Ravenal replied, clearly concerned that someone of Field Marshal rank would stoop so low. "Is it a matter I could take care of for you?"

"Well, to be honest, Captain, I'm not quite satisfied with the way my uniform is being ironed," I replied. "It takes a Northern man to know how to do it just right."

"I understand, sir," Ravenal responded, reassured and comfortable again. "I'll have your sergeant sent over right away."

I had requested from General Laclede the papers his staff was developing on possible courses of action, which arrived during the first solitary dinner I'd enjoyed since I came South. True to form, the Confederates had made sure my house had a first-rate cook, an old black mammy who could have stood in for Aunt Jemima and whose biscuits and cornbread would have made Escoffier swoon. After stuffing down a third piece of her ambrosial peach pie, I waddled upstairs, leaving her beaming. I'd put on a pound for each day I'd been in Dixie, and enjoyed every bite of it. I knew it would come off again as soon as I got back North, back to codfish cakes and boiled potatoes.

I settled in my study, lit my cigar and took up the papers. The old U.S. Army stared out at me from every page. It was endless, badly-written, jargonized nothing. With the best of intentions, hoping to find a diamond among the dung, I plowed on. But drivel on top of the dinner was too much for me. I last heard the great old grandfather clock, once the property of General Longstreet, chime eight. My brain swam lazily, back to The Basic School, to happy days playing in the mud and nights of beer and bullshit....

*

Someone was trying to get me up. Crap, it's o'dark thirty and I want to sleep. Tell the SPC to go play with himself. I'm too full for a company run. I'll throw up all that wonderful chow, and it never tastes as good the second time around.

I was awake. Someone was rapping at my second floor window. The clock said 9:15. If it was Poe's raven, I'd eaten my last piece of peach pie. It wasn't. It was Danielov, and he had somebody with him.

I threw up the sash and screen, and they scrambled in. "Glad to see you got my message, Dano," I said. "But this place does have a front door. Or were you just testing our security?"

"It's Southern security," Ron replied. "Sentries in perfect uniforms walking a regular beat. Let's just say we didn't have a problem getting in. I came this way because I wanted you to meet someone. This is Captain Walt Armbruster, 3rd Texas Rangers."

"Happy to meet you, Captain," I replied, "and happier still to dispense with the usual Southern formalities."

"I'm more than happy to meet you, sir," he replied. "We've been down on our knees praying you'd come."

"Who's we?" I asked.

"The real soldiers, sir," he replied.

"Are there any in the Confederacy?"

"Yes, sir, there are," he answered, meeting my eyes. "Despite what you've seen here in Richmond."

"It was to discuss what I've seen here in Richmond that I asked Sergeant Danielov to meet me tonight," I said. "I find myself in a somewhat awkward position, since what I have to say may appear poor return for lavish hospitality. Captain, would you excuse us if we go in the other room to talk privately?"

Dano answered before the captain could. "No need, sir. I know what you've found here, and I know it through Captain Armbruster. It's the worst of the old U.S. military: bloated staffs, meaningless briefings, commanders who can't make decisions, all process without content."

"But covered in syrup," Captain Armbruster added. "That's the Southern touch."

"That about sums it up," I replied. "Make no mistake, Captain, the Northern Confederation is with the True Confederate party all the way

when it comes to the important things, to morals and culture and religion. But I was sent down here to help win a war. At the moment, I
have some difficulty seeing how I'm going to accomplish that, since your
leaders seem unable to make up their minds about anything important,
like what to do."

"Sir, our leaders don't have any minds to make up," the captain
replied.

Having been a captain in the American military, I knew what I was
dealing with in Captain Armbruster. He was a warrior himself, but he
was more than that. He was a warrior who realized that most of his
superiors were not warriors. I didn't figure that out until right at the end
of my brief and lusterless Marine Corps career. This guy was well ahead
of where I had been.

"Captain, I think I understand where you're coming from. Earlier,
you used the pronoun 'we.' Are there any more like you?"

"Yes, sir," he replied. "There's a lot of us among the junior officers.
We never belonged to the old U.S. Army, so we never learned how to be
feather merchants. We joined up with the Confederate States Army for
the same reason our ancestors did: to fight. We're eager to get at these
New South traitors to our Cause. But what can we do? Some of us have
even thought about a coup, sir, but we don't want to turn the Confederacy
into some Latin American banana republic. Frankly, we're stumped."

"Are you in touch with each other?"

"Yes, sir. We've got our own network. We can get the word out, if
you've got a word for us."

"Do you have a base?"

"Yes, sir, a couple, wherever we have a commanding officer who
thinks like we do. My unit is on one of our bases. We're in Savannah,
right where the old 3rd Ranger Battalion of the U.S. Army used to be

stationed. We're all Texas boys, and our colonel, Colonel McMoster, is on the right side."

"How do you know that?" I asked sharply. Trust demanded deeds, not just words.

"During the burning of New Orleans, Colonel McMoster came to Richmond with a plan for our battalion to jump on the city and take it in a *coup de main*. He couldn't get an answer from Richmond, so he decided we'd do it anyway. We were commandeering civilian aircraft at the Savannah airport when the word came over CNN that we were too late. The city was already gone."

"Why wasn't he relieved for disobedience?"

"His wife is distantly related to President Yancey's wife. This is the South, sir," the captain replied.

Nepotism occasionally has its virtues, I thought. "All right, Captain, I trust you and I'll have to trust your colonel as well. I'm going to head down to Atlanta myself and see what's going on there. Once I've done that, I'll come see you and your CO over in Savannah. You get there first and tell Colonel McMoster that I don't plan to go home until I've done something. What, I don't know yet, but whatever it is it's not going to happen here in Richmond."

"Nothing ever happens here in Richmond," Captain Armbruster replied. "I'll head back tonight. Sir, I speak for our colonel when I say I hope you will regard the 3rd Texas Rangers as under your command."

"Thank you, Captain," I replied. "What's the old Texas Ranger rule, 'One riot, one Ranger?' Maybe here we can say, 'One civil war, one Ranger battalion.'" In any case, you can count on some action."

I turned to Danielov. "Dano, go with him. We're going to need some aircraft. See if you can find a former Marine or two who has some."

"Aye aye, sir," Ron replied.

*

The next morning, when Captain Ravenal came to pick me up for another visit to another useless headquarters, I told him I had a special favor to request.

"President Yancey has personally directed that we assist you in every way, sir," he replied. "If it can be done, we will do it."

"I want a Pullman berth on tonight's train for Atlanta," I said.

The captain stiffened. "Sir, I cannot advise that. It would be extremely dangerous."

"That is my request, Captain. Will you meet it, or do I have to give you the slip, find the rail yards and hop a freight?"

Captain Ravenal's face was a study as he wrestled with the greatest of military challenges, the need to make a fast decision in the face of unexpected events. Finally, he said, "Sir, President Yancey's order was quite clear. Your ticket will be waiting at the station. I will of course have to inform my superiors of what I have done—tomorrow."

Maybe Captain Ravenal had the makings of a real military officer after all.

That night, at 8 PM, at Richmond's Broad Street station I boarded the Southern Railway's crack express for Atlanta, Birmingham, and Mobile, the *John Wilkes Booth*.

CHAPTER THIRTY-FIVE

In the fine fashion of Agatha Christie mysteries and the old *Orient Express*, I was traveling incognito. When George the Pullman porter asked my name, I gave it as Mr. McWhorter. I was dressed in the uniform of the New South—expensive suit worn over a shirt with open collar—and I trusted to a Panama hat pulled low and Italian sunglasses to make a sufficient disguise. So long as I didn't slip into State o' Maine speech, I figured I was safe enough.

The train was fast but the Southerns' track was smooth, and I got a good night's sleep as Mr. Pullman's guest. George woke me at 7 o'clock on the 25th of March in time to shave and dress, and we arrived in Atlanta's Peachtree Street station on the advertised at 8 AM.

The only way to see a city is to walk it. I traveled light, with one shoulder bag, so I could do just that. Coming out of the station, I took a right on Peachtree Street toward downtown.

Immediately I got a powerful sense of *deja vu* all over again. I'd been here before, in the Corps, in places like Lagos, Mombasa, and Maputo, and later in Washington, Baltimore, and other American cities. Atlanta reeked of disorder and decay.

It wasn't just the garbage piled high on the street corners, uncollected, or the trash littering the potholed streets. It was the smell of fear. Even in the morning, when the worst elements were usually asleep, my nose wrinkled with it. All the windows and doors were barred, including upper stories. The better establishments had armed guards out front. The lesser made do with "Beware Of The Dog" signs. The few pedestrians scuttled furtively, like people in a kitchen full of cockroaches.

I picked up the day's *Atlanta Constitution*—now a double entendre, since Atlanta's New South government had its own constitution—and dove into a diner to get some breakfast. The few other patrons looked up briefly without any expression as I sat down at the counter. The young black counter-man turned to take my order, and on his face was written a familiar attitude, that cultivated stare of defiance and menace I hadn't seen up north since CORN solved our black problem, that had also vanished from Old South Richmond. He took my order for a three-egg omelet with ham and sausage without saying a word, then barked it to the cook at the grill.

As I waited for my chow, I unfolded the paper to find an unpleasant reminder of the bad old days. Murder and mayhem, rapes and riots filled the front page. Even with the New South Congress in session in the city, the political news took second place to crime. That reflected reality. When order is lost, the important news is all local.

My breakfast, when it came, was good. Atlanta was still Southern, in its way. I was through the sausage and starting on the ham when I heard pop, pop, pop, from somewhere out in front, mixed with the harsh staccato of an AK on full automatic. The waiter and cook dove behind the counter and the rest of the breakfasters ran toward the back. I grabbed the Walther .38 I carried in a shoulder holster, bent low, and made for the front door. I waited a few seconds—all quiet—then opened the door carefully a few inches, just enough to be able to look up and down the street.

About 100 feet away, south toward the downtown, a police cruiser stood, its windows shot out and one door, toward the sidewalk, hanging open. I could see a cop stretched out beside it, on the sidewalk. His Glock was in his hand. He wasn't moving.

"Call 911," I shouted back into the diner. "I think a cop's been shot. I'm going to check it out."

From behind the counter, the counter-man replied, "Fuck the cops and fuck you too, motherfucker. I ain't callin' nobody."

Boy, you just lost your tip, I thought.

I crouched and ran, keeping behind the parked cars, toward the cop. People in shops closer to the scene must have seen him, but nobody came to help. I figured whoever had done the drive-by was long gone, but you never know. I kept checking six, a useful lesson from Marine aviators, but in this case six stayed clear.

As I got in closer, I saw a pool of blood around the officer's head, not a good sign. Dropping down beside him, I checked for heartbeat and breath. He had both. He had a nasty gash on his right temple, but I quickly saw it wasn't deep. He'd been winged and knocked unconscious, but unless there was something I couldn't see, he'd live to collect his retirement.

I pressed my handkerchief into the wound, held it in place with the cop's cap, and leaned into his vehicle to see if the radio was still working. It was. I pressed talk and gave the signal every cop regards as sacred, and dreads: "Officer down, officer down!" The dispatcher came on immediately. Glancing at the street numbers, I gave him an address. I knew other cops and an ambulance would be there fast.

Returning to the downed cop—a good-looking kid, white, Kearney according to his name badge—I held the bandage tightly to stop the blood flow. As I did so, I looked up the street to see one of the other patrons leaving the scene of my breakfast, carrying my bag. A white guy, too. I yelled, but he just ran the other way. Blood is thicker than baggage, I thought. No way could I leave the cop. Thanks, New South. I'll get even, some day.

Kearney started to come to. His mind was still where it had been when he fell, and he started to move. I held him down. "It's OK, kid. You're covered. Help's on the way," I told him. But he was going into shock.

Even where everything else has fallen apart, cops still take care of each other. A cruiser smoked by in less than a minute, slammed on the brakes, and backed up on the sidewalk. Just one guy was in it—another dumb practice in the jungle. He saw the Walther in my right hand, reached toward his own weapon, then realized I was helping his buddy and cooled it. "Better get that out of sight," he said to me as he ran up. "It's illegal here for a private citizen to carry a weapon."

"Did the city council bother to tell that to the guys with the AK?" I asked.

"Effing politicians," he replied as he moved quickly to check his buddy over. "I hate all of them."

He found no other wounds. As usual, the drive-by boys couldn't shoot, they just sprayed.

The new cop guided in a couple other cruisers, a motor and, somewhat later than I expected, an ambulance. The cops didn't say anything to the EMT guys, seeing as they needed them, but their body language told me they weren't happy.

We saw Kearney lifted into the ambulance, and the motor and one cruiser gave it an escort to the nearest hospital. The remaining cops asked me a few questions, and I told them what I'd seen, which wasn't much. "Are open attacks on police something regular down here?" I asked a sergeant.

"Every day," he replied. "In case you didn't know it, you're in a war zone. And it's gonna get worse, fast."

"You think so?" I replied as casually as I could. The best way to find out what's going on in a place is from the cops. The problem is getting them to talk to you, if they don't know you.

"I know so," he replied. "Look, we owe you one. You came to the aid of an officer who was down. I can tell you're not from around here, because none of the SOBs in this lousy town will lift a finger to help a cop. I'm afraid Kearney bled all over that nice, expensive suit. Why don't you ride with me down to the station and get cleaned up?"

"Thanks," I replied. "I'll enjoy being safe for a little while."

"You think so?" the cop, a Sergeant Randall, replied. "They've mortared our station twice in the last month."

*

The police station was walled off for a full block around the actual building with Concertina wire, street barricades, and blockhouses in which I saw machine guns mounted. "Welcome to Fort Zinderneuf," Randall said as we drove in. "Isn't the New South gracious?"

The word had spread that Randall was bringing in a citizen who'd helped a cop in trouble, so I was met with friendly smiles and strong handshakes from all the other cops. Nobody said anything about the Walther. Randall showed me to the shower room, where I cleaned up while another cop did some quick work on my jacket. "Cold water will take the blood out if you get it before it dries," he told me. Somehow, it felt good being back among men who knew that sort of thing.

After I'd scrubbed up and the suit coat was hung to dry—my shirt was a lost cause but a cop my size gave me one of his—Randall stuck his head back in. "Can I invite you upstairs for a cup of coffee? There are a few other folks here who'd like to thank you for what you did."

"Sure," I answered. "But no thanks are needed. You guys are out there for us all the time. I'm happy to have a chance to return the favor. How's Kearney?"

"The hospital says there's no damage beyond what you saw," Randall replied. "A transfusion, some IVs, and a couple days in bed and he'll be OK. Thanks for asking."

Upstairs was officer country, as I could see by the "I love me" pictures as we walked down the second floor hallway. Sergeant Randall led me into the office of the police captain who ran the station house. There, about a dozen cops were gathered.

Again, it was smiles and handshakes all around, along with good southern coffee. The captain gave a little speech formally offering his gratitude and that of his men. At the end of it he said, "I've got a small present for you," and handed me an official looking piece of paper. It was a permit to carry a sidearm. "You may find that useful, Captain Rumford."

I jumped. At least I did inside. I immediately hoped it hadn't showed. I realized denial would just make me look foolish. "It's nice to be addressed by my real rank again," I replied with what was intended to sound like nonchalance. "I think you have to be German to carry off this Field Marshal business. I feel like I'm playing in *The Student Prince at Heidelberg*."

The cops smiled, though in Dixie I doubt many got the reference.

"Don't worry, sir, you're safe with us," the police captain replied. "You would have been even without your help to Kearney. We know what you all have done up north, and we only wish we could do the same down here."

I'd learned long ago that liberal cops are very, very rare. Cops see too much of life to believe in bullshit.

"But now we do owe you for Kearney, too," he continued. "So our question to you is, how can we help you do whatever you came here to do?"

"I came here to find out what's going on in the capital of the so-called New South," I replied. "The best way you can help me is to tell me."

"You've already gotten a good taste of it," one patrolman replied.

"I have," I answered. "But on my own, I can only see what's on the surface. What I need to know is what's going on that I can't see. The situation here can't endure. Human nature can't tolerate disorder indefinitely. Which way is it going to turn, restoration of order, or chaos?"

My question met with uneasy silence. The cops looked at each other, looked at me, then looked at each other again. They were pregnant with something. Could I get it to drop?

Finally, the station chief said, "I'm going to give you an honest answer. We owe you that, and one thing more besides."

"For more than a year, we've been tracking a conspiracy here in Atlanta. We've told the mayor, the city council, even the New South government, but they won't listen. They just call us racists and tell us to go away."

"The conspiracy involves the gang leaders, some local politicians, some members of Congress, all black. To put it simply, they plan to take over the city, kill all the whites and Asians, and proclaim something they call The Commune."

"When?" I asked.

"We don't know that," the police captain replied. "But the pieces all seem to be pretty much in place. My guess is the only reason they're still waiting is that the Congress is importing more arms for them. The gangs are now formally part of the New South Army, which should tell you what that army is worth."

"What are you going to do when it happens?"

"Run," one officer replied.

The captain nodded. "We've all gotten our families out of this place long ago, into the Old South, the countryside. We've only stayed because we need the paychecks. We don't owe the SOBs who run this town, white or black, the time of day. When the place blows, we hope it takes them with it. We're getting out."

A picture was forming in my mind. The Commune. The Paris Commune in 1871. If Atlanta became the Paris Commune, the whole South would have to unite against it—and act, just as the French had to do then. From my standpoint, the sooner it happened, the better.

"Are you willing to set this bomb off?" I asked.

The cops looked startled. That was not a response they expected. "Why should we do that?" one cop asked.

"Because it will finally force the True Confederate government in Richmond to act," I replied. "As you've probably noticed, they aren't the most decisive sorts. This would leave them no choice."

Again, the cops looked at each other. One spoke up, "Why not? We know it's coming. If we set it off, we can be sure we'll get out."

"How could we set it off?" the police captain asked.

"Am I right that you've been recording this meeting?" I said.

The officers looked a bit sheepish. "You're right," the captain answered. "We record everything. We have for years. It's the only way to cover our own asses. If the wrong people found out about this, we could always say we were just setting you up."

"OK, here's how you light the fuse," I told them. "Make a dozen copies of the tape, get one to each of the chief conspirators, then get out of town. Once they know I've been here, and that I know their plan, they'll set their coup in motion. They'll have to, because they'll think I'll move to stop them. Delete the portions of the tape after I asked, 'What are you going to do?' so they won't know what you're planning either."

I knew the cops would need to palaver on this one. I'd made their day a little more interesting than they had anticipated. I was asking them to play for high stakes, and to take risks, which cops don't like. At the same time, I was giving them a chance to get back at politicians they hated and a citizenry that looked on them with indifference if not contempt. Which would win out, fear or righteous anger? I gave them some time to think about it by asking directions to the head.

When I returned from an extended head call, the cops had made their decision. "We'll do it," the captain announced. "We know what's coming and we sure can't stop it. Plus, we know your war record up north. If you think this is the right thing to do, we probably ought to listen to you. We'll time it so they get the tapes day after tomorrow, March 27th. That will give us a day to get clear."

"And we still owe you something. We need to get you out of town, too. If the New South government or the conspirators nab you, you'll have seen your last New England autumn."

"Can you get me to Savannah?" I asked.

"Sure," he replied. "We'll just dress you up in one of our uniforms and have you ride with one of our men. Nobody stops a cop car, and if they do, no one looks at a cop's face. They just see the uniform."

So the bomb was armed. I spent the night in the station house. The next day, March 26, in the uniform of Atlanta's finest, I left town in a plain brown wrapper, driven by a patrolman whose family was in Savannah, a secure bastion of the Old South. At the outskirts, I turned around in my seat for a last look at the Atlanta skyline. "Kind of makes you wish old Sherman could come back, doesn't it?" the officer who was driving me asked.

I thought about Kearney left bleeding on the sidewalk and my stolen travel bag. "Ayuh, it kinda does," I replied.

*

The Atlanta cop drove me directly to the 3rd Texas Rangers' base camp, where our uniforms and his ID got us through the gate. Still Southern security, I thought. He dropped me at the CP, where I quickly found Captain Armbruster and Sergeant Danielov. Armbruster wasn't quite sure how to react to my latest avatar as an Atlanta cop. Dano just grinned. "Looks like you've been doing some spec ops on your own," was his comment.

"Ayuh, you could say that," I replied in good Maine fashion.

"You bring the rest of my trash down with you?"

"Got it all," Ron replied. "Though I'm afraid your uniform might need ironing." He'd obviously gotten the word from Captain Ravenal.

"We can take care of that, sir," Captain Armbruster volunteered.

Dano and I looked at each other and broke up laughing. No one up north ever thought of ironing a uniform. We seldom thought of washing them. We were wary of the Sukomlinov Effect: the side with the best uniforms always loses.

"Don't sweat it, Captain," I replied. "I assume Southern regulations forbid a Field Marshal's uniform to wrinkle itself."

The battalion commander, Col. McMoster, was out leading some training, but he would be back around dinner time. I suggested we meet in the mess, then retire to someplace quiet where we could talk. I told Armbruster we had some sensitive material to discuss, and left it up to him who should be there. Meanwhile, I could shower up and change into something more comforting.

Dinner in the mess was steak, barbecued pork South Carolina style, or both. Dano and I both took both. It would be some time yet before we had our guts and our arterial deposits back up to normal.

Col. Bill McMoster, CO of the 3rd Texas Rangers, joined us halfway through chow. He knew I had arrived, and I was glad to see he'd put training above hospitality. His utilities were muddy and he stank, which were also good signs. His conversation over dinner was direct, honest and self-critical.

We gathered afterwards in his office, which was paneled with books, most of them military histories. Their condition suggested somebody had read them in the field. Cigars and bourbon quickly went around. It was funny to think back on the old U.S. military, with its "no smoking, no drinking" rules. If your armed services have become a girls' school, you probably need rules like that.

I shared with the assembled Texas officers and NCOs the story of my minor adventures in Atlanta. The point, as I saw it, was that all we had to do was wait. When Atlanta erupted and the blacks proclaimed their Commune, the Confederate government would have to act. "I guess I should probably head back to Richmond tomorrow," I concluded. "They shouldn't need any advice as to what to do, but from what I saw there, they might."

Colonel McMoster sipped his bourbon for a bit, then responded. "I'm afraid you still don't understand the depth of the problem in Richmond, Captain. You weren't there during a crisis. I was. They didn't act when New Orleans burned, and they won't act when Atlanta goes up either. With the people they've got in charge, they can't. All they know how to do is nothing, so nothing is what they will do."

"That leaves me with a question for you," McMoster continued. "If the blacks proclaim this Commune and Richmond doesn't respond, what do we do then?"

The colonel's question hit me in the face like a cold, dead flounder. I didn't have an answer. I immediately realized I had just played the game of High Seas Fleet.

Prior to World War I, Germany had built a powerful force of battleships, the High Seas Fleet. Britain's Royal Navy was stronger, but the Germans were certain that, when war came, the British would steam up close to the German coast to blockade it. There, mines, submarines, and torpedo boats could whittle them down until the German battleships could engage them on equal terms. In May of 1914, Admiral Tirpitz asked the High Seas Fleet's commander, "What will you do if they do not come?" He received no answer. And when war erupted three months later, the British dreadnoughts stayed far away from Germany's home waters, supporting a distant blockade, and the German High Seas Fleet proved useless.

With my stomach in free-fall, I looked at Colonel McMoster and the other Confederate officers and gave the only answer I could. "I don't know," I admitted.

I could feel the room deflate. Here I was, their best and brightest hope, "the new Moltke," caught with his pants down like some second lieutenant in his first tactical decision game. Nobody said anything, but I knew what they were thinking and they were right. I hadn't thought the situation through to the end.

The one advantage experience gave me over a second lieutenant was that in a moment like this, my mind didn't freeze up. I asked myself the question, "If I were back up north and found myself in a fix like this, what would I do?" Immediately, I knew the answer.

"Now hold on, I don't know just means I don't know yet. Can you get me a secure communication link with our Governor Kraft, back up in Augusta, Maine?"

"Yes, sir," their commo replied. "We have secure comm with the military attaché in our embassy there. He can patch you through."

"OK, set it up," I said. I gave the commo the governor's private number. "Gentlemen, I'm afraid my guilty secret is out. I'm not a Field Marshal. But I know someone who is. God willing, he'll have the answer I don't."

It took about 20 minutes to put the call through. I took it privately in the XO's office. After a fair amount of crackling and hissing in the phone line—Confederate Bell, I thought—I heard Bill Kraft's welcome voice come on. "Is this the vaunted Southern Field Marshal on my phone?" he asked.

"No, sir," I replied. "This is one very junior captain calling to say he's screwed the pooch and needs some help."

"Well, well, the prodigal returns," Kraft chuckled. Luckily I'd caught him in a good mood. "Fear not, we shall kill the fatted calf. What can I do for you?"

I explained the situation to the governor. "We have an embassy in Richmond, as you know," he said. "Their estimation of the Confederate government tallies with that of your colonel there. I suspect he's correct that when Atlanta erupts, they still won't act."

"So what do I do then?" I asked.

Kraft was silent for about thirty seconds. The way his mind

worked—instantly or not at all—that was a long time. I was relieved when his voice came back up on the net. "Act for them," he said. "Act in their name. Present them with a *fait accompli*, an action so bold they have to repudiate it or take credit for it. If it works, they'll take the credit."

"You have any thoughts on what that action might be?" I asked.

"It has to resolve the situation in Atlanta," Kraft replied.

"How do I do that with one Ranger battalion?" I inquired. "They'll go into Atlanta if I ask them to, and they'll go down in a blaze of glory, but against a whole city, they'll still go down."

"You've got to use them to generate other forces," Bill said. "Exactly how to do that I can't say from up here. You're the one at the front, so you'll have to answer that question for yourself."

I thanked the governor for his advice, which did help put the puzzle together. But the key piece was still missing.

I hung up the phone and turned to go back into McMoster's office, where the Rangers were still waiting for a brilliant solution. Sergeant Danielov was standing in the doorway. "I took the liberty of listening in on the phone in the S-3's office," he said. "I've got an idea that might do the trick."

"What is it?" I asked, hoping I'd been right that if I got myself into trouble, a sergeant would get me out of it.

"Why don't we ask the Rangers to steal us a nuke?"

CHAPTER THIRTY-SIX

I T took me a few seconds to make the mental connection. What does stealing a nuke have to do with—holy shit! My jaw dropped. "You mean nuke Atlanta?" I asked Dano, astounded.

"Why not?" he replied with the typical sergeant's sang-froid.

Why not? The idea was mind-boggling. It was absurd. It was horrifying. The public would go crazy. The fallout. Possible retaliation. It was—it was the proposal of a madman.

Then, as the mental gears turned, an involuntary smile began spreading across my face. It was brilliant.

We needed to strike a single, decisive blow. A nuke would do that. We didn't have much conventional strength. This would give us the multiplier for our single Ranger battalion. We needed an act so dramatic Richmond would have to respond. This filled that bill, too. The more I looked at the problem, the better Dano's solution sounded.

Could it be done? Our Ranger friends would have to answer that one. We needed a bomb, and they'd have to get it. We also needed a bomber.

A deed such as this would would be a mouthful even for old Hans Von Seekt. But the SAS motto also came to mind: Who dares, wins.

"Well, I don't have a better idea," I said to Dano. Together we walked back into Col. McMoster's office. The Rangers looked up at us with expectant faces. "Well, we've got a solution to our problem," I said. "What would you boys think about dropping an atomic bomb on Atlanta?"

The body language told me they were going through the same reaction I did. And they ended up in the same place. After the initial shock, I saw grins spreading across the room. "Hot damn," the S-3 said. "We could call it Operation Sherman!"

"I never did like that city," chimed in a company commander.

"You can nuke Dallas too, as far as I'm concerned," a first sergeant added. "We're all country boys here. We don't like cities much."

New South versus Old South, city versus country. Mao was right, I thought. Take the countryside and the city will fall.

Col. McMoster's reaction was more thoughtful. "It would be a decisive action," he said. "The question is, how would the public react? Use of a nuclear weapon on our own soil would be a tremendous shock. On the other hand, so was New Orleans."

"What will Richmond do?" I asked.

"First, they'll diddle," McMoster replied. "Then they'll go with public opinion. It all comes back to that. If the public reacts negatively, we'll have won on the physical level, but the New South will have a moral victory. The moral level of war is far more powerful than the physical."

"I see you've also read John Boyd's stuff," I said to the colonel.

He nodded. "Boyd was probably the best military thinker the United States ever produced," he said. "His reward was to be retired as a colonel. I guess the old rule still holds: No prophet is honored in his own country."

"Not when his country is without honor," I replied.

After chewing for a while on his cigar, McMoster said, "Well, we're not without honor. I'm sick of watching these New South neo-Marxists and their gang-banger trigger men terrorize the rest of us. Terror must be answered with terror. Atlanta has earned a fiery end, no less so than Sodom or Gomorrah. It's risky, but I think the people of the Old South will go with us. We'll do it."

The Colonel's decision was greeted with a round of rebel yells from his officers. I hoped they represented the people they came from. If they did, and if we could get the weapon we needed and get it to Atlanta, the South's civil war might be over a lot sooner than I thought.

We turned immediately to the practical problems. "Getting a weapon is fairly easy," McMasters said. "The South has put all its nuclear warheads in one place, right here near Savannah, on the site of the old reactor where the stuff for warheads used to be manufactured. It's guarded by a battalion of Air Police."

We all smiled at that bit of information. I remembered the U.S. Air Force Police from my Marine Corps days. The warheads would be more secure guarded by a swarm of dachshunds.

"What about the danger of retaliation from the New South?" I asked.

"They'd have to get a warhead from the same place," McMoster replied. "When Atlanta goes up, I'll send a company to the storage site to provide some real security."

"It's downtown Atlanta we need to vaporize," the colonel continued. "We want to minimize damage to the suburbs. Most of the people there are really on our side. So we want something small, maybe five kilotons. We also need to minimize fallout. Ground detonation would stir up tons of radioactive dust and debris, so we need an air burst. That means a bomber aircraft, and where we get that I don't know. The Confederate Air Force has a lot of New South types in it—the high tech boys stick together, you know. We can't go to them for help."

"I think I have a solution to that problem, sir," Danielov said. "Captain Rumford sent me down here to hunt up some airplanes. There's a former Marine aviator in town named Terry Daktile. He got out years ago and made heaps money in real estate. When Washington fell and everything was being looted, he used some of that money to secure the Arado 234 he had seen in the Air and Space Museum. He's restored it to flying condition and takes it up on occasion. It would carry a weapon of the size we're talking about."

The Arado 234 was the world's first jet bomber, built in the waning days of World War II for a desperate Luftwaffe. I remembered seeing the one in the Smithsonian. It was a small aircraft, but a five-kiloton bomb was a small warhead. And the Arado was a bomber.

"Do you think this guy Daktile will go along with us on nuking Atlanta?" I asked. "We'll need him too, since nobody else will know how to fly the Arado."

"I'm confident he will, sir," Dano replied. "We talked politics a bit, and he's from the Attila the Hun school."

Well, Attila will get his skull pile out of this operation, I thought.

"OK, it's settled," McMoster said. "We'll have the weapon within 24 hours of Atlanta going up. Sergeant Danielov, I'll rely on you to get Daktile and his Arado here on our airfield in the same time-frame. Operation Sherman is a go—if the radicals of Atlanta do their part."

*

They did. Two days later, Dano got me out of bed at 3 AM to turn on CNN. The blacks had acted overnight, and parts of the city were burning. That morning at 07:00 the leadership of the Free Commune of Black

Atlanta staged a news conference to announce "the beginning of the liberation of the Black Man from the White Devils." Whites, Asians, and Hispanics were being slaughtered throughout the city. The New South Congress was besieged by its erstwhile allies in the Convention Center, where it issued repeated pleas for dialogue and understanding. The Commune's response was mortars and Katyusha rockets.

True Confederate President Yancey came on with his own announcement at nine that morning. He warned that "Richmond is prepared to take strong measures" to restore order in Atlanta, but also promised "to hear the grievances the people of Atlanta wished to present." It was clear Richmond was dithering, as usual.

We did not dither. The next day at dawn's early light, the Arado was on the Rangers' airfield, fueled and ready. A five-kiloton warhead was on board, with the fuse set for detonation at 3,000 feet. Terry Daktile more than filled his old Marine Corps flight suit, but his grin was that of an 18-year old kid.

The Arado was a two-seat aircraft, and while Daktile could do all that was necessary, I volunteered to fly with him. "I made the proposal for this attack, and if the public reacts badly, you can blame it on me," I told Col. McMoster.

"Thanks, but no thanks," the colonel replied. "This has to be an operation by the Confederate Armed Forces. Even if Richmond disavows it, it will show the New South that some of us can and will act. If Richmond decides to hang someone for it, it should be me they hang. You made a recommendation, as the General Staff should. But the decision to go through with Operation Sherman was mine."

I couldn't disagree with McMoster's logic, so reluctantly I stood aside. I'll confess that the little boy in me was disappointed. I'd miss the biggest light show anyone had seen since Nagasaki.

With the Texas Ranger battalion, Dano and myself standing attention on the airfield and holding the salute, the mission took off at precisely 10:00 hours. The Arado was a fast aircraft, and after it gained the necessary height, the flight would be a short one. We joined everyone who could cram into the ready room to watch CNN.

Justice occasionally does a strange little jig. By an extraordinary coincidence, CNN was devoting the morning of March 29, 2034, not to news but to a long-planned retrospective about its own early days. At ten o'clock, the network's prime news anchor welcomed to its Atlanta studio none other than the ancient wife of its founder, Ms. Jane Fonda.

At 10:43 AM, while the near-centenarian Fonda was attempting to justify her anti-war activities during the Vietnam years with an eye toward history, she became history. The former Hollywood actress, the studio, and the headquarters of CNN, along with downtown Atlanta and the entire New South government, were at that precise moment vaporized by a nuclear detonation. All we saw was the screen go dark, but we knew what it meant. The rebel yells around me were deafening.

The celebrations grew into a full triumph when the Arado returned, zooming over the airfield in a victory pass before it glided in for a three-point landing. Daktile and the colonel were soaked in bourbon as they climbed out of the cockpit, then carried shoulder-high into the ready room amidst the loud hoo-ahs of the Rangers.

Once things quieted down a bit, Colonel McMoster reminded us of the facts of the situation. "I hope you saved some bourbon for the real victory—if we win one," he said. "At this point, we don't know whether what we've done will help us or destroy us. The real fight is for the minds of our countrymen. We don't yet know how they will react. So let's cool it."

He was right. We had to wait for the news of Operation Sherman to reach the Southern people, then gauge their response. Dropping the bomb was the easy part. We now faced the real risk, public revulsion.

CNN was gone, but the other networks quickly picked up on the fact that something big had happened in Atlanta. With a bit of creative computer hacking, the Rangers got out a message from "Confederate Army units on the scene" stating that a nuclear weapon had been detonated over Atlanta. By 2 PM, the networks were reading that statement to their viewers, which by this point included almost everyone.

It took people a while to assimilate the news, get over the shock and react. By 5 PM, in Savannah and elsewhere, crowds of people were gathering in the streets.

Captain Armbruster had gone back up to Richmond to give us a direct report from the Confederate capital—now the only Confederate capital. He called in at 6:23. "Monument Avenue is packed with people," he reported. "They are waving Confederate battle flags, singing Dixie, and cheering the government. The Methodist bishop was on the tube, saying that all the churches would hold thanksgiving services at eight o'clock for, as he put it, 'delivering us from the Satan of the New South.' "

It was the same everywhere. People held torchlight parades to celebrate their liberation from New South cultural Marxism and black terror. Atlanta had been the symbol of everything they hated, and its destruction came as a great release. Finally, they thought, their leaders had acted like men.

Except, of course, they hadn't. As of nine PM on the 29th, the Confederate government had still failed to issue a statement. The people were crowded up to the Confederate White House, pushing at the front door, calling for President Yancey. But he did not appear.

During our interview, with typical southern courtesy Mr. Yancey had given me his private cell number, saying that if I needed his assistance I should contact him directly. I didn't need his assistance, but it was evident he needed mine. At 9:17, I texted the following message:

> *Mr. President: You must act, and you must act now. You can unite your people behind you by taking credit for Atlanta, or you can tear your nation apart by denying it was an act by your government. There is no other option. As Cavour said, you can do anything with bayonets except sit on them. Field Marshal Rumford.*

Just after ten PM, President Yancey finally appeared on the front steps of his official residence. His statement was brief, but it sufficed. "Fellow citizens, today your government did what had to be done. We could tolerate this sedition no longer. We regret that it had to come to this, to the destruction of a Southern city. But the choice was made by the New South, which was determined to destroy our Southern culture and replace it with the weakness and decadence of the former United States. We did not escape from that enemy in order to become it. Confederate forces are now moving to restore the authority of this government throughout the South. From here forward, there is only one South, the Old South, the True Confederacy."

Old Sam got shaken up a bit as the crowd carried him through the town, in adulation and in gratitude. But he smiled and bowed and waved his hat. No one would know that his greatness had been thrust upon him.

*

The Rangers wanted me to go up to Richmond myself, where the real story quickly became known within the inner circles. I could look forward to another round of tours, parties, and dinners. But my work was done, and my thoughts were turning homeward, toward the glories of a New England summer and the peace of a quiet farm. This time, the boys would be home before the leaves fell.

On April 6, 2034, Sergeant Danielov and I took ship at Charleston for Portland, Maine. The Rangers saw us off, after a dinner of she-crab soup, back country ham, and pecan pie at one of Charleston's better establishments. That was all the send-off we wanted.

Our voyage home again gave me time to think. I'd learned some things, including thinking an operation through to its conclusion before setting it in motion. I'd done what I was sent down there to do, and gotten pleasantly fat in the process, which was payment enough. The Confederacy still had weak leadership, especially in the military department. Laclede was hailed as the "new Jackson" after he publicly took credit for our operation.

But when I compared the South's wealth and inherent power to that of the Northern Confederation, I wasn't sure I wanted it any different.

On the way back home to Hartland, I stopped in Augusta and gave Bill Kraft the full story of what we'd done, and why. On the way out of his office, I pulled my Confederate Field Marshal's insignia from my pocket and put them on his desk. "You'll have more use than I will for these, I reckon," I said.

"The day may come when that isn't true," he replied. "You've got what it takes to run a campaign, or a war, in terms of your potential. And you're still learning, which is the most important thing. Yes, that day may come."

Then he reached out, picked up the crossed batons and put them in his desk. "But it's not here yet."

CHAPTER THIRTY-SEVEN

I'D missed the big Atlanta light show, but as if to compensate, in the Fall of 2034 the forests put on a brilliant exhibition of their own. Nature was New England's noblest artist, and she blazed the hills in orange, gold, and scarlet that year. We old-timers remember it as one of the half-dozen best vintages of our lifetimes.

I wanted to drink my fill, so after checking in at the Old Place, where my cousins had gotten my crops in, stored and sold, I headed out. The Texas Rangers had given me a surprise going away present of ten drums of gasoline, so I got the truck down off its blocks, tuned it up and drove over to New Hampshire's White Mountains to do some hiking. The White's are like an endless gallery of Winslow Homers. With the rest of the leaf-peepers long gone, I could enjoy them in the solitude art demands.

Ten days in the wilderness restored the granite of New Hampshire in my muscles and my brain. I still had plenty of gas, towed on a trailer behind the truck, so I drove across Vermont to Ft. Drum in upper New York state. We had an active battalion of light infantry there, along with our light infantry school. Unannounced inspections are the only useful kind.

I was pleased to discover nobody got nervous when I arrived unexpected. John Ross was in command of both the battalion and the school, so I anticipated I'd find both in good shape, and I did. I turned the Southern campaign I'd just come from into an Operational Decision Game for the young officers and NCOs, forbidding them to use the real solution, which made it tough for them. It was tough for me to tell the story as it happened, including my own brain fart when McMoster faced me with his "What now, Field Marshal" question. But it was important for our young soldiers to hear me admit to my own error. Only honest commanders can build honest subordinates.

Trains have the advantage of being social. You meet people on trains, talk with them, and often develop the strange intimacy that comes from knowing you will part in a few hours, never to meet again. Travel on back roads opens other windows. You see people at work in their fields, factories, and homes. You develop a sense whether towns are prospering or decaying. You get an earful from hitchhikers (astonished and delighted to get a ride in a truck, not a wagon) and town drunks and old men in the diner and young women running inns. You can take the temperature of the land you're passing through.

What I found that fall in the Northern Confederation gave me courage, and hope. People were beginning to make things work again. There was still great dislocation, and hardship. Most people were having to learn new and different ways, different from the modern, and build new lives. But the bottom was no longer falling out of everything, as it had seemed to do though the last decades of the American republic and the first years after it fell. On the streets of the small towns, people were looking out again instead of down.

Everywhere, the land was being reclaimed from wilderness for farms.

With Asia populous and growing rich, world food prices were rising fast. A small farmer could make a good living. Chinese and Japanese freighters were loading our wheat, corn, oats, cattle, and sheep as fast as we could get them to our ports.

Inland, shipping meant the railroads, and along their steel spines the Metropolitan Corridor was coming to life again. As the auto-driven malls and strips lay crumbling, the towns along the railroads were reviving. People again came to town to sell their produce and crops and to buy the manufactures they needed. Each town's railroad sidings were full of freight cars, and they didn't sit there long. Merchants, too, began to earn livings, as "Saturday night in town" saw the sidewalks thick with people and stores open. More people window-shopped than bought, but they wanted to buy, and as they got money, they would.

Some found jobs with the railroads, the single greatest employer in the 19th century. The small town station agent was again a busy man. Wherever the capital could be assembled, trails were being converted back to rails. In Schenectady, the American Locomotive Works was turning out Consolidations, Mikados, and Ten-Wheelers.

Motoring in the Northern Confederation was a slow business, not just because of the state of the roads, but because the roads had people in them: people in wagons, people on bicycles, and, mostly, people on foot. Morning and evening, the crowds of kids walking to school swarmed the highways.

Because kids can't walk very far, most of the schools they went to were local, one-room affairs. I stopped in and visited a number of them. There was one schoolteacher, usually a woman. She taught the older kids, and they did most of the teaching of the younger kids, which meant they really had to learn the material. Most communities had again posted the Ten Commandments up front by the blackboard—these schools relied on chalk, not computers—and everyplace I visited, the children were hard at work. No one need fear sending their kids to these public schools.

The roads were also full of people, walking, on Sundays. Dressed in the best clothes they had, they were going to or coming from church. Often, they did so twice, for morning and evening services, often with a big meal at someone's house along the way. Like most else, the churches didn't have much money—the priest or preacher got paid in hens or firewood or eggs, most of the time—but they did again have people in them. Lots of people. Along most of the roads I traveled, new churches were going up, even when nothing else was. Priorities were changing.

Life was becoming local again, and local means real. The scale of most things was small. People found they could get their hands around their lives without everything running through their fingers. News was what the neighbor said over the back fence. The economy was the price of eggs or corn or butter. The girl's heartthrob was the boy next door. Music was grandmother at the piano.

Most of the new ways people were discovering were old ways. Sometimes they knew that. Most often they probably didn't, not then, not yet. But they were discovering what worked, and what worked was usually old, because we now lived under the same conditions people had known for many generations. And those generations had learned some things.

Poets write odes to the sweet air in Spring. I found a sweet smell in our air that fall. It wasn't just the wood smoke.

*

By the time I got home to Hartland on the 14th of November, the leaves were gone, the fields were brown and the sky was speaking of snow.

I wanted to spend the Winter at home, working on the General Staff histories of the Northern Confederation's campaigns and an assessment of the Confederacy's forces. I put the second first, partly to do it while it was fresh in my mind and partly because it was shorter. I had a draft by Thanksgiving, enough to send to Augusta. My mind was eager to get into the campaign histories like a kid is eager for Christmas. Everything in the way of it seemed tedious and exasperating. My ear's dread of a phone call summoning me to another von Sander's mission added to my impatience.

The phone call didn't come. Instead, on the bright, prematurely frigid morning of December 5, 2034, someone knocked on the front door. I knew it had to be a stranger, because the locals all came around back to the mud room behind the kitchen. Maine front doors were reserved for formal events, and Maine didn't have many of those.

I opened the door to find a big, square-jawed, blond-haired, blue-eyed kid, obviously military, but not in uniform. My first take was that it was one of our sergeants or junior officers, come to pay a call on his CO. If he wanted to see me enough to make his way to Hartland in winter, he was welcome to some of my time. He might learn something, and so might I. Here again, Maine wasn't formal.

"Good morning, Captain Rumford," the kid said, snapping a salute. "I'm *Hauptsturmführer* Halsing of the Wisconsin *Landwehr*. I have a letter for you from our Leader, Herr von Braun."

I was astonished to find a foreign officer at my door with no heads-up from our Border Control people. "Where did you come through immigration?" I asked sharply.

"I didn't, sir."

I looked at him wonderingly. "Are you saying you infiltrated across our border, then E-and-E'd your whole way up here without getting caught?"

"Yes, sir."

"Why? We would have let you pass."

"Those were my orders from Leader von Braun, sir. We do not question our Leader's orders."

"Sounds like I have a problem with the Border Patrol. You should have been shot."

"Your Border Patrol was good, sir. But I'm better. Triumph of the will, sir."

"And the future belongs to you, I suppose. It sounds to me more like the triumph of some first-class field craft," I said. "Well, you've earned some breakfast, anyway. Come on in. I'll take a look at Herr Braun's letter while you help yourself. There's bread, apple butter, and oatmeal, and you're welcome to boil an egg."

We headed for the kitchen, where the captain gave me the letter. I sat down at the table while he secured some chow, which he did like he not only knew my kitchen but owned it. No shy puppy this, I thought. That was seldom a Nazi failing.

I knew of Leader Braun. He had put together something called the Party of Will out in Wisconsin and Minnesota. Thanks to cities like Milwaukee and St. Paul, those states had gotten a good taste of the disorder that engulfed the rest of the Midwest. It wasn't as bad as Illinois or Pennsylvania, but it was bad enough to get the local Germans and Scandinavians riled. Northern peoples haven't much tolerance of disorder, and when they get mad, which they don't do easily, they don't just sound off. They kill.

Braun was trying to organize the killing. His Party of Will spouted a vaguely Nazi ideology, built around the usual Aryan superiority, the need for order, extermination of the *Untermenschen* and so on. He'd organized a militia, which was hardly unique, but his seemed to have a more serious military edge than most. They'd sustained a major, month-long cross-border operation into the Chicago area to wipe out black gangs raiding up into Wisconsin. That meant they had a serious supply-and-maintenance organization, among other things. Halsing's rank, which was straight out of the SS organization chart, told me what they were using for a model.

Herr Braun's letterhead was a black eagle with long, straight wings, beneath which was a funny three-legged device I recognized as the symbol of the Dutch SS division during World War II. He wasn't quite to the point of resurrecting the swastika, it seemed. But the content of the letter suggested that would come soon enough.

Dear Captain Rumford!

Greetings from the Aryan Heartland! I write first to express my personal approval for your brilliant actions in defending the White Race and Aryan Culture in eastern North America. I am personally admiring of the Germanic decisiveness of your successful campaigns.

I guessed I was supposed to be grateful for Herr Braun's personal whatever. He would be disappointed to learn it had not previously entered my calculations, nor was it likely to.

For us, the decisive moment is coming also. The Black-Jewish-Freemason conspiracy is yet alive on our soil. But its fate will soon be determined. Hourly, our Landwehr and Freikorps swell with eager Aryan recruits. The Will to Power is in their blood, and it cannot be denied. Everything inferior will be reduced to ashes under its feet.

When that moment comes, a Fourth Reich will arise from our rich Northern soil. All that was lost in 1945 will stand forth again, cleansed and renewed, stronger and harder for the experience of temporary defeat. The Will of the Leader and the iron discipline of those who follow him will prove to all time that Racial Mastery cannot be denied. It is an Iron Law of History.

My personal Will to Power ensures our victory. However, I am aware that others have roles to play in our Aryan Triumph. Your achievements in the Blood-sacrifice of War grant you the honor of joining us. I have personally ordered that a place on our muster rolls be reserved for you, with the rank of Obergruppenführer. Hauptsturmffführer Halsing will escort you to our Free, Aryan, Unspotted land where the Will Triumphs.

Sieg Heil!

Von Braun

Under this humble petition was a postscript, in Braun's handwriting, perhaps to avoid appearing on the archival copy:

Please regard this as a formal request to your government for your assistance as an advisor to our Party and its armed forces.

Von Braun, indeed, I thought. Where did he get his "von," from, a cereal box? An image swam unstoppably into my mind: Charlie Chaplin in *The Great Dictator*.

My first reaction was to throw the letter in the stove and send Captain Halsing on his way, this time with a *laissez passer* so he wouldn't embarrass our border guards again. I glanced at him across the table, where he was working on his third boiled egg. His expressionless face and chiseled features gave the contradictory impression of an android feeding. After weeks on the lam dodging our patrols and everyone else he met, he was clean, carefully shaven, immaculate. In World War II, American soldiers always wondered how the German officers they captured managed that.

Halsing caught my gaze. "Thank you for breakfast, sir. Do you have any work I can do while I'm here?"

"After what you went through to get here, I'd expect you'd rather take a long nap. Is this part of the Iron Man competition?"

"We are all iron men in the Party of Will, sir," Halsing answered.

"Work makes you free, eh?" I took a good look at the *Hauptsturm-*

führer's bulging biceps and ox-like shoulders. "Waal, I got a couple cords of wood out back that need splitting. You're welcome to make a start on that chore if you really want to work."

"Thank you, sir," Halsing said, in a voice without a hint of irony or anything else. Which of La Mettrie's books applied to him, I wondered, *Man the Machine* or *Man the Plant?* I watched as he methodically took his dishes to the sink, washed them and put them all away in the right places. He then went straight to the maul, which was hidden away behind the kitchen door to the barn.

"Excuse me Captain, but I've got to ask you a question. How do you know my place so damn well?" I said.

"I had you under observation for three days before I came in, sir," he replied.

"You must have been in awful close to know where things are in my kitchen."

"Yes, sir. I was in your kitchen, sir, among other places."

I glared at him, then at the house dog, an old mixed shepherd bitch named Brunnhilde who was stretched out as close to the stove as she could get. "Nice work, girl," I said to the dog. She rolled her eyes and beat her tail feebly. "Nice work on your part too, Captain," I added quite sincerely. He was the perfect Nazi, cold and competent.

"Thank you, sir. I'll get to the woodpile now," he responded, picking up the maul like a 20-pound toothpick and heading out the back door. Shortly thereafter came the sound of a pile-driver at work. The intervals were short, and the regular rhythm told me no log took more than one blow. The wood was ash and locust, with plenty of knots in it. The thought crossed my mind that I might not want to disappoint this captain too deeply.

I looked at the letter from Halsing's Leader as it lay among the crumbs on the breakfast table. My inclination was still to toss it into the stove. But I'd learned the hard way that first impulses were not to be trusted. I picked the letter up, took it with me into the study where my barely-begun history looked up invitingly, and lit a cigar. I knew a cigar before lunch was garment district, but I needed to think and tobacco wakes the mind.

The reasons to refuse Herr Braun's request were easy enough to catalogue. I didn't like Nazis. I thought the past, what America had and was from around 1865 to about 1965, was better than what had followed, better even than what we had now in the N.C. Bill Kraft's Retroculture appealed to me. The Nazis were nothing if not modern. Hitler would have loved computers and color television and the rest of the video screen infernal devices.

The Nazis also disliked Christianity—Nietzsche's "slave religion"— and had tried to revive Norse paganism in the Third Reich. Funny how the real pagan revival had come from the radical left, the goddess-worshipping feminists and the Gaia-worshipping greens, in the last years of the American republic. Little did they realize whose hand they were holding. My own Christian faith had grown stronger, year by year, as realities like war and poverty and the deaths of too many friends stripped away my spiritual *impedimenta*. Besides, I knew enough history to know where Nietzsche's philosophy came from: his syphilis.

There was the Holocaust to reckon in the account. I didn't put as high a value on that as some people did. History, ancient and modern, was full of holocausts, one people wiping another people out. Met any Carthaginians lately? Jews had carried out plenty of holocausts of their own. The Old Testament was full of them. As a butcher and a tyrant, Hitler ran a distant second to Stalin. That didn't excuse him, but I found it difficult to put a higher moral value on six million Jews than on eight million Ukrainian Christians, not to mention the other 52 million killed by Soviet communism. Or the 78 million Chinese and Tibetans killed by its Maoist strain.

Of course, I was also partly responsible for nuking Atlanta, so some might question my moral own abacus. With reason.

What made the Holocaust unique was its impersonal, industrial efficiency. That, more than the killing itself, got towards the heart of why I didn't like Nazism. In an ideal Nazi state, every aspect of life would be icily efficient. The whole place would be one vast factory, with every machine working perfectly, and every person merely another, identical machine. My Utopia came from Tolkien: The Shire, where fuddy-duddy hobbits smoked their long pipes, endlessly re-told the same stories and liked their meals regular. The Nazis would have built an autobahn through The Shire and turned it over to the Strength Through Joy department, with mandatory calisthenics at 05:30.

But there was another side to the coin. Leader Braun and his boys were up against the same canaille we'd had to fight: Black Muslims, the Dykes on Bikes Motorcycle Cavalry Brigade, the Theban Band, Deep Greeners, the whole zoo. Minnesota had long been loony-left country, and they had a real chance of winning out there. If the lunatics won, the Christians would go up the chimneys. This wasn't the kind of war where anyone took prisoners.

Nazi efficiency had its hellish aspect, but chaos was a greater hell. It wasn't called pandemonium for nothing. The first need of any people is for order. In most of the old industrial Midwest, chaos had already claimed hundreds of thousands of lives. Nazism would restore order, no question about that. More, it would restore competence. Captain Halsing was probably one of their best, but he was also a model. There would be more Captain Halsings in a Nazi state, and they would bring relief to a people groaning under a hopeless present and a future of despair. That was, after all, why Hitler came to power in Germany, through an election, not a coup. And he delivered in a way, he made Germany work again and gave hope to a beaten, suffering people.

There was also the possibility that, if I were to go out with Halsing and help put Farmer Brown in power, he wouldn't last. The fact that he aspired to be an evil genius like Hitler didn't make him one. This looked like history first as tragedy, then as farce. A Nazi regime that decayed quickly would probably not return to chaos. The forces of chaos would have been liquidated quickly, as its first order of business. More probably, it would evolve into something authoritarian, but not totalitarian. In an authoritarian state, everything that is not permitted is forbidden. Under totalitarianism, everything that is not forbidden is compulsory. The latter was unbearable, but the former tolerable, and in a time of general collapse it might be a fair trade-off for order and competence. Nazi ideology was empty enough that it also might collapse, leaving a vacuum that could be filled by a return to tradition.

Half-way through my second Upmann, I made a decision. My decision was that this was above my pay grade and I'd buck it up the chain. There were more subtleties in the situation than my Marine brain could untangle. I turned to reach for the telephone, and caught Halsing standing in the doorway, still holding the maul. An image of Trotsky's fate flitted through my mind.

"Had enough wood-chopping for one morning's PT?" I asked.

"No, sir. I've split all the wood you've got out there," Halsing answered.

I glanced at the clock, which said twenty before twelve. "You got through almost two cord in just over two hours?" He wasn't sweating, either.

"Yes, sir. Do you have any more work for me?"

"Waal, I got a couple acres of trees that ought to come down some-time," I replied. "Think you could handle that this afternoon and be done by supper?"

"Yes, sir. Where away?"

"That was a joke, Halsing," I said. "Not even Nietzsche's superman himself could work that fast."

"We are *Übermenschen* in the Party of Will, sir," he replied. "And we don't joke about work."

"What do you joke about?"

"Jews."

"Yeah, I might have guessed. Well, I expect we'll be traveling this afternoon, so the trees will live another day. I'm taking you and your letter down to see Governor Kraft. He'll decide our response."

I called Bill Kraft and got an appointment with him the next morn-ing. I still had a good supply of Confederate gas, so we took the truck down to Waterville to catch the afternoon train. Being with me would cover Halsing's lack of entry documents, if he were challenged. I half hoped he would be; it would be fun to watch someone ask a Nazi, "May I see your papers, please?" As it happened, the trip was uneventful, be-yond my watching Halsing take careful mental note of the terrain along way. Androids never sleep.

*

At 07:30 the next morning, Captain Halsing and I presented our-selves at Bill Kraft's office. Bill wasn't a morning person, which is why I'd requested an early meeting. I figured he'd be in a surly mood and thus more likely to say no to Leader Braun's request. I really didn't want to go on this one.

I explained the case briefly, and handed Bill the letter. He read it silently, without expression. After taking a few minutes to think, he turned to *Hauptsturmführer* Halsing. "Are you familiar with the contents of this letter?" he asked.

"Yes, sir," Halsing replied.

"What do you think our answer will be?" Bill inquired.

"You'll refuse, sir," Halsing answered.

"You're right," said our Governor. "You may inform your Leader to that effect. I would rather not enter into correspondence with him myself. Let's just say we State o' Mainers believe in maintaining standards. But I do want him, and you, to understand why we refuse you. It won't do him any good, but it might do you some.

"It's not just the usual Nazi stuff, the ranting, the anti-Semitism, the demand for total control of every aspect of everyone's life. It's more basic than that.

"You see, Captain, your 'ism,' and every 'ism,' is an ideology. Ideology itself is wrong —always, everywhere.

"The word 'ideology', and the thing itself, came from that Pandora's Box of the Enlightenment, the French Revolution. An ideology takes a set of ideas, from one philosopher or another, and from them constructs an abstract ideal of how society should work. Invariably, the ideal runs afoul of human nature and of reality itself. Perhaps you remember the Third Reich joke that the ideal Nazi is slim like Göring and blond like Hitler.

"When an ideology attains power, it attempts to force reality to conform with its vision. But reality cannot do that. In response, the ideology becomes fiercer in its methods of compulsion: from fines and expropriations it moves to jail sentences, labor or re-education camps, random terror, pogroms, relocations of peoples, and finally simply to organized slaughter.

"In response, the people learn to live a lie. A façade of Communism or Fascism or political correctness or whatever is laid over reality. But reality itself does not change, because it cannot. People remain people, and human nature is constant.

"Eventually, a generation reared under the lie comes to power, knowing it is a lie. It clings to power, but no longer believes. Mere cynicism governs. Eventually, that collapses in on itself, and society is released. But in the meantime, grave damage has been done to culture and civilization, and people have perished in the thousands or millions, all to no purpose. No ideology can escape this fate, because of the nature of ideology itself."

"What about your own ideology of Retroculture, sir?" Halsing asked. He'd obviously been well briefed for his mission.

Bill Kraft smiled. "That's not an ideology, Captain, but an escape from ideology and a return to organic society. Up until the early 1960s, when the ideology of cultural Marxism began to take over, America had not been an ideological society. Like our English forebears, we thought and lived the way we did because those ways had grown up naturally, over many generations. That kind of society is philosophically untidy, but it works as well as human society can. Instead of contradicting human nature, it develops from it. Burke's analogy was to the root system of a great tree. It follows no apparent pattern, but it is deep, and strong, and gets the job done. Have you ever read Burke, Captain?"

"No, sir," Halsing replied.

"You might want to do so. He would give you some things to think about," Bill said.

"My Leader does my thinking for me," Halsing answered.

"Ah yes, the True Believer. Well, remember my warning: Your children will laugh at you, and your grandchildren will despise you."

"I've got a question, Captain," I interjected. "You said you expected us to refuse your Leader's request for assistance. I'd be interested in knowing why."

"You lack will, sir," Halsing answered.

"What makes you think so?" Bill asked.

"What I saw on my way from your western border to Hartland, sir," Halsing said. "You're allowing niggers to move into your countryside. I saw ads for kosher products in some towns. You don't have the will to exterminate the unfit. Captain Rumford didn't have the will to shoot a dog that let me into his house. You're supposed to be the military leader here, and you don't have the will to keep yourself in shape. You're fat."

"*Stillgestanden!*" Bill roared at the top of his lungs. Halsing came to German attention, feet at a 45 degree angle, fingers straight down his legs.

"I will have you know I am in perfect shape for the operational level of war," Bill barked. "I am fully capable of boarding the train that will take me to the next chateau. I will convince you, Captain, that the leadership of the Northern Confederation does not lack will." Bill reached over and pushed a button on his desk. Immediately, half-a-dozen big soldiers from the battalion stationed in Augusta—no ceremonial troops these—came in from the outer office. Two were carrying a full set of leg irons and chains.

"Captain, you are under arrest for illegal entry into the Northern Confederation," Bill pronounced. "You will be cast in chains and escorted directly to Portland harbor, where you will be put on the first ship leaving for a foreign port, regardless of destination."

Halsing remained at attention while our boys chained him fast. Then they frog-marched him out of the governor's office. Bill had a sparkle in his eye, but I felt sorry for the captain. He had carried out his mission perfectly, and it was one that had been far from easy. I would have liked to offer him a commission in our own Spec Ops unit, Nazi or no Nazi.

I knew the governor didn't usually have troops in his outer office, ready and waiting with a set of chains for anyone who referenced his ample girth. "I guess you saw that one coming," I said to him.

Bill smiled sarcastically. "Good theater always requires a bit of work behind the curtain," he replied. "Nazis used theater brilliantly—remember the Nuremburg rallies—and I thought it appropriate to turn their own tool against them. The captain will remember his experience longer than he will remember any of my words."

"Well, I'm glad you decided as you did. I would have had trouble keeping a straight face if I'd had to work with 'Führer Braun'."

"Fear not, my boy, we won't waste your talents," Bill replied, and with that I knew I was dismissed.

I figured I'd spend a few days in Augusta taking care of this and that before I headed home, finally to get into writing the history. The next day, as I was making marginal notes on some training reports, most having to do with maintaining the proper balance between training in techniques and training in tactics—the two are opposites—someone knocked on my office door. It was my adjutant, and with him were three of the troops I'd seen in the governor's office the day before. They'd had the shit kicked out of them.

"What happened?" I asked one, Lance Corporal Rollings, who had a broken nose and missing front teeth.

"He jumped us, sir," the Lance Corporal replied.

"He being whom?" I inquired.

"Captain Halsing, sir."

"How can one man in chains jump six?"

"Only three of us went down to Portland with him, sir."

"So one man in chains jumped only three of our men. That's reassuring. Precisely how did he take such unfair advantage of you?"

"Well, sir, we were on the train, sir, in a box car with some freight, and I guess we were smokin' and jokin' when we shouldn't have been. But he was all chained up, so we didn't think about it much. Somehow he got loose."

"Sir, we found a nail in the lock on the leg irons," the adjutant said. "He probably picked it up in the freight car."

"And, despite being in handcuffs, picked the lock," I said. "How did he get the cuffs off?"

"He didn't, sir."

"So still in handcuffs, he beat the crap out of three of our biggest men?"

"Yes, sir," Rollings answered, his expression reminding me very much of Brunnhilde's, back in my kitchen. "He knew how to use his boots, sir."

"Where is Captain Halsing now?" I was going to offer this guy a commission whether Bill Kraft liked it or not.

"We don't know, sir."

"You mean he got away?"

"Yes, sir," the adjutant replied. "He apparently timed his move so that he broke free just before the rail bridge over the Androscoggin. He jumped from the train into the river."

Good map recon, I thought. "Has anybody searched in the river and along the banks?"

"Yes, sir," the adjutant answered. "We didn't find anything. We assume he died in the fall or drowned."

"Remember, Lieutenant, that assume makes an ass of you and me. I suspect our young Nazi is alive, well, and on his way home."

"Do you want us to search again, sir?"

"No. He earned his getaway fair and square. Let him have it. As for you," I said as I turned to face our three stooges, "Private Rollings, you and your two fellow privates are in charge of cleaning the barracks' heads until further notice. You are obviously incapable of any higher responsibilities."

*

About three months later, I got a nice letter from Captain Halsing, postmarked Milwaukee, thanking me for my hospitality. He was the model Nazi, cold, competent, and perfectly polite.

CHAPTER THIRTY-EIGHT

As it turned out, the Nazis took over Wisconsin while the cultural Marxists conquered Minnesota. Jews, blacks, Hispanics, and feminists fled Wisconsin for Minnesota, running headlong into whites and Asians coming the other way. Leader Braun set up a concentration camp at Oshkosh, with gas chambers, ovens, the whole works, and began building a new state capitol in the form of a swastika so huge it would be visible from space. In Minneapolis, the Catholic bishop, the Orthodox Archimandrite, and the pastor of the First Baptist church were crucified together in front of city hall, while the city of St. Paul was renamed Saul.

Neither regime lasted very long. Braun, along with most of his top henchmen, fell victim to an unexplained release of Zyklon-B during a "Beer Hall Night" in the Rathskeller of the new state capitol building. In a brief but bloody civil war, the remaining Nazis were defeated and locked up in their own concentration camp, where they escaped only as smoke. The victorious militias actually held a clean, statewide election for governor, which was won by a former mayor of Milwaukee known for his love of traditional architecture and desire to bring back streetcars. Wisconsin remained orderly and set about recovering its past.

Minnesota, on the other hand, disintegrated into the usual chaos of ethnic urban gangs, shoot-on-sight rural militias and wandering, bizarre cultic tribes. No central authority arose that could make anything work. On the whole, of the two states, Minnesota had the worst of it. Order, even from a defective source, is better than anarchy.

But order carries its own bad seed: totalitarianism. Totalitarianism did not come to Wisconsin, because it's hard to revive a dead ideology. The corpse may dance, but the wires always show and the ultimate effect is comic. Live ideologies, however, were not in short supply in the early 21st century. We in the N.C. watched with growing concern as one brought totalitarianism to Cascadia: the ideology of Deep Green.

Cascadia itself was the foal of a bastard and a witch. The illegitimate father was centralized government planning, and the hag on a broomstick was Gaia, the Earth Goddess of extreme environmentalism. Both had long fattened in Oregon, Washington, and British Columbia, which as early as the 1990s were calling themselves Cascadia and flying their own flag.

Portland, Oregon, the Cascadian capital, had a deserved reputation for the most intrusive government in the old United States. Red Bureaucrats dictated land use, housing densities, racial balances, environmental protection, you name it, not only for the city but for the rest of the state as well. The urban-rural split that played so large in America's second Civil War was established early in Oregon. Well before the end of the 20th century, the rest of the state hated Portland. But Portland had the numbers and the votes, so it got what it wanted.

The pieces to the puzzle of environmental totalitarianism were also on the board early, though few people put them together. The environmentalists portrayed themselves as simple, peaceful people who loved furry little animals and green, growing things, who wanted nothing more than clean air and water, deep forests to roam in and craggy shores free of unsightly commercial development. Most other people wanted these things, too, so environmentalists came across as the good guys.

What they really wanted was power. They knew that everything ultimately comes from the earth, and whoever controls the earth controls everything else. More, every human action affects the environment, so in the environment's name, every human action can be controlled. Environmentalism was the perfect justification for totalitarian power.

As with communism or Nazism, there were plenty of warnings. As early as the 1980s, factories were being closed, large tracts of land made off-limits to humans, and thousands of jobs lost to protect nominally endangered species like snail darters, which turned out to be more prolific than thought, and spotted owls, which weren't even a separate species. Property rights were overturned with abandon but without compensation. Farmers went to jail for filling in low spots along a fence because someone called them protected wetlands. The EPA became America's Gestapo, but because its agents didn't wear leather trench coats and black fedoras, few people saw them for what they were. The few who did were labeled extremists or friends of pollution.

Just as Hitler did in *Mein Kampf*, the enviro-Nazis published their grim vision of America's future. At a huge eco-conference in Vancouver, B.C. in 1990, U.N. Envirocrat Mostafa Tolba said, "I am advocating The User's Fee—a fee for using the environmental resources like air." Earth First! co-founder Dave Foreman said, "A human life has no more intrinsic value than an individual grizzly bear life. If it came down to a confrontation between a grizzly and a friend, I'm not sure whose side I'd be on. But I do know humans are a disease, a cancer on nature." Australian eco-freak Richard Jones added, "An ant is as much a part of God as a polar bear, or a koala, or you and me…I think they're all spiritually equal."

They were even open about their lying. In October of 1989, *Discover* magazine quoted one of the many professional prophets of environmental doom, Stephen Schneider:

> *We need to get some broad-based support, to capture the public's imagination. That, of course, entails getting loads of media coverage. So we have to offer up scary scenarios, make simplified, dramatic statements, and make little mention of any doubts we may have.*

The prophets of global warming in the 21st century were often the same people who in the 1970s had warned about a coming ice age. But most of the media were caught up in the environmentalism fad, so the contradictions were ignored and the real scientists whose work debunked the fanatics received no mention.

It didn't take long for the binary munition of government power and environmentalist ideology to begin spewing poison. Cascadia became independent in 2027, elected its first Green Party majority in 2029, and by 2030 had outlawed nuclear and coal-fired power plants, gasoline-powered automobiles, fireplaces and wood stoves, backyard grills, lawnmowers, and pets. In the enthusiasm ideology begets, most Cascadians put up with cold, dark houses, sore feet, weed-lot lawns, and boiled wieners. But when the government started grabbing their dogs and cats on the grounds that it was "degrading for an animal to be owned by a human," some resisted. Those who did were sent to sensitivity camps where they were compelled to go naked except for a dog collar, walk on all fours, and bark or meow for their suppers.

Cascadia had yearly elections to its governing body, a 3,000-member General Assembly that met only once, to elect a thirteen-member governing board called Paleopitus. For the rest of the year Paleopitus ran the show. The election of 2031 put four Deep Greeners on the Paleopitus. That year, Cascadia introduced an annual Air Tax of 20 percent of total assets, in return for which the taxpayer got a license that allowed him to breathe. It adopted the French Revolutionary calendar, in which the names of the months reflected the seasons and all Jewish and Christian holidays were eliminated. All cars except those propelled by electricity or pedals were banned, and by law, if a car hit an animal, the car had to be destroyed. One amendment even ordered the removal of all automobile windshields on the grounds that they killed beneficial insects.

In 2032, the Deep Greeners attained a majority on the Paleopitus and the gloves came off. All killing of animals was forbidden and the sale, possession, or eating of meat was outlawed. Anyone caught "carnivoring" was executed with a sledgehammer blow to the head. Pedestrians were compelled to sweep the sidewalk in front of them lest they step on a bug. Worship of the Earth Goddess, Gaia, was made Cascadia's state religion. People who refused to dance around the sacred Maypole had their children taken from them to be reared as Gaian Vestals—boys as well as girls—while the parents were condemned to slave labor demolishing Cascadia's dams, its only remaining source of electricity. The dams, it seemed, were offensive to fish.

By 2033, Cascadian cities and towns were organized into "goves" where everyone was encouraged to denounce everyone else for the crime of "Ecocide." Swatting flies or mosquitoes, pulling weeds, or owning a flush toilet all counted. Trial came before Green Courts where animals made up the jury. A seer interpreted their votes, which were always guilty. The automatic penalty was revocation of your breathing license, followed by tying a plastic bag over your head.

The bag, of course, was reusable.

That summer, at the Solstice Festival, the eleven Deep Green members of Paleopitus pushed the two remaining Light Greeners into the grizzly bear pit, annulled the elections as a waste of paper and announced they were gods. The official pronouncement of their divinity stated that "all creatures are filled with the Goddess, but some are fuller than others." There was no hint of irony, probably because humor had been outlawed as a Waste of Air.

*

By this time, a majority of Cascadians had learned their lesson about environmental ideologues. They were cold, hungry, and frightened. But they had another lesson yet to learn: Getting rid of totalitarians is a great deal harder than inviting them in. The Deep Greeners had created an efficient police state, enforced by stooges who received "Gaia's Offerings" of fuel, warm clothes, food—including meat—"given by a Nature grateful for their worship." In Cascadia as in Stalin's Russia, mass deprivation was itself the most effective tool for control, because anyone exempted from it was utterly loyal from the understandable terror of being hurled down again amongst the hungry masses.

The winter of 2033–2034 was a harsh one in the old American Northwest, and mass suffering graduated into mass starvation. Except for the gods and their Deep Green enforcers, no one had power, heat, or fat in their diet. As in a POW camp, the fat got thin and the thin died. There weren't many fat people after a half-decade of Deep Green rule, so the deaths were counted by the thousands. The government began distributing protein packs of flat, flabby "nutrients." Guessing its origin, people called it Soylent Green.

Normal tyrants might have eased up at this point. But the gods of the Paleopitus were not satisfied by thousands of human sacrifices. Humans were, after all, still a cancer on the Earth. The Western World, to which Cascadia had once belonged, had "criminally deprived their brown and black brothers on Gaia of a rightful share of Gaia's gifts." The goddess was still angry over this injustice. So Cascadia would pay reparations. Her remaining resources—her timber, old and new growth, her minerals, her agricultural products—were offered as gifts to whatever Third World countries would take them.

That winter, the stripping of eastern Cascadia began. Work parties of starving men and women began hacking down the trees, digging up the earth (topsoil being one of the natural gifts on offer), packing up the apples and other produce and hauling it in man-drawn carts to Cascadian ports. There, Chinese ships were waiting to take it away—all of it. There was no Spring in Cascadia that year. There was nothing left to bloom.

The tiny elite at the top of the ideological heap still lived well. It soon became known that Cascadia's riches weren't actually going to her brown and black brothers. The ships in Portland, Seattle, and Vancouver harbors were all Chinese for a reason. Cascadia had been sold to China, for gold. The gods of the Paleopitus all had Swiss bank accounts. Absolute power had once again corrupted absolutely.

Ideology had come full circle, as it always did. Communism promised a classless society and created a ruling class unparalleled in its selfishness, greed, and brutality. Nazism promised the mastery of the *Herrenvolk* and ended up with Germany incinerated and occupied. Deep Green promised a natural paradise and turned a beautiful country into one vast, hideous strip mine, a place of dust and ashes. A Shire had become a Mordor.

People resisted as best they could. They ran away from the labor parties, or else did as little work as possible. Everybody stole what they could. Tools broke or disappeared. People raised illegal chickens, even cows, and bribed the inspectors with butter or eggs. Above all, people fled. Cascadia's borders were heavily patrolled by the EPA, renamed the Environmental Police Agency and *de jure* as well as *de facto*, but the countryside was wild and escape and evasion were relatively easy. The only thing that kept most people from walking out of Cascadia was physical weakness, the product of their scanty vegetarian diet.

One day in March of 2034, a party of high mucketymucks from Portland went out into the woods west of the Willamette to spur on the clear-cutting. Time was money, and Chinese ships didn't like to wait. Since the journey was easy and the weather fine, one of the goddesses of the Paleopitus deigned to go along. She led the mere mortals through the forest, giving clear orders about what was to be cut and how soon. Her tone did not encourage delay. Coming upon one stand of old growth, her petulance turned to anger. She specifically remembered ordering it cut down two months ago. The gold from that timber was destined for a statue of Ceres which was to adorn Seattle harbor. It was a matter of particular interest to her, since Ceres's face would be modeled on her own.

Turning to select a victim, she found herself alone. Furious, she started back down the trail, thinking blood. At the first bend she found it. Her chief attendant lay dead with an arrow through her throat. The feathers on the arrow, she noted, had come from a spotted owl. That wasn't surprising, since the owls were plentiful, but touching one was a capital offense nonetheless. Someone would pay.

It took half a minute for the goddess to realize that her own immortality might soon be put to the test. Running now, she found the rest of her entourage, slain the same way, spaced by bends in the trail. The column had been picked off one by one, from the rear, the last man falling as soon as his predecessor had turned out of sight. Arrows are silent, and the throat shots had prevented any cries.

The search party found the goddess just before evening. She, too, had died with an arrow through her throat. She had also been skinned, and her hide splayed and tacked up on a large tree just as animal skins had once been nailed to barn doors for drying.

Had the Cascadian Paleopitus possessed the slightest shred of wisdom, or even a morsel of healthy fear, they would have hushed the whole thing up. But, as tyrants will, they had cut themselves off from any hint or suggestion that they were less than wildly popular. Certain the citizens of Cascadia would rise as one person in horror and outrage over the vile crime, they trumpeted it from the housetops. But no one answered the trumpet's call.

Instead, a despairing people found hope. Resistance spread. Work parties plunged their picks into the backs of their guards instead of the earth. Firearms were scarce—gun control had been near the top of the Green agenda, since guns killed furry little creatures—and bows required skill, but crossbows filled the gap. They were easy to aim and shoot, and secret armories were soon turning them out in numbers. Ambushes became common.

The Paleopitus stripped Cascadia faster, now trying to deprive guerrillas of cover as well as earn a quick renminbi. The Deep Green's shock troops had always been kids, who were brought up on environmental ideology from their first day in kindergarten. Now, those teenagers were making environmentalism itself the object of their rebellion. So the Paleopitus began importing Green mercenaries from Europe. There, the movement hadn't gone so far as to expose its real nature, and a combination of ideological appeal and payment in gold sucked in Czechs, Spaniards, and Swedes. They called the foreign units "John Muir Brigades." And Cascadians learned why the Diet of Worms was what most Germans ate during the Thirty Years War.

*

High summer is wonderful in Maine. The mud's dried up, the black flies are slowing down and for at least a month you can ignore the depleted state of the woodpile. Some days you can even go without long underwear, so long as you don't have to spend too much time in the barn early in the morning.

The high summer of 2035 found me enjoying the squire's life in Hartland, working in my fields in the morning and on the campaign history in the afternoon. The sergeant who was helping me with the documentation even knew how to cook. Life didn't get much better than that, at least for those of us who like to think big but live small.

Still, I was not unhappy when Bill Kraft called. We'd both been watching events in Cascadia, and Bill shared my fears. The N.C. already had one brush with the Deep Greeners, and the fact that Deep Green made a mess of Cascadia didn't eliminate the danger. Ideologies so blind those who swallow them that facts don't matter, and they move across borders easier than other plagues. If Bill wanted me to head West, I was ready to go.

He did. The resistance in Cascadia was mostly leaderless resistance, because that was the hardest kind for totalitarians to fight. But the local groups were beginning to coordinate. They had set up a support network in Montana and Idaho, both of which had remained orderly and democratic thanks to long established and self-disciplined militias. That network had contacted us and asked for our help.

The train ride from Waterville down to Augusta on July 8 gave me time to think. The more I considered the situation, the more I realized the strategic center of gravity might lie further west than Cascadia itself.

So long as the Deep Greeners could export Cascadia's resources, they could get foreign exchange. So long as they could get foreign exchange, they could import mercenaries. The 21st century offered plenty of armies for rent. In this as in many other things, post-modern was pre-modern. So long as the gods of the Paleopitus could import troops, the best the Cascadian resistance could hope for was some sort of stalemate. I had no interest in fighting for a stalemate, so as I saw it, the problem couldn't be solved locally. The enemy's hinge was the link to Chinese money, and the way to strike it was from the other end.

I had arranged to meet the governor over dinner on July 10th. This time, I wanted Bill to be in a receptive mood, which meant a good meal, a decent wine, and a late hour. July 9 was my birthday, and when Father Dimitri, our indefatigable Russian ambassador, heard I was in town he invited me for dinner. Over a summer meal of iced vodka, cold borscht, and cucumbers in sour cream I laid out the Cascadian situation as I saw it. If we were going to act in Asia, we would need Russian help.

"One of our Tsar's highest priorities is restoration of Russia's land, water, and air," he replied. "The Communists were pigs, and like other pigs they uprooted, dirtied and stank up everything. The first pillar of the Russian state, now and always, is the Russian Army. The second is the Russian land. He restored the first, and now he is bending every effort to restore the second."

"At the same time, he is deeply worried about this other environmental poison, the poison of Deep Green ideology. Better than any other country, we know the price ideology exacts. Russia is a Christian nation, and the Tsar's guiding concept is Christian stewardship, not environmentalism. People should respect the land and its creatures, but these exist for people, to serve people. Man has lordship over creation, under God. Man is not a cancer, but God's highest creation, for which He sent His only Son to die on a cross."

"Give me a day to think about this," Father Dimitri concluded. "Perhaps there are some ways we can help."

"Will you join me tomorrow for dinner with Bill?" I asked.

"Of course," the good priest replied. "I had a tin of caviar ready for you tonight, and then I remembered your fond feelings about fish. We will put it to good use tomorrow instead."

*

When I got to the governor's house at the appointed time of 18:30—a fashionably late dinner hour by Maine standards—Father Dimitri was already there. Bill was in a jovial mode, thanks to the caviar. I gave the Ambassador a look that said, "Good prep fire," and he smiled.

As Bill ladled out the iced cucumber soup that was one of his favorites, he looked at me and asked, "All ready to travel west?"

"I'm ready to travel, but I think I need to go in the opposite direction," I replied. One of Bill Kraft's virtues was that he was always open to unusual, counterintuitive approaches to problems. His expression told me to go on, so I laid out my view of the strategic situation.

He grasped my point at once. "You're right," he said. "I hadn't seen it that way, but you're absolutely correct. If we can cut off the exchange of Cascadian resources for Chinese money, the Deep Green leadership's whole game collapses. The question is, how can we do that? Our navy has no such reach."

"But Russia's navy does," I said, looking toward Father Dimitri.

"The Tsar would be extremely reluctant to confront the Chinese," Father Dimitri replied. "Remember, we share a long border with China, and we want that border to be a friendly one. Moreover, we and the Chinese are cooperating extensively to confront the Muslim threat we both face. Islam is an even greater danger than the Deep Green ideology, and we would not be so short-sighted as to sacrifice a greater objective for a lesser one."

"I'm glad to hear the Imperial government is wiser than in the days of Bezobrashoff and Izvolsky," Bill responded.

"The Tsar learns from the experience of others" Father Dimitri replied.

"But without Russian aid, I see no way we can interrupt the exchange between China and Cascadia," I said. "Are we back to square one?"

"I did not say Russia would not assist," the Ambassador answered. "I only said she would not do so by confronting China. I think there may be another way."

"As you are aware, China and Japan are now bitter rivals," Father Dimitri continued. "Especially they are rivals for raw materials. In the time of the United States, the American Pacific Northwest was a primary source of raw materials, especially timber, for Japan. That is why Japan financed the U.N. effort to preserve the federal union. The Japanese are angry at the loss of those resources. Worse, those same materials are now flowing to her main competitor, China, and China is getting them at less than the world market price. Japan is losing her ability to compete, and MITI is not happy."

MITI, I knew, was the most powerful ministry in the Japanese government, more powerful even than the Finance Ministry. MITI effectively controlled Japanese industrial and trade policy.

I also knew that in a naval confrontation, Japan would have the advantage over China. Since the beginning of the century, both countries had built powerful, blue water fleets. But the Imperial Japanese Navy was a real navy, one that could go places and do things. Japan was by geography a maritime country, and the Japanese were first-rate sailors. The Chinese navy was merely a collection of ships. It spent little time at sea and Chinese naval officers still found oceanic navigation something of a challenge. The Chinks were lubbers, and as history had shown time and again, it's the people that count, not the ships.

"Why haven't the Japanese already done something?" I asked Father Dimitri.

"That would be too direct," he replied. "Remember, we're talking about the Orient. The indirect approach is the preferable approach."

"Where do we come in?" Bill Kraft interjected.

"You provide the flag," the Ambassador replied.

Bill and I both had to think about that one. He got it first. "Are you suggesting we rent the Japanese navy?"

"Precisely," Father Dimitri answered. "In today's world, what military isn't for rent, if the price is right?"

"What might the price be in this case?" I asked, thinking that our entire treasury might suffice to rent one gunboat.

"My guess, and it is only that, is one Pine Tree dollar—and the understanding that Cascadia would resume its previous place in the Greater East Asia Co-Prosperity Sphere."

International law, if the term still had any meaning, now recognized forces hired on contract as belonging to the country that contracted for them. Usually, such forces were provided by private entrepreneurs. But states had rented out parts of their own militaries—"Hessians" was again the term of art—and the rule still applied: The state that had contracted for them was responsible for their actions, not the state that supplied them. A Japanese fleet under the Pine Tree flag of the Northern Confederation was legally an N.C. Fleet.

"The Cascadian rebels aren't organized enough to make a commitment to the Japanese," Bill said. "But I'm prepared to make it on their behalf. It's a natural relationship, since Cascadia has looked toward the Pacific since well back in the 20th century, and Japan is the dominant maritime power in the Pacific.

"If the Cascadians won't honor the commitment, well, we'll just have to rent another fleet and make them see reason."

"Meanwhile, are you still packed and ready to travel east, this time?" Bill asked me.

"Aye, aye, sir," I replied.

"The Imperial Russian Air Force aircraft that keeps me supplied is due here the day after tomorrow," Father Dimitri said to me. "I have taken the liberty of reserving you a seat on it—Admiral Rumford."

CHAPTER THIRTY-NINE

Russian punctuality had long been a proverb, in the same vein as Italian efficiency. It was a testimonial to the new Russia that Father Dimitri's resupply flight landed right on schedule at Portland airport, at 5 PM on July 12, 2035. The big white Ilyushin 76 carried the pre-1917 white-blue-red roundels on its wings and fuselage and an immense, black Orthodox cross on its tail. The latter was by the Tsar's ukase. If the Muslims wanted a religious war, they could have one. It was good to see Christianity once again willing to fight.

Father Dimitri met me at the airport with my Russian and Japanese visas and quarantine waivers. Without the waivers I would have faced a three-month quarantine to enter Russia and another six months to get into Japan. As usual, when governments wanted something for themselves, the rules proved easy to bend.

The Russian aircraft took off at 7 PM, just as the flight plan indicated. They had a bunk ready for me, which I appreciated. From Maine to Tokyo was a fair ways. I would change planes in St. Petersburg, at a restricted military airfield. The Russians didn't want my fingerprints on them when the Chinks started to howl. Lenin on the sealed train again, I thought.

The flight was uneventful, as every air passenger always hopes it will be. I remembered a party years ago where some silly woman asked an airline pilot if his job was exciting. "Not if I do it right," was his reply. I slept most of the way, thanks to the vodka that was part of Russian military rations plus a Marine's ability to sleep anywhere. At St. Petersburg, I was only on the ground long enough to shit, shower, and shave.

On the St. Petersburg-Tokyo leg, my body clock said day, so I went up to the cockpit. The co-pilot spoke some English and told me a bit about the country we were flying over. As we came across the Urals, two SU-41 fighters appeared alongside as escorts.

"An honor guard?" I asked the co-pilot.

"Nyet," he replied. "All Russian aircraft flying through this region receive fighter escorts. Sometimes the Islamics send a single fighter of their own north, flying low to avoid our radar, to shoot down our airliners. After we lost four, and almost a thousand civilian air passengers, we realized we had to provide escort. Once we reach the Russo-Chinese border we will be out of their range."

"Airborne pirates," I said.

"Assassins," the co-pilot responded. "Remember, assassin is an Arabic word. It is the way the Islamics have always fought. Now they do it with airplanes, bombs, rockets, and bioweapons instead of daggers. Nothing really changes with them."

As we began our long descent toward Japan, I went aft to change into my admiral's uniform. We didn't actually have any admirals in the Northern Confederation Navy, but Orientals were big on rank and my time in the Confederacy had taught me to play along. For a uniform, I took our plain Navy blues and threw on handfuls of gold braid, fruit salad, and gee-gaws. My adjutant took one look at it and said, "Boy, get me a cab," so I figured it was about right for the Japs.

We landed on a Saturday afternoon at a military airfield on Hokkaido. I was met with full honors, but the remoteness of the location told me the Nips also wanted to keep things quiet. After greeting a variety of big-wigs, I was introduced to the officer who would be my escort, aide, and keeper, Captain Yakahashi Tomo IJN. He explained that the fleet—soon, the Northern Confederation fleet—would be ready to weigh anchor in about ten days. Until then, he and I would keep a low profile. Was I agreeable to spending the time at a *ryokan* up in the mountains, which we would have to ourselves? I was, so the two of us jumped into a new Mitsubishi Zero sports car and set off on back roads.

I had always appreciated the Japanese sense of beauty. Its spare harmony reflected its origin among a poor people. Perhaps I liked it because Maine too was poor. But it was also a masculine aesthetic: simple materials, subtle colors, precise ordering that took long thought and care not to look ordered. As Oscar Wilde said, the problem with being natural is that it is such a difficult pose to maintain.

Our ryokan fulfilled my long ambition to immerse myself in traditional Japan. It grew out of a rocky cleft in the mountains like the pine trees that almost hid it. It was very small, just three guest rooms. Inside, it had the minute perfection of a fine watch. The woodwork was all straight-grained, no knots or blemishes. The paper screens that made the walls glowed like unimaginably thin sheets of ivory. The tiny courtyard garden was grey sand and grey rocks, with a single mountain laurel. I knew the laurel's twisted trunk was no accident. It had been shaped carefully as it grew, like a bonsai. The garden was stark, and peaceful.

My mind and body were in a variety of time zones by this point, and Captain Yakahashi kindly suggested we postpone any business. Instead, we soaked in the *ofuro*, the steaming hot Japanese bath, then enjoyed a long, slow, dinner of many tiny courses, served with absolute grace by three geisha. I recognized the food as *kaiseki*, the court cuisine of Imperial Kyoto. The important thing was not the taste but the beauty of the presentation. To a degree unapproached and incomprehensible elsewhere, the culture of Japan was dominated by a visual aesthetic. I drank it in like cool mountain water, and that night I slept as if in hibernation.

Japanese summers are hot, but up in the mountains, I awakened Sunday morning to a cool crispness that reminded me of home. The only sounds were the wind in the pines and the calling of birds. Captain Yakahashi and a Japanese breakfast of rice, vegetables, and green tea were waiting on a small porch overlooking the garden.

"Bit of a nip in the air this morning," I said to the captain.

"Just like one Sunday morning at Pearl Harbor," he replied, and he laughed. I hadn't expected an irreverent sense of humor in a Jap, and I was happy to find one.

After breakfast, still sitting on the porch, I read the Morning Prayer service in the old 1928 Book of Common Prayer. I always did that when I couldn't get to church.

Then the glories of the morning and the mountains beckoned. Could we go for a walk? The captain said we could. I was a guest, not a prisoner. That day began an idyllic week of walking, talking, and soaking in rural Japan.

To my relief, the Japanese military had not caught the old American "briefing disease." They didn't think it necessary to tell me what we were going to do in some damned slide show led by a talking dog major or commander reading from a script. Tomo—we were quickly on a first name basis—knew his stuff and we just talked.

The fleet would be a powerful one. I would have two aircraft carriers, the *Zuikaku* and *Shokaku*, one with fighters and ASW aircraft and the other carrying ground support planes and transports. We'd have ASW destroyers as escorts, since if the Chinese responded it would probably be with submarines, plus two amphibious transports without troops. Six Japanese subs would also operate in support.

"Why the amphibs without troops?" I asked Tomo.

The troops would be provided by the Cascadian Resistance, he replied. The op plan was that the fleet would arrive, blockade the Cascadian coast and fly the transport aircraft across Cascadia to Idaho. There, they would pick up the troops and bring them back to one of the carriers, whence they could be ferried to the transports. No Japanese would go ashore. Beyond the blockade, the Cascadians would liberate themselves.

It was a good plan, and I said I'd go with it. I didn't really have much choice. Tomo made it clear that my role was as a fig leaf only and I would have no real command over the fleet. I told him I would go ashore with the Cascadian troops where I would be more in my element. He said that would be agreeable to Tokyo.

The big question was the Chinese reaction. Japanese naval intelligence didn't think there would be one. While the Chinese had a big navy on paper, it seldom went to sea, and when it did it was always something of a Chinese fire drill. Tomo hadn't heard that expression before and howled with laughter when I used it. For more than a century the Japanese Navy had been a real navy, and if the Chinese took them on it would be the Battle of the Yalu all over again. Both sides knew it, too, so Tokyo expected Beijing to keep quiet.

Of course, China's interests would have to be accommodated. A revenge-minded China would not be good for Japan. The Japanese plan was to let China bid for Cascadian resources along with everybody else. She'd still get her share, she just wouldn't get everything. And she'd have to pay market price. The Japanese Foreign Service thought China realized her current game was too good to go on forever and would be willing to recognize reality. Besides, at the rate the Deep Green government was stripping the place, there soon wouldn't be any Cascadian resources for anyone.

That all made sense from the Japanese perspective. Unfortunately, China had another option. The fleet that would cut her off from the Cascadian honeypot would legally be a Northern Confederation fleet, not a Japanese fleet. How might China strike back at us? She could cut off trade, but the raw materials that made up most of the N.C.'s exports were in hot demand in a resource and food-short world. What we didn't sell to China we could sell as easily to someone else. Geography protected us from the Chinese Navy. But a Chinese ICBM could reach N.C. territory. What would our response be if the Chinese gave us an ultimatum to raise the Cascadian blockade or get a Chinese nuke on, say, Buffalo? We had nukes of our own, taken with the old U.S. Navy sub base at New London, Connecticut, but the Chinese might calculate that we could not deliver one on China. How could we demonstrate we could?

I spent most of a week thinking about this one. I didn't say anything to Tomo because I didn't want to screw up the Japanese plans. But unless I had an answer, my responsibility to my own government meant I would have to call the whole operation off. We'd look like fools who'd gotten in over our heads, then lost our nerve.

Maybe it was the serenity of the ryokan that let my Marine brain work better than usual. Thursday evening, sitting on a rock that looked down at the inn from higher up on the mountain, an idea came with my third cigar. I walked down the mountain and found Tomo in the inn's *ofuro*. "Captain Yakahashi, I have a formal request to make on the part of the Northern Confederation government," I said as he soaked in the deep tub.

Thinking I was playing a joke, Tomo bowed deeply into the bathwater and replied, smiling, "I have been instructed to meet every request of the Northern Confederation or die in the attempt."

"Good," I said. "I want you to set me up a meeting with a *yakuza* leader."

"This is an example of New England humor, I trust," Tomo replied, his eyes telling me he wasn't sure.

"Nope. It's just what I said it was, an official request," I said. "If you want, I'll put it in writing."

"Why do you want to meet with a gangster?" Tomo asked, now worried that he faced an Oriental's deepest dread, embarrassment.

"Remember, Tomo, the line between war and crime is thin. In our time, it is growing ever thinner. We're about to walk into a war, and I think a gangster might make a useful ally. More than that will have to remain a Northern Confederation military secret."

Tomo hissed. I recognized the involuntary gesture as something Japanese did when presented with an unexpected and unpleasant situation. But Japanese also did their duty, unpleasant or not. "Will tomorrow afternoon be soon enough? It will take a little time to make the necessary connections."

"Tomorrow afternoon will be fine," I answered.

"May I make a personal request?" Tomo asked.

"Of course."

"Would you be willing to consider meeting the yakuza somewhere on the mountain rather than here in the ryokan?"

I knew Tomo would embarrass the ryokan if he arranged for a yakuza to come here, and embarrassing them would embarrass him worse. I had no desire to do either. "On the mountain is fine with me."

Tomo did another bow into his bathwater, this time a deep one that said "Thank you very much." I couldn't keep my mind from seeing an officer of the Imperial Japanese Navy bobbing for apples.

The next day, on a fine, clear afternoon, I went hiking. Tomo had told me to take the Willow Trail, which followed a small stream. At a miniscule pavilion, so artfully constructed that it almost vanished into the ferns and trees around it, the gangster was waiting. He wore the trademark zoot suit and sported heavy gold rings on all nine fingers, the missing tenth serving as his formal ID. Being a Japanese gangster, he proved exceedingly polite. My request was a reasonably simple one, and the yakuza's price was not excessive. We sealed our deal with an exchange of business cards, *meishi*. In Japan, there was still honor among thieves. I was as certain he'd come through as that a new Toyota would start.

That evening, Tomo had ordered us a special dinner. The *kaiseki* was beautiful, but truth be told, my weight was dropping. After a day of mountain hiking, coming in and sitting down to a meal of Fabergé eggs had its drawbacks. So that night, the ryokan swallowed its pride and fed us meat: big *donkatsu*, Korean *bulkogi*, and Peking duck. At the end the three geisha, giggling madly, processed in with an enormous *Malakofftorte*. I have no idea where they found one on Hokkaido. I stuffed myself to just short of the terminal bloat point, then said what the hell, had more cake and went over the edge. I knew I'd have nightmares but the Malakofftorte was worth it.

I suspect the dinner was Tomo's way of thanking me for not embarrassing him or the inn. I understood the oriental desire to save face, and he in turn knew that gaijin like to stuff themselves on gross fatty food. I didn't mind a bit of multiculturalism with Asians, because their culture, like Western culture, had earned respect. It wasn't as if they were just down out of the trees.

Besides the courtyard garden, the inn had a back yard, less formal and therefore the product of even more painstaking conception and care. Tomo and I waddled out there after dinner to sit on a rustic bench by the tiny stream whose gurgles might mask our guts' groaning. I offered Tomo an Upmann, which to my surprise he took.

"Have you heard yet when we sail?" I asked, not in any hurry to leave a place whose beauty I would always remember, yet anxious to get my business done.

"The fleet is already at sea," Tomo replied. "The day after tomorrow, we will leave here, pick up a flying boat at a small fishing village on the coast and fly out to the *Zuikaku*. That is the point when the charter will begin and you will take command. I hope you remembered to bring some Northern Confederation flags."

"I did." I'd brought a couple dozen naval ensigns, our Pine Tree flag with a blue anchor in the upper left quadrant.

"You also need to re-name the ships," Tomo added.

"I don't like giving weapons names," I answered. "Once you name a weapon—and that's all a warship is, another weapon—its loss becomes a big deal, so you become afraid to take risks. I'd rather just give the ships numbers."

Tomo hissed again. "Perhaps you could do that with the escort ships and the amphibious transports, but please, not the carriers! It would be a terrible humiliation to their men."

"OK, then, let me think." This was another point where compromise was in order. "How about *Nature's Revenge* for one of them? That would send the Deep Greeners a message."

Tomo coughed. "Most regrettably, that is the name of the best-selling Japanese laxative."

"Then I guess the crew wouldn't care much for that, either. I sure don't want them to run."

"Why don't you name one of the carriers for your Governor Kraft? I am certain he would be pleased," Tomo suggested.

"We don't believe in naming anything for people who are still alive," I answered. "That's flattery." Toward the end, the U.S. Navy started doing that with its aircraft carriers, naming them for politicians who'd given them pots of money. It turned my stomach.

Then the light bulb went on. "We do have some dead men who have earned the honor. The carriers will be the *John C. Adams* and the *John Kelly*." I knew John Kelly would have preferred an amphib, but I'd make sure his name went on the carrier that flew the ground support aircraft. There was enough Marine Corps in that.

"Excellent choices," Tomo replied. "Real American heroes."

Now it was my turn to ask a question. "How does it feel to be sending a fleet east again, to attack part of the old United States?"

"Please do not take offense if I give you an honest answer," Tomo said. "It feels very good. Even though this fleet is under a flag that is not the Rising Sun, that is merely a stratagem. For every officer in the Imperial Japanese Navy, this action wipes out a long-standing shame."

"Shame for the attack on Pearl Harbor?"

"No, shame that we lost the war."

"Whose fault was that?"

"It was our own fault. Japan was impatient. We had already conquered most of China. All we had to do was hold on to that and wait for you to collapse from your own internal contradictions, as eventually you did. Now, America is gone, but we face a powerful China, which is a greater danger to us than you could ever have been. You were an ocean away, and China is on our doorstep."

"So you think the world's future will be decided in Asia?"

"Yes. Asian culture is superior to Western culture, and in the long run, culture determines everything else. The West had its day in the sun, but that day is over. The future belongs to those who eat rice."

"I agree culture determines whether a society works or fails. We learned that the hard way. But at least in the Northern Confederation, we are recovering our old culture, and it does work. What makes you think Asian culture is superior to Western?"

"Because you believe the individual is everything, and we know the individual is nothing. It is the group that achieves, not the individual. Oh, I know you will point to what Western individuals have done: Newton, Napoleon, Einstein. Even your religion is built around an individual, Jesus. But in recalling the few who were great, you pass over the millions who were not. Yet each of these little Western men, ignorant and foolish, still thought the world should revolve around him. To the degree he could, he made it do so. In the end, these little people achieved nothing on their own, and because they were working only for themselves, they left behind no achievement but disorder.

"In Asia, we are all little people. But we know that. So we devote ourselves to the group, and the group accomplishes what no one person could. I will give you your few great men. In the end, millions of little people working together, anonymously, will achieve vastly more than your handful of heroes."

Tomo then offered me a haiku:

*

"I watched a colony of ants
Efficiently
Strip a butterfly."

*

Looking down at the intricately fitted stones of the path in front of our bench, I saw an ant wending its way home at the end of a hard Japanese ant day. I stepped on it with the toe of my hiking boot, grinding it under the lugs until there was nothing visible left of it. Then I looked at him.

Tomo only smiled. "The colony will not notice the loss."

"Perhaps," I replied. "But perhaps that ant was bringing the word about a wounded butterfly."

*

We left the ryokan at 03:30 two days later. The whole staff in their best kimonos were lined up outside in the darkness to bow us farewell. I always hoped someday I'd go back there, but I never did. It's probably for the best. Nothing is the same the second time around.

We drove over back roads for a couple of hours until we came down a mountain into a small fishing village. One of the big Kawanishi flying boats was anchored in the harbor. A sampan rowed us out, we boarded through the side door, and the plane took off straight into the sun.

After a couple hours in the air, Tomo told me the pilot had something to show me. We went up to the cockpit, where everybody was looking at me and grinning. The pilot motioned for me to watch the wing, then pushed a button on the dash. As I looked, the big orange Rising Sun insignia vanished and in its place appeared the Northern Confederation's Pine Tree. Apparently the insignia were all on some kind of LED display. Sovereignty now changed at the push of a button.

About an hour before we were due at the rendezvous, I changed into my admiral's uniform. It made me feel like some organ-grinder's monkey, but the Jap aircrew aft all bowed deeply.

It was hard to remember that America's military leaders had all been in love with this kind of crap too. Maybe that is as good a sign as any that a nation's days are up.

Just after 16:00 hours the fleet came into view from the aircraft. It was all drawn in tight as if for a photo op, the two carriers just a few hundred yards apart and the escorts not much further out. Japanese ship handling was good enough to do that without much risk of a collision, but one tac nuke would have vaporized the whole lot. I wondered how good Chinese military intelligence was.

The sea state was moderate, but we landed to the lee side of the *Zuikaku* anyway, which gave us a duck pond with minimal wave and wind action. A launch met the flying boat and we transferred to the ship the old way, missing only the oarsmen. I was piped aboard and escorted immediately to the bridge. There, in a brief ceremony, the Japanese flag was hauled down, the Northern Confederation ensign was hoisted and the fleet passed to my nominal control. I saw Japanese seamen being lowered over the side to paint out the characters for Zuikaku and paint in *NCS John C. Adams*. I was relieved to find they still used paint instead of electrons.

From the Japanese standpoint, I was an honored passenger, nothing more. Tomo had made it clear the fleet would remain under Japanese control while performing the agreed mission. But I'd grown up in the school that said a military problem is a military problem, and somebody has to solve it. The tight grouping of the fleet was dangerous.

I had relieved the two-star Japanese admiral as commander of the fleet, but a Japanese rear admiral remained in real command. With Tomo in tow as interpreter, I headed below to the CIC.

The Japanese sentry at the CIC hatch came to a smart salute, put his hand on the hatch handle, then looked at Tomo. His question was implicit but obvious: Am I supposed to let this gaijin in here? Tomo nodded imperceptibly, and the sentry swung the hatch open. Inside, everybody immediately froze in rigid attention, regardless of what they'd been doing. I'd have to remember not to enter the CIC in the middle of an emergency.

The man in charge, Rear Admiral Juichi Tanaka IJN, came over, bowed deeply, and through Tomo thanked me for the honor of my presence. Would I do him the further honor of leaving immediately? It wasn't put that way, of course—"Would I join him in the senior officers' mess?" was the line—but I understood what was going on .

"Tell Admiral Tanaka I would be delighted to join him in the mess, just as soon as I have had the exquisite pleasure of being shown what is going on in his honorable CIC," was my message back through Tomo.

Tomo hissed and translated. The Admiral hissed in return, and his staff officers hissed in succession, like a fleet of ships-of-the-line wearing. The admiral motioned toward the hatch. I started to move deeper into the CIC. The staff officers formed line abreast to block me. I bowed deeply to them, which meant they had to bow more deeply to me. While their heads were down, I went around the left of their line and headed toward what the wall chart told me was probably their G-2 section.

At this point there was a lot of rapid-fire jabber between Tomo and the admiral. As Tomo explained later, he told Admiral Tanaka they had to let me into my own flagship's CIC, they just didn't have to tell me much. That compromise did the trick, and Tanaka was soon hurrying after me, alternatively bowing and hissing.

I'd guessed right and found myself in the G-2 section, Intelligence. The electronic map had some units in blue, others in red. The icons were recognizable as subs, aircraft, and surface warships. Guessing that blue meant friendly, a quick map recon told me no Chinks were where we were headed. "It looks as if we've got clear sailing," I said to Tanaka.

"Hai" was his reply after Tomo translated—"Yes." OK, I knew how to play Twenty Questions.

"Are we under Chinese satellite surveillance?" was my first.

"Hai."

"Do the Chinese have ballistic missiles that can target a moving fleet?"

"Hai."

"Do some of those missiles have tactical nuclear warheads?"

"Hai."

"Would a single nuclear warhead wipe out a fleet as concentrated as this one?"

"Hai."

"If you were the Chinese, would you drop a nuke on this fleet right now and solve your problem?"

This brought a new round of hissing. After a lengthy back-and-forth, Tomo said, "The Chinese would never dare attack a Japanese fleet with a nuclear weapon."

"This is no longer a Japanese fleet. Legally, it is a Northern Confederation fleet. Would the Chinese dare attack that?"

More hissing, a lot more, and a lengthy conversation between Tanaka, Tomo, and the G-2. At the end of it, Tanaka turned to me, bowed very low, and through Tomo said, "The fleet will be dispersed immediately."

"Please tell Admiral Tanaka that I would be delighted to join him in the mess."

From there on out, I was no longer just the Honored Passenger.

CHAPTER FORTY

I F you overlook the occasional typhoon, the Pacific usually lives up to
its name. So it did for us. The fleet had calm winds and a following
sea all the way. About 500 miles from the Cascadian shoreline, we
split up. The carriers, amphibs, most of the escorts and two submarines
headed for Portland, the Cascadian capital. The rest of the destroyers
and subs established the blockade, the tin cans as visible agents and the
subs in case the Chinese navy tried anything. Two of each were stationed
off Vancouver and one pair went to Seattle. Two more DDs made up a
roving patrol, and we left one sub about 300 miles out to ambush any
Chink interlopers.

By August 15, everybody was in position. That morning, back in Augusta, the Northern Confederation government proclaimed the blockade
of Cascadia. It was a bold step. Under international law, a blockade is
an act of war, so in a sense we were now at war with Cascadia. That
technically went beyond what the referendum had authorized and risked
another referendum to force our withdrawal. Just two days later a group
began gathering signatures to put the matter on the ballot.

But Bill Kraft had calculated well. He reasoned that once people saw no actual Northern Confederation forces were involved beyond myself, and our flag was mostly a fig leaf for the Japanese, they would understand. The press, which was fathoms more serious than the media in the old American republic, presented the facts thoroughly and without any slant. The public considered the matter thoughtfully, free from the old assumption that their leaders were scoundrels with a hidden agenda. Everybody knew what was going on in Cascadia, and there was a consensus in favor of helping Christians there and elsewhere so long as we didn't get in over our heads. People knew they could pull the plug whenever they wanted through a referendum and recall leaders who failed. So for the moment, most folks decided to wait and see. The petition drive stalled.

Back with the fleet, I officially informed the Cascadian government their coasts were under a blockade. There wasn't much they could do about it. The gods of the Palaeopitus had put all their resources into suppressing their own people and had neither air nor sea defenses. Aircraft from our carriers dropped leaflets telling the Cascadian people what we were doing and why. We sought to create conditions under which they could liberate themselves.

All Chinese ships already in Cascadian harbors were allowed to leave, with their cargoes. That didn't stop Beijing from denouncing the blockade as piracy. On August 17, we stopped the first Chinese ship attempting to enter a Cascadian port and ordered it to turn around. Beijing's rhetoric got hotter. Tokyo referred the Chinese protests to Augusta and the Chinese played along, holding the Northern Confederation "fully responsible for acts of war against China." That worried me, because it was a smart move. China was going for the weakest link in the chain.

One of the things I learned from John Boyd is that war is waged more in time than in space. At this point time was not on our side. We needed to wrap things up quickly in Cascadia before Chinese reaction overwhelmed us. But the realities on the ground in Cascadia forced us to move slowly. We needed time for the Cascadian people to understand what was happening. We needed time for the Resistance to get its act together. Above all, we needed time for the Cascadian government to run out of money and stop paying its mercenaries.

So, we waited. But waited actively. By August 21st, we had established regular contact with the Resistance all along the coast. Our reconnaissance aircraft roamed freely through Cascadian skies, but what they brought back had limited value. This wasn't a conflict where you could count armored divisions. The important intel was about people and could only be learned from people, and for that we depended on the Resistance.

On the 24th, we began flying in Resistance troops who had gathered in Idaho. They numbered just under a thousand men, giving us a one-battalion landing force. It wasn't much, especially in view of Resistance reports that gave the government more than 30,000 mercenaries. I figured that number was probably high by at least one-third, because most people overestimate their opponent's strength. Plus, the government's troops were scattered throughout Cascadia. But intel from refugees suggested the gods had retained about five thousand mercs around Portland as a Praetorian Guard. That meant we would be pitting a battalion against a brigade. I knew the old Lanchestrian rule requiring 3:1 superiority for an attack was bullshit, but 5:1 against was cause for concern.

Another concern was that the Cascadian government would flee Portland and hide inland where we would have trouble finding them. The Resistance told us that was unlikely, because the gods were too afraid of their own countrymen. The more rural the area, the more dangerous it was for anyone connected with the Cascadian government. The guerrillas already controlled the countryside. It was our job to bring about the fall of the city.

A question the Resistance could not answer was how much money remained in the Cascadian treasury. The mercs demanded payment in hard currency, and we had to wait for the government to run out of it. Usually, once a war is on, money is flowing out as fast or faster than it comes in, and the Palaeoptus had been hard pressed by the Resistance for some time. My guess was that they didn't have much of a financial cushion, but we couldn't know.

By early September, the Resistance was reporting a noticeable slacking off by the mercenaries. Whenever they could, they avoided action. Nobody wants to be the last man killed in a war, especially a losing war, and that went double for mercenaries.

As usual in this kind of war, neither side had taken prisoners, unless it was to torture them to death for information, or amusement, or both. At my demand, the Resistance changed that policy. On September 9th they announced that any mercenary who surrendered would be treated well and returned promptly to his home country. By mid-month, they were getting deserters. On September 20, the entire garrison of Yakima came over. Desertion by whole units was an excellent sign, and the commander of the garrison, a Dutchman named van Leeuwin, told us they hadn't been paid since early August. With Tokyo's approval, on the 23rd I announced that any mercenary coming over would be paid all his back wages plus a bonus. We also began putting deserters on the Cascadians' tac nets to confirm to their former colleagues that we kept our word. The pace of desertions picked up. By the end of September we were averaging more than a hundred a day.

A blockade is a form of siege, and like any siege, the question is who runs out of time first, besieged or besieger? On the ground, time was now working for us. But our problem wasn't the Cascadians. It was the Chinese.

Through the month of September, Chinese rhetoric became steadily more shrill. Both Tokyo and Augusta assured Beijing privately that China would not be cut out of Cascadia, that she could still trade for Cascadian resources like anyone else. The assurances seemed to have little effect. Each day the Chinese media whipped up the public further, presenting the issue as one of China's Great Power status. Our blockade was denounced as "humiliation by foreign devils." China was an authoritarian state without a free press, so the stuff appearing in the papers was there because the Chinese government wanted it there.

It took the Chinese Navy about a month to react, but by mid-September its deployments were increasing steadily. Three submarine squadrons of ten boats each were in or on their way to the mid-Pacific. A carrier task force was assembling off Tsingtao. Amphibious transports from as far away as the South China Sea were moving to northern ports, where troops were gathering.

Tokyo quietly told Beijing that a Chinese attack on a Japanese warship would be met in kind, regardless of what flag the Japanese ship was flying. The Imperial Japanese Navy was not about to be pushed around by its Chinese counterpart, for which it had complete contempt. Japanese subs deployed across the lines any Chinese task force would probably take. The Japs had figured out that a sub's worst enemy is an airship, and Japanese ASW flying boats and dirigibles began tracking the Chinese submarines in the Pacific.

From my standpoint, all this was good news. The more the contest was between China and Japan instead of China and the Northern Confederation, the more confident I was of the outcome. Both China and Japan were nuclear powers with full arsenals, which meant that in the end neither would do anything to provoke a direct confrontation with the other. As Martin van Creveld wrote long ago, nuclear weapons are stabilizing. Not only did mutual deterrence prevent nuclear war, it made conventional war between nuclear powers impossible. In the end, all this dispatch of sub squadrons and trailing with zeppelins was mostly kabuki theater.

Not only did logic tell me this, so did the Chinese themselves. By the end of September, we were reading the message traffic between Portland and Beijing. The Chinese had not given the Cascadian government its best cyphers, and in about six weeks the Japanese broke the code. The messages from the Palaeopitus to Beijing were increasingly desperate: Guerrillas controlled most of the countryside, the mercs were deserting in droves and the Cascadian treasury was almost out of hard currency.

More important was the Chinese response. China told Cascadia that no warships or troops were coming. Chinese merchant ships had been ordered not to attempt to break the blockade. China would not risk a crisis with Japan for Cascadia. All the Chinese pledged was "increased pressure" on the Northern Confederation. Exactly what that meant wasn't clear, but so long as it was restricted to ranting and raving, we could take it.

Instead of Liman Von Sanders, I spent most of my time playing von Steuben, training the Cascadian battalion on our amphibs. They were good material and potentially good light infantry, but they needed a lot of work on weapons skills and tactics. We could drill live-fire with most of the weapons on the ships, shooting over the sides, but we had no ground on which to practice tactics. Instead, I ran them through TDGs and refereed commercial board war games, of which *Advanced Squad Leader* was still the most useful for infantry tactics. Gradually, they became accustomed to making military decisions. I even did squad-on-squad freeplay exercises on the ships, which made adequate substitutes for urban terrain. By the end of September, I was gaining confidence in them and they in me.

It looked like the final stage of the operation, taking Portland and overthrowing the Palaeopitus, would go sometime in October. The total Cascadian force was down to under 20,000 men. The Palaeopitus had concentrated its best troops, those who were still motivated by Deep Green ideology rather than greed, around Portland. They would be a tough nut to crack, but the hopelessness of the overall situation made me believe even the Deep Greeners might not put up too much of a fight. We continued to stress that anyone who surrendered would be treated well, and on October 3rd we twisted the arms of the Resistance leaders into promising foreign sanctuary to native Cascadians as well as mercenaries, if they wanted it.

On October 5th, the conference to set D-Day met on board the *Adams.* Attendees included Resistance leaders from both Idaho and Portland, the Japanese naval staff, Admiral Tanaka and myself. I still wanted to go slow, preferring to spend time rather than blood since time was now working for us. But the Resistance scented victory and wanted to move fast. Tokyo was also pressing Admiral Tanaka to get the whole thing over with so they could begin to restore normal relations with China. I hoped to get a compromise, aiming for about the 20th.

The conference was due to start at 10:00 hours. At 09:51, Tomo knocked at my door.

"Admiral Rumford, Admiral Tanaka asks if you would join him immediately in the CIC." Tomo's use of my title and his tone both told me something was up.

"Sure, let's go on down," I replied. Since our first headbutting over the question of fleet dispersion, Tanaka had involved me in all the important decisions. I was careful not to press too hard, and he in turn took my input seriously. Looking at the clock, I realized this meeting would almost certainly make us both late for the conference. In view of the Japanese stress on punctuality, that meant rocks and shoals ahead.

The atmosphere inside the CIC confirmed my guess. I'd been with the Japanese long enough that I could begin to read their body language. The staff officers were moving like marionettes, in short, jerky motions, punctuated with rapid-fire, overloud talk. Admiral Tanaka almost ran over to me, bowed deeply and apologized for delaying my arrival at the conference.

"No sweat," I replied through Tomo, although the admiral was in fact sweating. I hated councils of war. "We have an unusual development," Tanaka continued. "A Chinese military transport aircraft is flying toward Cascadia."

So far, the Chinese had not challenged our blockade in the air or on the water. "Maybe it is to pull their people out," I replied. "If they are withdrawing their embassy and military mission, that's a good sign for us. It means they know the game is up."

"Unfortunately, that does not appear to be the aircraft's mission," Tanaka replied. "We have intercepted a communication that suggests another purpose."

Commander Yahashi, the Signals Intercept officer, stepped forward. "Yesterday afternoon, we intercepted a radio message from the Cascadian government to Beijing. The message read, 'Confirm three tons AU 173.' Three hours later, Beijing replied, 'Confirmed 173.' Forty-five minutes ago, a Japanese air station on Hokkaido queried the Chinese aircraft now heading for Cascadia. It identified itself as Flight 173."

"In other words, the Chinese aircraft is bringing the Cascadian government three tons of gold to pay its troops," I replied.

"That is our interpretation," Yahashi replied.

"The question is, would three tons of gold enable the Cascadian government to reverse the trend on the ground?" Tanaka asked. "And if so, should we intercept the aircraft?"

"That's two questions," I replied. "And there's a third. Were we meant to intercept this information?"

"What do you mean?" Tanaka asked.

"Is this a set-up? Do the Chinese want to create an incident, as a pretext for escalation?"

Once Tomo translated, that brought a general round of hissing. "Yes, that is also a possibility," Tanaka said.

"If China wants an incident, it wants one with the Northern Confederation, not Japan," I said. "So the decision is my responsibility." I took a few moments to think. That much gold would enable the Palaeopitus to stabilize its forces, at the least. We would lose time—a month? two months? three? I was counting on time to work for us, to reduce the odds against us in Portland. Now, we would lose the time advantage.

"I'll take the risk," I told Tanaka. "It may be a trap, but sometimes the only way out of a trap is first to fall into it." When the other side faces you with a dilemma, that's sometimes the only choice. Score one for them, I thought.

"So you think we should intercept the aircraft?" Tanaka asked.

"Yes," I replied. "Are you willing to do that?"

Now it was Tanaka's turn to think. After a pause, he said, "The aircraft making the intercept would carry Northern Confederation markings, but in fact, Japanese aircraft would be shooting down a Chinese aircraft. I do not think Tokyo would look favorably on that."

"I understand," I said. "But I said intercept, not shoot down. You have highly skilled pilots. Can they maneuver their aircraft so as to continually force the Chinese plane off course?"

Tanaka turned for a quick conversation with his air boss.

"Yes, we can do that."

"The Chinese pilot will be a long way from home. His eye will be on his fuel gauge. If you force him into constant maneuvering, he'll have to calculate the possibility that instead of landing in Portland, he'll have to make it all the way back to China. I think he'll make that decision pretty quickly," I said. "And I'll bet he heads for home. That means no gold and no incident."

After some more jabber with his staff, Tanaka turned to me with a smile and bowed. "We will intercept the Chinese aircraft as you suggested."

"When will the intercept take place?" I asked.

The G-2 replied, "The track of the Chinese aircraft will put it in our range in about four hours."

"Intercept as close to the carrier as possible," I suggested. "We want the Chink to go bingo before our own fighters do."

After Tomo translated, the air boss looked at me, grinned, and said "Roger!" I was glad I'd spent enough time with Marine aviators to learn their lingo.

That problem solved, Admiral Tanaka, Tomo, and I headed for the D-day conference. The admiral was upset by his tardiness and half-jogged along the corridors and up the companionways, rehearsing his *gomens* for being ten minutes late. We entered the conference room adjacent to the admiral's quarters to find a bunch of nervous Japanese officers and no Cascadians. The Cascadian landing force commander had already come out from Portland, and we flew in a delegation from the Resistance Council in Idaho yesterday. So they were here, but not here.

The explanation sauntered in more than an hour later, with the rest of the Cascadians. The Idaho delegation was headed by a god-damned woman! Shit, I thought, here we go. Not only are women never ready on time, they absolutely hate taking responsibility and making decisions. I should have guessed that even the Resistance in Cascadia would be infected by the old nonsense from the latter days of the American republic, including putting women in men's jobs.

Her ladyship offered the slenderest of excuses for keeping us all waiting, something about not being able to sleep with so many armed men around. That was a double entendre, I thought. Then, she bloviated for most of another hour about how she hated war, agreed with the Deep Greeners about green growing things and furry little creatures, deeply regretted the need for foreign assistance, and just felt so unhappy that things had some to such a pass. The Japanese were polite as always, but I could tell the Cascadian Resistance military men wanted to crawl under the table. By the time the dingbat finished, lunch was ready and we had not moved one inch closer to making a decision. How wisely Clausewitz wrote against councils of war—and he'd never dreamed about including a woman in one, not even in his worst nightmares.

I was supposed to sit next to the silly bint at lunch, but I motioned a Jap lieutenant into my place and took his at the far end of the table. He didn't speak a word of English, which in this case was a comfort. Tomo, who was stuck up there with the admiral, told me she spent most of the meal refusing to eat any meat or fish and lecturing the Japanese about hunting whales.

I ended up sitting next to a young Cascadian resistance leader from Portland. "Is she typical of what we're supposed to put in power in Cascadia?" I asked him. "If she is, I'm wondering why we're here."

"She's typical of the so-called Resistance Council in Idaho, but not of the people in Cascadia who've done the fighting," he replied. "The

Council thinks they'll just walk in once it's all over and tell us what to do. Worse, what they want is not all that different from Deep Green, a paler shade maybe, but at root the same stuff. It's all pagan, but the fighters in the Resistance are almost all Christians, and we're not going to take it."

I knew the troops on the amphibs were Christians to a man. Maybe this broad didn't represent much beyond herself and the Council. If that was the case, maybe I could find a way to tilt the game for the good guys and against her and her pagan friends.

It was 13:30 before we got back to the conference room, and before we'd all sat down she was on her feet again. "Before this goes any further, I want to take some time and make sure you all understand just how the Council feels about the situation."

"Lady, cut the crap," I said from my end of the table. "Nobody in this room gives a rat's ass how you or anybody else feels. We're here to make a military decision, and you've already made it more than clear that you have nothing to contribute. So let's get on with business."

The Japanese looked inscrutable, the Cascadian landing force CO gave me a thumbs up, and the dumb broad began to say, "I am deeply offended that—"

"SIT DOWN AND SHUT UP!" I bellowed in my best Marine parade ground voice.

She sat down and shut up. With women, as with many things, the old ways usually work best.

We then got a useful discussion going on the pros and cons of moving now or waiting. The deck was stacked against me, but I had some strong arguments and by around 15:00 I felt the group was beginning to move my way. At the least, I should be able to get the compromise October 20 date.

It was just after seven bells that the carrier air boss came into the room and whispered something to Admiral Tanaka. Tanaka looked at me, then spoke quickly to Tomo. "Would you join Admiral Tanaka in the CIC, please?" Tomo translated.

We hurried back down to the CIC, jogging again, now faster than when we'd been late. I figured we had news about the intercept and hoped they would tell us the Chinese aircraft had turned for home. But our pace and Tanaka's face both said the news wasn't good.

Once again we entered a tense CIC. The Japanese staff officers avoided looking at me, which also suggested something had gone wrong, something that was my fault. I suddenly understood where the term "losing face" came from. It was as if I didn't have one.

The air officer explained the situation while Tomo translated. "Four Mitsubishi fighters from this ship intercepted Flight 173 just after 15:00 hours. As we agreed, they began close maneuvering to force the Chinese aircraft to take evasive action. Whenever the Chinese aircraft attempted to head west, they cut it off."

"At approximately 15:20 hours, the Chinese aircraft made a clear turn east and stayed on its new course. Our aircraft formed a close escort around it, but took no more maneuvers. Our pilots have reported that our message must have been clear to the Chinese aircrew: If you head for home, we will stay out of your way."

"At approximately 15:25, our fighters were preparing to take a more distant escorting position, with the intention of accompanying the Chinese aircraft to the limit of their range. Without warning, the Chinese aircraft turned to the right as hard as possible. Our closest fighter did the same, but our pilot apparently was taken by surprise. The right wing of his fighter touched the tail of the Chinese aircraft, and both aircraft plunged toward the sea out of control and crashed."

"Were there any survivors?" I asked.

"Our pilot did not attempt to eject." Transport aircraft, I knew, generally had no ejection seats. But fighter planes did.

I had to try to put myself in the Oriental mindset. I understood why the Japanese pilot had not ejected. He felt he had failed, so he went down with his plane. What about the hard right turn of the Chinese transport? The Chinese crew knew they were all dead men if they had a mid-air collision. Were their orders to create an incident? Would Chinese commit suicide in order to carry out their mission, as Japanese would? Ever since the Sino-Japanese War of 1895, the Japanese had always beaten the Chinese. Did the Chinese crew find death preferable to another Chinese defeat? Or would worse have been waiting for them it they came home having failed?

Whatever their intention, one thing was clear. We now had an incident between China and the Northern Confederation, an incident with Chinese casualties. My plan for the intercept had failed. I'd been hooked by one horn of the dilemma, and my first task now was to avoid the other one.

Turning to Admiral Tanaka, I said, "In view of this change in the situation, my judgment of the appropriate timing for our attack on Portland is also changed. We must act to resolve the situation in Cascadia as swiftly as possible, to present China with a *fait accompli*. That may forestall further Chinese action as pointless."

"I agree," Tanaka replied. After a short talk with his staff, he said, "We can be ready the morning of the day after tomorrow, October 7th."

"The landing force is as ready as it will ever be. Let's do it," I said.

On the way back to the conference, I had to make some more quick decisions. Trust was vital in any military operation, especially a combined operation with forces from two countries. But I did not trust the Idaho crowd.

Walking into the conference room, I did not sit down. "Gentlemen," I said, ignoring the woman, "we have had some developments in the military situation which concern only those who will be taking an active part in the operation. This conference is concluded. The delegation from Idaho will report to the flight deck immediately, where an aircraft is waiting to take them home. I will ask the Cascadian Resistance military leaders to remain here for some further discussions."

The broad at least knew when to cut her losses. "It is imperative that the Resistance Council arrive in Portland as soon as possible after fighting is concluded," she said.

"We will send an aircraft to Idaho as soon as Portland is secure," I replied.

"Thank you very much," she said stiffly.

The Idaho delegation filed out, and the rest of us sat back down. I explained the incident with the Chinese aircraft and why it was now necessary to move fast. Everyone saw the point. "I know the landing force is ready. Can the Resistance units in and around Portland move by the day after tomorrow?"

The consensus was that they could. Their job was to tie down as many enemy forces as possible while the landing force went after the Palaeopitus.

"OK, it's a go."

*

The last big question was the weather. In Cascadia, it rains a lot, the weather changes almost hourly, and fog is common. Rain we could handle, but fog was a problem, since we were coming by air straight into downtown Portland. Like the old German airborne, we would land right on top of the objective to cause maximum confusion among the enemy.

By 03:00 on October 7th, the fleet's chief weather boffin gave us a go. The ceiling should be about 3,000 feet, which was perfect. They wouldn't see us coming until we were on top of them.

Overnight, the fleet had steamed up close to the coast to minimize flight time. We had enough helos to carry a third of the landing force in each lift, with about two hours between lifts. Our target was the former campus of Portland Community College, located on top of Mount Sylvania, which the Palaeopitus had turned into their compound.

At 05:00 the local Resistance forces were to hit Deep Green barracks and checkpoints throughout the Portland area. Their mission was to keep the enemy occupied so he couldn't shift his forces. At 05:30, our first lift was to hit the compound. The timing was tricky. We needed to tie down enemy forces before we went in, but not give the Palaopitus time to skip town.

It didn't work. I went in with the first lift, and we found the former community college deserted. Food, clothes, and abandoned vehicles spoke of a hasty flight some time in the night. They'd obviously gotten the word we were coming, probably from a double agent in the Resistance. I was disappointed, but I knew that when you worked with local forces this kind of thing had to be expected.

Elsewhere in the city, the remaining enemy didn't put up much of a fight. They knew that if they surrendered they'd get their back pay, a bonus, and a safe trip wherever they wanted to go. The government they were fighting for couldn't offer them any of those things, much less all of them.

By about 11:00 the city was in our hands, but not the Palaeopitus. The local Resistance leaders trickled in to the former campus where they knew they'd find me. I needed them, because their humint was the only source for what I needed to know: where had the Palaeopitus fled? I had air reconnaissance up, but in typical Cascadian fashion, the ceiling was coming down. The air boss called to tell me that by 13:00, they'd have to suspend air operations.

We established our headquarters in the old gym of the community college and the Cascadians worked their nets from there, trying to piece reports together. As always, many of the reports were false, and we couldn't know which were good. We ended up graphing them, trying to determine where the most sightings were being reported. If the bad reports were spread evenly, the density of reports in a given area should still give us a clue. By mid-afternoon a pattern was emerging: a steady build-up of reports from west of the city, toward the sea.

I got on the horn at once to the ship. "Tomo, tell our ASW boys to put everything they have into the areas along the coast due west from Portland. I'm betting they'll find a Chinese sub. If they do, let me know, but don't attack it." The Japs would be embarrassed if a Chinese submarine had gotten through to the coast undetected, but I knew subs were real good at that. If I were right, we had to grab the local gods before they got on board. The last thing I wanted was another incident with China, so we couldn't attack the sub. If the Paleopitus did make their escape, the Chinese would have a government in exile they could work to put back in as soon as we were gone. That Chinese task force with amphibs suddenly took on a new meaning.

Meanwhile, we were in a tail chase with no aviation thanks to the weather. And we were infantry with no vehicles. It didn't look good.

The Resistance forces set to work scrounging some trucks and fuel from what the Paleopitus had abandoned, and by late in the day we had a column ready to go. I didn't have much hope of success, but I figured I'd head out with it anyway. Just after 17:00 hours, as I was getting ready to roll, Tomo came up on the radio. I figured they'd found the sub.

They had, and it was where it should to be to pick up the Paleopitus. But that wasn't why he was calling. "I have an urgent message for you from Governor Kraft," Tomo said. "At approximately six this morning, a Chinese ICBM hit the center of Portland Harbor. The missile carried no warhead, but it was followed by a Chinese ultimatum demanding compensation for the loss of their aircraft and the withdrawal of all Northern Confederation forces, ground, naval, and air, from Cascadia within 24 hours. Failure to comply will bring 'full retaliation on the Northern Confederation with all the means at the disposal of the people of China.' Request advice."

No wonder Sherman said war is hell, I thought. But this time the Chinese hadn't taken me by surprise. Now it was my turn.

"OK, Tomo, get this back to Governor Kraft immediately. 'Response to Chinese ultimatum: You will have our answer in Shanghai.'"

"OK, I've got that," Tomo said.

"Now, I've got a second task for you. You remember the yakuza I met with near the ryokan?"

"Yes."

"Call him. You still have his number?"

"Yes."

"Give him this message: 'Illuminate the Great Wall.' Got it?"

"Yes, 'Illuminate the Great Wall.' But what does it mean?"

"Just do what I say, Tomo. Please. I don't have time to explain. Can you get that message to him immediately?"

"Yes."

"Good. I'm heading out with a truck-borne Cascadian Resistance force in chase of the Palaeopitus. Keep an eye on that sub. You'll have continuous comm with me."

Unlike American military radios, I knew Japanese military radios always worked.

A few days after I joined our fleet, a small freighter flying the Malaysian flag had steamed up the Whangpoo river into Shanghai's outer harbor. In the world's busiest port, it had gone unnoticed. A few hours after my talk with Tomo, its crew went ashore and melted away in the fleshpots of the Bund. At approximately six AM Shanghai time, the 300 tons of explosives on board blew up with a roar audible for fifty miles around. The ship was anchored far enough out that there was no damage to port facilities, just as there had been no damage in Portland.

The Chinese government knew the Northern Confederation had nuclear weapons. They had doubted our ability to deliver them on Chinese soil. I hoped we had now resolved those doubts. Where megatons are concerned, a fishing boat is as elegant a delivery system as any rocket.

The Chinese had wisely kept their ultimatum private, so they could ignore it without publicly humiliating themselves. But we still needed to wrap up the NC's involvement in Cascadia fast. It was evening by the time our column got out of the Portland suburbs, and a slow tail-chase by night was almost hopeless. But we pressed on nonetheless, crawling along the barely discernible remains of old Highway 26 at an average speed of less than 10 miles per hour.

About an hour before daylight, I got a call from the SIGINT officer on the *Adams*, Commander Yahashi. They had picked up a rapid exchange of messages between a shore party and the sub, in a different Chinese code. He suspected it was from a Chinese military liaison party accompanying the fleeing Palaeopitus. After the final message from the shore party, the sub had turned away from the coast and was maintaining a course due west. Yahashi's Direction Finder put the on-shore source of the signals about ten miles east of Tillamook.

The night had remained wet and fog-shrouded, and we'd lost the remains of the road more than once. We had to turn south toward Tillamook and we missed the junction three times, hunting back and forth across it like dogs on a weak scent. Of the surrounding countryside we could see nothing.

A clammy dawn snuck in around 05:00, and it revealed a vision like nothing I'd ever seen, except maybe in pictures of the areas around Verdun or the Somme in World War I. The landscape was a bare, blasted ruin of mud and tree stumps and skidder trails. Through it on both our flanks marched columns of infantry: animals, dozens of them, coyotes, wolves, mountain lions, bears, emancipated household dogs and cats, emaciated, staring but keeping a safe distance of about 50 yards.

Deep Green, in its dual worship of nature and power, had stripped the landscape bare but strictly forbidden the killing of animals. Deprived of habitat, the animals had turned into quadruped Hell's Angels, forming vast packs of mixed species, that moved from one government feeding site to another. Animal welfare working much like human welfare, they continued to breed until their numbers outstripped Cascadia's ability to feed them, and then they kept breeding anyway. Sometimes they ate each other, but mostly they roamed, slowly starving.

Deep down in the ancestral dungeon of the human mind lies a powerful fear of being eaten. We fingered our triggers and wondered how soon we would run out of bullets. But the animals didn't attack. They kept their distance, following us as we marched along.

A little after ten o'clock in the morning, heading south-southeast, our human convoy and its animal escort crested a rise. The motorcycle outrider on point held up his hand to halt us. I jumped down from the lead truck and walked forward. Just over the rise lay our objective, the gods of the Palaeopitus, along with their last-ditch Deep Green bodyguard and the Chinese liaison team whose calls to the submarine Yahashi had intercepted.

Their gnawed bones, stripped nearly clean of flesh, lay scattered in a circle about a hundred yards across. Crows flapped their wings and picked at the remains. Around the bones was a wall of dead animals, shot down in a charge that even modern firepower could not stop. Beyond the quadruped dead was another circle, of more predators of every kind, male and female, facing inward, standing at rest or sitting on their haunches. They turned their heads to watch us, but not a one moved.

Two armies faced each other, one human, one animal. I wondered what we would do if they attacked. All our firepower could do was build another wall of furry bodies before we too went down before their numbers.

But it seemed they had fed well enough that day. Inhuman eyes stared at us as we cautiously retreated, leaving the battlefield to its victors.

*

Our column retraced its steps toward Portland, mission accomplished, thanks to our unexpected allies. The weather lifted shortly after noon and a helo from the ship soon found us. I took my leave of the Cascadian Resistance, reminding them of our promise to put it all back the way it had been before Deep Green, and flew back to the *Adams*.

Yahashi met me at the aircraft door as soon as we set down. "We've managed to break that Chinese military code, most of it anyway. The last message from the liaison group reported they were being overrun. We don't seem to have the whole code, since our translation says they were 'being eaten.'"

"You got the whole code," I replied. Yahashi looked at me quizzically.

"Don't worry about it," I said. "The Palaeopitus is dead. That's the important thing. Now, the Chinese have no exile government they can scheme to restore. They've got nothing but empty hands and an empty submarine, and an ultimatum that they'll find it convenient to forget about. The game's over."

Right behind Yahashi was Tomo. "You have an urgent message from the Resistance Council in Idaho. They say Portland is now secure and you promised you'd send an airplane for them. They are very anxious to come and set up a new government."

"Yeah, I'll bet they are," I replied. "Well, I've got two promises to keep." I'd promised Idaho an airplane, but I'd also promised our four-footed allies that we'd make things right. The Idaho bunch were still Greens, and I knew where their agenda led. I also had an idea of how I'd keep both promises.

"Tell the air boss on the *John Kelly* to get a transport ready along with four dive bombers as escorts." The *Kelly* carried our ground support air wing, which the Japs called Jaeger Air, using the old German word that meant both "hunter" and "light infantry." It included two squadrons of Val II prop-driven dive bombers. They were slow but deadly accurate, and unlike fancy PGMs you could stock a lot of 2,000 pound bombs because they were cheap.

I grabbed a quick meal and shower on the *Adams* while the *Kelly* got my flight ready. Over a bowl of fish and rice, I told Tomo, "Let the Resistance Council in Boise know our ETA and tell them to assemble everyone in the old air terminal building." Idaho wasn't important enough to have any regular air service, but the field was still operable for occasional flights and the terminal building was open.

We'd take off around 5 PM, and there would still be a little daylight when we got over Boise around 7. I transferred by helo to the *Kelly*, where my flight was being prepped. In the ready room I met with the ship's air boss and my flight crew and briefed them on the mission. My plan brought a few initial hisses, but after I explained the political situation in Cascadia they turned to grins.

We took off just after 17:00 hours, as planned. The Vals each carried their usual armament of one 2,000-pound bomb. I rode up front in the co-pilot's seat of the transport to direct the show, if any direction was needed.

Once we were over the Cascades, we found clear skies and plenty of sun. The evening light gave shadows that made it easy to pick out features on the ground. Just after seven we came over the Boise airfield. The Vals stayed high while I did a low pass over the airfield, then confirmed by radio that the Resistance Council was duly assembled in the terminal building. I could see their faces pressed up against the glass of the main waiting room.

Over the radio, I told the Vals, "Good to go." With that, they dived in succession, planting their eggs in a perfect rectangle on each corner of the air terminal building. With the final flash from the last 2,000 pound bomb, the remains of the roof pancaked onto the remains of the floor, entombing the mortal remains of the last of Cascadia's Greens.

So I kept both pledges. I'd only promised the Resistance Council one airplane, and I gave them four.

*

We got back to the ship just before ten, and I slept away the rest of my last night as Lord High Admiral of the Ocean Sea. The next morn-ing, after a short ceremony, the Northern Confederation ensign came down from the ships, the Rising Sun with streaming rays went back up the masts, and the Northern Confederation's Pacific fleet was no more. Alongside the *Zuikaku*, a long-range flying boat waited to take me home, this time flying straight across the old United States.

Tomo went with me in the launch to the flying boat. We'd become friends, and we parted with genuine wishes we could get together again some time.

"John, there is one ceremony we never performed, and I would be remiss if we did not do it now. We never exchanged *meishi*." Tomo handed me his card, on which he had given me a rare honor: his home address and phone number, written on the back.

I took out my simple card, turned it over and wrote on the back. As I stepped through the door of the Kawanishi, I handed to Tomo. He turned it over and read it.

*

I watched a butterfly
Soar unconcerned
Above a chain of ants.

CHAPTER FORTY-ONE

IKE most flying boats, the big Kawanishi was slow. By the time
we reached Buffalo, the Northern Confederation's westernmost
city, the sun was long gone from the sky. The Japanese pilot
switched on the powerful landing lights, made a pass over the harbor to
find a clear stretch of water, then set her down. We'd radioed ahead that
the Chief of the General Staff was on board, so the local militia had sent
a sergeant to meet me at the dock.

"Welcome home," the sergeant said, offering me his hand and a grin.
"Understand you were having some fun with the loonies out west."

"Some," I replied.

"All's well that ends well, eh?"

"Ayuh." The sergeant's "eh" told me he was a former Canadian who'd
come across. The ones we took were solid stock, plain folk and hard
working, with the friendliness that had characterized English Canada.
We didn't let in the French Canadians.

"How's the hockey 'round heah?" I asked. Hockey had allowed
Canada to export its two great surpluses: Canadians and ice.

"Good. Plenty of us Canucks to teach you boys how to play it."

"I'd like to head on to Maine tonight," I said. "What time does the Night Mail leave?"

"She leaves at midnight," the sergeant answered. Trains were always "she," which was odd since they were supposed to be on time. "But we couldn't get you a Pullman berth or even a seat. All filled up. Folks are traveling again, mostly on business."

"That's OK, I'll ride the RPO." The Railway Post Office car was another old idea we had revived. The mail was sorted en route. You could put a letter in the RPO's slot in Buffalo Tuesday evening and it would be delivered in Albany Wednesday morning.

I glanced at my watch and saw it was ten minutes past eleven, local time. "Can we get to the station by twelve?"

"No sweat," the sergeant replied. "The streetcars still run pretty often even this late." Thanks to Niagara Falls, this part of the N.C. had plentiful electricity, and streetcars had made a fast comeback. They were another good idea we had forgotten about in the Motor Age.

We walked down to the main road that connected the docks, and in a few minutes a big yellow Peter Witt trolley car stopped in front of us. With a growl of traction motors and clanking of Brill Maximum Traction trucks, we were off through the night.

Despite a change of streetcar in the town center, we made it to the station with seven minutes to spare. There waited the *Night Mail*, at her head a gleaming black Niagara fresh out of the Alco works. Like all steam engines, she was a thing alive, talking to herself in a monologue of hisses, roars and thump-thumps-thumps as she gathered her strength for the run to Albany. We'd be doing 80 within minutes of leaving the station, and she'd keep the *Night Mail*'s twenty cars at track speed steady through the night on the old Water Level Route.

The sliding side door of the RPO stood open as last-minute sacks of mail were thrown aboard. I thanked the sergeant for meeting me and swung myself up on the grabirons. "No room at the inn, gentlemen," I said to the postal clerks. "So I'm afraid you've got a passenger tonight."

I was in uniform, which meant I was welcome anywhere. "I'm afraid we don't have much to offer in the way of billeting, captain," said the head clerk. "You're welcome to a pile of mail bags to sit on, but that's all we've got."

"I've sat on worse," I replied. "Just wake me up when you need to sort my seat."

The RPO exploded with an immense WHUMPF as steam entered the Niagara's cylinders and the 80-inch drivers grabbed at the rail. I looked at my old Hamilton watch: right on twelve midnight. In the Northern Confederation, the trains ran on time. Soon the engine was belting out the steady TCH-tch-tch-tch TCH-tch-tch-tch that meant steam at speed. It proved an effective sleeping potion.

By the time I woke up it was daylight and we were in the Berkshires on the old B&A. I'd slept right through the division of the train and engine change at Albany. Up front now was an ancient ten-wheeler, a relic retrieved from some museum, and she was working hard to hit 50. No matter; the RPO door was open on a crisp fall day and the deep forests in orange and gold helped banish the grim Cascadian landscape from my mind. I'd be in Boston by noon and Portland in time for supper.

"We'll take those mail bags now that you're up, skipper," said the clerk.

"I told you to get me up when you needed 'em," I replied. "I don't want to hold up the mails."

"Don't worry, you won't," he said. "We just put those off for last. We know our soldiers need their sleep. If you'd like some breakfast, we've got a thermos of coffee and a cheese sandwich we picked up for you at Albany."

"Thanks. How'd you get coffee?"

"We Buffalo boys do a bit of trading across the river. Got some Cuban cigars too if you'd like one."

"Hell, yes. That's the best homecoming present anyone could give me." I sat on a sack of sorted mail in the open door, enjoying a mix of Havana and coal smoke, listening to the stack talk from our little engine and watching the world go by. Life's real pleasures turn up where you least expect them.

We made Boston on time, and after changing to North Station I got the afternoon train for home. This time I got a seat, in a new Maine-built wooden car. Maine craftsmanship showed in its inlays and arched windows. Now that we were poor, we made things right again.

I'd wired ahead that I'd be in on the six o'clock train. If any hot items were waiting my attention at headquarters, someone could bring them down from Augusta. If they did, I'd have to take another look at my staff, since they had full powers to act in my absence. I scanned the platform as we pulled in but didn't see any of my boys.

Then out of the cloud of steam and smoke a massive figure strode purposefully down the length of the train, obviously on the hunt: Bill Kraft. Shit, I thought, is this going to be another BOHICA homecoming? Yeah, I'd cut things a bit close with the Chinks, but I had all the bases covered. Now it looked as if I were going to get a rocket.

I grabbed my gear and jumped down from the train. The governor was two cars up dead ahead. Bill's face was perfectly masked, offering no clue as to what he was thinking. He steered for me like Tegetthoff at Lissa.

"Well, do I get an 'attaboy this time or should I turn around and bend over?" I greeted our Chief of State.

Bill stared me down, expressionless. Then he came to attention, saluted, and barked, "*Heil dir im Siegerkranz!*" "Hail to thee in the Victor's wreath!" It was the old song played at German military triumphs, the tune known elsewhere as "God Save the Queen."

"I guess this means I'm not in trouble?" I asked.

"You know the first law of war, my boy," Bill replied, grinning. "All's well that ends well. You got the result we intended, at virtually no cost to us. That's my definition of a brilliant campaign."

When a militia sergeant and the country's supreme war leader both see it the same way, in the same words, you've made some progress, I thought. Maybe we were finally free of the old American military preoccupation with process instead of results.

"Waal, I suspected that Chink rocket in Portland harbor might have ruined your day," I said to Bill as we turned to walk together toward the station entrance.

"I've had more welcome wake-up calls," Bill admitted. "But the folks you left in charge back here had foreseen the Chinese might do something like that. We had some responses working through both Tokyo and Moscow. But none were half as good as the light show you put on in Shanghai."

"I thought you might like that one. Of course, it depended on you, too. You had to trust me enough to give Beijing the reply I recommended."

"I did trust you."

"Why?"

"First, because your message told me you were ahead of the game. You had thought it through to the end this time, as much as anyone can in war. Second, because I've watched you grow. Some people can't, and their utility is limited. And third, because if I can't trust you I should replace you. There is nothing more counterproductive than a subordinate you can't trust, unless it is a superior you can't trust."

"I gather I can take all that as a compliment," I replied.

"You can take it however you like," Bill replied. "It's the truth."

*

The governor intended to stay in Portland for a few days, nosing about and taking the pulse in our busiest port. His duties as Field Marshal never detracted from his work as governor of Maine, which he regarded as his first responsibility. He understood that smaller, not bigger, is better.

Bill had arranged a room for me in his hotel, and after I got settled we headed for a little restaurant, really just somebody's house. He had finds like this every place he went, and they seldom disappointed. If, as Napoleon said, an army travels on its stomach, Bill traveled for his.

This *auberge* was run by one of our Egyptian Christians, and while I didn't know exactly what I was eating, it all tasted good. In Maine, that was unusual. Once we'd both gotten past the hungry stage and were eating for pleasure, Bill asked if I had any plans beyond checking in at Augusta.

"It's fall again, and while I've seen better leaf years, I thought I might go walking in New Hampshire."

"How about going fishing instead?" Bill asked.

"I might do some fly fishing along the way," I answered.

"I was thinking more of ocean fishing."

"Bill, I'm a Marine, remember? Ocean fishing means a boat. Marines hate boats."

Actually, I enjoyed a good sail, but I sensed I needed to get some defenses up.

"We've got some rather interesting boats sailing out of Portland now, schooners, some three-masted, heading toward the Grand Banks. It would be a real 19th century experience to crew on one," Bill said.

"Governor, are you telling me you're going to crew on a Maine fishing boat?"

"No, I'm telling you that you are."

I nearly choked on my falafel. "You mean my reward for a job well done is to be demoted from Admiral of the Fleet to cabin boy on some damned lobster boat? What's second prize, a moose shit sandwich?"

"Don't whine, not in front of wogs. The reward for a job well done is another job. Or were you expecting your little feat in Cascadia would bring peace in our time?"

"I take it we have a problem at sea?"

"No, I'm sending you out because I thought the sea air would be good for your complexion. Why do Marines always revert to the rank of lance corporal when presented with something new?"

"Probably for the same reason you get sarcastic. Why don't you stow the sandpaper and tell me what's going on?"

"Piracy. Our fishing boats are disappearing on the Grand Banks."

"Who's doing it?"

"We don't know. The little fishing expedition I've proposed to you is an attempt to find out."

"Why don't we just leave it to the Navy?"

"Because we don't really have one. Your magnificent Pacific squadron was a rent-a-fleet. Our real Navy doesn't have near enough ships or men to patrol the Grand Banks. Of course, you can leave this mission up to them if you want. I simply thought you might want to visit the front, as wise Chiefs of the General Staff have been known to do."

"Just what has the Navy proposed?"

"A Q-ship. A sailing ship with hidden guns."

"Shades of von Luckner! I've commanded a fleet, but I've never been in a real naval battle. Where would I find this Q-ship?"

"At the naval pier. Why don't you go have a look at her?"

"You know, I just might do that."

The next morning I walked down to the Navy Yard, where our High Sea Fleet of torpedo boats and converted trawlers was based. The subs were at New London. Alongside the pier was moored a three-masted schooner. I quickly spied Captain Rick Hoffman, the senior officer of the N.C. Navy, chewing somebody's ass on the quarter-deck.

"Ahoy, mate! Permission to come aboard?" I called out.

Rick turned and peered my way. "Shit, it's the Admiral of the Fleet hisself," he exclaimed. "Wait a minute, I gotta get the bo'suns' pipes up. Why aren't you in your admiral's uniform, anyway?"

"Cause if you saw it you'd laugh your ass off, and then what would you think with?" I answered. "You can belay the pipes, too, since I'm in mufti. I just came down to see what you're up to."

"What we're up to is creating the Northern Confederation's first ship-of-the-line. Come aboard and see for yourself. After a two-carrier battle group, she may not look like much, but I think she'll do the job we need her for."

I crossed the gangplank and climbed up to the quarterdeck, where I noticed a swivel mounted on the taffrail but no other armament.

"Welcome aboard, John," Rick said, offering his callused hand, "I'm green with envy, not seasickness. I would have given my right hook to command our Pacific fleet."

"You would have had to grow some slanty eyes to do that, my friend," I replied. "For the most part, I was just a bird in a gilded cage for all of the world to see. At least this tub is really an N.C. ship. Where'd you find her?"

"She's the former *Victory Chimes*, out of Castine," Rick replied. "She was built early in the 20th century as a lumber schooner, and later converted into a cruise boat that worked Penobscot Bay in the 1960s and '70s. She's got the lines of a barn and the speed of an old house darkey on a hot July day, but she's sturdy, and that's what we need most."

"She better be sturdier than *Old Ironsides* if you're gonna fight pirates with that swivel."

Rick grinned. "If you think that, maybe they will too. Come below."

Rick led me down to the lower deck where the passenger cabins used to be. In their place was a full gun deck. I could see a row of 120 mm breech-loading mortars mounted on each beam. Rick grabbed a line and pulled, and a port opened in front of the nearest gun. Putting his shoulder to it, he ran it out on a carriage that looked about right for a twelve-pounder. "We've got fourteen ports a side, with a mix of 120s and 50. cal. machine guns. Plus, fore and aft, we've got Sagger missiles on pivot carriages, which we can use on broadside or as chasers. What d'ya think?"

"Horatio Hornblower would be proud," I replied.

"That's it!" Rick exclaimed.

"What's what?"

"The name of our ship! We've wanted to rename her now that she's a man o'war, but couldn't come up with anything we liked. Admiral, you stand on the gun deck of the *NCS Horatio Hornblower!*" A ragged cheer went up from the men working around us. I was glad to know some people were still reading C.S. Forester. His books are excellent studies of military decision-making.

"Well, if she fights like Hornblower, we should have plenty of pirates to hang. Would you mind if I came along for the fun?" I asked.

"We'd be delighted to have you. Think you can still lead a boarding party?"

"That's the kind of party Marines like best. When do you sail?"

"In three days, if the wind is fair. Stow your gear aft in my cabin. There's an extra bunk. And John, there is one thing we still need for a proper sailing warship, if you can scrounge it for us."

"What's that?"

"A cask of rum."

*

Three days later, the morning calm gave way to a land breeze. A tug warped the *Horatio Hornblower* out from the dock and into Portland's outer harbor, where we hoisted our three big gaff mainsails. We were soon bowling along at a grand five knots. *HMS Lydia* would have been hull down of us in an hour.

But Fall's northwest winds didn't fail us, and the 20th of October saw us off the Grand Banks. There, we pretended to fish, which is what most fisherman I've observed seem to do.

It didn't take long for the first military problem to crop up. We saw some other Northern Confederation fishing boats, sailing ships like ourselves. But most of the fishing operations we encountered were foreign, motorized, and poaching the hell out of our fishing grounds. I knew what my first order of business would be once I got back to Augusta.

We drifted and fished and messed about for a week and more, finding nothing but fish. Our eleventh day out, we crossed paths with a Mexican trawler. She wasn't the first we'd seen, and we let her pass without hailing her.

About two hours after sunset, in the direction she'd gone, we heard sharp bursts of automatic weapons fire.

With a top speed of five knots, we couldn't chase much. All we could try to do was place ourselves in harm's way. Rick put the *Hornblower's* helm up, tacked and set a course in the direction of the gunfire. Below decks, we cleared for action and the crews stood to their guns.

As so often in war, nothing happened. Dawn revealed an empty sea. Had it just been fiesta time in old Mexico, with some weapons fired in celebration? We had no way to tell.

On a hunch, Rick turned south. The gun crews went to breakfast and then racked out. If something were in the neighborhood, we'd have warning enough. The steady northwest wind put us on a reach, which was a fore-and-after's best point of sailing.

Just after noon, as I was enjoying some cheese and hardtack with the daily grog ration, the foretop lookout cried "Ship ahoy! Two ships close abeam 30 degrees off the starboard bow. Range five miles."

Rick grabbed his binos and started up the foremast shrouds. Shortly, he called down, "One of them is the Mex from yesterday. Beat to quarters!"

Below, our crews lay to their guns. Above, we luffed as if we'd just found a good fishing spot, lowered the dory and began laying a net.

The two trawlers had seen us before we saw them, and neither had moved. Maybe they were just passing the tequila and comparing fish and whores.

Then, about forty-five minutes after we'd lowered our nets, the trawler behind the Mexican boat began to move. She cut across the other boat's bow and set a course straight for us.

We played dumb. Our lookout came down from his perch, and our oared dory continued spreading the net. I went below to the gun deck, leaving a minimum watch topside, as would be normal on a working boat.

The approaching trawler didn't seem in a particular hurry. He didn't need to be. It was obvious we weren't going anywhere. He'd probably figured we'd found some fish and he might as well help himself to our catch. There was nothing an old Yankee scow could do to stop him.

I heard Rick calling my name down the main hatchway and ran toward it. "What's up, skipper?" I asked.

"His flag," Rick answered. "He just raised it to his bridge, but I don't recognize it. It's red with some kind of white blob in the middle."

That threw me. "Can't help you. Probably some Caribbean ministate. Their flags all look like beer can labels. Where's he heading?"

"Like he's gonna come up on our port side."

"Well, we're ready for him."

The trawler suddenly shifted his helm and came starboard of us. The gun crews quietly moved from one broadside to the other. We could hear the trawler suddenly back engines as he came abeam of us. Above, Rick yelled, "Ahoy, what ship?"

The answer came back in a blast of automatic rifle fire. Below, we didn't need any order. The hidden gunports slammed up, strong Yankee shoulders ran out the 120s and .50s and the gun captain yelled, "Give 'em hell, men."

Through an open gunport, I got a clear look at the pirates' flag: red with three white skulls in a horizontal line, and above them a white, stepped pyramid. Aztecs?

The gunfire from the trawler was quickly drowned in a cascade of exploding 120mm shells. They ripped whole sheets of metal from her bridge and her hull. Our .50 cals smothered every point from which enemy fire had been observed. In a matter of seconds her bridge was a pile of flaming wreckage and we could see gaps in her hull that reached below the waterline.

One shell hit something in the engine room and caused a secondary. Then, with a roar, his whole aft end ignited in a sheet of flames and foul, oily smoke: Pemex diesel.

As soon as I saw the engine room go up, I yelled "Cease fire! Cease fire." I wanted some live pirates to take home with us to find out if we were really fighting sea-going Aztecs or just somebody else who found their flag convenient. Besides, public hanging of pirates was a nice old tradition that offered fun for the whole family.

"Enemy to port!" The cry came from somewhere forward on the gun deck. I ran to a portside gun and looked out to see the other trawler coming up. She was about 4,000 meters off, with a bone in her teeth. It was a brave but stupid move, especially since she probably carried only a prize crew.

I walked forward to find the bowchaser crew manhandling their Sagger on its pivot carriage from the starboard to the port side of the ship. By the time that muscle-intensive operation was completed, the trawler was in Sagger range. It was still a long shot. We'd see whether today's Yankee gunners were as good as their ancestors who served Preble and Decatur. The carriage extended the Sagger on a long arm to keep the back blast out of the ship. It was a jury-rig that made aiming awkward. I knew I couldn't have hit much with it, not at that range.

With a roar, the missile ignited, rose, then fell again, trailing its guide-wire. I watched the plume recede into the distance as the gunner stared and sweated behind his crude sight.

Flight time should be about 15 seconds. I leveled my binos at the oncoming trawler and counted: 11, 12, 13—a hit! The warhead flashed, smoke and parts of the ship flew upward and a dull boom echoed across the water. Then it was Beatty at Jutland all over again. With an enormous flash and roar, the trawler exploded. When the smoke cleared, nothing was left.

We wouldn't be getting any guests for a necktie party from that trawler, so I raced topside to see what the other ship had delivered. I heard rifles cracking as I came up the hatch. The Aztec boat—if that's what it was—was going under, the survivors of our broadsides were abandoning ship and our boys were shooting them in the water. The 21st century didn't stand on ceremony with pirates.

I yelled "Cease fire! Cease fire!," but too late. All the figures in the water were face down and trailing blood.

Except one. "That's a woman, sir," one of the sailor-snipers said. It probably wasn't an accident. Most men don't like shooting women.

She'd been trying to swim away, even though there was nothing to swim to closer than Labrador. When the firing stopped, she turned around and looked our way, then struck out again. "Launch a boat and pick her up," I ordered. "Maybe she'll tell us who we were fighting."

"We'll get it out of her, sir," a sailor said, grinning, Men may not like shooting women, even in war, but there are plenty of other things they enjoy doing to a woman caught on a battlefield.

"Not that way," I replied with an icy look. "Remember, we're a Christian country. If anybody needs God's favor, it's men at sea on a sailing ship."

The woman flailed frantically as our boat approached her, but she was at the end of her strength. I saw a sailor reach out and grab her, then watched other arms haul her aboard.

As the dory approached the *Hornblower*, the woman looked up. I could see her features, and she was clearly no Indian. "Get her towels and a blanket, and some hot soup," I ordered. The water off the Grand Banks is frigid year-round.

The dory crew led the woman up on deck, where we wrapped her tight in a warm blanket and handed her a mug of steaming chowder.

"Do you speak English?" I asked her.

"Yes, Señor." She mouthed the words almost soundlessly, like a cat's silent meow.

"No one here is going to hurt you. Drink the soup and get warmed up. When you're able to move, someone will take you below where you can get into dry clothes." I noticed a crucifix around her neck and pointed to it. "We are also Christians. You are safe now." Then I left her alone and made sure everyone else did the same.

One of our crew, Sam Medelli, was a paramedic when he wasn't a topman, and I asked him to keep an eye on our prisoner. After a while I saw him lead her below, and soon thereafter she was topside again in dry dungarees and a flannel shirt. Sam hung her clothes in the rigging to dry. I motioned him over to me and asked how she was.

"She's exhausted and frightened, but she has nothing physically wrong with her that I could see. If she can eat and then sleep, she should be all right."

Not long after, the cook rang the dinner bell. Sam went over to the woman and spoke with her, and she followed him down to the gundeck where we had our mess. There, she tasted the food, then pushed it away.

"Try to eat, ma'am," I said to her. "The sea took a lot out of you, and some food will help."

"I am sorry, señor, but your food is very bad," she said.

"We know. Yankees generally don't make good cooks."

"I was the cook on the *Nuestra Señora de Guadaloupe*," she replied. "If you want me to, I will cook for you also."

"Was that the name of the pirate ship?" I asked, surprised.

"No señor. I was not on the pirate ship. I was cook on the trawler, the one the Aztecs took. The ship you sank with a rocket, señor. It was my brother's ship. The Aztecs took me aboard their ship for their pleasure, señor."

"I'm sorry," I said. "I guess I am also a little surprised that you are willing to cook for people who just killed your brother."

She shrugged. "We are used to these things, señor. He is not the first brother I have lost. We are killed by everybody, enemies and friends alike. It is our fate. I have learned to accept it."

"Who do you mean by we?"

"We are Cristeros, señor. My father is a leader of the Cristeros in the province of Tamaulipas. We are at war with the Aztecs. That is why we were here."

I knew about the war in Nueva Hispania, as the Spanish-speaking remnants of Mexico and the former American Southwest were now known. After the Indians took Mexico City they renamed it Tenochtitlan and brought back their old religion. That meant the cult of Huitzilopochtli, the Hummingbird Wizard who demanded an endless diet of human blood and hearts. The Cristeros had been Christian rebels against the Marxist, secular PRI dictatorship in early 20th century Mexico. Putting two and two together, I figured the new Cristeros were the Christian Resistance to the pagan Indians.

"Just why were you here?" I asked. "There are plenty of fish in the Gulf of Mexico. You didn't need to come to the Grand Banks for more."

"Yes, señor, but the Gulf of Mexico is also full of Mexica ships. It has become too dangerous for us. Sadly, our enemies found us here also."

The Aztec flag on the pirate ship was real, then. But why had Aztecs—Mexica, to use their own name for themselves—come so far north? "Do you know why your enemies were here?" I asked her.

"Yes, señor. They do not search for fish, nor for ships, nor for treasure as we understand it. They have come to take captives for Huitzilopochtli. In the time of Cortez, Huitzilopochtli preferred Indian blood. But through his priests, he has told the Mexica Tlatoani, their priest-king, that he will no longer accept the hearts and blood of Indians. He demands white hearts and white blood now. So the Mexica go ever farther in their quest for those things."

Once again, someone else's fight far away had reached out and touched us. We couldn't figure what pirates would want with our fishing boats, which were almost all sailing ships with nothing on board but fish. We also wondered why we didn't get any ransom demands for their crews. Now, we knew. It didn't make me happy to think of those good Yankee boys having their beating hearts ripped out of their bodies with obsidian knives on top of the Great Temple of Tenochtitlan.

"Just one other question, ma'am, if I may. What's your name?"

"I am Maria Mercedes de Dio de Alva," she replied. "And I would like to cook for you."

Maria Gift of God of the House of Alva, one of the noblest families of Spain. I had no idea any of the Alvas had gone to Mexico. Good thing for her she was rescued by an N.C. ship and not a Dutchman, I thought. Well, if an Alva wanted to cook for us, who were we to say no?

"We would be grateful, ma'am," I replied.

*

By the next day, Maria was up and working. She didn't have much to work with. The *Hornblower's* galley wasn't fancy. But I found at breakfast that she knew how to soft-boil an egg without turning it as hard and green as a Martian's testicle. Dinner proved chowder didn't have to be fish mush. Maybe we should rename our ship *Babette's Feast*, I thought.

We cruised for three more weeks, but came up empty. It seemed we had stomped the one roach in the kitchen. As usual, I enjoyed being at sea under canvas, even if we didn't get any action. As the days grew shorter the winds grew stronger, and in them was more than a hint of winter. I found myself drawn to the warm galley, whence instead of cooky's curses came the soft aromas of fresh bread, good stew, cinnamon buns, and apple pies.

As Maria kneaded and chopped and stirred, we talked. At first we talked about our wars. She knew more about mine than I expected. It seemed the example of our success helped motivate the Cristeros of old Mexico. If Christians in one part of the Americas could not only fight but win, perhaps Christians elsewhere could do the same.

At first, it had seemed as if the Cristeros' hope might triumph. They drove the Aztecs back almost to Mexico City. But in the night before the climactic battle, the Christian left wing melted away, and morning found an Aztec hoard in its place. The battle was lost, the Cristeros fled and in Tenochtitlan, Huitzilopochtli feasted.

"Why did it happen?" I asked Maria.

She shrugged. "It was a plot, señor. More than that I do not know. But now we are reduced to guerrilla warfare, trying to hold on to a few places in the hills."

I was always puzzled when someone used the phrase, "reduced to guerrilla warfare." Even brain-dead attritionists with their Lanchestrian equations thought a superiority of three-to-one enough to attack a conventional opponent, when a superiority of ten-to-one was the minimum required against guerrillas.

"Mexico has lots of hills," I said to Maria. "You should be able to grind up one Aztec army after another with guerrilla warfare. Why do you speak as if the situation is hopeless?"

"We have no leader, señor," she replied. "Remember that we are Latins. With us, everything depends on one Great Man. Without such a one, there may be ideas, hopes, even efforts, but in the end nothing happens. If we had a leader like yourself, then we would have hope. But as it is…" Again, she shrugged. "Would you help us?"

Well, here I go again, I thought. The Hispanics had driven the Anglos out of the old American Southwest, and killed plenty of us in doing it. Was I now supposed to go in and help pull their tamales out of the fire? On the other hand, the Hispanics were Christians and the Mexica religion was pure devil-worship. One of the problems with war is that people keep changing their hats: black for white and vice-versa.

It's always hard for a man to say no when a woman asks for help. That's as it should be. But this was a strategic decision, and it wasn't even mine to make. "I'll think about it," I replied to Maria's question. "There's someone else we'll need to talk to when we get back to Maine."

Getting back to Maine was on my mind. I needed to ready our fishing fleet to defend itself and take pot-shots at foreign poachers. But those hours in the galley talking with Maria exerted a growing hold on me. We talked of many things: our families, growing up, our hopes and dreams before our countries came apart and the strange twists and turns in our lives since. It had been many years since I'd spent much time with a good woman, and Maria was a good woman. She took life as it came, doing whatever woman's work needed to be done, including cooking on a warship that had sunk her brother's boat with him on board. She didn't demand and she didn't complain. She had none of the excitability of Latin women, for which I was thankful. The blood of the Alvas had left its mark on her. She had the quiet strength and genuine humility that mark a real aristocrat.

I didn't shirk my shipboard duties for the pleasure of Maria's company. I hauled lines, stood to the capstan, worked gun drill and in the end fished, once we decided we weren't likely to find any more pirates and might as well fill up with cod. The N.C. still needed every codfish it could catch to get through the winter. As we worked, winks and nods and occasional sly comments from the rest of the crew told me they thought Maria and I had something going.

Well, maybe we did, I thought. Being a Christian, something had to mean marriage. It seemed eons ago that I'd last thought about marriage. I admired Maria, and I liked her. Could I love her? I had no expectation of romantic love, nor any desire for it. By its nature it was a flash in the pan, the only effect of which was to lead incompatible people into marriages that didn't last. A better question was, were Maria and I two people who would grow to love each other over time? I couldn't answer, but I found it interesting that I was asking myself the question.

By the 11th of November, our hold was full up with codfish and we turned our bow toward Portland and home. We made landfall on the 19th, and that afternoon saw us safe in harbor and auctioning off our catch. Rick Hoffman appeared on the dock as the last of the codfish were being winched up out of the hold.

"Nice catch, Admiral," Rick shouted above the din. "But we were hoping for something more than fish."

At that moment Maria appeared on the quarterdeck to ask how many people would want dinner on board. "A very nice catch indeed," Rick added. "Or did you have a stowaway?"

"Come aboard, you looby, and let me make a proper introduction," I yelled back. Rick ran up the gangplank, mounted the quarterdeck, doffed his cap and bowed to Maria. "Allow me to introduce Maria—of the House of Alva. Maria, please meet the distinguished commander of our fleet, Captain Rick Hoffman. Rick was a SEAL. Toss him a ball and watch him balance it on his nose."

"Charmed, madam," Rick replied, bowing again. Maria curtsied in return, looking at me with a quizzical expression. Humor is hard in a foreign language.

"Maria was a captive on a ship we had a bit of a tussle with," I explained.

"So you did see some action?" he replied, looking around for signs of damage, which were few, thanks to our fast shooting and a good ship's carpenter.

"Aye, we did. Sent Davy Jones a little present, too. Unfortunately we couldn't bring any pirates back for public entertainment, but we did find out who's been messing with our ships."

"My guess was frogs out of Quebec," Rick said.

"Guess again."

"Philadelphia orcs?"

"Good try, but too far north. The pirate craft we sank was Aztec."

"Aztecs? Shit! You're kidding! Up here? What in hell for?"

"You put that question better than you know. Why don't I explain over a piece of Maria's apple pie?"

"It figures you'd pull some waif out of the ocean only to find she's a pastry cook. Are all the Rumford's born dumb lucky?"

"Mostly just dumb. Anyway, come down to the galley and I'll tell you the whole story."

I did, and when Rick realized what had happened to the crews of our missing ships, he lost his sense of humor for a time. "Good God, John, we don't have much of a navy, but isn't there some way we can pay those bastards back? We've got some nukes. Why don't we just fry Mexico City, their stinking temple, and them with it?"

"As Chief of the General Staff, I'd have to advise against using nuclear weapons unless our survival is at stake. Any country that looks like it's loose with nukes invites pre-emption. Remember, Rick, it's a nervous world out there."

"There's gotta be something we can do, John. General Staffs are supposed to come up with solutions, not just objections."

"That's correct. The people who only offer objections are the JAGs, which is why we don't have any. Maria said that the Cristeros' main weakness is that they lack a strong leader. She asked if I would go down there and be one."

"If you'll do it, I'll go with you, if that's any help. I had two cousins on the *Edwin Drood*, John, one thirteen and one sixteen. It was hard enough thinking of them as lobster kibbles, and what you've just told me is a whole lot worse."

"So you think I ought to do it?"

"Hell, yes. We voted to help Christians against their enemies. All these people want is one of us. They're not asking for an army—or even a fleet." John was still rankled that he'd missed out on our here-today, gone-tomorrow Pacific squadron.

"I wouldn't say this about Maria, Rick, since she is a Spanish Alva, but its mestizos we're talkin' about helping. *La Raza*. Mexicans."

"I guess that doesn't bother me so long as they aren't planning to come up here. You know we won't make that mistake again."

"I know." I was thinking that I hoped we might make one exception. "Well, we're seeing this along the same lines. But there is someone else I need to talk to before I make up my mind."

"Bill Kraft?"

"Ayuh."

*

I asked Rick to look after Maria, and the next day I took the train to Augusta. From the station I walked directly over to the governor's office. I told Bill Kraft the story of our cruise, our new enemy and why I thought I ought to be packing my hot weather utilities and jungle boots to head south.

Bill puffed on his pipe for a while. "I think I'd like to meet Señorita de Alva," he finally said. "It would be an honor to be introduced to a member of her house. Can you arrange for her to come?"

I knew Bill had more than courtesies in mind.

"We talked a good deal on the *Hornblower*, and I don't know what you'll get out of her that I didn't, but I'm sure she'll be willing to meet you. And cook for you too, if you'd like a good dinner."

Bill smiled and bowed from his chair. "I'm certain Mrs. Kraft would be happy to have a de Alva's assistance in the kitchen."

Rick Hoffman brought Maria up to Augusta on the early afternoon train the next day. A Hispanic traveling alone in Maine would have been questioned, and maybe stopped, by Maine citizens. That was as it should be. With Rick along in uniform everyone figured it was government business and left Maria alone. I had a two-week visa for her when I met them at the station.

The Krafts had invited Maria to stay with them, and she was happy to join Mrs. Kraft in the kitchen. Mrs. Kraft was a first-rate cook, but she gamely demoted herself to scullery maid for the evening and let Maria take over. She knew her husband was both catholic and venturesome in matters of the table, and as a good wife she always looked first to his pleasures and comforts.

As usual, I was counting on a good dinner to put Bill in the best mood toward my proposed adventure, and Maria did not disappoint. Bill was more enthusiastic about the squid cooked in its own ink than I was, but

Maria's chicken *molé* left everyone purring like cats with cream. Dessert was a *flan* as rich as Ebenezer Scrooge. When the ladies retired to the kitchen to clean up, Bill brought out the treasures he reserved for happy occasions: Uppmanns and *Grand Marnier.* The omens were favorable.

Even governors ate early in Maine, and we had sat down at five. Nonetheless, it was almost eight before the ladies rejoined us. "Miss de Alva, we are in your debt for a splendid dinner, and life offers few joys that surpass a splendid dinner," Bill said graciously.

"Regrettably, the nature of our times require that we now face some business. Captain Rumford has told me about the situation in your country, but it would help me greatly if I could ask you some questions directly. Would you be so kind as to join Captain Rumford, Captain Hoffman, and myself in the study?"

Maria nodded. She was nervous, but she was game.

Bill's study was small but comfortable, a place where a man could be at ease alone or in company. If Bill had to play the Inquisitor now, at least he kept the rack and thumbscrews out of sight.

"Miss de Alva, Captain Rumford has told me that in the early stages of your war, the Cristeros were very successful."

"Yes, Señor Gobernador. We defeated the Indios everywhere, even when the Mexica and Maya were joined together. Before the great battle, my father could see the cathedral in Mexico City from his camp on El Popo, the volcano. The Mexica had not yet destroyed it to rebuild their temple."

"Then the left wing of your army ran away?"

"No, señor, they did not run. Our Cristero soldiers are very brave, because they are fighting for Christ. That part of our army was ordered to leave its positions, in the night. The soldiers were just obeying orders."

"Who gave that order?"

"Their captain-general."

"Who was he?"

"My father's brother."

"Why did he give such an order?"

"It was a plot, señor. The nature of the plot I do not know."

"What happened to your father's brother after his treachery?"

"He was assassinated."

"Did you then put your army back together?"

"That was not possible, señor. The assassins were from another family, the Ocampos. They made one of their own the new captain-general. That left blood between our families, so we cannot work together. We both fight the Indios, but when our men meet, they also fight each other."

"How large is the Cristero army, or armies?"

"We have many men, tens of thousands, and we have weapons also. Just a few weeks before my boat left, a ship flying the Pope's flag came in to Matamoros with more."

"How much do you know about the fighting?"

"I see our men go out, señor, and I hear them talk when they get back. My father tells us about the war sometimes. The men do not believe women should go with them near the fighting."

"They're right about that," I injected.

"Indeed," Bill said. "What do the men say about the war?"

"It is very difficult. We can only do small things."

"If you have plenty of weapons and tens of thousands of fighters, why can you only do small things?"

"Señor, it is Mexico. It is possible to make great plans, but nothing happens. You go to meet someone and they do not come. The man who was to bring the bullets got drunk last night and is still in bed. Nobody told another man to put gas in the truck so he did not do so. In your country, when things go wrong, people make them right. In my country, they find a place in the shade and wait for someone else to do it. Many people have tried to change Mexico and make it like other places: Maximilian, Dias, Cardenas, Salinas. But in the end, they go away or die, and everything is the same."

"And you think a new leader would change this and win the war for you?"

"Perhaps. I do not know. But I can see no other hope."

"Who leads you now?"

"A junta. But it does very little."

"Why?"

"There are always plots, señor. You can trust no one. When you Yankees have a problem, you put a group of men together and they solve it. In Latin countries, if you do that, the people do not think of the problem. They think of how they can please other men who might be useful to them. They look for patrons or clients. They support one against another. The problem is not important and is soon forgotten. That is our culture, señor."

"Yet, as you know well, Miss de Alva, Spain became the first true world power. At the time of your famous ancestor, the Duke of Alva, the Spanish army had not lost a single battle for more than a century."

"That is true, señor. But we were a different people then. In the time of the Emperor Charles V, a Spanish nobleman was honest, blunt, forthright, even to the king. But then the court grew in power, and favor at court became more important than courage or honesty or the ability to so something. So new men rose, smooth, polished, full of flattery and lies, men who cared only for themselves. And Spain fell."

"We know something of that story here, señorita, in the old United States. But we have taken much of your time, and I'm sure you are tired.

What you have told us is most helpful."

Bill stood up, and the interview was over. Rick escorted Maria from the room, closing the door behind him.

"John, I could tell you what to do, but I'm not going to," Bill said to me. "Instead, I'm going to ask you to think carefully about what you've heard here, and answer one question, not as Maria's friend, but as Chief of the General Staff of the Northern Confederation. Is it probable that your presence with the Cristeros would make a decisive difference in their war, or not? If your answer is yes, you may go. Think on it tonight, and give me your decision tomorrow."

"Yes, sir," I replied. "And thank you."

*

I thought on it most of that night. No matter how I looked at it, the answer was always the same. Bill's questions had gotten straight to the heart of the matter: culture. Culture was the basis of everything else, and if the culture didn't work, nothing else would either. Mexican culture—more broadly, Latin culture—didn't work. Oh, it worked better than some others. I'd rather live in Mexico than Africa. But I remembered a joke a Spanish Marine Corps officer told me at Quantico. "People talk about the German economic miracle or the Japanese economic miracle, but those aren't miracles at all," he said. "Germans and Japs work like crazy. Spain is the real economic miracle. The place is booming and nobody works at all."

If I went to Mexico to be the Cristeros' *caudillo*, nothing would change, because it couldn't. Oh, I might kick and drive and even inspire their troops to do better than they were doing. But the more I succeeded, the faster plots would grow against me. And I couldn't be every place at once.

I still wanted to go. But Bill hadn't asked me that. He'd asked for my professional judgment. The same self-discipline we demanded from every private required that I set my own feelings and desires aside. As Chief of the General Staff, there was only one answer I could give: no. The overwhelming probability was that if I went, the Cristeros would continue to lose, for the same reasons they were losing now.

But that answer left me facing another question: what about Maria? What did I owe her? What did she want from me? Anything, now that I had to refuse her request to help her people? Was I really thinking about marriage?

The problem was that I was already married. I was married to Bellona, goddess of war. Bigamy would quickly become a burden. Back in my Marine Corps days, most of my fellow officers had been married. They still did their jobs, but the Corps and war wasn't their life the way it was mine. If they took an evening or a weekend or a month to hear Bruce Gudmundsson lecture on stormtroop tactics or walk the Valley with Jackson or follow Rommel's 7th Panzer Division through northern France, they left at home a wife in tears or in a snit. And their sweet little wifey knew just how to make their life a perfect hell unless they kept her happy. Though it was usually only the aviators who came home from a six-month deployment to find the toilet seat up.

Maybe Maria, as a de Alva, would be different. But every man since Adam who got married did so thinking his girl would be different.

The next morning I went to the governor's office right after breakfast and gave him my answer to his question: no. Then I walked over to his house and asked to see Maria. It was a fine Indian summer day, and she met me in the garden.

"Maria, I have to tell you something I would rather not. I will not be going to Mexico. I do not think my presence would make a decisive difference, even if the Cristeros were to accept me as a leader, which they might or might not. I cannot justify leaving my duties here in the face of that fact."

Maria smiled, reached out and took both my hands in hers. "Señor John, please believe that I understand. It is what I expected. If my ancestor the Duke of Alva were here, I think he would decide the same way. A soldier must know when to fight and when not to fight. If he does not know that, he will lose many battles."

"Maria, there is another question, and it is one I cannot decide. I have enjoyed our time together, more than I have enjoyed a woman's company in a long time. If my life belonged to me alone…well, it does not. I cannot grant the one thing you have asked of me, but perhaps there is something else. What do you want to do now, and how can I help you?"

"My duty is to return to Mexico and my family."

"Do other Mexican fishing boats come up this far?"

"Yes, a few, but…the *Guadeloupe* was my brother's boat, so my honor was safe. On another Mexican boat, it would not be safe. I am sorry, Señor John, but that is Mexico."

"I understand." I took a minute or two to think. "Do the Cristeros have any contact with the Confederacy?"

"Yes. My father goes to Houston sometimes, and there he meets with a Confederate officer. They have supplied us with some arms."

Though neither side recognized it officially, the new border between Texas and Mexico left Houston, Dallas, Austin, and San Antonio in Confederate hands, while the Cristeros held west Texas. The Confederates were smart enough to realize that Aztecs would be difficult neighbors.

"I have some friends down south who I'm sure will help you get to

Houston. Your father could pick you up there?"

"Yes."

If I'd been talking to a man, I would probably have left it there. Problem stated, solution identified. But I was talking to a woman, a woman I cared about. "Maria, you said your duty was to return to your family. I know women have their duties also. But I asked you a different question. What do you want to do?"

Maria looked down at the ground, then at me. Softly and hesitantly, she said, "I would like to stay here, with you."

"I would like that too, Maria." I knew now how much I wanted that. But all my desire and hers did nothing to change reality.

"Maria, I'm a soldier in a world in which there is no peace. I hardly have a home. At least I'm seldom there. I could not do my duty to my country and a wife, and I'm already sworn to my country."

"You do have a home, Señor John?"

"Yes. We call it The Old Place. It's been in my family since we Rumfords came to Maine, and that was a long time ago. It's near a little town called Hartland."

"Who keeps your house for you?"

"No one, I guess. It's just there, empty most of the time."

"I will keep your house for you, John, if you will let me. I do not mind being alone most of the time. I will keep your house well. I can clean as well as cook. My family also lives on the land. I will keep your house for you, and someday, if there is peace…"

Lead us not into temptation, I thought. What about when I was home? Maria and I alone under the same roof, liking each other, perhaps in time loving each other, unmarried. Could I maintain her honor and God's law?

Sometimes we don't even realize we're praying, but God hears anyway.

His answer was clear and strong: yes! Maria was Christian also, and the three of us, her, me and God, could do it.

"Very well, Maria. The Old Place has always been a refuge for those in need of one. It was for me, and now it can be for you. Yes."

Maria smiled, with the soft, sad smile of those who have seen too much of life. "Thank you, Señor John."

I walked her back through the garden to the kitchen door. Mrs. Kraft opened it, smiling. Perhaps she had known something of Maria's hopes, and mine.

For once, I thought, I've done something right, and it wasn't just fighting a battle.

CHAPTER FORTY-TWO

I took Maria up to Hartland for Thanksgiving that year. I wanted to settle her in at the Old Place before winter, and I also thought I should be there when she met the rest of my family.

I couldn't say they were pleased with what I'd let follow me home, but they had good manners and minded them. The name Alva helped; we Rumfords knew the best families of Europe had not come over on the *Mayflower*.

After thanking God for another year of life, good health and victory and feasting in His honor, I left Maria and went back to work. My family would keep an eye on her and help her adjust. We all knew a señorita's first Maine winter would be a pretty intense learning experience. I left the larder well-stocked, and at Maria's request I brought my livestock back up from Cousin Sam's place: two Percherons for the wagon and the plow, a Jersey cow for rich milk and half-a-dozen Rhode Island Reds for fresh eggs. Maria said the animals would give her all the company she desired. For a Yankee farmer-soldier and a Spanish doña, we were surprisingly alike.

Back in Augusta, I found plenty to keep me occupied. Good intelligence work was the first requirement for security in the New World Disorder, and while my staff was good, they tended to get lost in the weeds. Intel types always do. I needed to be involved personally to ask the man from Mars questions that sometimes draw meaning from mere information.

I also expanded our contingency planning. We had concentrated our efforts on situations where the Northern Confederation might be attacked directly. But I also wanted plans for intervening, with advice, force, or both in situations beyond our own border where our assistance might be requested. I'd had to pull the Pacific campaign out of my butt, and while the Japs had taken care of most of it, I often wished I'd had a tad more to go on.

The next couple years saw order re-established in the Mid-Atlantic and Midwestern states, sometimes bloodily, more often not, as sources of disorder were given the option to repent or die. The biggest source of disorder had been the blacks, but inspired by what our blacks in the N.C. had done, the good ones took their communities back. Then, most of them followed our example and left the cities to become farmers. They knew there was no other way they could rear their children in a healthy environment, physically healthy and morally healthy.

Most Mexicans and Central Americans headed home. All the states passed laws forbidding the preaching, practice, or profession of the Mohammedan religion. Regular crime became rare as hanging became the usual penalty, at least where violence was involved. We remembered that if you hang a thief when he's young, he won't steal when he's old.

All this made my life easier. By the end of 2037, a wild-eyed optimist might have allowed himself to think that the lone Teutonic knight, order, had a fighting chance against Old Night. In all of North America, there was only one place where things were still getting worse: California.

When the American republic blew itself to pieces in 2027, the Hispanics promptly seized southern California, which they had long occupied. They drove the remaining Anglos out, then slaughtered the blacks, who had been slaughtering the Orientals until Korean marines landed at Long Beach to get their people out. A new border between Mexico and Anglo California eventually established itself just north of Bakersfield.

Northern California had it all. It had resources, timber, and minerals it could sell in Asia. It had high-tech industry. Its farming country remained productive. But the first sign that it would turn itself into a colossal mess came early. In 2028, the government moved the capital from the pleasant and historic city of Sacramento to Berkeley. The stated reason was that Sacramento included the word sacrament, "an exclusive reference to the phallocentric Christian cult." Berkeley, in contrast, was a shrine to the cultural revolution that broke out in the 1960s and, in time, broke apart America.

The new venue soon made its spirit felt. Because offices such as state governor were deemed "hierarchical," northern California—officially now the Azanian Democratic Republic, a name soon unofficially abbreviated to Zany—adopted a popular assembly form of government. There were no officers or committees, all matters being debated and decided by the whole assembly. The assembly itself was vast, more than 1,000 members, the better to ensure democracy. Since, in the time of crisis, men had real work to do, the delegates were soon mostly women.

In happier times, tasking hundreds of women with thousands of decisions might have set the stage for a delicious comedy. One can imagine it in the hands of Moliere, or Gilbert and Sullivan. But ours were not happy times. Where nature intended comic chaos, ideology produced disciplined fanaticism. The ideology that grabbed hold was radical feminism.

By 2030, the Feminists had a solid majority in the Human Gathering, as the assembly was named. Their early actions were a mixture of the predictable and self-satirizing. Women were given preference in all hiring, and the Azanian national flag became a pair of bloomers hoisted up the flagpole.

Ideology, by its nature, demands purity. Any compromise is hypocrisy, weakness, and betrayal. The pursuit of purity can have no limits, least of all limits on the power of the state. Intentions, not results, are the measure of all actions. Where reality contradicts ideology, reality must be suppressed.

The ideological imperative exposed itself quickly in Azania. In 2031, the assembly was renamed the Womyn's Gathering and the male members were expelled. Later in the year, men were stripped of the right to vote. Only San Francisco's homosexuals were exempt as the new law made them "honorary women".

2032 saw the beginning of what the feminists called Fair Discrimination. All pretense of equality between the sexes was thrown out. It had never been more than a cloak for power, anyway. Under Fair Discrimination, girls got higher grades in school than boys for the same work, plus a monopoly on the playground while boys spent recess inside where they were forced to play with dolls. All executive positions, including in private businesses, were legally reserved for women. Only women were allowed to be policemen, firemen, judges, attorneys, or clergymen. In all jobs, women received higher pay for comparable work, and where a job required physical labor, the woman was assigned a male secretary to do the heavy lifting while receiving half her pay.

Men had to pay more to ride the bus or subway. When a male columnist for the *San Francisco Chronicle* wrote that the government "couldn't seem to tell the difference between Fair Discrimination and fare discrimination," he was thrown in Alcatraz for the crime of public sexism and the paper was shut down.

In 2033, a new law made all sexism, along with ageism and lookism, felonies punishable by imprisonment, "alteration," or both. Alteration was a euphemism for castration. Conviction required no evidence beyond a woman stating that she had been offended. Only women were permitted to serve on juries.

In order to break down stereotypes, sumptuary laws were enacted. Pants were reserved for women, and men had to wear skirts. In what was called the "stud muffin amendment," muscular young men were exempted. Instead, they had to leave their chests bare and wear leather.

But these measures proved insufficiently pure. Men were reduced to second-class citizens, but they were still there. Their very presence was soon deemed "offensive to women" by the more radical feminists. The only solution was their removal.

Early in the year 2037, the radicals bullied the Gathering into mandating the abortion of all male babies. They argued this was a moderate measure, since it allowed men to die out gradually. Even so, it passed by only a narrow margin, and for the first time a feminist decree met widespread resistance from Azania's people.

The resistance was led by mothers. Many mothers and prospective mothers, it seemed, liked the idea of having sons as well as daughters. Mothers started marching and protesting. Ten thousand mothers gathered in Berkeley to make their views known. The Gathering turned dogs, fire hoses, and tear gas on them.

But the radicals realized they had a problem. The solution, as always, was more ideology. First, the radicals slipped frying pans and rolling pins into the Gathering. Then, in the mother of all cat fights, they physically drove their opponents out. The Gathering duly cleansed, the radicals passed a series of new laws called the Gender Purity Acts.

First, motherhood was outlawed. Any woman who got pregnant was required to get an abortion, regardless of the sex of the baby. Reproduction would henceforth be by cloning. Then, sex between men and women was also outlawed. Only lesbian sex was permitted, though male homosexuality was winked at. Finally, the vote was restricted to "women of full consciousness," that condition to be determined by precinct committees made up entirely of lesbians.

In response, the resistance strengthened. Men and reasonable women rallied, marched, and organized. They denounced the Gathering, said it no longer represented them and called for new elections.

When Azania first formed, it had a military similar to those of most former states and state fragments: the old National Guard, some local regular military units and a few militias. The Fair Discrimination laws had reserved all military positions for women and the men had been dismissed. This eliminated at one stroke almost the entire Azanian army. What it left were a variety of women technicians and a cadre of pilots left over from the final senility of the U.S. Air Force, when it had begun training women to fly fighters and bombers. Now, the only real military force the Zany Gathering had was an air force.

So it used it. On July 4, 2037, opponents of the Gender Purity Acts gathered on the lawn of the old State House in Sacramento. They rallied to demand universal suffrage and a restored state government like the one they used to have. They were husbands and wives and kids, grandmothers and babies in prams, armed with nothing more dangerous than signs, petitions, and sparklers.

The rally began at noon. At just a quarter after, two F-35s, formerly of the U.S. Navy, flew over. The first dropped cluster munitions, the second a Fuel/Air Explosive device. Over a thousand people died on the spot.

Unlike Cascadia, Azania had not closed its borders. Those who opposed the radicals could vote with their feet, and they did. They left by the hundreds of thousands, most heading west into the Rocky Mountain states. The people there did not have much themselves, but they shared what they had, including their homes, with the newcomers.

In Berkeley, the Gathering debated what to do about the exodus. On the one hand, a nation without people wouldn't last very long. On the other, they welcomed the departure of the ideologically impure, the mothers. Borrowing from another Brave New World, they had made "mother" their term of abuse for women who did not share their view of men, a view summed up in Azania's official motto: "A woman needs a man like a fish needs a bicycle."

Their ideology informed them that, across North America and around the world, millions of oppressed women were desperate to be free from men. So the Gathering issued a clarion call to feminists everywhere to come to Azania, the world's first "Man-free Zone." And come they did, by the thousands. Soon, the inflow of feminists exceeded the outflow of normal people. Azania, it seemed, would represent ideology's long-sought triumph: a triumph over human nature itself.

Down east in Augusta, I hadn't paid Azania much mind. It was a long way away, the Christians had all fled, and I couldn't imagine our own women getting a case of the zanies. Oh, we had a few. Maine's Episcopal "bishop," Ms. Cloaca Devlin, was one. A leftover from the last apostate days of the Episcopal Church of the U.S.A., she still ranted and raved, though her following was minuscule. Most Episcopalians, myself included, had long ago joined the Anglican Church, established with the help of orthodox Anglican bishops from third world countries.

But I had miscalculated about the Northern Confederation's women. They were deeply interested in what was going on in Azania. They were interested and appalled. In their eyes, Azania represented the ultimate degradation of women, worse even than the whorehouse or the female soldier or the crooner who in the old American Republic had dared to call herself "Madonna." Marriage and motherhood represented women's highest calling, and in Azania women had turned their back on both. They felt something had to be done.

Northern winters leave plenty of time for tongues to clack, and among the sewing circles and quilting bees during the winter of 2037–38, a plan was hatched. When spring came and the roads were again passable, women began making their rounds, gathering signatures. Their goal was a ballot referendum on the question, "Resolved, that the Northern Confederation shall undertake any and all actions short of a declaration of war to overthrow the wicked and unnatural feminist government in Azania and return northern California to the civilized world."

I was as contemptuous of Azania and all it represented as anyone. Still, I wasn't sure we should involve ourselves out there. Looking back on it, I felt that Cascadia would have fallen of its own weight without our assistance. It would have happened more slowly, but it would have happened. I wasn't the kind of soldier who was looking for wars to fight. If time would do the work for us, why shouldn't we let it?

*

One fine spring day in the year 2038, I waded through the mud over to the governor's office to get his take on it. The women's petition drive was moving fast. After the third straight dinner of cold fish hash and colder looks, most husbands found it prudent to sign. I laid out my

doubts to Bill Kraft, and asked him whether, as Maine's governor and the
N.C.'s Field Marshal, he perhaps should speak out against the petition.

Bill sat back, puffed on his pipe and thought over what I had said.
When he replied, he put a different light on the matter. "First of all,
regardless of my own views, I don't think I ought to try to influence the
petition process, or even the referendum itself, when the initiative comes
from our people."

"Remember, our government is founded on the idea that the people are sovereign. Unlike the old American Republic, we're serious about
that. That's why we have the referendum process and a weak central
government. If our women can convince a majority of voters that we
should intervene in Azania, then we probably should. If I thought we
were putting our national existence at stake, I might feel differently, but
I don't see that in this case."

"Azania has nuclear weapons," I warned.

"I know that. But it doesn't have missiles that can reach us. They
have bombers, but I trust the Boys from Utica to take care of that threat.
They might smuggle a weapon in here, but our border controls are pretty
darned good. I'm not saying there's no risk. Anything worthwhile has
risks. But the risks are not so great that I should try to thwart the political
process."

"Second," Bill continued, "I think you misunderstand the situation
in Azania. It's different from Cascadia. In Cascadia, by the time we intervened, a small, corrupt elite was running the place by force and terror.
Most of the people were just waiting for a chance to rise up against them.
That's not true in Azania. The radical feminists drove their opponents out
and brought more women like themselves in to replace them. The whole
country is made up of True Believers. In time, of course, you are correct:
All ideologies fall in time, because eventually reality reasserts itself. But

where the whole population has caught the ideology bug, that time will probably be measured not in years but in generations."

"So what?" I asked. "Why can't we wait for generations?"

"Because ideas have consequences," Bill replied. "For a time, through the first generation, Azania will seem to work. In fact, it's a perfect hellhole, as our women recognize. But not all women will be so wise. Remember, Azania intends itself to be a beacon to the whole world. The poison it has imbibed will spread elsewhere."

"Think of the damage the French Revolution did, not only to France, but to all the West. In a sense, Azania is its final and most bitter product. It is part of the price paid for the Duke of Brunswick's fatal decision at Valmy."

Bill had told me about that before. More than once. "*Hier schlagen wir nicht.*" With those words the Duke lost the chance to strangle the French Revolution and "The Rights of Man" in their cradle. That was exactly what I was saying now: we're not going to fight this one.

"OK, then what do you want me to do?" I asked.

"Start planning a campaign. I expect the referendum will get on the ballot and pass handily. I certainly wouldn't want to tell Mrs. Kraft I voted against it."

"Where should I start?"

"What do you know of the Azanian military?"

"They've been building it up as fast as they can. They've gone the high-tech route, the stuff the U.S. military was losing itself in toward the end. Information warfare, computerized systems of systems, remote sensors, stealth. They believe technology can tell them everything an enemy is doing and allow them to hit him with stand-off weapons. Push-button warfare."

"Then plan to defeat that."

"With what, Bill?" I asked plaintively. "The referendum says we should do everything short of declaring war. Where am I supposed to find troops?"

"In the Vendee."

CHAPTER FORTY-THREE

THE Vendee was a province of France. During the French Revolution, it remained loyal to the king, and paid the usual price in lootings, burnings, murders, and massacres by those devoted to the Rights of Man. To this day, July 14 is no holiday in the Vendee.

The English had raised a French Royalist army from the Vendee. Bill Kraft was telling me to recruit my army from among the Azanian refugees.

But history told me something more. The army the British cobbled together from among the French Royalists was a defeat waiting to happen. It was torn by factionalism and petty jealousies, commanded by incompetents who thought rank was leadership and motivated by regrets and recriminations. The French Revolutionary army kicked its butt clear out of Europe.

That Royalist army was the prototype of all exile armies. The Whites in the Russian Revolution, the Chinese Nationalists, the anti-Castro Cubans, the Iraqi exiles who lured America into that quagmire were all cast in the same mold. Maybe Bill Kraft thought it sufficient to train would-be soldiers in sound tactics and techniques. I knew that for trained men to become an army took much more. It took cohesion, motivation, and belief in a cause strong enough to sacrifice ego on the altar of Mars. I hadn't a clue how we could find or create those virtues among the Azanian exiles.

But I'd long ago learned that when I faced a problem I couldn't solve, the best course of action was to work on the parts I understood. The General Staff should be able to think through how to fight a high-tech opponent. So that was the place to start.

In April, 2038, the Northern Confederation General Staff numbered 23 officers and one NCO. Ten officers were assigned to the General Staff in Augusta and the rest to the field forces. Of the ten in Augusta, four were on leave—spring planting—so the group that gathered on the 20th in the General Staff ready room was six officers, plus myself, plus Danielov, our single Staff Sergeant on the General Staff. By our standards, that was a large meeting.

The referendum was scheduled for May 15, and everybody knew it would pass. Our job, as I explained to the assembled multitude, was to answer two questions: How could we find or create an army to retake Azania for civilization, and how should that army fight a high-tech opponent?

"What exactly do we mean by a high-tech opponent?" John Ross asked.

I turned to our intel officer, Major Erik Walthers, to explain. "The Azanian military has realized the wet dream of the French Army of the 1930s," Walthers explained. "The whole thing has been reduced to artillery and forward observers. The artillery is high-tech, with stealth bombers, missiles, and logic bombs to hit enemy computer systems, and the FOs are automated sensors, but the concept is the same. The centralized headquarters is now banks of computers, a fusion center that automatically targets any enemy the sensors detect. It's the same crap the Pentagon was pushing in the 1990s. The U.S. Marine Corps called it 'Sea Dragon,' the Army called it 'Force 21' and the Air Force called it 'Global Reach, Global Power.' Or collectively, 'Transformation.'"

"Why have they gone this way?" Ross asked.

"Because it's the only way women can fight," answered Danielov. "It's clean, air conditioned, and comfortable. No mud, no bugs, no humping packs or squatting in poison oak to take a shit in the woods. They'd rather buy it than do it."

"The Azanians have a few battalions of what they call infantry," Walthers said. "They're recruited from among the bull dykes. As you can imagine, they're not anything we would recognize as infantry. Their actual function is as security guards for airfields, computer centers and headquarters."

"How effective is Azania's high-tech military?" I asked Walthers.

"It can hit stationary targets if it can find them," he replied. "It can easily drop a bomb or put a missile on a building. It's deadly against large concentrations of troops camped in the open or caught moving in columns on the roads."

"But that's all it can do. Camouflage defeats it, deception defeats it, digging in and dispersion both defeat it. You'll take some attrition, of course. The easiest ways to beat it are stay dug in, like the Serbs in Kosovo, or move too fast and covertly for it to track. But the latter is difficult."

"It sounds like Desert Storm," said Mike O'Hearn, our Air Officer. "We were great at hitting telephone exchanges in downtown Baghdad but never got a single mobile Scud launcher."

"The whole high-tech warfare business was an extension of the propaganda about Desert Storm," Walthers said. "By the late '90s anyone who followed the literature knew the initial claims from Desert Storm were bullshit. But if the lie is big enough, the truth never catches up. Azania has swallowed the lie. I think that is to our advantage."

"The way to fight high-tech is with low-tech," I agreed. "But if there are any exceptions to that rule, we need to know them. What about stealth?"

"Azania has four operable B-2s, about 20 F-117s, and around 50 F-35s," O'Hearn said. "Thanks to the fact that our Russian friends never throw anything away, we've gotten our hands on some of their old long-wave radars. They were built in the 1950s, and they pick up stealth perfectly. The F-117s can't reach the N.C., and if they send any B-2s our way, I'll have F-16s on 'em long before they reach our borders."

"What about the F-35s?"

"They are horrible air-to-air fighters. They have a higher wing loading than the F-105, and less than a 1:1 thrust-to-weight ratio. They're Thuds. Our long-wave radars will pick them up. We'll use GCI to vector in for visual kills with Sidewinders and guns. And remember, we're facing women pilots."

"How will you counter their AMRAAMS?"

"Formation effects." Every radar-guided missile ever built was a sucker for enemy fighters flying a box or diamond formation. They all went for the centroid.

"OK, it's obvious you're on top of the air side," I said. "What about their sensors?"

"The key to enemy sensors is to capture one of each major type early, take it apart and see how it works. Once you know how it works, it's easy to design counters. I've got my guys ready to go out there right now and start scarfing them up," Dano said.

"Go to it," was my order. In the Vietnam War, the high-tech "Mc-Namara Line" had tried to catch NVA infiltrators with sensors so sophisticated they could distinguish human from animal aromas. The North Vietnamese foxed them by hanging buckets full of piss in the trees. Most fancy sensors had simple counters. But Ron was right: you first had to know how they worked.

"What about all their computer crap?"

Our data dink, Capt. Christian Patel, grinned. I knew the N.C. military wasn't vulnerable to information warfare, because I had forbidden it to own or use computers. That was the only real electronic security, plus it kept people thinking about the enemy instead of some damned system. The one exception was Patel's department: Offensive Information Warfare, or as it was usually known, the Goatscrew Office.

"We're already having fun," Patel said. "We started hacking their system the day after I heard about the petition drive. Info war against women is more fun than a hog-calling contest in Pakistan. They talk all the time, they can't keep a secret and they're conspiratorial, so when we mess something up they blame each other. It's the first time I've ever seen hair pulled electronically."

"What vulnerabilities do we have in our civilian sectors?"

"A few, but no show-stoppers," Patel replied. "Thanks to the power shortage, almost everything has been de-computerized. Most communication is by mail. Banks rely on ledgers, as do businesses. Transport is horses and steam locomotives, neither of which find much use for data. The area that gets hydropower from Niagara Falls is a partial exception, but the power system itself has put in manual back-up for its computerized systems. I would recommend they switch to that before we open hostilities."

"Agreed. Draw up a directive to them and I'll sign it. What else is there on the technical side? What about missiles and nukes?"

"They've got both, but they know we also have nukes, which means neither we nor they can use them," Walthers replied. "Their missiles are short range, and missiles are only useful against fixed targets."

"OK then, what about the big question: How do we fight this bunch of Amazons?" I asked.

"With infantry." The reply was from Major Van der Jagd, our tank specialist. "Light infantry, on foot, on bicycles, and on dirt bikes. The largest unit should be a platoon, which is too small for high-tech systems to find, target, and hit, especially if it keeps moving. It doesn't have to be very good infantry, since there won't be any infantry facing it. Low-quality militia can do most of the job, which is stomping sensors and scaring women. We'll need a few high quality units to cut through quickly to the key targets: airfields and missile storage sites, computer centers and headquarters. Dano, can your guys handle that?"

"Sure, with augmentation from some of our own light infantry units. Can we use our own personnel?"

"Yes, a few," I replied. "Remember, we have the public with us in this war. How many men will you need?"

"A few hundred, no more," Dano replied. "I'm not worried about Dykes on Bikes."

"What this sound like to me is essentially a large-scale Special Operation," I concluded. "The militia absorbs the attention of their centralized, computerized system, while we slip in a few small units to bring that system down by hitting its central nodes. Does that make sense?" I saw nods all around the table.

"If anyone disagrees or has a better idea, speak up now. If you don't, you share equal responsibility for the result." That was the old General Staff rule. Nobody spoke. "OK, write it up in a paper of less than ten pages, double-spaced. That will be our campaign plan. Now all we need is that militia army."

*

Sometimes when a problem seems too hard, the best thing to do is walk away from it for a while. So that's what I did. The next day, I headed home to Hartland, the Old Place, and Maria.

Other than a couple days at Christmas, I'd stayed away from Hartland. I needed to let my emotions about Maria cool down. At Christmas, I'd been on the go so fast between relatives that we weren't together much. This time would be different.

The railroad now ran to Hartland, as it had many years ago. Cousin John met me at the station with his wagon, which we needed to haul all the books I'd brought with me up to the farm. While every military situation is unique, none is wholly so, and I wanted time and quiet to study some campaigns with similarities to ours: Von Lettow-Vorbeck in German East Africa, T.E. Lawrence against the Turks, the Tet Offensive from the North Vietnamese side.

By the time two massive Clydesdales had dragged and skidded us through the mud to home, pulling as if they themselves were powered by steam, it was evening. Maria met us at the door, welcomed me home, and said she had dinner ready for John and me both. Her manner was friendly but also formal, as befitted both her heritage and her present position. That came as a relief, as it would help keep some distance between us even at close quarters. I expect she knew that.

John took the horses to the barn, curried them, and fed them while I unloaded the wagon. He would stay the night. No point is going out on bad roads after dark if it could be helped. In the old days, he would probably have thought that a was waste of time. But people didn't think that way any more. The world had slowed down, and few regretted it.

The house was clean, ordered, warm, and welcoming. I could feel a woman's touch, and perhaps the house could as well. Maria served our dinner in the dining room, waiting until we were done to eat her own alone in the kitchen. Again, the distance was welcome.

Dinner was excellent: a roast chicken, tasting as only a free-running, fresh-killed bird can, oven-browned potatoes, and fresh fiddleheads. The food was Yankee, not Mexican, but it wasn't cooked Yankee. Some sage here, some chives there, a piquancy in the skin of the chicken suggested a touch from somewhere south of New England. I looked forward to what summer and a garden might bring.

Cousin John's presence made the first night easier. By the time he left the next morning, Maria had made the rules clear. Whatever we felt about each other, our relationship was that of Holmes and Mrs. Hudson: intersecting but separate spheres. My responsibility was my work as Chief of the General Staff, and her responsibility was to create an environment where I could do that work without distraction.

Yet as the days went on, Maria showed me there was more to it than that. Despite my books, I could still see no solution to my problem. In the best of times, California had not been famous for its martial vigor—if the United States had been Europe, California would have been Italy—and now I was supposed to create an army from Californian men who had run away from women.

My frustration grew. But it didn't boil over into calling Bill Kraft and saying it couldn't be done. Maria created an atmosphere in the Old Place that helped my Marine brain to remain calm, open, and functional. Good meals were part of it, and domestic order was also a part. But there was more, something I could feel but not put my finger on. Perhaps it was the suggestion that if she could do her duties so well, I should be able to do mine.

And we talked. Some people work best in silence and isolation, but I was not that kind. By laying a subject out for others, I enabled myself to see it in new ways. And so, in breaks from my books and her housework, I explained to Maria what we were planning in Azania and the problem I was up against.

Maria understood that I did not expect answers from her. She was my sounding board, from whose echoes I might spot something new. She was content to be that. But the blood of the Duke of Alva still flowed in her veins.

On the evening of April 7th, after a fine omelet of six fresh eggs, potatoes, and onions, Maria brought me my usual apple brandy and cigar, on a small silver tray. But instead of retiring to the kitchen to eat her own meal, she pulled out a chair and sat down opposite me.

"Señor John, you have spoken to me of your great difficulty in finding an army for this war against the crazy women. As a woman, I understand nothing about how to fight a war. But there is something women do know that men do not always understand."

"What is that, Maria?"

"Men fight when women want them to."

I took a few minutes to think about that. Years ago, I'd heard the Israeli military historian Martin van Creveld explain why war exists: because men like to fight and women like fighters. As a Marine, I knew men liked to fight. But I'd never really thought much about the second part, probably because I was too busy fighting.

"Well, sure, we're getting involved in Azania because the women of the Northern Confederation want us to."

"But what about the wives and daughters of the men from Azania, the men who you want for soldiers?"

"What do you mean, what about them?"

"Señor John, if those women want their men to fight, they will."

Now that was a new idea. The dim green bulb in my own brain housing group began to flicker. Assuming they weren't all gay, Maria was right: Not even California men would want to appear weak and fearful to their own women.

"How could we get the women to want their men to fight?" I asked Maria.

"I do not know," she replied. "But I helped your sisters and your mother and aunts carry the petition for the referendum from door to door, here around Hartland. One woman we visited said her sister was a member of the Council of Conscience, the group of women who co-ordinated the petitions. She heard her say that they were corresponding with some of the women among the Azanian exiles. Perhaps they could help you."

*

The next morning I was on the train again, heading for Boston. That's where the Council of Conscience met, and a quick call to Bill Kraft had secured an invitation for me to meet with them that same evening.

I had been given an address on Commonwealth Avenue. It proved to be the apartment of the Council's chairman, Mrs. Rutherford P. Bingham. I rang promptly at eight, and was met at the door by Mrs. Bingham's butler. The Brahman's trust funds had made it through another revolution intact.

The Council was made up of two representatives from each state in the Confederation, for a total of twenty-two. The ladies were gathered in

Mrs. Bingham's ample parlor, and Mrs. Bingham herself was waiting for me at the parlor door, smiling warmly. "Welcome, Captain Rumford," she said. "It's always such an honor to have a man in uniform here. We're all looking forward to hearing you, but I'm afraid you may not have had time to get dinner on your way down. A place is set for you in the dining room. May I tempt you with some lamb chops while we transact some dreary business?"

"You may, ma'am," I replied. "No real soldier ever passes up chow."

"Good. Alonzo, bring a bottle of the Chateau Lafite '82 for our distinguished guest. Captain, just ring if there is anything you need. It's such a delight to have you at our table." The butler bowed, and I thought how nice it was to once again have women who could set the course of state while preserving the graces of ladies.

Mrs. Bingham escorted me to the dining room, excused herself and left me facing an entire rack of lamb. I wondered briefly if I had done the right thing in accepting the offer of dinner, then reflected that there wasn't much point in fighting for civilization, yet refusing it.

At about half-past the hour, Alonzo came in to tell me that when I was finished, I was welcome to join the ladies for dessert. I'd already packed most of the lamb under my belt, and not wanting to hold things up, I said I was ready. I hoped the rest of the Chateau Lafite wouldn't go to waste. The color of Alonzo's nose told me that wasn't likely.

Mrs. Bingham again welcomed me and introduced me around the room. Some names were from the history books—Mrs. Thomas Weld, Mrs. John Cabot, Mrs. Russell Sage, Mrs. William Schermerhorn—and others were new to me. But all were ladies, in hats and gloves and some, in the cool of a Boston spring, wearing those little fox stoles with the head and beady little glass eyes. No stringy-haired, horse-faced, jeans-clad professorettes here. The words matrons came to mind.

Then there were éclairs and coffee and, for me, a cognac and a David-off Churchill. "We do hope you smoke, Captain," Mrs. Weld said. "We so enjoy the aroma of a good cigar."

"It is a very good cigar," I replied. "I will smoke it with pleasure." For so many decades, things had only changed downward. Now, they were changing up again.

After dessert and some pleasant drawing-room conversation, Mrs. Bingham took the floor. "Captain, let me say again how honored and delighted we all are that you would take from your valuable time to visit with us. We think we know why you are here. You would like us to withdraw our ballot initiative, so our country does not face war. I am not certain we will agree with you, but we are most eager to hear with respect what you have to say."

"You show remarkable hospitality to someone you think is here to argue against you," I replied.

"Captain, among ladies hospitality is always more important than politics," Mrs. Bingham chided gently.

"Well, as it happens, I have nothing to say against the referendum. That is for the people of the Northern Confederation to decide. If they choose to intervene in Azania, I will do my utmost to accomplish the task they set. In fact, I am here to ask your assistance with that task. Are you in communication with the women from Azania, the ones who fled and are now in exile?"

I saw some uneasy glances around the room. "Yes, Captain, we are," Mrs. Cabot finally said. "Some of their women heard of our effort and wrote to us. We wrote back. At our urging, they have formed Committees of Correspondence, and we have communicated our progress to them. We thought that if our initiative passes, we would need some type of support out there. I hope we have not done anything wrong."

"Not at all," I reassured them. "In fact, what you've told me is very good news. You were looking down the pike before I was."

I then laid out my problem, and Maria's proposed solution. I needed to get the men among the Azanian exiles to fight, and the key to the men was the women. Would the Council of Conscience be willing to write their correspondents among the exiles and promote the war?

The answer required little discussion. Matrons knew their own minds. "Of course we will, Captain," Mrs. Bingham replied. "But as a woman, I know the importance of the personal touch. I cannot speak for others, but I am fully prepared to go out to the Rocky Mountain states myself and help inspire the people there." Old Hiram Bingham would have been proud, I thought.

"Mrs. Bingham speaks for me as well," Mrs. Schermerhorn said. Quickly, the rest of the room chimed in with their agreement.

"Thank you very much," I replied. "But I am not at all certain that sending women to a war zone is consistent with what the Northern Confederation represents. War is properly a man's business. Bombs and missiles will be falling in the Rocky Mountains as soon as the Azanian feminazis figure out what we're up to. Men's duty is to keep that sort of thing away from their women, not send women into it."

"Captain, no woman in this room has any illusion that women can be soldiers," Mrs. Bingham replied. "But that is not my intention. You will never see me in camouflaged fatigues, unless a floral print dress counts as such when working in the garden. But as the people who have brought on this war, we also have duties to perform in it. The women of London and Berlin did their duty under bombs and missiles, as I dare say did the women of Hanoi. We aren't sissies, Captain. If you think we are, I invite you to join us at a sale in Filene's basement. I tell you, I'm going."

A good soldier knows when to beat a retreat. "Very well, ladies," I replied. "As Chief of the General Staff, I am prepared to accept volunteers." In fact, I knew their on-scene efforts would make my task a great deal easier. "How soon after the referendum passes can you be ready?"

"Alonzo, pack my valise!" Mrs. Bingham ordered her goggle-eyed butler. "I can leave this very evening."

"That won't be necessary," I replied. "But if the women exiles from Azania will show as much spirit, I think I'll soon have my army."

*

Come May 15, the Northern Confederation's men offered a conditional proof of Maria's theorem. Not wishing to seem less bellicose than their women, they pushed the referendum through to victory with an overwhelming 86 percent. As the returns came in, the radio stations began playing, "California, Here I Come." The eternal war between men and women was about to become the shooting kind.

As always, we sought to move quickly. Some pieces of the puzzle were already in place. The Rocky Mountain Confederation had consented to let us use their territory as a base, even though it guaranteed they would suffer missile and air strikes from Azania. They were also a Christian nation, and regarded Azania as the perversion it was. All they asked from us was air defense, since they had only a handful of operable fighters. The Boys from Utica were already deploying their ground crews and antique, anti-stealth long-wave radars. F-16s would soon follow.

Dano's guys were already in action, roaming the hills of eastern Azania and collecting sample sensors. Some they found by setting them off, but the Azanians couldn't believe we'd be there so soon so they filtered the returns out as noise. Our wireheads had set up a skunk works in an old garage outside Portland and were starting to disassemble the first of

Ron's little presents.

On May 21st, Mrs. Bingham and 81 other ladies—our 82nd Airborne Division, some wags called it—boarded a Russian Antonov for the trip to Salt Lake City. The Tsar also didn't think much of a nation of harpies. If the feminists could find international support, so could we.

Once in Salt Lake, the ladies paired off in two-woman teams to evangelize the countryside. The Mormon Legion sent a sergeant with each team whose job was to prevent the Azanians from targeting them. At first, that looked like a difficult problem. The meetings needed to be publicized so the exiles could find them. We had to figure the Azanians would pick up on the publicity and send a missile as their *carte de visite*. Against a fixed target like a meeting hall or even an open field where people were gathered, their hi-tech weapons were deadly.

A Mormon NCO came up with the solution. When people got to the advertised site of the meeting, they found a sign directing them someplace else. There was no way the Azanian gizmos could pick that up real-time. Cardboard and magic markers triumphed over high-tech.

By the end of May, the ladies' circuit riding had become a triumphal procession. They were welcomed by throngs wherever they went. War was in the air, not only among the Azanian exiles but among the local residents as well. The women were galvanized when they saw genuine ladies taking the lead against the Azanian feminists, and the men were shamed. By early June, a cadre of men from the Azanian exiles had signed up to fight, and they followed our ladies wherever they went, offering the King's shilling. Large numbers of Rocky Mountaineers were joining too, with the blessings of their states.

Maria had been right. I would have my army.

On June 12, the Azanians responded. They did so in exactly the way we anticipated. That evening, a dozen cruise missiles hit the locations in a dozen cities and towns where our rallies had been advertised. Because the meetings were never held in the advertised locations, the blow fell on air. But the missiles had their usual effect. They made the local people angry and helped our recruiting.

After that, the missiles kept coming, with similar results. At our advice, the Rocky Mountain states announced the missile strikes and the handful of casualties, but did not explain why the casualties were so low. We wanted to draw the Azanians out.

At first, the Azanian response was more missiles. When that didn't work, they took the bait. On June 22, they sent aircraft. They figured aircraft could give them immediate BDA and solve the mystery of the low body count.

Our radars had been netted into a good GCI system, and we watched six flights of four F-35s each come over the mountains. We positioned two F-16s, flying in trace with a couple miles separation, high and behind each flight of F-35s. The first F-16 drew off the rear pair of F-35s, which were escorts. Then, the second F-16 went for the bomb-carrying F-35s. It was a tactic the North Vietnamese had used with good success against the U.S. Air Force.

It worked for us, too. In every case, when the lead F-35s came under attack from the second F-16, they had to jettison their bombs in order to maneuver. That was the end of the air strike.

More interesting was what happened next. Once the second F-16 had done its job, the first turned back into the escort while the second continued to mix it up with the bombers. We got what we wanted: furballs where we could gauge the quality of Azania's female fighter pilots.

As expected, they stank. As soon as the unexpected happened, they started to come unglued.

Everyone kept yelling "Break!" so often no one knew who was warning whom. Three-dimensional maneuvering—the Boys from Utica made lots of use of the vertical—was more than the female sense of space could handle.

It ended up a turkey shoot. The F-35 was as bad as its pilots, a real flying piano. We lost one F-16 to a mid-air collision when a befuddled and panicked woman turned into our aircraft. Eleven of the 24 F-35s were shot down, most with cannon fire, and some of those that made it home were pretty shot up. Our guys came back to their bases whooping and hollering.

The Azanians went back to missiles. By way of revenge, they hit and destroyed the Mormon Temple and Amphitheater in Salt Lake City. Not only did that bring swarms of Mormons to our recruiters, the state of Utah declared war on Azania. That put the superbly trained Mormon Legion at our disposal. I had planned to send military training teams from the N.C. to teach the newly-recruited Azanian exiles and Rocky Mountaineers, but when Utah entered the war they volunteered to take over that task.

Back in Augusta, I felt events were moving well and, more important, quickly. It was time for me to get in on the action. On July 3, with the rest of the General Staff, I boarded an Ilyushin at Portland for Salt Lake City.

CHAPTER FORTY-FOUR

A N endless, howling rain of cruise missiles had obliterated Salt Lake City's airport. The tower and hangers were rubble. The terminal building somehow still had one wall standing. Through its gaping windows showed the smoke-blackened artifacts of early 21st century travel, heaped like broken toys in a bad boy's toy box.

Nonetheless, we landed. Using pushcarts, the Mormons filled holes in the runways as fast as Azanian missiles could make them. All you really need for an airport is a runway. It was the oft-repeated story of high-tech warfare. It kicks the enemy in the shins, not in the head.

A couple of Mormon Legion trucks were waiting for us. We piled in and they hauled ass out the urban danger zone, then began a long, slow climb on dirt roads up into the mountains. Toward evening, we turned off into a Mormon cattle ranch, pulled into the barn and stopped. We had arrived at the Legion's headquarters. To a satellite, one cow barn looks like another, and the Zanies didn't have enough missiles to hit all of them.

The Legion was a first-rate infantry outfit, and we quickly established a good working relationship with them. Our strength was staff work, so that's what we did: Refine the campaign plan, issue the necessary orders, organize the logistics, schedule the deployments. They focused on training our newly recruited troops.

The time schedule was tight. Our army had to be through the passes before the snow came. D-Day was set for September 1. But the work went smoothly, despite the Azanian reprisal weapons. The relatively few casualties they caused in the small, dispersed training camps helped harden the troops.

Dano's boys continued to collect enemy sensors, and our skunk works had little trouble developing ways to fox them. Compared to men, even the most brilliant machine is stupid.

But boys will be boys, and ours didn't stop with collecting. They started clearing the sensors from key passes. Usually, the devices were poorly camouflaged and easy to find. Women have shitty field craft.

One afternoon early in August, Sergeant Danielov turned up at my headquarters, which for the moment was in an abandoned silver mine outside Virginia City, Nevada. I'd gone forward to check on the supply build-up. The reports said it was going well, but I'd long ago learned that reports had to be checked by personal inspection. In this case, thanks to Mormon honesty, most were accurate.

Dano sauntered up to the old farmhouse table that was my desk, stopping briefly on the way to stomp a visiting rattlesnake. "Want him for dinner?" he said, holding up the still-twitching snake with its bloody head ground into a disc by the heel of the jungle boot.

"No thanks," I grimaced. "I don't eat snake unless it's in aspic. Besides, Mormon country is rich in victuals. There's turkey, ham, and fresh bread sitting on top of a barrel over there. Make yourself a sandwich, unless you prefer rattlesnake tartare."

"I'll save him to scare a POW with," Dano replied, tossing his kill aside. "Besides, I just ate an MRE."

"Ugh. Meals Rejected by Ethiopians. If that's the alternative, I'll take the snake. Anyway, I assume you came back here for more than a bad meal. What's going on?"

"The Zanies are starting to re-seed sensors in areas we've cleared."

"How are they doing it? They're not sending out the Dykes on Bikes, are they?"

"Nope, not yet. Hope they do. I've always wanted my own Harley. For now, they're sending in teams by helicopter, in broad daylight."

"Ha ha."

"Yeah. But maybe a good opportunity."

"What are you thinking?"

"It'd be nice if we could whittle down their air strength before we go in. Even with a broad flying it, an airplane is smarter than a missile. Since they tried that F-35 strike and lost their asses, their Air Force has stayed in the kitchen. Maybe we could use this to draw 'em into some more furballs."

"What's your plan?"

"My guys can put more effort into collecting sensors. Since the Zanies don't have any infantry, we can push on west of the passes, policing up their gizmos along the way. Then, when they send their helos out, our F-16s can ambush them. They'll have to stop re-seeding the sensors or give the helos fighter escort. Either way, we win."

"Now I remember why we put a sergeant on the General Staff. That's a shit hot idea! The airedales will eat it up. I'll get a courier off to them right away. If this works, Dano, I'll see you get the Air Medal for it."

"Thanks, but I wouldn't want to trash up a good infantry uniform."

*

It took just over a week to put all the pieces together. The long-wave radars were too big to move forward, and their continuous emissions would bring HARMs. But our flak outfit also had some small, single-ping radars adapted from the MiG-47 for ground employment. They put a few on peaks just west of the passes. They would pick up stealth because they'd be looking straight up at the F-35's huge, flat bottom.

The Boys from Utica, now unofficially the Condor Legion with Utah Air Guard markings and uniforms, cheered when they heard Dano's plan. They figured a game of aerial grabass against women pilots among the peaks of the Rockies would be a demolition derby. As one fresh-faced lieutenant pilot put it to me, "If you think women have any sense of spatial relationships, next time you're in a supermarket, see who always leaves their shopping carts in the middle of the aisles."

The challenge was bringing aircraft forward into Nevada without making them missile targets. Our aviators knew they'd have to keep the numbers down. They finally decided to go with just eight F-16s, for four two-ship *rotte*. By flying them in at night, letting the engines cool down, then hauling them into hides with horse teams, they effectively hid them from eyes in the sky, even eyes with thermal imaging. Meanwhile, Ron's guys laid land lines back from the radars to an improvised GCI site, which communicated to the fighters from dispersed burst transmitters.

On the bright, clear morning of August 12, one of those days where you could see fifty miles around from any peak, the Zanies fell into the trap. They sent a flight of two big, fat CH-53 Echoes out to run down the passes, north to south, installing new sensors.

Two Condor Legion F-16s caught them right over their second LZ. They shot down only one, making sure the witches in Dash 2 got a clear look at them. We wanted them to go home and tell their tale.

Three days later, another sensor replacement mission came out. This time, there was just one helo, but it had four F-35s as escorts. We hit them with all eight of our forward F-16s. Again we left one survivor to go home and weep her debrief.

We didn't need superior numbers to pick Azanian grapes. But we had used them for a reason. The last thing feminists could admit was that women couldn't fly fighters. So the problem had to be numbers.

Two days later, one helo had sixteen F-35s along for the ride. Our F-16 jockeys were happy as Irishmen at a distillers' convention. Five of the F-35s didn't even require an AIM-9 or cannon shells. Two had a mid-air and three flew into mountains. Again, we let one get home, the same little lady our boys let go the first time. Her aircraft was easy to recognize. She'd had the whole fuselage painted up as a cut-off penis.

It took the witches five days to figure out what to do next. On August 22, they came out with two helos and twenty-four F-35s. So many more little figures on broomsticks to paint on our F-16s, our pilots figured. Then, just after our diamond formations had foxed their barrage of AMRAAMS but before the merge, our pilots got a warning from one of Dano's boys that he had a visual on four fighters, high and fast, behind us and starting to turn. GCI didn't have them. I was listening on the net, and we all knew at once what the report meant: F-22s, the old U.S. Air Force's ultra-hot stealth fighter. We didn't know the Zanies had any.

So our F-16s ran away. Holding their diamond formations to guard against AMRAAM tail shots, they turned, dove for the deck, went to afterburner and fled all the way back to Utah.

Our SIGINT heard the Azanian pilots giggling and cackling as the helos made their inserts in safety. They'd given those pricks a licking, all right. Hi-tech had triumphed over testosterone.

One of the most basic rules of warfare is, don't fall into predictable patterns. But women don't understand war, and high technology does the same thing over and over.

Our recon troops quickly cleared the fresh Azanian sensors, so two days later, early in the morning, the ladies came to replace them. They had two helos, just eight F-35s, and four F-22s again protecting the whole gaggle.

High over the Nevada desert, at the max altitude an F-16 could fly and as slow as they could go, two of our fighters waited. Behind them, at low altitude, two ancient F-4 Phantoms of the Utah Air Guard were circling. Both our aircraft and the Zanies used old USAF IFF. Early that morning, Patel had personally hacked the day's Azanian squawk code, which was entered in the F-4's boxes.

As the four F-22s swung back west, fat, dumb, and happy, the two F-16s came slashing down, huns in the sun, blowing past the rearmost F-22s and pouring cannon fire into their cockpits. The witches were blown into dog meat before they could utter a syllable. Typical of bad pilots, the other two F-22s never bothered to check six. The F-4s, which had moved up on burner as soon as the F-16s began their attack, slid in behind them. They stayed there all the way back to the Zanies' base.

War after war, air force after air force lines its aircraft up wingtip to wingtip. They look so pretty that way. Ladies especially like things neat. Two thousand-pound cluster bomb dispensers on each F-4 turned the whole Azanian F-22 inventory into scrap metal in thirty seconds.

Women always fight dirty, but they are surprised when men do. It had never crossed the minds of Azania's aviators that our skedaddle on the 22nd had been a set-up. As John Donne wrote, "Hope not for mind in woman; they are at their best, but mummy possessed."

*

Drawing the Zanies' attention to the air battle helped cover our deployments, which by mid-August were well underway. Ten thousand troops were positioned forward in Nevada to advance through the Donner Pass; five thousand were set to go through the Feather River Canyon, following the old Western Pacific Railway, and another five thousand waited to move down the valley of the Tuolumne. Each had an Operational Maneuver Group behind the lead elements: a high-quality unit, all Northern Confederation troops, mounted on dirt bikes for speed. Like the prototype Soviet OMG, they were to be injected early to collapse the enemy operationally while the tactical battle was still underway.

All indications were that getting through the passes would not be a problem. Dano's recon troopers had cleared out most of the sensors, and the skunk works had provided us with counters for the few that might remain.

Still, my German-educated gut was uncomfortable. What we were doing was predictable. The geography left us little choice. Only high-quality mountain infantry could hope to enter California except through the major passes, and we didn't have much of that. Our Azanian exiles had grown up in cities and suburbs, and two months of training was far from enough to make them into good infantry, much less mountain troops. The Mormon Legion was broken up in small units to provide stiffening to the exiles, and most of Dano's boys provided the core of the OMGs.

There was one unit left: the Jefferson Davis Brigade, a 3,000-man unit of volunteers from the Confederacy. Paid and equipped by ladies of the South, who reviled the Azanians as strongly as our own women did, the Brigade had asked if it could join our war. The men were all well-trained regular soldiers from the Confederate Army, and they were in Light Armored Vehicles, the most operationally mobile weapon system on the market. The campaign plan envisioned using them as the operational reserve.

Instead, on August 25, I ordered them to move north. A phone call secured permission for them to cross into Cascadia, and I directed the Brigade to laager around Goose Lake. When the balloon went up, they were to advance as rapidly as possible down the difficult valley of the Pit River to Lake Shasta, then drive south through the Sacramento Valley. It was the long way around into northern California, but it was also Azania's back door.

X-hour on September 1 was 04:00. The missile threat meant our forces, though in range of the passes, could not mass until the night of the 31st of August. Satellite imagery told the Azanian fusion center what was up. Our forces could disperse, shift, and dig in sufficiently to avoid most of the missiles, but we could not conceal the fact that we were there.

On August 30, I had moved forward to a small OP set up by Ron's guys overlooking Donner Pass. That was the initial *Schwerpunkt*, and I needed to see what happened there. The sensors in Donner had all been cleared. No Azanian missiles had been fired at the pass itself in more than ten days. Our radars on the peaks hadn't seen an F-35 within 75 miles since August 24th. If we could get through the passes with small loss, the game was over.

*

Back in the Azanian photo analysis shop, a witch had been putting the puzzle together. She saw hundreds of platoons swarming east of the passes. She made their call: We would come through on the night of the

30th.

At about 01:00 on the 31st, a barrage of at least one hundred missiles hurtled down out of the clear night sky. The pass was scoured of every living thing in one tremendous barrage, a barrage out of the Somme or Passchendaele. Absent an unlucky round, we were safe enough in our OP, if soon somewhat deaf. But I offered a quick prayer of thanks that the Azanians had gotten it wrong by a day. Our infantry would have been slaughtered.

I soon got calls from similar OPs in the Feather River and Tuolumne valley passes. The Blitz was underway there also. I heard nothing from the Jefferson Davis Brigade: They were under strict radio silence.

As my mind began to recover from the first barrage, I noticed a couple of interesting things. First, the missiles were ballistic, not cruise. Second, while the barrage lightened, it didn't stop. As I continued to observe, I saw a pattern: The bombardment would let up, almost stop, grow a bit, dwell, then yield to another tremendous surge, which would last about fifteen minutes, then diminish. It was like a rolling barrage from the First World War.

I wasn't overly worried. The Azanians' timing was wrong. They were shooting their wad, and we weren't under it. Hi-tech missiles were expensive, slow to build, and inevitably available only in small numbers. In fact, the bombardment was an act of desperation: Their sensors destroyed, all the Azanians could do was use their smart weapons like dumb ones and fire them in barrages. We just had to wait for them to run out.

At around 06:00, just after first light, a missile came into our OP. It wasn't a lucky hit for the Azanians. It was carried in by six of Ron's boys, with Ron himself holding up the tailfins. The warhead was missing, or seemed to be until I saw another N.C. recon trooper, a Maine boy I recognized, following along behind holding it and grinning.

"Afraid they were going to miss us up here?" I asked Ron

"Yep," he answered. "I thought you ought to see one of these up real close. Corporal Eakins here spotted it, a dud, got some friends to help haul it back and took the front end apart."

"Nice to see you still among the living, Eakins," I said to the corporal with the warhead. "You sure you got that thing disarmed?"

"No, sir," he replied, "but I don't plan to drop it either."

"And just what qualities of this rocket do you wish me to admire?" I asked Ron.

"What it isn't. It's not hi-tech. There's no homing device, no fancy guidance system. It's a FROG, Free Rocket Over Ground. A Katyusha, in effect."

Eakins quickly showed me the rocket's simple front end, just a fuse and a warhead. I got the point at once. A simple rocket like this could be produced easily, quickly, in large numbers. The Zanies could have tens of thousands of them, and they could keep this bombardment up for days, maybe weeks. Maybe even indefinitely if they had production lines going.

"There's more," Ron said.

"You're just the bluebird of happiness this morning, aren't you?"

"Bad news is still news. Have you been listening carefully to the detonations?"

"All I'm hearing at this point is lots of ringing in my ears."

"The Zanies are also using artillery."

"Shit. We didn't know they had any."

"Well, they got some, somewhere."

That was bad news indeed. Artillery made it easier for them to keep up a prolonged bombardment. It was clear we'd had a big-time intel failure. It must have been early, months ago, that a voice of sanity had penetrated Azanian high councils and they had decided they needed low-tech as well as hi-tech. We should have picked something up from their computers about this. I'd have a word with Patel later on.

"You got anything else?"

"Just one little thing," Ron replied. "I sent a few of my men in deep, way deep. One team got within ten meters of one of the FROG batteries. The personnel were men, and they're speaking Spanish."

Welcome to 21st century war, I thought. The Mexicans wanted our help against the Aztecs and at the same time hired themselves out to our enemies.

"Okay, that's good work, Ron, as always," I said. "We'll just have to adjust."

From the OP, I ordered the attack to be postponed indefinitely. Then I spent the rest of the day and most of the next night working my way back east out of the pass. The enemy fire stayed in the valley, except for an occasional wild round, and I was safe enough so long as I moved on the high ground. Lucky I'd spent all that time climbing in the Whites.

*

The GHQ for the operation was outside Carson City, in another abandoned mine. Borrowing a dirt bike from an infantry unit, I got back there early in the afternoon on September 1st. My order had been received, and in addition to the rest of the deployed N.C. General Staff, the CO of the Mormon Legion was there, along with the commander of both the Feather River and Tuolumne brigades. It was not a group of happy campers.

A quick discussion confirmed that all the passes were effectively blocked. "Well, gentlemen," I said, "an angel has pissed in the touchhole. That's how war goes. Seldom does a plan survive its first contact with the enemy. Any ideas as to what we should do now?"

A battalion commander from the exile militia spoke up. "Sir, my men want to fight. We're willing to try to get through the pass, rockets or no rockets."

"I'm glad to see such strong fighting spirit, colonel," I replied. "But bodies have no effect on firepower. We could fill every pass up with bodies and the fire wouldn't slack off. You wouldn't get through."

John Ross spoke up. "We've heard nothing from the Confederates up north."

"The valley of the Pit River is just that, a pit," I replied. "LAV's can take some artillery and rocket fire—frag and shrapnel won't stop them—but they can't handle cluster munitions. There's no way to avoid fire in that valley, and they'll be in it for 200 miles."

"If the Zanies know they're there."

I thought about that for a minute. Satellite imagery would show an LAV force strong and clear. But only if someone was looking in the right place.

"Okay, John, get us a helo and put two dirt bikes on board. Let's go up north and take a look. Meanwhile, all forces are to remain in position. You've got good resupply where you are and there's no reason to pull back. We still don't know when the girls may run out of ammo. If they do and I'm out of comm, go for it."

By the time we found a Blackhawk and got out of Carson City, it was evening. That was fine. Night still offers concealment. Just to be sure, we flew back to Utah, up to Idaho and across into Cascadia. The helo put us down near the South Fork of the Sprague River, where a ridge line gave cover from radars looking north from Azania. It was dawn when we got on the dirt bikes.

By about 07:30 we arrived at the Jeff Davis Brigade's laager on the north side of Goose Lake. It was empty.

We swung south around the lake and picked up the Pit River. Even under the press of things gone wrong, I couldn't miss the beauty of the morning, clear and cool with a mist floating above the river and sharply-angled beams of sunlight refracting the colors in the rock. I also couldn't miss the LAV tire tracks everywhere and the absence of any destroyed vehicles.

It was forty-five minutes or so before we got confirmation of our growing hopes. We came around a sharp bend and almost ran into our first casualty: a LAV that had broken down. The Confederates had the trail covered with a light machine gun, but it was easy to identify us as friends: We were men.

One of the Jeff Davis troopers recognized me from my earlier adventures in Dixie. "We're honored to see you again, suh," he said, saluting smartly.

"Thank you, soldier. Is your whole force up ahead?"

"Yes, suh, goin' balls to the wall for the Valley, just like ol' Stonewall. Only this time, it's the Sacramento instead of the Shenandoah."

"Any sign of enemy action?"

"No, suh."

"I assume you're still in radio silence."

"Yes, suh."

"Okay, we'll just have to catch 'em."

"You got some catchin' to do, suh. These heah LAVs is fast as a coon with a dog on 'im."

That was good news, not bad. Speed was the key. If the Davis Brigade could get through the Pit valley and past Lake Shasta before the Zanies spotted it, we'd be through the back door.

Fast as the LAVs were, dirt bikes were faster. That's why LAV units had motorcycle scouts. Steadily, we overhauled the Davis Brigade from the rear. I stuck a small N.C. Pine Tree Flag on the handlebars, and a good many Southern troopers recognized me, so they made way for us. We rode all day and well into the night.

At around 02:00 on September 3rd, we finally caught up with the Confederate command group, which was near the head of the column. To my surprise, it was small, just a CO, XO, S-2, 3, and 4, in two LAV command vehicles. The CO was up in the lead vehicle's hatch, and when he caught sight of me in his NVGs he pulled over to the side of the road.

John and I pulled up alongside him and dismounted. God I was stiff. The CO jumped down from his LAV. He knew me, but I didn't know him.

"Colonel John Mosby of the 1st Virginia at your service, sir," he said, removing his plumed helmet and bowing cavalier style. "We are honored by your visit, sir, though I will confess surprise at seeing you here at our minor front."

"Your front's the only front, Colonel," I replied. "At least the only one that's going somewhere. The other passes are sealed by Azanian fire. You are now the *Schwerpunkt* for the whole operation."

"I didn't catch that word, sir."

"*Schwerpunkt*. Focal point. It means everything depends on us, Colonel. We make it or break it." The voice was that of a Confederate major who'd dropped down from the other Command LAV and was striding up fast to coach his CO. I recognized it, and when he took his helmet off I recognized him in the chemlight: It was none other than Charlie Ravenal, my old escort officer during my Confederate escapade.

"So you're speaking German now, Charlie?"

"Been doing a little reading, sir. Some of us officers have been trying to get a bit more serious about our profession."

"Glad to hear it. Gladder still to see you where you are. I take it you didn't receive my order to stop?"

It was an order I shouldn't have given these guys, since I didn't know the situation up here.

"Well, suh, I'm afraid I have a confession to make," said Colonel Mosby. "We did receive the halt order. But seein' nuthin' and nobody in front of us, we figured we'd just go until we did. Then, we'd think about haltin'."

"Colonel, you have the most important quality in a military leader," I replied. "You know when to disobey orders."

"That's what Major Ravenal said you'd say."

"And as a consequence you've saved the day," I replied. "Speaking of which, can you be through the Pit valley and to Lake Shasta by daylight?"

"Yes, sir," Ravenal answered. "At least most of the column can be." It had continued to stream past us as we talked by the side of the road. "May I ask what your orders will be at that point?"

"We have two options. You can advance straight down the Sacramento Valley until you come to the Feather River, then turn east and begin clearing the enemy's fire support systems out of the passes so our main force can come through. Or you can go straight for the strategic targets yourself: the airfields, the missile dumps and depots and, above all, the Azanian 'fusion center' that ties all the parts together. What's your preference?"

Major Ravenal turned to Colonel Mosby. "Sir, the purpose of an Operational Maneuver Group is to strike as directly as possible at the strategic level. I think that's what we'd like to do."

"Remember that you are only 3,000 men," I cautioned.

"Yes, sir. It's a high-risk approach. But we're fighting women."

I thought about it for a bit. The bolder approach was always tempting. But here, if it failed, it would not fail gracefully. The remainder of our forces would still be stuck in the passes, hoping the Zanies ran out of ammo before snow closed the roads. The risk was great and the pay-off relatively small.

"I'm sorry, gentlemen, in this case I have to decide otherwise," I ordered. "If your bid for a strategic decision were to fail, we'd be out of tricks. I need the options our main force provides. I want you to open the passes for them from the rear."

"What if the Azanians turn their rocket launchers and artillery around and try to keep us out?" Colonel Mosby asked.

"You'll have to cut their logistics line, so their ammo supply would dry up fairly fast," I replied. "The ammo they have appears to be anti-personnel rounds, which won't do much to your vehicles. Most important, they'd be trapped, and it takes real guts to be surrounded and still keep fighting. I think they'll run."

"What about their air?" Charlie Ravenal asked.

"The 25mm guns on your LAVs are good anti-aircraft weapons," I replied. "And once your column is out of the Valley and the Zanies know you're here, I'll break radio silence and designate you the air *Schwerpunkt*. That'll give you fighter cap, and the Zanies have learned not to tangle with our fighters. If this time they do, so much the better."

"That's good enough for me," said Colonel Mosby. "If you don't object, suh, I'd like to mount up and keep movin'. I feel a need to be up front. You're welcome to a seat in my command LAV if you want one."

"Thanks," I said, thinking of my aching butt. "But as an old infantryman I feel better with a vehicle I can get off of in hurry. Let's say we rendezvous at Project City, on the south side of Lake Shasta. I'll get on the horn there and call for air."

"That'll be just fine, sir. Don't hold it against us none if we get there first." With that the good colonel mounted his LAV, waved "Forward!" with the plumed helmet and joined the race for the lake.

*

As Major Ravenal had predicted, sunrise saw the long column of grey LAVs mostly out of the valley and reaching around to the southern side of Lake Shasta. Colonel Mosby left a command vehicle with its extensive commo suite waiting there for me, but he and his men didn't stop. He was entering a populated area, which meant the Zanies would soon know of his presence. He needed to get out into the wider Sacramento Valley where he could disperse to avoid air and missile attack.

By 07:00, I had established radio comm with my staff back in Carson City. Within 45 minutes, we had F-16s providing cover over the lead LAVs. Better still, an A-10 squadron from Idaho had flown in to volunteer their services, and by mid-morning I had two loitering over the Davis Brigade. They were the only aircraft in the old U.S. Air Force that could make a difference in a ground fight, and while I didn't expect much fighting, the first Principle of War is: "You never know."

At the same time that I switched the air *Schwerpunkt* to the Confederates, I asked that a helo be sent to pick me up. The Jeff Davis Brigade had a commander who could make decisions and, in the metamorphized Major Ravenal, someone who could serve as his brain. I already knew what gunpowder smelled like and had no need to be at the front. With our three other thrusts about to go, my place was back at the operational level, which for the moment meant Carson City. I left John Ross to serve as my liaison with the LAVs.

It was around 11:00 that a Montana Air Guard Blackhawk—all the

Rocky Mountain states now wanted into the fight— dropped me off outside our mine. Before I was even clear of the rotor blades some fresh-scrubbed Mormon kid in utilities was in my face, screaming, "Sir, we're through! We're through! The fire lifted along the Feather River and we're through!"

As we moved away from the helo I caught sight of a butterbar on his collar. "OK, lieutenant, simmer down. When did you get the first report of the fire lifting along the Feather?"

"About 10:00 hours, sir."

Even if the Mex mercenaries had high-tailed it when they heard the LAVs were coming, that still meant the Jeff Davis Brigade was making good time. "Any word from further south?" I asked.

"Sir, as your bird was coming in I heard a radio saying the fire was slacking off in Donner Pass."

Good. The Zanies were about to learn why armies had stopped hiring their artillery a few centuries back. The gunners first loyalty is to their guns, not their temporary employer. Of course, there were more bearded ladies in circuses than women who read military history.

I soon got settled back at my old table in the mine, with a heaping plate of Mormon goodies in front of me. If all American women had cooked like Mormon women, the old U.S.A. wouldn't have had a divorce rate.

Then, John Ross was on the horn with more good news. A company of LAVs had caught the Mex arty as it was trying to get out of the Feather River canyon and captured the whole lot. The A-10s had gone ahead of the ground units into Donner Pass and shot up a bunch of rocket batteries. The survivors were packing up and getting ready to run for it. The Zanies had sent in F-35s but they were grapes for the F-16s. "The main air threat now is F-35s falling on our heads," John said.

Even the A-10s were shooting down Azanian fighters. It looked as certain as anything in war can be that by the end of the day, we'd be through all the passes unless the little ladies had a lot more long range cruise missiles than I thought they did. So long as the LAVs were focused on taking the passes, there wasn't much we could do about the long-range stuff controlled by the enemy fusion center.

About mid-afternoon, I again spotted Sergeant Danielov working his way toward me through the headquarters' creative chaos. "Sir, I think it's about time for our special op to go," he said.

"What special op?" I inquired.

"Well, while you were tooling around on your bike chasing the Confederates, I got to thinking I'd like to stomp the head off another snake. So I sat down with a few guys and some of the airedales and we came up with a plan to go after the fusion center. We figured that if we could take that out, the whole Zany hi-tech war would collapse with it."

"Good reasoning," I said. "How are you going to get there?"

"By air."

"As long as the fusion center is still functioning they'll know you're coming. They've still got radars, plus SAMS aplenty around San Francisco airport, which is where the fusion center is located. Even women pilots in F-35s can shoot down transports. You'll need every fighter we've got as an escort, and that will leave our other forces uncovered."

"I'll only need four F-16s for escort, and they're only if we get real unlucky. The Zanies won't know we're coming. We've got stealth transports."

"Stealth transports?"

"AN-2s."

The AN-2, I knew, was an ancient Russian aircraft, a small, biplane transport designed in the 1940s. It could operate out of rough fields, and for decades had been Aeroflot's luxury liner for out-of-the-way places. Like biplanes of World War I, it was mostly made of fabric. The only thing for a radar to pick up was the engine.

"Where in the hell did you find AN-2s?" I asked.

"A Colorado airline bought a dozen a few years back to provide local service. Colorado asked how they could help in the war so we asked for the AN-2s. Eight came in this morning. I can get ten guys with gear into each. Eighty men is enough."

"How sure are you that the Zanies hi-tech radar won't pick you up?"

"The higher tech it is, the less likely it will pick up an AN-2. Not only does a flying engine without an airplane not make any sense, the AN-2 only flies about 60 miles per hour. The Intel shop is pretty sure the highly automated Azanian systems will wash it out as a false contact before any human even gets it on a scope."

It was the old high-tech story: An automated system can't deal with any situation not anticipated by its designers. High-tech designers didn't build their systems to detect World War I airplanes.

"Well, pretty sure is as good as it gets in war. I don't see any downside, other than you and 79 other guys coming home in body bags. If you're ready to risk that, so am I."

Dano knew me well enough to guess what my answer would be. He had his men already packed into their string-bag AN-2s and ready to roll. The mission took off at 15:40 hours Mountain time, September 3rd.

Operationally, Dano's spec op was not critical. If it worked, it would shorten the war, which was always good. Speed kept casualties down. If it didn't work, we still would get through the passes, even if some cruise missiles kept coming. The broad-front advance was a sure thing in this case, because all it would meet would be hordes of panicked women.

At the same time, it's hard watching an old friend and fine soldier head off on a high-risk mission. I knew my stomach would be in knots until we had some word from Dano about success—or failure.

As we waited, I occupied my mind by calling Major Walthers over to my ersatz desk. "What do we know about this Azanian fusion center?" I asked him. "Assuming our guys get there alive, can they get in?"

"They can get in," Walthers replied. "The question is how far down they can get. I gave Ron everything we know before he left, of course. But it isn't much. On the surface, the fusion center is just a big, two-story building with no windows. Assuming Northern Confederation Special Forces can get past the Dykes on Bikes, entering the building is not a problem. It has doors and we can blow them."

"I somehow doubt the dykes will delay us much. Assuming we get in, what then?"

"Then's when it gets interesting. The building itself is a decoy. Like all militaries, the Azanians thought symmetrically. Since they use long-range precision weapons to destroy buildings, they figured someone attacking them would do the same. So the building is designed to be destroyed. They planned to let the enemy think he had destroyed the fusion center along with the building. But the workings of the center are actually underground, far enough under that blowing up the building doesn't have any effect."

"So the building is military make-up, in effect?"

"Exactly. A false face. A natural female ploy."

"How far down does the actual fusion center go?"

"That's what we don't know. Dano is going to have to find out the hard way, layer by layer. I told him to take plenty of C-4 and some big shaped charges."

Erik's intel work didn't make me feel any better as I hung around all alone by the telephone. An idle mind soon decides to amuse itself with mischief, and I remembered I owed Captain Patel a rocket for missing the Hispanic mercs, not that they'd done the Zanies a lot of good anyway. I rang him up on the intercom and told him to report to my desk.

He soon came waddling up, wearing a sheepish grin. That didn't tell me much, since it was his usual expression. "How's your Spanish today, fat boy?" I inquired.

"Non-existant, sir. Where I grew up, we spoke to the servants in Bengali."

"How did you let a big one like that get by you?"

"To be honest, sir, we figured that if it was in Spanish, it couldn't be of much military significance. I don't think Spain's won a battle since the Thirty Years War. Plus, I've had virtually all our assets chasing something else."

"What?"

"Medusa."

"What's Medusa?"

"It is something discussed at the highest levels of the Azanian government and military, and only at those levels. Beyond that we don't know, except that as the war has turned to shit for them the word has turned up with increasing frequency. Since early this morning, there have been intensive discussions between the Zany state house in Berkeley and the fusion center on whether to use Medusa or not."

"That suggests it's some sort of weapon."

"Clearly. But we don't know what sort. So far, we haven't found the key word that gets us into the file."

"Have you tried Perseus?"

"What's Perseus?"

"God save us from data dinks! Perseus is the Greek who slew Medusa. Didn't you study mythology?"

"Sure, the Bhagavad-Gita."

"Multiculturalism strikes again, eh? Don't worry, it won't last more than one generation in the Northern Confederation. Your kids will learn about Greeks and Romans, not Ganesh and Kali."

"I'd hope so. Remember, my family didn't go to all the trouble of leaving India because we liked the place. If my kids want to experience their ancestral culture, they can go out in the back yard, take off all their clothes, sit in the dirt and starve."

"Okay, then I guess we'll let you stay. Meanwhile, try Perseus on the Medusa file. And Patel—next time you catch some Spanish on the net, don't assume it's always someone trying to sell their mother."

"Aye, aye, sir."

After Captain Patel headed back to his infernal machine, I kept thinking about the password. Perseus seemed less likely the more I considered it. Not only was it obvious to any educated person, but Perseus was a man and a bunch of feminist banshees wouldn't be likely to use a man as a key to a woman.

But if not Perseus, what? Maybe a suitably feminist word that sounded like Perseus? I began doodling on a notepad: Persia, pussy—nope, scratch that one—percale, Percival—feminists should like men named Percival—Percheron—definitely too masculine—percolate—too domestic—persecute—what women complain of yet do, cuts too close to home—persiflage—women were good at that—persimmon—sour enough for this lot—persnickety—too appropriate—personality—few feminists had one—purse.

Purse. Perfect. The one thing no woman could do without and no man could comprehend. Nor find anything in.

Patel had secured his computers and their pencil-necked geek operators in a shaft off the main mine. I sauntered over with my notepad. The sign in front of his department read "Nerd's Nest." Humor was always a good sign in a military outfit, as its absence was a warning. "Here, try these," I said, dumping the pad on his keyboard. "Start with purse."

The roly-poly little captain's fingers flew over his keys and buttons as weird signs blinked on the hideous orange screen. Real men prefer steam, I thought to myself. After a few minutes of blinking and beeping, he said, "No go. Doesn't work."

"Try the plural." Perseus/purses. It was a closer homonym, and lesbians ought to go for homonyms.

More stroking of the machine. This time, it took longer. "Hm," Patel said. "It's not rejecting it right up front like it did everything else. That may or may not mean something. Let me play with this one for a while."

"Okay, buzz me at my desk if you come up with something. I'd rather get away from your computers while I can still father children."

"It's microwaves that affect that, not computers," Patel shot back. "And you can still have girls."

"How reassuring," I replied

Back at my improvised soldier's desk, I found no word from Ron. That left me facing a strong temptation, one that beguiles every commander: the temptation, when idle, to interfere in his subordinates' business. I could start asking for reports from the battle groups in the passes, briefs from the staff, "information," that late 20th century soma. Instead, I remembered again von Rundsted's reaction when he learned the Allies had landed on the beaches of Normandy: He went out into the garden and trimmed the roses.

I rummaged in my pack and dug out a volume of Xenophon. Xenophon was the perfect travelling companion: He was always a delight to read, and no matter how many times you went through him, you always found something new. I put my feet up on my desk, lit a cigar, and got lost in Athens.

A few minutes after 17:00 the phone on my desk rang. "Sir, we've got Sergeant Danielov on the horn," the Mormon Legion commo said.

"Put him through," I replied. At least he was still alive. The next voice was Ron's. "We're in. The ruse worked. All the aircraft made it in. It's a go!"

"Are you in the building?"

"Yes. We're down to the third level. The fusion center is gone. It's out of action for good."

"Casualties?"

"Just three dead, from booby traps. Eleven wounded. The booby traps are the only real problem. The Dykes got on their bikes and ran as soon as we started pouring out of the aircraft. The people in the fusion center were all women, so there was no organized resistance. We've got a lot of POWs."

"Have you hit bottom in the building yet?"

"Negative. There is at least one more level down. We don't know what's there, or who. We've already rounded up the whole Azanian command and staff."

At that moment Patel came flying up to my desk, panting from the short run through the mine. "Sir, sir, we've cracked it! We're into the Medusa file! It's not—"

"Hold on, Patel, I've got Danielov on the line."

"No sir! He has to know this! Medusa is right under him!"

"Hold on, Dano," I said into the phone. "What do you mean?" I asked Patel.

"Medusa is in the fusion center, sir," Patel answered. "It's in a bunker in the basement. The spec op is going to hit it, sir."

"What is Medusa, Captain?"

"A Q-bomb, sir. A doomsday device. It's every nuclear weapon the Azanians could get their hands on, all tied together to go off at once. It's at least 1,000 megatons, sir. If it blows, the whole of North America is going to get bathed in radiation. It'll be worse than 1,000 Chernobyl's. And the Zanies' email has told whoever is in charge of it to set it off if the bunker is breached."

Shit, I thought. It was the mother of all booby traps. Just like women to want to take everyone else with them.

"Dano, listen closely," I said into the phone. "We just found out what is in the lowest level of the fusion center. It's a nuclear doomsday device. Stop your operation! Repeat, stop your operation!"

Silence on the other end of the line. Please, Jesus, don't let the comm go down now. "Ron, do you read me?"

"I read you," he said. "OK, we'll stop where we are. But then what do we do?"

"You hold tight 'til I get there. You said you have POWs, including the top Azanian military leaders. Start interrogating them. Tell them we know about Medusa. Some of them probably aren't looking forward to being vaporized. Get out of them everything you can, especially anything on how the device is triggered."

"Roger. All right, we'll get to work on the prisoners and otherwise hold tight. How soon can you get here?"

"I don't know. But for God's sake and the future of this continent, don't press on any further. Wait for me."

"Roger, we'll wait. Out here."

We had a couple Blackhawks fueled and ready to go, waiting under cammo nets just outside our mine. Even at the operational level of war, you never know when you'll need to get someplace in a hurry. We'd be a grape for any Zany fighter or SAM, but war is dangerous, even war against women.

The helo crews were hanging around the mine's entrance in typical lounge lizard aviator fashion. I ordered them to get one bird ready to leave for San Francisco in three minutes. Then I yelled for Patel.

"Are you still seeing email flow from the Medusa bunker to the Zany government?" I asked as he came scurrying over.

"Yes," he answered. "In fact, we're hacking some right now."

That told me Medusa was controlled by people, not by some automatic mechanism. Somebody was still down there with it. I wasn't sure whether that made the problem easier or harder.

"Okay, here's what I need from you. Try to break in to the net and give the bunker good news: fake reports that we are retreating, plans by their Air Force for new strikes, rumors that the Mexicans are about to intervene to help them, that sort of stuff. So long as the folks minding the bomb think they have a chance to win, they're not likely to set it off. Do you know enough of their codes to do that?"

"They aren't using code," Patel replied. "They are so confident in their electronic security that everything's in plain English, or at least in politically correct English, which isn't too hard to figure out once you realize words like 'peace,' 'freedom,' and 'justice' mean their opposites. We haven't tried breaking into the nets yet, but I think we can do it."

"If you can't, you'll probably be heading back to India, because this continent will be uninhabitable."

"That's motivating enough."

"Get on it now!"

"Aye, aye, sir." As he ran off on his fat little legs, Patel was grinning. Like all good officers, he enjoyed a challenge.

As I walked out of the mine toward the Blackhawk, I saw two birds, not one, with their rotors spooling up. "We don't need the second bird,"

I yelled to the cockpit as I got into the nearest one. "It's just me you've got. We Yankees don't go much for entourages."

"The other bird's a decoy, sir," the captain in the pilot's seat shouted back. "If we're intercepted, he'll try to draw the enemy off on him."

The helos were from the Montana Air Guard. As usual, the Guardsmen had both brains and guts. I gave a thumbs up and buckled myself in, and we were on our way.

The FLIVO with my headquarters was in on the plan, and he diverted two F-16s to provide close escort in. It turned out we didn't need them. With the fusion center down, the Zanies were paralyzed. That's one of the problems with centralized control. When it goes down, everything just stops. Whatever initiative and adaptability the Azanian pilots might have had was long since drilled out of them.

The SAM and AAA threat worried me more than fighters. We countered as best we could, flying nap-of-the-earth and letting the other Blackhawk lead. If he took fire, we could break. Again the precaution proved unnecessary. It was clear that the whole Azanian military was down. I hoped that whoever was minding Medusa didn't know that. A lot was riding on Patel.

Helos are slow, and the sun was hanging just above the Pacific Ocean when we touched down at San Francisco International Airport, right next to the still-smoking fusion center. Dano ran out from the blown entrance toward the helos and met me just beyond our bird's rotor blade.

"What's the situation?" I asked without preliminaries. A line from an old Tom Lehrer song came to mind: "We'll all go together if we go, in one great incandescent glow."

"We got the fires out quickly and kept the noise and commotion down, so whoever's on the final level or levels thinks the assault is over. They may think we don't know they are there."

"What have you gotten out of the POWs?"

"We know who's down there with the bomb."

"Who?"

"Lt. Col. Molly Malone, Azanian Air Force."

"One woman?"

"Just one woman."

What a dumb move, I thought. The first thing a soldier learns is never send anyone out alone.

"What do we know about her?"

"A lot. According to the POWs, she was selected because she is an absolute fanatic. A 'feminist's feminist,' an 'ultra,' were some of the terms the POWs used. One even called her a 'Lady Macbeth', which was apparently intended as a compliment. She was disappointed in love early in her life and has hated men ever since."

"I've always suspected that being disappointed in love was the origin of most feminism," I replied. "At least she's not a lesbian."

"There's more. One of our troops is the man who disappointed her."

"What! How? Is she from New England?"

"Nope. But I brought along half-a-dozen of the Azanian exiles. They're all former cops with SWAT backgrounds. I figured they'd know enough at least not to get in our way, and having someone with local knowledge might prove useful. Turns out I figured right this time."

"Where is this guy?"

"Right here."

Standing just inside the blasted, smoke-blackened entrance to the Azanian fusion center was a somewhat overweight, 40ish guy in gray utilities and high-tech boots, typical cop gear.

"Captain Rumford, this is Sergeant Willy O'Toole of the Sacramento Police Department. Willy, Captain Rumford is Chief of the Northern

Confederation General Staff."

"Pleased to meet you, Willy," I said. "So you know the broad downstairs who is sitting on the Q-bomb?"

"Yes, sir," Willy replied.

"How well?"

"Pretty well, sir. We were in love."

"How long ago was that?"

"Twenty years, sir."

"It's a remarkable coincidence that you just happen to be here now."

"It's not a coincidence, sir. I knew Molly was a senior officer in the Azanian military, sir. When I heard a special op was being put together to go after the Azanian headquarters, I thought she might be there. I thought I might have a chance to get her out alive. So I signed up."

"And now she's all set to blow up a continent because you left her at the altar? I hope to God she doesn't find out you're here, or she'll push the button for sure."

"I don't think so, sir. It wasn't like that. It didn't happen that way."

"Why don't you tell me how it did happen?"

"Yes, sir. Molly grew up a few houses down from where my family lived, in a typical Sacramento suburban neighborhood. We were kids together, played together, went to school together. From pretty early on, we knew we liked each other. By high school, it was more than like. We knew we were in love."

"My dad was a cop, and I always knew I would be a cop. That was fine with Molly. But not with her mom. Molly's mom—her dad had split just after she was born—was a schoolteacher. She bought into all the political correctness stuff and ran the sensitivity training sessions at the high school. She was a big-time feminist. And she hated cops."

"And Molly had to choose between you and her mom?"

"Yes, sir. Her mom was all she had growing up, and she was real close to her. All through college, Molly and I still hoped to get married. But when I graduated and came home and joined the Sacramento Police Academy, her mom said she had to choose between her and me. She chose her. She told me she had to, because otherwise her mom would have no one and I could always find another woman. But I never did."

"Did she find someone else?"

"No, sir. After she broke off our engagement, she dove into all the feminist stuff with her mom. She hadn't been like that before. I guess she figured that if she couldn't have a normal life, she might as well go all the way into a weird one. I saw her name in the paper a lot, promoting abortion, leading demonstrations and so on. She became the local head of Planned Parenthood, then got elected to the State Assembly about the time the country was breaking up."

"Have you had any contact with her since she dumped you?"

"No, sir."

"But you still love her?"

"Yes, sir."

"Does she still love you?"

"I don't know."

Well, as Stan would have said, this was a fine kettle of fish. We were sitting on top of 1,000 megatons of nuclear weapons with the former boyfriend of the trigger woman, who might still love him or might hate his guts. All that was at stake was the ability of the North American continent to support life for the next thousand years.

"OK, Willy, I want you to stay right here with me. Dano, have you got comm with my headquarters?"

"Yes."

"Get Patel on the horn."

It took about thirty seconds for Patel to waddle over to the comm center. His PT was a cake a day.

"Patel, were you able to get the good news into the Zany fusion center?"

"Yes, sir. We blocked everything from all the other sources and have been feeding our stuff in. It's tough coming up with ways the Zanies could be winning, but we've done our best."

"OK, stay on the line," I turned to Danielov. "Do we have any voice comm with Lt. Col. Malone?"

"We might. There's an intercom right outside the vault door leading to the lower levels. We haven't blasted there, so it's intact. I don't know whether it works."

"Willy and I will go find out. Meanwhile, get your wirehead to rig a land line to this radio so I can still talk to Patel."

"Aye, aye, sir."

The cop and I headed into the fusion center and down, climbing through the usual wreckage of war. It was reassuring to see that in a contest between computers and hand grenades, grenades still came out on top.

The massive, sealed door to the lowest level was near the back of the third level. The women were already surrendering by the time Dano's boys reached that level, so the damage wasn't too bad. Boots were sufficient to take out computer screens. The area even had power.

The intercom was just outside the framing of the vault door. When I pushed the button to talk, a red light came on.

"Hello?" The voice was female.

"Lt. Col. Malone?" She wouldn't know my voice, but she'd know it was a male voice.

"Yes. Who is this?"

"Captain John Rumford of the Northern Confederation. The war's over, Colonel. Can we talk?"

"I don't know how you've broken into this system, Captain, but I know a trick when I hear one. The Azanian Armed Forces are doing well. I'm not surprised you need to pull some tricks at this point."

"Sorry ma'am, but the trick was played earlier. This is for real. The info on your email has been coming from us."

"You're lying, Captain, and you're not good at it."

Just at that moment one of our troops came running up with the land-line connection to the radio to Patel. "Patel, come clean with your customer. Tell her who you are and what you've been up to."

"Yes, sir."

"Ma'am, I think your computer screen will soon have a different message on it. But before you go take a look at it, someone here would like to say hello."

I put Willy on the intercom. "Hi, Molly."

A long silence. "Willy?"

"Yes, it's me."

"Where are you?"

"At the door."

"You can't be."

"I am."

Silence. Was she consulting her computer or reaching for the button?

"Willy?"

"I'm still here."

"Is it true that we've been beaten?" She had gone to her computer.

"Yes, it is. It's over."

"Not quite."

"Molly?"

"Yes?"

"I still love you. Will you marry me?"

Silence. A long, long silence. What would being vaporized feel like, I wondered? Then, a low, quiet, little-girl voice. "Yes. Yes, Willy, I'll marry you."

The war was over. North America was saved. Human nature had again triumphed over ideology. And I needed to take a whizz.

*

Before we Yankees could go home, we still faced a mopping-up operation. This time, the problem wasn't enemy units that were still holding out. It was several million panic-stricken women.

Propaganda in the world's first, and last all-female state had a single theme: Men are horrible. All males are born rapists, torturers, and murders. They are capable of only one relationship with women: as abusers. Now, the nation that called itself "the planet's safe house for women" was again ruled by armed males in battle uniforms. Some even had armored vehicles with big phallic cannons on them.

As usual, the Azanian propaganda's main victims were its inventors. Azania's women were terrified. Some hid, others fled into the hills and the bush, knowing the first male who found them would rape them, slice off their breasts and notch their ears and noses like a sow's.

None of those things happened, of course. Ours was a Christian army. But it was a Christian army with a big problem. If we simply left northern California, the feminists might take over again. If we stayed, women would die of hunger, thirst, and exposure. The dilemma had to be resolved quickly. Winter was coming on.

We set up our headquarters and a new Government of Northern California, chosen from among the exiles now returning home, in the old capital, Sacramento. Berkeley, birthplace of so many demons, we burned and bulldozed before we symbolically sowed it with salt. I was sitting at my desk in the old capital building on bright mid-September day when my corporal announced a female visitor. I rose from my chair to greet none other than the formidable Mrs. Rutherford P. Bingham of Boston, Massachusetts.

"Good afternoon, Captain Rumford," she intoned in a rich voice that suggested the stage more than Back Bay. "I am so delighted to be able to congratulate you on your splendid victory."

"Thank you very much ma'am," I replied. "We couldn't have done it without you. Your ladies were the real focus of this operation."

"Why, you are too kind, Captain!"

"May I offer you a seat?"

"Yes, thank you." Mrs. Bingham sat with the dignity of a camel getting down on its knees.

"Captain, as I said to you when we met in Boston, I know women have no place on the battlefield. But when the din of battle has died, it is time once again for women to come to the fore. It is a woman's duty to bind up the wounds of war, to succor the injured in body and spirit, friend and foe, and to spread the bounty of peace."

"I think I go along with that," I replied.

"Good. As you know, the women of this sorry place are in a most unfortunate condition. Most are suffering, and some are dying. It is all their own fault, of course. But we must not hold that against them. They were led astray, and now it is our duty to lead them back."

"That's proving something of a challenge," I replied.

"Captain, your men cannot reach out to these women. It is quite unjust that they fear you, but the fact is, they do. But they will not fear us—ladies of the Northern Confederation. I have been in touch with our organization back in our own country, and thousands of our women are prepared to do as we few did and come here. But they cannot do so without your permission and your assistance."

"What would they do if they came?" I inquired.

"Go out into the countryside, find these poor, deluded creatures and bring them home."

The maternal instinct at work, I thought. That might be just what the situation required. Most of the former Azanians were hard-core feminazis, or had been. But when a cause collapses, it loses its hold on many of its former adherents. By 1995, there were more believing Marxists on American university faculties than in the former Soviet Union.

"You realize there will be risks? Some of the former Azanians are armed, and a few might even be able to shoot."

"We took risks in Utah and the other Rocky Mountain states, Captain."

"Indeed you did," I replied. "Very well, you have my permission to proceed. But I'd like to start on a small scale and see how it works. How many of the other ladies from the N.C. are still with you?"

"Every one, Captain. None of us is willing to go home while there is still work to be done here."

"Is that enough to try your approach in one location?"

"I should think so."

I turned to my map of northern California. I wanted to pick a relatively small town, but one with countryside around it where a fair number of Azanian women would likely be hiding. There: Fort Bragg. Odd that America had not one but two places named for the Confederacy's worst general. The Azanians had renamed it Fortress Bragg. They seemed to have thought that a fortress was a female fort. Was their offspring a bastion?

"How's this?", I said to Mrs. Bingham, putting my finger on the map.

"I'm sure one place is as good as another."

"OK, I'll arrange an escort. An infantry company should be sufficient to protect you."

"Captain, we cannot take any of your soldiers with us. They would frighten the refugees away."

"That leaves you pretty open. I don't suppose any of you would want a shotgun?"

"Captain, the only weapons a lady needs are her elbows, her purse, her umbrella, and her sense of indignation."

I could sense the latter was on the verge of rising, and I was more comfortable facing a flight of Zany F-22s than a single indignant Back Bay matron. "Very well, Madam. I will arrange transport. Will the day after tomorrow be convenient?"

"It will. Thank you, Captain." Mrs. Bingham rose majestically, like an airship. I came to attention at my desk and offered a crisp salute. The thought floated through the room that it would be easier to be Alonzo than Mr. Rutherford P. Bingham.

*

There were a whole number of ways this could go bad, I thought to myself as Mrs. Bingham receded down the corridor. If it did, I would be responsible. But that was what authority entails. If it bothered me, it was time to retire.

Our 82nd Airborne left on commandeered buses the next day. The no-men-allowed rule meant I couldn't send a trusted agent to serve as the commander's telescope. I supplied the ladies with comm gear, which, for once in female history, they didn't use.

It was ten days before we heard from them. On the 27th of September, I was again in my office when the phone rang. On the other end was Mrs. Bingham, patched through from our comm center.

"Good morning, Captain Rumford."

"Good morning, ma'am. I hope this isn't a request to be ransomed?"

"Indeed it is not, Captain. Things are going splendidly, just splendidly. I want you to come and see for yourself."

I didn't have anything particularly pressing to deal with at the moment, other than the refugee problem. Maybe our ladies had something to show me that would solve it. "I would be delighted. But won't my presence scare off the refugees?"

"I don't believe so, Captain."

"OK, I'm on my way."

If Mrs. Bingham thought she accomplished something, the least I could do was test it. So I called for a couple of LAVs as transport.

Along the way, we saw a few furtive female figures, which promptly vanished when they spotted us, like feral cats. Nothing was working. No stores were open, no cars were on the roads, no fields were being tended. Northern California was a ghost town.

Until we rolled into Fort Bragg. Suddenly, we saw normal life. People were on the streets, walking, shopping, talking. Lawns were being cut, houses cleaned, gardens watered. Of course, everyone we saw was a woman. Strangely, they weren't just women. They looked like ladies. Instead of jeans and tee shirts, they were all wearing dresses and skirts. Downtown, most had hats and handbags. The place looked as it might have in 1950.

We pulled up to the town hall, which was serving as a soup kitchen and reception point for refugees. We parked the LAVs, and the crews, all in battle dress, dismounted with me. Nobody ran away.

"Welcome, Captain Rumford," I heard in an unmistakable voice from the women gathered in front of the building. "You and your men are just in time for dinner. Please come in."

Mrs. Bingham led us through the growing crowd. I noticed a few admiring glances from some of the women, clearly former Azanians, directed toward my young stud troopers. What miracle had our good ladies wrought?

More refugees were gathered inside. Shyly, they welcomed us. Again, each and every one was dressed as a lady. No feminist "unisex" here. We sat at a long table and were served, not by Northern Confederation women but by locals, ex-refugees.

"Well, this is quite a transformation," I said to Mrs. Bingham. "How have you managed it?"

"By being ladies ourselves, Captain," Mrs. Bingham replied. "You see, every woman really wants to be a lady. When the refugees saw us, dressed properly and behaving properly, they were drawn to us. Oh, they came in great numbers, poor things, dirty, half-starved, quite desperate. We fed them, bathed them, gave them proper clothes to wear, and explained that no one was going to hurt them. On the contrary, we were here to help celebrate their freedom, freedom from all the unnatural, nasty things that had deluded them. Now, they are preparing to go out to other places and bring in more women like themselves."

I turned to one young woman who was serving our soup. "Is what I'm hearing true?" I asked.

"Yes, sir," she replied. "We're all happy it's finally over. And, well, it's nice to see men again, and to be real women again ourselves."

At Mrs. Bingham's request, we began an airlift, bringing in more ladies from the Northern Confederation and also from the Rocky Mountains states. The Mormon women were especially eager to come, and they made wonderful role models. Word spread quickly throughout northern California that the terror was over and normal life could resume. By the time winter set in, the refugee crisis was over. More than a few former Azanian feminists became blushing war brides, heading back to the N.C. with their new soldier husbands.

There were a few hold-outs, of course, women so poisoned by feminism that they could not let go of it even after its failure was evident. We quietly rounded them up and sold them into the slave market at Aden. Muslim husbands would be good for them.

Among the volunteers from the N.C. was Maria. She thought her Spanish might be useful, though few Hispanic women had been sucked into feminism. Once her work was done, we spent a quiet Christmas together in San Francisco, which remained a beautiful city. On January 2, 2039, we headed home to Hartland.

What new war awaited me, I wondered. Would our country and our continent finally know some peace? If it did, what might that mean for me…and for Maria?

CHAPTER FORTY-FIVE

W ERE symbols chosen by men of action rather than poets and painters, they would be very different. The symbol of war would be a hand reaching out toward another, for war makes brothers of men. The symbol of peace would be a sword, for peace divides.

War had brought the Northern Confederation into being and given it purpose and direction. War had cleansed our country of America's vices, the silliness, selfishness, and sluttiness that had overflowed the late United States. We had fought together, scrimped together, and huddled together in our cold, dark houses for more than a decade. Now, with the coming of peace, I feared we would never again be so coherent or so content.

I had to shovel four feet of snow before we could get to the door, but once I settled Maria in again at the Old Place and brought the livestock up from my cousin's farm, I headed back down to General Staff headquarters in Augusta. There I moved swiftly to begin the lessons-learned critique for the Azanian war. Unless the man at the top insists on a rigorous, honest, air-all-the-dirty-linen review, even the best army tends to reach for the whitewash. Then, the next time, it makes the same mistakes all over again and the lance corporals pay the bill.

The second thing I did was tell Bill Kraft to cut the defense budget. The continent was as quiet as it was likely to get, quiet enough we could reduce the burden on our taxpayers. I figured we could cut our spending at least by half.

Third on my agenda was improving our officer education. War is always the best training ground for officers, because you can promote the men who get results. Peacetime makes it harder.

In late March, I wandered over to Bill Kraft's office to get his take on an idea. The best officer education the world had known was in the old German *Kriegsakademie*. I wanted to set up a War Academy of our own, modeled on the original German one. I knew the right man to do it. Colonel Mike Fox, formerly of the United States Marine Corps, was a neighbor of mine up in Hartland. Mike had been one of the leaders of the last, doomed attempt to make the U.S. armed forces think seriously about war, the Military Reform Movement of the 1980s. There was no one better on the subject of officer education. Mike was well along in years, but in the Northern Confederation, old people worked, and wanted to do so. Retirement killed a lot more men than work ever did.

The governor received me graciously, as he usually did now. He seemed to be mellowing some, though he wouldn't have taken it as a compliment if anyone had dared tell him so. He understood German officer education thoroughly, and immediately approved my proposal and the choice of Mike Fox to head the new school.

"Is there any reason we can't name it the *Kriegsakademie*?" he asked.

"None I can think of," I replied. "It's about time somebody brings back the name. Germany calls its General Staff academy the *Führungsakademie* now. They're afraid some idiot will call them Nazis if they use the old name, even though the Nazis hated the place and everything else about the old Prussian officer corps."

"Well, then, consider it done," Bill replied. "I'll be happy to put on my Prussian uniform again for the opening ceremonies."

"Are you going to wear it for the ceremonies opening the Fundy project? The first power is due to start flowing in May, if I remember right."

"Are you certain that is something to celebrate?" Bill asked.

"I can't imagine why not," I replied, taken aback. "Our industries have been starved for power. With this, they should be able to take off. It's clean power, too. Why shouldn't we celebrate?"

"Television, computers, and cars, to give three good reasons up front," Bill shot back. "The best thing the war has done for us, beyond guaranteeing our survival, is shattering the virtual realities created by television and computers. Cars and television together destroyed community in the old U.S.A., and without community there is no way to prevent moral decay except by the power of the state. That's another road we don't want to go down."

"Waal, I have to admit, I haven't thought much about that side of it. I was just looking forward to central heat, hot water without heating kettles on the stove, and lights that go on when you flip a switch. Not to mention ice cream."

"Well, you'd better think about it, because we all face some tough decisions. If we decide wrongly, we may end up right back where we were. Remember, technology isn't neutral. Some technologies are inherently evil in their effects. And there is no record of a modern society being able to say no to a technology."

"What you're telling me is, we have to find some way to kill Faust."

"Exactly. Or he will once again kill us. And I don't know how to do it."

If Bill Kraft didn't know the answer, he wasn't the only one asking the question. Slowly, through the war years, the Retroculture movement had been spreading through the N.C. In wartime, a return to past ways of living had been natural, often unavoidable. Our poverty and our loss of many of the "necessities" of early 21st century life had compelled people to go back. The Retroculture folks, along with the Amish, had become everybody's teachers because they knew how to do things in the old ways.

But a return of electric power and prosperity would change that. For many people, it would be all too easy to slide back down into the modern age. They'd buy one of those nice, new electric cars that gave 300 miles on a full battery and recharged in 15 minutes. That would free them from their town, their local merchants, and their neighbors. Then, they'd get a big TV and DVD player, so instead of spending their evenings on the front porch with family and friends they could solo in whatever imaginary world promised the most sensual pleasure. Or they could lose themselves on the internet, opening up to utter strangers about matters they wouldn't feel comfortable sharing with their priest. That would be the natural trend of things, and if the Retro folks wanted to stop it, they'd have to stop it before it got started.

Fortunately, they knew it. Even while the wars were still underway, they had been preparing for it. It was no secret that Fundy would begin producing power early in 2039. And they had an idea about how to kill Faust.

As the roads began to dry out, in that Spring of 2039, they again bore citizens carrying petitions. The return of real democracy meant that when our people wanted to do something, they could. The proposed new law was simple and clear: "Resolved, that it shall be unlawful in the Northern Confederation to use any technology not in common usage in the year 1930."

That meant radio was legal, but not television. Electric cars and trucks were all right, but only with lead-acid batteries and that made them short range forms of transportation. The price of oil still made gas cars unaffordable. No computers, DVDs, Xerox machines, cell phones, sat phones, none of that witches' brew of technologies that had so undermined the old ways of living. An exception was made for the armed forces and for medical technologies, but nothing else.

The opposition was considerable. A few folks argued we should let anyone do whatever they wanted: liberty confused with license. Memories of the American republic and its final decadence were too strong for that to go very far. Most opponents put forward a different case: that we had learned our lessons and could now be trusted to use modern technologies in the right ways. We could produce decent, uplifting television, television that would bring high culture to average people. We could own cars, but leave them in the garage when we didn't really need them, still walking to local stores and taking the train on longer trips. We could use computers, but understand that the connections we made through them were to a virtual reality, inferior to the reality that awaited beyond the front door. The case seemed reasonable, practical, and moderate. At least, it did for those without much understanding of human nature.

I wasn't sure where I stood. Experience in war leaves a pretty good grasp of human nature, and I could not share the optimism of those who believed we could surround ourselves with temptations and not yield to them. On the other hand, I wasn't sure I liked government dictating what technologies I could own or use. Here too human nature came into play: I foresaw an enormous black market, an underground of people who defied the law and owned TVs and computers or souped-up their cars with better batteries. And what then? Would we have Northern

Confederation police in black ninja suits and body armor breaking down doors in the middle of the night to seize forbidden devices and arrest people for possessing them? That wasn't the kind of country I fought to create.

There were easily enough Retro people in the N.C. to get the signatures and put the issue on a ballot. That was how our political system was intended to work. It required only a demonstration that a matter was serious, then it put it before the people to decide.

On May 15th, the power began flowing from the Bay of Fundy, just a few thousand kilowatts at first. But more would follow.

On May 18th, the Board of Elections ratified the petitions and set the vote for August 15th. The first political crisis of the Confederation was the oldest a people ever faced, in its most literal form. We had power; what would we choose to do with it?

Through June and July, the campaign grew steadily more intense. Tempers sometimes flared, especially when families were divided over the issue. That happened a lot, because older folks, those who remembered the American past before the final, worst days, tended to favor television and cars. Their children were more radical. They inclined toward Retroculture, especially the Victorian period. It wasn't uncommon to see families on an outing where the old folks were dressed in jeans and tee-shirts while their kids were all in Victorian clothes, carrying a Victrola with a big horn on it and a wicker picnic basket filled with cold lobster and champagne. Old things were becoming new again.

I was buried in my work to the point where I didn't pay the business much mind. But when the Retro folks announced a rally and torchlight parade in Augusta on July 22, I noticed that Bill Kraft would be the speaker. Knowing of his earlier doubts, I decided to see how he had resolved them. That might give me a clue about how to resolve mine.

The rally began at 8 PM on the State House lawn. Thousands of people came, some from as far away as Vermont. Most were in Victorian dress, although some were in clothes from almost every period from colonial up through the 1950s. The cut-off point for Retroculture was 1959: Anything before that year was acceptable. After that came the '60s and cultural Marxism.

The program began with the hymn the Retroculture movement had adopted as its anthem, "Turn back, O man, forswear thy foolish ways. Old now is earth, and none may count her days. Yet thou, her child, whose head is crowned with flame, Still wilt not hear thine inner God proclaim, Turn back, O man, forswear thy foolish ways." Then came a succession of speakers, leaders of the Retroculture Movement and organizers of the vote. Most were women, many the same women who had pushed through the decision to go to war in Azania. One of them, Mrs. William P. Hamilton of Gilman's Corner, New Hampshire, told the crowd, "In Azania, we saw the terrible plight into which the modern age led women. It is therefore right and proper that women should lead this nation back, away from that poisonous age to a better time when women and men both knew and did their duties."

Governor Kraft was the keynote. By the time he mounted the bunting-draped platform, the sun was gone from the sky and the torches were lit. The sea of flames, stretching well on beyond the lawn down into the principal streets of the town might have been an omen. Just how deeply would this law divide us if it passed? And if it didn't pass, how would the Retro folks react? The speeches suggested they weren't about to return to life splattered across a video screen like a bug on a windshield. The Confederacy had fought its own civil war. Would we?

The governor's silence in the campaign had surprised many of the Retroculture people, since he had been one of them almost since the movement began. Or perhaps even before; I don't think Bill Kraft ever belonged to the modern age. Now, they were eager with anticipation, certain he had waited until the last to give his advocacy the greatest possible impact. They knew the public was closely divided, and they doubted not that Bill's immense prestige would put them over the top.

The governor's vast bulk towered over the puny podium, and with a final fanfare from the brass band the crowd grew quiet. There was no microphone; Retro politicians were expected to have a voice. Bill never lacked one. He could have shouted down a convention of moose. No one would miss his words that evening, nor forget them.

"Ladies and gentlemen," he began. "It is a measure of how far we have come that I can address a gathering of fellow citizens as ladies and gentlemen, and not lie. Thanks to you and to the spirit of Retroculture, of recovering our past, civilization has replaced barbarism faster than barbarism previously displaced civilization.

"I speak this evening as one of you. I have been Retro since long before the term was coined or a movement imagined. From my earliest childhood I loved the old and passing and detested the new and modern things. Before I was ten, I mourned the passing of the steam engine and the trolley car. I loved the town and loathed the suburb. I answered rock and roll with Strauss waltzes played on my wind-up gramophone. In my teens, for a whole year I gave up electricity, lighting my room with kerosene lamps and washing each morning from a bowl and pitcher.

"The culture of late 20th and early 21st centuries America was a landfill of lies. But the greatest lie of all, the foundational lie, was the lie that said, 'You can't go back. You can do anything you can imagine, but not the things you already have done!' It was nonsense. What we did once we can do again. But it was repeated so often that, like most of the other lies, almost everyone believed it. Those of us who did not were seen first as cranks, then as monsters.

"But the truth will out, and it has. We can go back. Of course, we do not recapture the past exactly, nor do we seek to. But we can recover its essence, its best, its foundation and framework. And much of its charm and grace and beauty also. We cannot be our grandparents. But we can live very much as our grandparents did by honoring them and emulating them and learning from them. That we have done, all of us gathered here tonight.

"This movement, Retroculture, embodies my most daring hopes and boldest dreams. Throughout the hideous final years of the American republic, I prayed such a turning would take place, impossible as it seemed. As we cut our chains to that republic's corpse, I began to think this day might come. Now it has. In it, in the movement to reconnect with our own past, lies our best chance of recovering civilization and fortifying it so strongly no future savagery dares approach its walls.

"It is from that perspective that I tell you tonight that I am unalterably opposed to this ballot measure."

The crowd had been getting what it expected and swaying along happily with the speaker. Now, it thought it had misheard something. It was suddenly edgy, focused, intent.

"You have heard me correctly," Bill continued. "I am as opposed to this measure as to anything I ever fought against in my life. I am opposed to it so strongly that if it passes, I will retire at once from this office and from all public life."

That brought gasps and shouts of "No!"

"I am opposed not to the end, but to the means. I realize as well as anyone the dangers inherent in video screen technologies and in automobiles. I do not doubt that, if they proliferate in the Northern Confederation, they will set us on a course not unlike that of America in its final decades. They must be stopped. But not this way.

"Cultural degradation and decay are not the only diseases once rampant in America that still could sicken us. Another is loss of freedom to an intrusive, meddling, evil-stepmother state. Have we so quickly forgotten that by the 1990s, the federal government in Washington told you what kind of toilet and shower head you had to have in your own house? If this measure were to pass, it would mandate that the government of the Northern Confederation become that kind of government: overweening, ever-present, a daily, oppressive force in the life of the citizen. I won't stand for it.

"There is another way, and a far better one. It is a way taken by our forefathers, the people we seek to learn from and emulate. In their hands, it had great power without coercion by the state. I am speaking of the pledge.

"The Victorians battled with success against some of the most powerful demons lodged in human nature, including the demon of habitual drunkenness, with the pledge. We can fight these technological demons with the same weapon, and defeat them. Instead of passing a law and setting the state on your neighbor like a dog, I am asking you tonight to go to your neighbor yourself. Ask him to pledge that he will join you in refusing to own or use a computer, a cell phone, a television, or an automobile capable of traveling more than 25 miles. Ask him to join you in making life real and local.

"You have a strong base from which to build. You have us, every practitioner of Retroculture in the land. You have everyone who signed your petitions.

"And you have me. While I must oppose to the utmost of my strength this misconceived attempt to inflate the power of the state, I will eagerly serve a drive to convince our fellow citizens to take the pledge. I will begin now, by taking that pledge myself."

With that, Bill pulled a pledge card from his coat pocket, drew his fountain pen from another and signed.

"As we among all people know, words precede action, they do not substitute for it. So I will sign something else this night as well."

At these words, Bill's immaculate 1948 Buick Roadmaster, long his proudest possession, drove slowly across the lawn from somewhere behind the speakers' platform.

It stopped, and the driver mounted the stage.

"Let me introduce Mr. Josef Licht, of Portland. As some of you undoubtedly know, Mr. Licht is in the import/export business. I will now sign over to him the title to my Buick. It will be exported to the Confederacy for sale, where I have no doubt it will secure a good price."

Mr. Licht did a little dance and said, "You should see what price a car like this will get down south. It would make me a rich man, if I weren't a rich man already."

"I have instructed Mr. Licht to put all my profit from the sale into a fund to promote the pledge," the governor continued.

"I know many of you are disappointed. You will still have the opportunity to vote for the ban, of course. I could not remove it from the ballot if I wanted to, and I do not want to. That is also part of the meaning of liberty. But I urge you to vote against it, as I will vote against it, remembering that where moral choice is impossible, there can be no virtue. Then, let us join our efforts to convince our fellow citizens to do by choice what I would not have the state compel them to do: Renounce these infernal devices."

The audience was too much in shock to react as Bill left the stage. Some understood that, in the face of the governor's opposition, their initiative was now unlikely to pass. Others saw a yawning fissure in the

Retroculture movement and wondered if it would survive. Only a few grasped the real picture: Bill Kraft had saved them from making an immense strategic mistake, a blunder which would have forced every citizen to choose between Retroculture and liberty, between our past and our future.

He had also set two precedents that have since become sacred in this country. The first was that our lives would not be politicized. Because government touches us seldom, and then lightly, beyond demands war may temporarily impose, politics doesn't matter much. We elect our officials, and more importantly, we vote directly on any major matter of state in referenda. But custom now limits what even a referendum may impose. Any proposed law that goes beyond those limits, that threatens government interference in average people's daily lives, is seen as illegitimate and has no chance of passage.

Indeed, human nature being what it is, cranks still come up with such proposals from time to time, but usually fail to gather even the few signatures needed to put them on a ballot. They are rightly seen as the fruit of diseased brains.

The second nation-shaping precedent Governor Kraft set that dramatic evening was the pledge. At first, it did not seem like much, merely a clever device to sidestep a political problem. But it turned out to be much more. The pledge revived and made part of our culture the very essence of liberty: voluntary self-discipline.

As the American republic spun into the ground toward the end of the 20th century, "freedom" came to mean simply doing whatever you want. "If it feels good, do it," was what the vanguard of the cultural proletariat said in the 1960s. But that was license, not liberty, and no society could long sustain it or survive it.

As the American Founding Fathers knew and incessantly preached, liberty really meant something else: substituting self-discipline for the imposed discipline of the state. They called that self-discipline "virtue." Through virtue, men would do the right thing even though the state would allow them to do wrong, up to a point, anyway. Of course, in the late 18th century, Americans understood the difference between right and wrong. Even those who were not practicing Jews or Christians respected the Ten Commandments.

The pledge became the tool with which the Northern Confederation recreated right and wrong. When people took a pledge, they accepted the action to which they pledged themselves as defining right conduct. Because pledges were public, backsliders were known. Social pressure came to provide the sanctions the state would not, and far more effectively, too. Those who pledged and faltered became objects of scorn and shame, cut off from their neighbors, their community, even their families. As it must, virtue had an edge to it.

As Bill left the platform that evening, I worked my way through the crowd to him and walked him home. I could read him pretty well after all we'd been through, and I knew it had cost him some to say what he did.

"I know it hurt to give up your Buick," I said by way of a Marine's clumsy consolation.

"It did."

"How do you think people will respond?"

"I don't know."

"You've taken a risk."

"I have."

We walked on in silence. I remembered a Viking friend's description of an Icelandic salon. Everyone sits around looking at the table; at fifteen-minute intervals, someone says, "Ja, ja."

As we neared the governor's house, Bill turned to me, very intent yet also somehow far away. "John, the war was our nation's course of instruction. It taught us life's most important lesson: what is real and what is not. Now, in what I proposed tonight, we face our final exam. Have we grasped reality firmly enough that we can reject both illusions that drove America to suicide, the illusion of beneficent government power and the illusion that decadence can be indulged? If we fail the exam, we will fail as a nation, and swiftly too, I think. Never have we, have I, taken a greater risk than this. Yet there is no other way."

More than once during the wars I envied Bill his chateau campaigning. This night I realized chateaux can be cold and lonely places. At his gate, we parted with a nod. That's Maine for I think I understand.

*

The shock waves from Bill's speech spread quickly throughout the Confederation. His opposition gave great encouragement to those who wanted modern life back again, and it left the Retro movement in the dumps. Both assumed, rightly, that it tubed the referendum. By the time it was held, on the 15th of August, it was of little interest. Only 34 percent of voters came to the poll, and of that 34 percent, only 22 percent voted in favor.

Both sides misread the vote, because neither calculated that most of the Retro folks simply stayed home. Or at least stayed away from the polls: Many were out and about. This time, instead of electoral petitions, they were carrying pledge cards.

The very evening Bill spoke, the first groups met to design and carry out the pledge drive. Some did so because they regarded the governor as their leader. Others realized a voluntary pledge was more powerful than state imposition, not less. Many came forward, then and later, because Retroculture itself warned against the power of the state. The world Retroculture sought to recapture had been one where the American federal government was small and unobtrusive.

The advocates of television and computers and cars dismissed the pledge campaign. They were sure the convenience of easy travel and the allure of instant entertainment would be irresistible.

They were wrong.

By the end of August, more than a million citizens of the states that made up the Confederation had signed the pledge. Many not only signed, but joined the drive to get more signatures. The numbers jumped exponentially: 5 percent of the population in September became 25 percent by the end of October. The Retro folks set a goal: They wanted a majority of the population to take the pledge by Thanksgiving.

Dr. Faust struck back with all he had. The mails were stuffed with glitzy brochures pushing TVs and computers. Toyota offered its fast, sleek, long-range electric cars at a loss, priced lower than a decent wagon and a pair of Percherons. Men in raincoats lurked outside schools, offering children violent video games for free.

The Retro movement responded with a series of simple posters, just black type on white. The first asked, "Did We Fight for Nothing?" The second, "Have We So Soon Forgotten?" The final poster, which went up early in November, simply read, "Turn Back, O Man."

They got their majority by November 15th. Throughout the Confederation, Thanksgiving was celebrated with a special fervor that year. By Christmas, an amazing 85 percent of the people of the Northern Confederation had taken the pledge.

Of course, those who did not were free to buy TVs and computers and cars, and many did. Television stations sprang up in most of the larger cities. A few places began installing cable.

But such actions had a cost. As the pledge drive grew, so did the understanding that these technologies were immoral. If a family got a TV or a computer, it found its neighbors growing chilly. They wouldn't allow their children to go to that house. In Boston, the Catholic Archbishop excommunicated television owners. When people drove their fancy new Toyota to a store or restaurant, they were often refused service. Sometimes, children threw stones.

Dr. Faust's party tried to put a good face on it, hoping that with time, folks would loosen up. But the fact was, they were beat. The new television stations went broke. The long-range cars were sold for export. When the telephone operator detected a modem, she pulled the plug.

Oh, a few madmen in cabins in the woods kept their toys; you can find some even today. New England has always had its eccentrics. But, the hopes of Henry David Thoreau notwithstanding, we've always been able to tell a loon from an owl.

*

The summer of 2039 marked a change in the life of our country, and in my life as well. For the first time since Maine declared its independence, I could start something with reasonable hope I could finish it. That meant I could farm.

I didn't try to do too much that first year. In late May, I put most of the good bottom land into potatoes, and the rest into feed corn. Hartland now had a potato chip factory. The labels on the cans were in Chinese as well as English, and most of them were sold to the Asian market. The feed corn would enable us to add a few more cows; Maria knew how to make cheese.

Up behind the house was an ancient orchard. It had been there as long as anyone could remember, and the apples were antique varieties, all now nameless but some with unique flavors. I pruned and fed the trees, and got in a small cider press. Come fall, I'd press the apples from each tree separately, identify the best flavors, then do some grafting from those trees. I figured I could build up a small business in specialty ciders, which sold well both at home and overseas. It wouldn't be too many years before the Old Place again offered its inhabitants a decent living.

Maria and I were together a lot that summer. That's the real test. Does time in close company draw people together or cause them to rub each other raw? Nature usually decrees the second. But farming reminds us of another fact, which is that labor can overcome nature. Maria and I were both old enough and mature enough to work at getting along. So we did, and time smoothed the rough edges rather than sharpening them. Which is another way of saying we were growing into love.

One afternoon late in August, when days were growing cool but not yet noticeably short, Cousin John drove up to visit in his new Baker Electric car. John had gone Retro, and the car was Retro, too. It was a duplicate of the china closet, the electric car favored by old ladies early in the 20th century: black, upright, with a short sloping hood and a trunk filled with lead-acid batteries. It had window shades and flower vases and was driven from the back seat with a tiller. Instead of a horn, it had a bell. It was a perfect lawyer's car, which is what Cousin John was. Even in summer, he always wore a black homburg hat.

I'd finished the milking and was coming out of the barn when he pulled up. "Evenin', Cousin," I said. "That's a fancy new buggy for these parts."

"There's money in these parts now, Ire, for the first time in almost a century. We're making things people want to buy, people in foreign parts.

I assume you've seen the sheep all over the hills. And the expansion of the tannery, and the potato chip plant, and the wagon works and soon, with the new electric power, a Nestlé's cannery. It'll be Swiss money putting that up."

"But that's all honest business. What I want to know is, how's a lawyer makin' money?"

"Contracts. Business contracts. Many with foreign suppliers or buyers. Not lawsuits much any more, I'm glad to say. Nor impossibly complicated dealings with government agencies."

"Waal, that's all right then, I guess. It's suppertime now for us. We farm folk eat early, as you probably know. You're welcome to join us."

"We town folk eat late, as you should know. The Baker will get me back home in time for our dinner, at eight."

"So even in Hartland we now have town and country?"

"We do, Ire. Hartland is a real town again, with town manners. We want to keep it that way, or at least I do. That's what I've come to talk to you about, if you've got a minute."

"In the country, we always have a minute, or an hour. Come on in and at least have a beer—Pittsfield brewery—so we don't feel inhospitable."

"I trust that's not a bad pun about ambulance chasing."

"I know why you're a good lawyer. You don't miss a word, do you?"

"Not often."

We went through the back door into the kitchen, which summer or winter was the family room of any Maine house. It smelled of warm apple pie, made from our own Transparents. John sat down and pulled out his pipe while I poured us each a mug of Porter.

"So what can I do for Hartland, John?" I asked. "I hope nobody is planning to attack it."

"Well, Ire, they are in fact. In a manner of speaking, anyway. Now that cars, short-range ones anyway, are making a comeback, a fellow wants to re-start all the ugliness cars brought with them. He wants to put in a strip mall along the road between Hartland and Pittsfield. Not only do those things look like hell, they suck the life out of towns. I don't want to see our towns die a second time, so I and a few other folks are going to fight it. I was hoping you might join us."

"I'm not sure that's my kind of fight, John. Unless you're planning to let this fellow put up his strip of stores, then bring up artillery. Remember, John, I haven't gone Retro, not yet anyway."

"Haven't you? I'm not so sure about that."

"You won't catch me wearing a homburg, John. One of the most important principles of war is, 'Never trust a soldier who much cares what he looks like.'"

"Retroculture isn't about clothes, Ire. Period clothing is just an outward symbol some of us use to witness quietly to our beliefs. Retroculture is in part about what things look like, because ugliness breeds ugly behavior. Why do you think the cultural Marxists in the old U.S.A. so avidly promoted ugly architecture, ugly art, and ugly music? They understood that ugliness is a weapon. For us, beauty is also a weapon. Don't you see any difference between a harmonious, traditional New England town and a plastic strip mall?"

CHAPTER FORTY-SIX

W E couldn't know it at the time, but the course of events in the year 2039 set a pattern for the Northern Confederation. We had entered the period historians now call the Recovery.

Year by year, more turbines came on line in the great dam across the Bay of Fundy, the most massive engineering work in human history, surpassing even the pyramids and China's Great Wall. By the time it was all up and running in the year 2057, we had almost triple the total energy available to the same region at the height of the American republic. It was clean power. And it was cheap.

The combination of peace and inexpensive, abundant energy created a boom gaffers and gammers compared to America in the 1950s. As in the 1950s, the growth was real. Our boom was based not on corporate mergers and downsizing and exporting jobs to Third World hell-holes, but on making things.

All over the country, in cities and towns and villages, small factories sprang up. Some were high tech. We now lead the world in cold fusion applications, airship design, and wireless power transmission. In fact, we've created a whole new branch of electronics by developing the long-neglected ideas of Nicola Tesla. My department is one of the beneficiaries. Our Navy's zeppelins carry one device that will fry the electronic circuits of any enemy plane or ship within fifty miles, and another that will explode their on-board ordnance.

But most of our success lay in making improved versions of simple, old fashioned things: Retro-technology. Contrary to the Tofflers and other 20th century prophets, the world did not go high tech. The New World Disorder moved life in the opposite direction. What people needed were simple, useful technologies that could function under primitive, isolated, often chaotic conditions. In most of the world, the only use for a computer was as an anchor for a wooden-hulled, rowed fishing boat.

The Alco works in Schenectady, New York was our first big Retro-technology success. Drawing on the work of the brilliant Argentine steam engineer Livio Dante Porta, Alco designed and built steam locomotives that rivaled diesels in efficiency, yet could be maintained by a jungle machine shop. By the year 2047, Alco was the biggest locomotive builder in the world, exporting a thousand engines a year.

Some people worried that reindustrialization would again depopulate the countryside. That didn't happen. Thanks to our ever-growing railway network, there was little reason to concentrate industry. Labor cost more in cities, because most people didn't want to live there. And most of our industries were small; with the strangling net of government regulation gone, anyone with an idea could simply set up shop. Yankees had never been short on ideas.

More important, farm incomes continued to rise, to the point where a farm of a couple of hundred acres offered a comfortable, even a prosperous living. The rest of the world was a hungry place, and some of its hungry people could afford to pay well for food. Though our manufactured exports rose steadily, our overseas trade in farm products remained our main source of foreign exchange. Between the two, we built up our gold reserves and with them our money supply, to the point where by 2048 the standard interest rate in the Northern Confederation was a historically low three percent.

Returning prosperity was necessary for the Recovery, but prosperity was not itself the Recovery. Mere prosperity could easily have degenerated into another consumer economy where people poured their wealth into useless, time-wasting, mind-deadening gadgets that quickly broke or were made obsolete by yet another, more expensive gadget they "had to have."

But the fall of the American republic and early 21st century culture, coupled with the hardships of the war years, had wrought a vast change in the way people approached life. No longer did they exist merely to be entertained through ephemera, so many mayflies of the spirit. We had again become a serious people. Like serious people throughout the ages, we wanted to build.

If you are going to build, the first thing you have to do is clear the ground. Although the early 21st century was gone, we were surrounded by its debris: depopulated suburbs, abandoned shopping malls, empty strip developments, all the clutter of the auto age, most of it ugly when new and none improved by age and neglect. The fate of the suburbs showed how empty the heads of 20th century "futurists" had been. Not a one had predicted their demise, even though people had been fleeing them by the 1990s the same way (and for the same reasons) they had earlier fled the inner cities. Collapse, revolution, and war had finished them. The disappearance of white collar jobs and gasoline drove their inhabitants to the small towns or the countryside. Those who still worked in cities lived near downtown along the trolley line, just where their great-grandparents did.

So we made a desert and found it was peace. The early Recovery rang with the sound of demolition. Hundreds of square miles of former suburb become farmland once more. So did shopping centers, malls, and the endless Vegas strips along the highways. At first, the removal was utilitarian; the auto age wasn't coming back, and farmland was valuable.

But the spirit of Retroculture soon took over. In the cities, the cold, slab-sided International-Style buildings, created by the Marxists of the Bauhaus to be alienating, came crashing down. So, in the towns, did the churches and banks that looked like Dairy Queens, the cheap motels, the plastic facades on once-noble buildings. Everywhere, in an orgy of ordered destruction, we trashed the trash and restored the landscape and the streetscape. To us Tolkien fans, it was the Scouring of the Shire, only in reverse.

The Scouring continued up into the 2040s. The wreckage of half a century takes some clearing. But by the mid '30s, we were also starting to build. Here Retroculture gained its first universal acceptance. Retro or not, virtually everyone wanted to go back, back to the City Beautiful movement that had grown out of the Columbian Exposition of 1893, back to the Greek Revival or Victorian town, back to the old-fashioned New England or Pennsylvania Dutch farmhouse.

We were not without guides. The sheer ugliness of the last American built landscape had spawned a reaction, the New Urbanism. By the 1990s, pioneers such as architect Andres Duany had recovered many of the rules that shaped 18th and 19th century towns: grid street patterns, ratios of street width to building height that made pedestrians feel comfortable, the social role of front porches. Even then, people wanted such things: Duany's projects had been commercial successes. But the Establishment had been against him, as it was against anything true, good, or beautiful. Now, with the Recovery, the New Urbanism came into its own. We would have recovered our past without it, but not so quickly nor so well.

As in many things, Maine came out ahead, because Maine had always been behind. Beyond the usual detritus of strip malls and shopping centers, we didn't have to demolish much. Portland had been heavily into architectural preservation and restoration by the 1980s, and our few other cities mostly needed fixing up: The old buildings still stood. That was true even of small towns like Hartland. Poverty, the great preserver, had kept out the late 20th century crap. So the Scouring didn't take much work on our part, though I did join Bill Kraft when he went down to Boston for the demolition of the John Hancock building, I.M. Pei's turd in Beantown's punchbowl. It was a grand festive occasion. Today, the tallest structure in Boston is once again the steeple of Old North Church.

Maine didn't need to take much down, but it rejoiced in putting things up. Prosperity brought new building even in Hartland, and what we built was splendid. Cousin John's new house was one of the first. Just a ten-minute walk from the tannery, it was a fine Greek Revival, fan light over the door, center hall all done in native pine post and beam construction. Others like it quickly followed. By 2055, drab, sad old Hartland had become the kind of town the early 21st century tourist would have driven a hundred miles to see. Only no one had to go one hundred miles by then, because the same kind of thing was happening all over. The Northern Confederation was building a beautiful country.

It wasn't only in architecture that the Recovery was a recovery of the beautiful. Even more important was what happened in the culture. It was amazing how quickly and completely both the old pop culture and elite culture—rock music, soap operas, tabloids, obscene "art," Pinter's plays, atonal music, Dadaism in all its forms—simply vanished. We should not have been surprised. That culture was merely the vaporings of a bored, self-destructive people, a people that had lost touch with reality. We were that people no longer.

In its place, the Recovery brought back the beautiful. But it did more than that. The new popular culture that arose in the 2040s was participatory. People didn't want to lie back like lumps and watch or hear someone else do something. They wanted to do it themselves.

It started with music. In the Fall of 2040, a high school music director in Nashua, New Hampshire, put a notice in the local paper asking for volunteers for a choir to sing the music of Stephen Foster. He had been a secret Foster admirer all his life, and wondered if anyone else in the frozen North might share his eccentricity. More than two hundred people answered, and in March of 2042, he took his choir on a recital tour of New Hampshire and Vermont towns. The halls and churches where they sang of life in the antebellum South overflowed with people, and more stood in the snow outside, straining to hear.

Each place the tour stopped, a new choir sprang up. These weren't the tiny choirs of dying, early 21st century politically correct churches. These were Victorian choirs, hundreds of voices strong. Most of the people in them were young.

Choral singing became one of the rites of passage of youth in the Northern Confederation, and remains so today. With Dr. Faust dead and buried, once we find something we like, we stick with it. While the Victorian repertoire remains popular, new composers soon began to write in the Victorian style. One of the byproducts of that movement was a quire of splendid new hymns, many so stirring you'd think the tunes came from Sir Arthur Sullivan himself.

The return of 19th century choral music as popular music reestablished a long-lost connection, the tie between high culture and popular culture. The two were never identical, but in culturally healthy times, each had been influenced by the other. Now, in the 2040s, people began reaching beyond choirs to orchestras and the music that went with them: Mozart and Haydn, Mendelssohn and Brahms (and regrettably, Wagner, who to me always suggests elephants farting). Mahler marks the cutoff; after him it's merely an assault on your ears.

Here too people wanted to play, not just listen. As in the German-speaking countries, every respectable town now has its own orchestra. Even Hartland, a town with just two main streets, has a chamber group. Soon enough, the people in those little, local orchestras wanted something new, but not too new.

In 2047, the Boston Symphony proclaimed a contest under the rubric, "Old Mozart." If Mozart had lived his full four score of years, what else might he have written? That opened the door to both the fulfillment of the Classic style and the flowering of the early Romantic. The best entries were featured at a special concert in Boston's Symphony Hall. Every ear in the N.C. was glued to the radio for the premiers, and the sheet music was soon circulating even in backwoods Maine.

The light bulb soon went on for the artists. The Boston Museum of Fine Arts assembled a stunning collection of Winslow Homers, displayed them in a train of railroad cars and sent the train around the country. It made a special point of stopping for a day in small, rural towns. Farmers left their plowing and blacksmiths their forges to come and view. Today, it's routine for young ladies to paint and young men to draw, and average people decorate their homes with original artworks, good ones, painted by family, neighbors, or friends. Abstractionism is dead. I last saw a de Kooning at a gallery when the owner was repainting a room. It was in service as a drop cloth, which was also how it started.

Another Lazarus was the Christian novel. Of course, some people had continued to write and read Christian novels. Those of the self-diminutive Inklings, Dorothy Sayers in particular, had even retained a certain popularity. A few new writers quietly followed their path; Sally Wright was one with her *Publish & Perish* and *Pride & Predator*, Russell Kirk another. Kirk did it while bearing virtually unaided the corpus of Western culture through the blighted 1960s, '70s, and '80s. A large and flattering statue of him now stands proudly in Harvard Yard, and students doff their caps when they pass by.

But the mainstream of American literature had flowed with the rest of the culture to the sewer, the *cloaca maxima* that was prurience misla-beled "art." That made it easy for people with little talent and no skills to become "artists". In the 1990s, one potter in a magazine interview fittingly defined a craftsman as "an artist with skills", but reading their *ouevres* was like taking a bath in the sewage farm. So people stopped read-ing literature or much else and watched television instead, to the infinite amusement of Hell.

But that was over. People wanted to read again, read more than the newspaper or a tract. They wanted to be amused, but not shocked or horrified. They wanted to escape, but not too far, not beyond the borders of what was real and right. In short, they wanted Christian novels.

And lo and behold, it turned out there were people who could write them. The literary revival began in the Confederacy. The last great Amer-ican novelist, Walker Percy, was a man of the South; his *Love in the Ruins*, published in the 1970s, offered the first clear look at where the country ended. Something Southern seems to fertilize writers. Perhaps it's the time that hangs heavy and humid as a Mississippi summer night, time too slow for real work but too long for just nuthin'. Writing lies some-where in between.

In 2037, a new publishing house was founded in Baltimore, The Mencken Press. True to old H.L.'s name, it sought out new writers of merit, encouraged them, edited them strenuously, and by the mid-2040s deployed a stable of fine Christian authors. By that time we had some money, and Mencken Press books flowed North. In 2047, The Mencken Press established a branch in Boston, specifically to encourage writers of Christian fiction in the N.C. It was broad-minded of them and good for us. Soon, for the first time since television sprang upon us, authors found they need not join Dr. Johnson's lament about "the patron and the gaol." They could again make a decent living by their craft. Now, most homes have a good-sized library of well-thumbed fiction, and even Hartland has a prosperous bookstore.

The revival of literature, music, and art and the recovery of beauty, a great and glorious part of the Recovery, put a bullet through the head of the cultural despair that had infected the nation. No longer did we wallow in endless self-pity, alienation and anomie. No more did we celebrate the deformed, degraded, and degenerate. Bad news was no longer good news.

Everyone now knew where all that crap had come from. It was another road apple left on the highway of life by the Frankfurt School, those *hosti humanis generis* who had all too successfully translated Marx from economic into cultural terms. From Lukacs' call for an "abolition of culture" through Benjamin's command, "Do not build on the good old days, but on the bad new ones" to Adorno's worship of atonal music on the grounds that it was sick, these harpies trashed everything beautiful and elevated the alienating. They set the tone and direction of elite culture in America for half a century. Not coincidentally, the same half-century that marked the end of America.

But the Frankfurt School was history, and with its game out in the open, no one fell for it any more, not even academics. A new Zeitgeist was abroad, and it had a remarkable resemblance to England's longest-ruling monarch, Good Queen Victoria. Recently, rummaging in the attic at the Old Place, I came across a quote that summed up the spirit of the N.C. in the 2040s and '50s.

> *The power necessary to obtain a most unexampled growth is secured to our country. And we speak in this tone of confidence because the power itself dwells in the mind and character of the people. It is not derived from external circumstances...If this grandeur is realized, it will place a gigantic sceptre in our hands. Such a spectacle as the near future is opening its portals to disclose has never charmed the vision of the world. It will be the miracle of modern life.*

The quotation is from *Harper's Magazine*, January, 1855. Retroculture was working.

Along with everyone else, I immersed myself in the pleasure of a normal life. That was something none of us had known, except those old enough to remember the 1950s. They enjoyed it all the more, because it represented what they had always been told was impossible: the recovery of something that had been lost. It didn't hurt that when they started the kind of story old folks all love to tell, beginning with "I remember when..." young people wanted to hear it.

For me, normal life meant summers spent at the Old Place, farming, and most of the rest of the year in Augusta, attending to the duties of the General Staff. Those weren't too heavy. We had occasional trouble with pirates, or with some tribe molesting one of our traders in the Mediterranean or off some African or Malay coast. But a visit from an N.C. zeppelin was something to be feared, and not many miscreants wanted a second one. If there were any left after the first. Most of my work consisted in keeping our forces from getting foutinized or bureaucratic, the usual consequences of peace.

Maria and I were together from planting through harvest and over the holidays in the winter. Time and practice had given us the rarest of relationships, the kind without friction. We loved each other deeply. But our love expressed itself not in passion but in consideration. Each knew what the other liked and disliked, and was careful to do the first and avoid the second. In short, it was Christian love, which is not what you feel but what you do.

For a while, I did wonder whether Maria was as satisfied with our arrangement as I was. So one fine July evening in the year 2045, as we sat out front on the half-log bench and watched the sun go down over the ponds, each mimicking its fade from orange to purple to black, I asked her to marry me.

She replied with her kind, frequent and slightly sad smile, the sort proffered by Botticelli Madonnas. "Thank you, Señor John. I am honored that you would ask me. But I have learned the lesson of our people. When you are happy, be content. Do not seek for more. I hope you will allow me to remain Mrs. Hudson." Of course, I did.

The Faustian dance was over, in small things as in great.

CHAPTER FORTY-SEVEN

ON November 23, 2053, N.C. Naval Zeppelin L-370, while patrolling the western Mediterranean against the usual Algerian pirates, was caught in a sudden squall at the same time she was experiencing engine trouble. The huge airship was blown onto the North African shore, where most of her crew had the misfortune to survive the crash.

They were captured, brought to Algiers, and in a public ceremony before a vast crowd, offered the usual choice between the Koran or the sword. The sword was a metaphor. When, to a man, they chose Jesus Christ over the Prophet, they were crucified. Some took three days to die of exposure, thirst, and asphyxiation.

This required more than the usual punitive air raid in response. The people of the Northern Confederation agreed, and on December 6, they voted overwhelmingly for war with Algeria.

The key to these affairs was always the same: Find someone on the other side who would like to become the local Grand Wazoo in place of whatever raghead held that dignity at the moment. By the time our small task force reached the Med, a revolt had broken out in Algiers. We quickly hooked up with the rebels. The government forces made the mistake of coming out of the city to fight, which made the job easy. While the rebels grabbed them by the nose, two N.C. Marine regiments hooked into their rear and rolled them up from behind. It was over in the course of an afternoon.

Our portion of the booty was the leaders who had ordered the crucifixion of the men from L-370. We put them aboard another airship, positioned it precisely over the public square where our boys died, and pushed them out the door, one by one, at an altitude of 1,000 feet. Observers on the ground reported that each landed with a satisfying splat. The new government made the usual Algerian peace and promised not to attack N.C. ships or citizens. They didn't mean it, of course, but they'd leave us alone for a while.

A correspondent from the Rochester, New York newspaper had accompanied our Marines. He reported that when they attacked, they'd done so yelling the age-old battle cry of German and Austrian troops: "Victoria!" I smiled when I read the account. It seemed our military traditions were taking a firm hold.

Public opinion is a funny thing. When the report from the Rochester paper was reprinted around the Confederation, the "Victoria!" battle cry struck a chord. Most people didn't know its origin, or much care. To them, it represented what we as a nation most respected, the Victorians, our astonishingly successful forefathers who now served as our models, mentors, and measure. It thrilled them that our Marines now swept to victory under the very name that inspired most of what we as a people did, or tried to do.

In the Spring of 2054, the voters of the town of Putney, Vermont adopted a resolution in town meeting: "Resolved, that in honor of our

Victorian forebears, the Northern Confederation shall henceforth be known as the nation of Victoria." Armed with their resolve, the people of Putney went forth to their neighbors in other towns, gatherings signatures for a ballot. The petitions lengthened swiftly, and by the end of April it was clear we'd have a vote. When the country went to the polls on May 15, the proposal carried by no less than 80 percent in every precinct in the nation.

On July 4th, 2054, we formally ceased to be the Northern Confederation and became the nation of Victoria. In every city and town, people gathered for fittingly Victorian celebrations, with grand parades, stirring oratory, civic picnics, and spectacular fireworks. We did not intend to displace the old July 4th holiday. In most places, the mayor or the governor read the original Declaration of Independence in addition to the official Proclamation of Victoria. Rather, we saw in one our beginning and in the other our completion, through the Recovery of what our 18th century ancestors had dreamed of and fought for: a nation that could be free because it was virtuous. Queen Victoria and Lady Liberty shared the same dais, each leaning on the other.

*

The year 2054 was a marker in my own life as well. It was the year I turned 66. That no longer meant retirement: We had neither the law nor the custom. I had my share of aches and pains, and I messed up more than I used to on names and dates, getting them wrong or just drawing a blank. But inside, I was the same person I'd always been, and my mind hadn't gone to the point where I didn't want to hear any ideas but my own. When that happened, it would be time to retire from the General Staff. As to farming, well, I continue to hope they'll find me some fine

Maine spring day, stretched out at the end of a long, straight furrow, the reins to Elise and Max Jr. still in my hands.

Age is strange for its silent swiftness, all out of sync with our internal calendars. If someone had told me I'd soon be fifty, that might have felt about right. But growing old is not a hard thing otherwise, much less difficult than being young and wondering if life will ever offer us challenges equal to our talents, or what we imagine our talents to be.

Except for the deaths of friends. I never got used to that. It was not a new experience. War had seen to that. But the shock was always fresh, as if it were happening for the first time. Maybe that was a grace.

On September 17, 2054, my cousin John's sons Ham and Seth were up at the Old Place, helping me get in the potatoes. It had been a good year, rain and sun in the right proportions, and we forked a wagonload out of the bottom land every hour. Maria came out early with our lunches, just after eleven.

"John, you had a call from Augusta. It was your adjutant, Captain Harlan. He asked you to call as soon as possible. He sounded upset."

"It'll wait," I replied. "Real work comes before paperwork." Harlan and the rest of the staff knew my rule: Act, and tell me about it later. Anyone who needed to talk to me before he could deal with an emergency was in the wrong line of work.

"No, Señor John, I think you should call him as soon as possible. There was something in his voice...I can't express it, but he had trouble talking. I think he was fighting to control himself."

That didn't sound like Captain Harlan, whom I chose as my adjutant because he had a personality that was both efficient and relaxed.

"I've just been cleaning the house and canning tomatoes this morning, Señor John. I can dig potatoes for a while. The exercise will help me sleep tonight. It won't take long to walk back to the house and call him."

"Anything to please a lady," I replied with a smile and a bow. I would do just about anything to please Maria. But I also knew her intuition was usually right. Women could hear things that the male ear didn't register.

I glanced at the clock as I placed the call; it said quarter of twelve. "Waal, Captain, you've got a way with wimmen," I said when Harlan picked up. "Maria's now out there forking spuds instead of me. If you're calling because you couldn't find the paper clips, you're gonna be chipping paint for the next three weeks."

"Yes, sir. I'm afraid I've got bad news, sir."

"Out with it."

"Governor Kraft was found dead in his study this morning, sir."

The only sound in the room was the ticking of the clock. The sun streamed in, illuminating the old, oiled wood floor, my cigar-stained worktable, Maria's needlepoint on her chair. Everything was the same as always. But nothing would be the same again.

"Sir? John? Are you okay?"

"No. No, Harlan, I'm not okay." My legs collapsed under me, and I fell heavily, awkwardly into my chair.

Maria and Seth found me there a little before one, sitting just as I fell. I couldn't move and I couldn't think. Maria said all the color was gone from my face, and my eyes didn't blink. She thought I'd had a stroke.

"Aiyee, Dios," she cried, dropping the basket of tomatoes and mums she had brought from the garden. "Quick, Seth, call the doctor!"

Maria ran over to support me, fearing I would slide off the chair onto the floor. Seth grabbed the phone to call Doctor Sturgis. Somehow, the thought of an unnecessary visit from the doctor made me react. I reached out my left hand and pushed down the buttons on the telephone.

"No, Maria." I could hear myself talking, as if it were someone else saying the words. "No. No doctor."

"John, please, what has happened? Tell me. You must talk."

Again, I heard my voice from far away. "It's not me. It's Bill. Bill Kraft is dead."

"Oh. Oh John, no." Then she couldn't talk anymore either.

Seth and his brother worked 'til nightfall, getting the potatoes in. When they finally brought the last wagonload up the hill, they found us still sitting in my study, holding on to each other, the house dark. Maria was crying softly. I couldn't even do that.

Bill was older than I was, of course, by more than 20 years. He'd borne the strain of our nation's birth more than anyone. But he'd carried it so well it almost never showed. He loomed indestructible, unconquerable, a mighty fortress that could and would stand against anything any enemy could hurl against it. Except time.

*

Governor Kraft's funeral was Victoria's first great event. Victoria was his gift to us, and we joined together, each and every citizen, to give back what we could. That didn't mean just pomp and circumstance, though we didn't stint on either. But we wanted more than that. We wanted what spoke of Bill Kraft, and we wanted to speak to him, each in his own tongue.

So everyone brought what he had to bring. The great room in the Capitol Building in Augusta where our governor lay in state filled with offerings. Children sent their favorite toy. Farmers sent their best bit of produce. Factories across the country stopped their production to build one, special example of whatever they made, built as well as they could build it, and sent it to Augusta.

Bill Kraft always loved his trains. So that's how he came home to

Waterville for the last time. But that too was an offering from a grateful nation, because all the railroad workers from all over the country came to Maine and laid a new track from Augusta to Waterville, another rail between the rails of the Maine Central, laid on the two-foot gauge. The little two-foot gauge lines that once served Maine had disappeared before Bill's time, and he'd always regretted missing them. So we gave him one, and he rode home behind a tiny teakettle of a steam engine, pulling a train of old, wooden cars. All along the railway, people from across the nation stood silently to watch him pass by for the final time.

As Chief of the General Staff, there was one thing I insisted on. Bill would have a Marine Corps funeral. I met the train at the Waterville station, dressed in my old United States Marine Corps dress blues. A company of young Victorian Marines was with me. They carried Bill's coffin from the train, through the vast, silent crowd to a waiting horse-drawn caisson, where I met them. I would have the honor of being the first man to walk behind the caisson for the trip of a couple miles to Bill's Anglican church and the churchyard where we would bury him.

The Marine body bearers brought his coffin to the hearse, then stopped.

"Put him aboard, men." I ordered.

"No, sir," the lance corporal body bearer nearest me said. "He wore a blue uniform too, sir. He's one of our own. We'll carry him."

I looked at him sharply. Bill Kraft was a lot to carry. He looked back at me just as sharply. I could see this was one of those situations where rank didn't mean anything.

"Okay, then that's what we'll do." I discreetly bumped the lance corporal out of his position and took the weight of the coffin on my own shoulder.

The caisson rolled ahead of us, empty, as we carried our old friend home. At the churchyard, a small group of black farmers was waiting. They'd dug Bill's grave, by hand, in the rocky Maine soil. That was their gift to him.

The Rector of the Church said the service from the old Book of Common Prayer, the short, stark, English service in which the name of the deceased is never mentioned. The God who numbers the hairs on our heads knows who we are.

Bill's family had asked me to say a few words at the gravesite. I was the only one they asked, and little as I felt equal to the task, I couldn't say no. But the governor himself had pointed me toward words better than my own.

"As all those who knew him know, our governor's great example and hero in life was Dr. Samuel Johnson. So I want to let Dr. Johnson's friend and biographer, Boswell, speak for me today. His words on the death of Johnson are mine also:

I trust, I shall not be accused of affectation, when I declare, that I find myself unable to express all that I felt upon the loss of such a 'Guide, Philosopher, and Friend.' I shall, therefore, not say one word of my own, but adopt those of an eminent friend, which he uttered with an abrupt felicity, superior to all studied compositions: 'He has made a chasm, which not only nothing can fill up, but which nothing has a tendency to fill up. Bill Kraft is dead. Let us go to the next best—there is nobody; no man can be said to put you in mind of Bill Kraft.'

That was it, but in Maine, that was enough. We're not much on words, and the fact that I borrowed somebody else's was considered to my credit. We Victorians know we are pygmies standing on the shoulders of the giants who came before us.

Chapter Forty-Eight

ILL Kraft's greatest monument was the fact that once he was gone, we discovered we no longer needed him. Life went on just the same. Unhurriedly but steadily, Victoria proceeded back down the road of progress, recovering the past.

The people of Maine still wanted to give our founding governor overt honors. Early in 2055, a petition drive began for a vote to rename Augusta "Kraft."

I was dead-set against it. So was virtually anyone else who had really known Bill. He wouldn't have wanted it. It reeked of the latter days of the American republic, with its phony holidays and politicized name changes (in New Orleans, in the 1990s, some worthless orcs even dared to strike George Washington's name from a school because he owned slaves). Worse, the symbolism was opposite to everything Bill stood for. In German, "Kraft" means power. We had fought to take power away from capitals and politicians and bureaucrats and return it to the countryside, to citizens. Bill Kraft himself had held enormous power, but his had been the power of moral example, not the corrupt and corrupting power of government.

When Bill's widow came out against the renaming, the proposal died. We did a few more appropriate things in his honor. "Turn back, O Man," was adopted as Victoria's national anthem, with a new third verse:

> *Our land shall be fair, Victoria's people one*
>
> *Nor till that hour shall God's whole will be done.*
>
> *Now, even now, once more from earth to sky*
>
> *Peals forth in joy our old, undaunted cry,*
>
> *"Our land shall be fair, Victoria's people one!*

The Maine Central Railroad inaugurated a crack, all-first-class Boston to Portland express named the "Governor Kraft," with beautiful wooden parlor cars all painted white like the New Haven's old "Merchants' Limited." Despite electrification of the railroad, it was pulled by a high-stepping Atlantic steam engine, the pride of the Alco works. That was a tribute Bill would have loved.

But the nation's finest gift to Bill Kraft came about in a strange way.

*

Cleaning up a culture takes some time, especially when it has trashed itself to the degree America's had. In the 2050s, we still had some dark and dusty corners where spiders lurked. One was the ancient hag who still styled herself the Episcopal Bishop of Maine, Ms. Cloaca Devlin.

Few institutions had degraded themselves more in the final decades of the American republic than the Episcopal Church. A pillar of propriety and comfortably stuffy rectitude as late as the 1950s, many a young bride was advised by her aunt to join the Episcopal Church wherever she settled, because she would meet all the best people in town. But it had sought to become trendy and ended up looking like an aging whore. It abandoned Cranmer's timeless prose for a Book of Common Prayer that read like yesterday's newspaper. It attempted to make priests and even bishops of women, which was impossible: There can be no such thing as a Christian priestess. It worshipped the "racism, sexism, homophobia" trinity of cultural Marxism in place of the Holy Trinity, priested open homosexuals, censored ancient well-loved hymns, and generally licked Satan's boots every way it could. People left the church in droves, but their loss meant nothing to the ideologues in charge. They harkened only to their Dark Lord's commandment, "Fleece my sheep."

That was history. With help from bishops and missionaries from Anglican churches in Africa and India, which had remained orthodox, the Episcopal Church returned to Christianity and its old ways. The neo-pagan clergy gone, the pews filled up again, and the sonorous language of the 1928 Book of Common Prayer and the King James Bible again instructed Sunday mornings.

Still, Ms. Devlin remained. She had only a tiny band of eccentric followers, aging apostates like herself. It would have been easy enough to wait a few more years until Hell claimed its own. But we Victorians were again a serious people who did our duty.

In January, 2055, the real Episcopal bishop of Maine, the Right Reverend Michael Seabury, brought formal charges of heresy against Ms. Devlin. An ecclesiastical court convened that spring and to everyone's surprise the false bishop appeared in her own defense. Or to be more precise, her own offense. On the witness stand, she denounced the Trinity as "phallocentric," consistently referred to God as "she," pronounced the writers of the Gospels "dead white males," said St. Paul was a "self-hating gay" and finally announced that for many years she had worshipped Astarte, not Christ. That, no one doubted.

There could be no doubt about the verdict, either. She was guilty as sin. The church, ever merciful, offered Ms. Devlin the opportunity to recant and be received as a penitent. Her answer was to spit in Bishop Seabury's face.

Then the ecclesiastical court did something unexpected. It voted that Ms. Devlin be turned over to the secular arm, and burned.

In Augusta, the decision was quickly made that burning a heretic required the consent of the people. A referendum was duly proposed, to take place in August. The people of Maine would have most of the summer to discuss the proposal down at the town store.

Discussion there was, aplenty. Some folks felt a burning would just give the bishopess unwanted attention. Others wondered whether the whole thing was a publicity stunt by the Episcopal Church, looking for new members. They needn't have worried about that. I recalled the comment of an elderly lady parishioner to the Rector of my church after he gave a sermon on evangelism. At the door she said, "But Father, all the people who want to be Episcopalians already are." Down at the store in Hartland, most of the men scoffed at the whole business. "Who the hell cares what some woman says about religion anyway?" seemed to be the general view.

But Maine's women did care. Ms. Devlin represented everything horrible women had done to themselves since feminists became cultural Marxists. She was an embarrassment and ladies do not like to be embarrassed. They wanted to make an example of her, and they worked on their menfolk.

Just before the referendum, the good Bishop Seabury made a final effort to save the bishopess from herself. All she had to do, he announced, was formally renounce Christianity. She had already said she worshipped a different god, or goddess. If she would just say was not a Christian, she could be bishopess or high priestess or a goddess herself for that matter in whatever cult she chose. The Episcopal Church would then be happy to recommend exile rather than flames. Her reply was that she didn't have to believe in God in order to be a bishop in the Episcopal Church. That had been true in the early 21st century. But it was true no longer.

On August 15, when the vote was taken, a solid 65 percent of the voters of Maine said yes to an auto-da-fe. Bishop Seabury requested the event be postponed as long as possible, in hope Cloaca would change her heart. Alas, by that point, she had none.

The governor waited as long as he decently could without compromising the voice of the people. When it was clear there would be no repenting by Ms. Devlin, the event was set for September 14, at just after noon.

I well remember the crowd that gathered for the execution, solemn but not sad, relieved that at last, after so many years of humiliation, civilization had recovered its nerve. The governor was prepared to light the pyre himself. But the day before, Bill Kraft's widow asked if she might have that right, as a representative of Maine's women. The governor agreed.

It was a perfect New England summer day, the sky blue, the air clear, temperature in the low 70s without a trace of humidity. A good day to die, I thought, even for a servant of Satan. The stake had been set in the ground the evening before, right out on the statehouse lawn, and at 11:30 a horse-drawn paddy wagon brought the self-proclaimed bishopess from her cell in the old town jail. She had asked to be allowed to wear her ecclesiastical robes, and with the consent of Bishop Seabury, the state agreed. After all, it was precisely because she insisted she was a bishop of the Episcopal Church that she was being burned.

She walked with some dignity to the stake, through a hushed crowd.

There, she was bound to it, and faggots were piled at her feet. Bishop Seabury walked forward and spoke to her, pleading earnestly that she either repent or renounce her claim to be a Christian. Either would save her life, and the former her soul as well. Again, she spit in his face.

Then Mrs. Kraft came forward. Behind her walked a policeman carrying a lighted torch. She turned and faced the crowd.

"I am sorry my husband cannot be here today to do what I am about to do," she said. "It is something he would have done joyfully. Not because he hated this woman. She isn't worth hating. He certainly hated what she represents, as should we all.

"But that isn't what would have made him happy to light this pyre. He said often enough in my hearing, to me and to many others, that no society, no civilization can survive that is not willing to die and to kill for what it believes. Somehow, in the early 21st century, our civilization lost that willingness. Because it lost it, it almost died itself. Now, we have it back. That is what the Recovery really is, a Recovery of the will to survive as a people and a culture. Somehow, I think Bill knows what we are doing here today, and he's very proud of all of us."

Neither I nor others had realized until that point that the burning of the bishopess was the best memorial we could offer to Bill Kraft. But Mrs. Kraft was right. I could see him looking down and smiling, with all the company of heaven rejoicing.

That said, Mrs. Kraft took the torch from the police officer, turned, and tossed it into the pile of faggots. The sticks were fresh pine wood, and they quickly blazed up in a tower of flame reaching well above the head of madam bishopess.

Exactly how Cloaca Devlin reacted to the flames neither I nor anyone else could tell. But the host of demons she carried within her took them badly. I doubt it was the temperature, given where they came from.

Perhaps it was the fact that this particular variety of fire, fire consuming a heretic judged by the Church and burned by a Christian state, had left them untouched for so many centuries. Its sudden return must have come as an awful shock.

In any case, they howled. The shrieks, moans, cries, and curses in tongues unknown to men or angels rose to the heavens. There, they were heard as sweet music, no doubt. To the mortals on the Maine statehouse lawn that September day they left no uncertainty. Ms. Devlin and her ilk had been shit straight out of the bowels of Hell.

The demons fled for more familiar fires, and the business was soon over. The Albigensians always claimed flames were the best way to go. The crowd dispersed before one o'clock, satisfied with a deed and a bishopess well done. The whole affair was, as Ms. Devlin herself might have said, liberating.

As I made my way through the multitude back toward my office, I heard a familiar voice I couldn't quite place. "Captain Rumford! Captain Rumford!" I turned and looked, but didn't see anyone I could connect with the voice. Then, hurrying along, I saw a form and visage from times past. It was none other than Father Dimitri!

I hurried over to meet the good priest. Though we had not seen each other in years, I knew he was a mere monk no longer, but Procurator of the Holy Synod in St. Petersburg. "Good heavens, Father, what brings you here?"

"Good Heaven indeed brings me here," Father Dimitri replied, laughing. "This is a great day for Christendom. Both my Tsar and myself rejoice in your nation's recovery of firm faith. What you had the courage to do here today repays all our investment in you."

"Are you saying this was the burning of the mortgage?"

"Exactly. Well put. And I wanted to be here with you to celebrate."

"I can't think of a more welcome surprise guest. Come on over to Stavka with me and we'll open a bottle," I invited.

"I hope you are free for dinner at our embassy tonight. No caviar, I promise." Father Dimitri replied. "But plenty of vodka."

"It's a deal."

On the walk over to my headquarters, we caught up on each other's lives. Father Dimitri asked me rather pointedly if I were still unmarried. When I told him Bellona was still my only betrothed, he smiled. I began to suspect there were more to his visit than celebrating an auto-da-fe.

Father Dimitri entered the General Staff building as a conquering hero. I'd sent a Marine running ahead to bay our arrival, and the younger officers and NCOs were clustered at the door, eager to meet a man who had played a key role in our short history as a nation. I led the mob into an empty classroom—our headquarters was in an old school building, which I had chosen because a competent general staff is a school—where our distinguished guest patiently took questions and told stories for more than two hours. I was pleased to hear that most of the questions revolved around Russia's strategy in helping the N.C. and how she arrived at it. We had not repeated Germany's error of halting the education of general staff officers at the operational level of war.

Then the good priest and I adjourned to my spare office for a bottle of my own cider and some talk about the future. Russian newspapers and military journals put a happy face on the endless war with Islam, but I detected whitewash.

"The problem, John, is that Christendom is everywhere on the defensive," Father Dimitri lamented. "Russia is holding the *limes* from the Black Sea to Vladivostok, as she always has. It is an endless drain on us, but our people are patient and know how to suffer. Every Russian understands what our fate would be if that line were breached. It will not fail.

But alone, we cannot do more, and wars are not won simply by holding lines."

"What does Christendom need to take the offensive?"

"In truth, John, that is the main reason I am here. We need your help."

"What's the plan?"

"Several years ago, the new Pope, Julius IV, initiated secret talks with the Patriarch in Constantinople. I have been party to those talks, as the Tsar's representative and mediator. The Pope and the Patriarch reached agreement last year, and since then the Archbishop of Canterbury and the German Emperor, representing the Lutherans, have also been brought in. Later this year, at the beginning of Advent, they will announce the reunion of Christendom. The bans and anathemas of 1054 will be lifted, and while each church will keep its own rites, each will recognize the clergy and sacraments of the others as valid."

"Wow! I'd say you just won the award as negotiator of the millennium."

"I am an unworthy and lazy monk."

"How are you handling the problem of the Apostolic Succession and the Lutherans?"

"There will be a ceremony of a mutual laying on of hands by all the parties to the agreement. That will be extended to any other Protestant denominations that join. With God's help, they will come."

"I'd say this is the best news for Christendom since the First Crusade took Jerusalem. But you said you needed my help. This event far overshadows me and anything I've done. I don't see where I come in, beyond rejoicing."

"John, at the time the announcement of reunion is made, the Pope, the Patriarch, Canterbury, and the Emperor will also preach a new Crusade. The goal will not merely be Jerusalem, which, as you know, has been closed to Christians since the destruction of Israel by the Arabs. It will include Jerusalem, but the larger objective will be the reconquest of the whole Mediterranean world. Turkey, the Levant, Egypt, and North Africa. As long as the Islamics hold most of the Mediterranean shoreline, Europe will never be safe. Of course, by putting the Islamics on the strategic defensive, it will also relieve the pressure on Russia."

"The military challenge is, of course, immense. The Crusade will require military leaders who really understand war. To that end, the leaders of the churches have agreed to found a new monastic order, an order of fighting monks. It will be called the Order of St. Louis, for the devout King of France who devoted himself to an earlier Crusade."

"If I remember right, on his deathbed he called for the reunion of the Eastern and Western churches," I said.

"Yes. That is why his name was chosen. John, what I came here for is to ask you if you will become a monk and a Knight of the Order of St. Louis."

So that's why Father Dimitri asked me if I had married, I thought. Perhaps it was the reason I never had. The Lord moves us in mysterious ways.

I'm sixty-seven years old, and he wants me to start over again. My body aches in places I never knew it had. I can't remember anybody's name for five minutes. I'm set in my ways and want nothing more than to go back to Hartland and Maria and farm.

"Of course I'll do it." It was the only possible reply. Father Dimitri had just told me the best news heard in Christendom in a thousand years and asked me to be part of it. My pains and fears were chaff in the wind. Dying in bed is a poor ambition for a Marine. "Where do I go and when do I start?"

"I don't know that. When the Pope and the Patriarch announce the founding of the order, Tsar Alexander will abdicate the Russian throne in favor of his brother and become the order's Grand Master. He will know what he wants from you."

"He's a great soldier, and I'll be honored to work under him."

"John, the Tsar and I know something you don't and probably shouldn't. You are yourself the greatest soldier of our time. You will work with him, not under him."

"Whatever he wants is okay with me. Just so long he understands I'll also be an unworthy and lazy monk."

On January 20th, 2056, I retired from the Victorian General Staff. On January 21st, I was knighted in Augusta, Maine, by the Papal Legate and the Russian Ambassador and admitted as a Commander of the Order of St. Louis and a neophyte monk in the one, holy Catholic and Apostolic Church. Crusade was being preached from every pulpit in Russia, Europe, and North America, and for the first time in centuries, all Christendom was stirring.

At the end of the ceremony, the ambassador handed me a letter from the former Tsar Alexander, now my superior. It was my orders.

Dear Brother John,

We have not yet met, but I feel I know you well, from your exploits and from Father Dimitri's many words about you, words of deep admiration. What the Order of St. Louis needs most are more men like you. So that is my order to you: prepare such men. Teach them what you know. Teach them how to think, about war and in war. Teach them how to make decisions quickly, welcome responsibility joyfully, and above all, to act.

I will send you the raw material, young men of promise from every land in Christendom. Go to your farm and there build a school for them, and teach them. Make them into the commanders and leaders we need to fight for God. Make them you.

Brother Alexander

So that's what I did.

POSTSCRIPT

J UST after noon on May 6, 2072, Maria found Brother John face down in the soft bottom land of the Old Place behind his plow. He ended his days where and as he hoped he wou'd, which is as good a definition of victory as any. He was buried just up the hill from where he fell, with a simple graveside service, read from the 1928 Book of Common Prayer. At his request, there were no military honors. Besides his name and dates, there is one word on his tombstone: "Farmer."

*

The peace of God, it is no peace, but strife closed in the sod. Yet, brothers, pray for but one thing—the marvelous peace of God.

CPSIA information can be obtained
at www.ICGtesting.com
Printed in the USA
BVOW06s1636230517
484635BV00013B/49/P